# Eminence

# MORRIS WEST

Harcourt Brace & Company

New York   San Diego   London

# Eminence

Requests for permission to make copies of any part of the work should be mailed to: Permissions Department, Harcourt Brace & Company, 6277 Sea Harbor Drive, Orlando, Florida 32887-6777.

Library of Congress Cataloging-in-Publication Data
West, Morris L., 1916–
Eminence/by Morris West.—1st ed.
p.    cm.
ISBN 0-15-100439-0 (hardcover)
I. Title.
PR9619.3.W4E65    1998
823—dc21    98-21838

Designed by Lux Design, San Diego, California
Printed in the United States of America
First edition
F E D C B A

*For Carol and David Ashley-Wilson,*
*good companions, friends of the heart*

I offer a special word of thanks to my two editorial consciences: my personal assistant, Beryl Barraclough, and my wife, Joy, companion of many voyages, sharer in many literary enterprises. Between them, they have kept me as honest, consistent, and self-critical as any man can be in a confusing world.

# Eminence

The Church in Argentina and we, its members, have many reasons to confess our sins and to beg pardon of God and society: for our insensitivity, for our cowardice, for our omissions, for our complicities [in respect of] illegal repression.

*Monsignor Jorge Novak, Bishop of Quilmes, Argentina*
*quoted in Clarin, 29 April 1995*

Where law ends, tyranny begins.

*William Pitt—speech, 9 January 1770*

# 1

On his bad days—and this was one of his worst in a long time—Luca Rossini fled the city.

His staff were accustomed to his sudden exits and entrances. They could reach him at any moment on his mobile number. His peers, who could recite by rote his titles and offices, knew also that he was a special man commanded from the highest place. They accepted that he was charged with secrets—they had secrets of their own. They understood also that gossip was a dangerous pastime in this city, so they kept any resentments for private and comradely moments. His master, a curt man, never called him to account for his movements, only for his official transactions.

He traveled widely and generally alone. Few were able to chart his movements or the reasons for them, yet wherever one turned one was conscious either of his presence or of his influence. His reports were laconic. His actions were brusque. The reasons he offered were clear and precise, but he declined to argue them with anyone except the man who commanded him. He could be agreeable in society but he committed himself rarely to intimacy. Before he left the city, he would change into jeans, walking boots, a scuffed leather jacket, an old cap. He drove an elderly Mercedes, which he kept garaged at his apartment, twenty minutes walk away from his office.

His refuge was always the same: a small holding in the foothills, which he had bought twenty years before from a local landowner. The property, invisible from the road, was enclosed by an ancient stone wall pierced by a heavy wooden gate studded with hand-forged country nails. Inside the walls was a small cottage, once a barn, with a roof of barrel tiles. It consisted of one large living space onto which he had built with his own hands a country kitchen and a paved bathroom. There was water and electricity and the gas was delivered in bottles. The furniture was sparse: a bed, a dining table, a set of chairs, a battered sofa and armchair, a modern CD player with a large collection of classics, a bookcase over which hung an olive-wood crucifix with a grotesquely agonized Christus. The garden contained a vegetable plot, a stand of fruit trees, a trellis of vines, a pair of rosebushes in pots. During his absences, which were many and long, the garden was kept by a villager, whose wife cleaned the house. When he came, as he was coming today, he lived a hermit's life. When he departed, he left money in an envelope propped against the table lamp to pay the custodian.

This was the one place in the world where there was no curiosity about his identity or his station in life. He was simply Signor Luca, *il padrone*. Heaven or hell—and sometimes he had wondered which it was!—this was his true home. No one could look in on him. He could not see beyond his own garden wall, but he recognized that this was a place of healing. The cure had been slow. It was not ended yet; perhaps it would never be ended. But as he pushed open the gate and walked into a garden rich with the first flush of autumn fruits, he felt a sudden surge of hope.

His rituals began the moment the gate closed behind him. He walked into the house, laid out the few purchases he had made along the way: bread, cheese, wine, mineral water, sausage, and ham. Then he made the circuit of the room. It was clean; dusted every day, as he required. There was fresh linen on the bed, and towels in the bathroom. He tested the pressure in the gas cylinder and checked the pile of wood in the locker by the fireplace. He would have no need of it in this mild weather, but there was comfort in the thought that he could make a fire if he chose. He paused by the bookshelves and looked up at the twisted figure on the olive-wood cross. He talked to it in a sudden burst of Spanish.

"It still isn't settled between you and me! You're out of it—out of it and into glory. That's what we claim, anyway! I'm still here. I'm held together with string and sticking plaster. The moment I got out of bed this morning, I knew it would be a bad day. I'm in flight again. What else can I do? I'm still in the dark."

He pushed aside the volumes on the top shelf of the bookcase. Behind them was a small steel safe in the wall. The key hung around his neck. He opened the safe and took out a pile of letters held together with faded ribbon. He did not read them. He knew every line by heart. He held them in his hands, rubbing his thumbs over the thick paper as if he were handling an amulet. Then he put the letters back into the safe, relocked it, and replaced the books.

Isabel and he still corresponded; but her letters now were evanescent texts on a computer screen, read and erased, leaving only a trace of her in his memory, like the track of an insect on desert sand.

The disk on the CD player was Mozart's *Prague Symphony.* He switched it on and let the music take hold of him. Then he moved to the bed. He stripped off his jacket and his shirt and laid them carefully on the bedspread. Although the air inside the house was warm, he shivered. He wrapped his arms around himself so that his fingertips touched the first ridges of the scars that covered his back and reached around his rib cage. He could not see them. He did not want to see them. He could only feel them. After a while, he released himself from his own embrace and walked out into the sunlit garden.

Outside the door, a number of simple country tools were stood against the wall: a spade, a mattock, a fork, a rake. He picked up the mattock, feeling, as he always did, a pleasure in the touch of the rough handle. He laid the mattock over his shoulder and began to work his way around the garden, grubbing out weeds between the lettuces and the bean rows, chopping back grass from the edges of the plots.

All the time, he was aware of the sun upon his back, of the trickles of sweat along the raised surfaces of the scars. That, too, was a comfort, but the greatest comfort of all was to be able to expose the scars and feel no shame, because here there was no witness to what so many years before had diminished him to a nothing.

He worked for more than an hour, finding new tasks, even in the well-kept garden. He raked leaves and burned them. He clipped dead flowers from the rosebushes. He picked tomatoes and salad leaves for his supper. He inspected the ripened fruit and tamped the ground under the vine trellises. By the end of it, his jangling nerves were quiet and his familiar demons had stopped their chattering. He was where he needed to be: in the quiet of a physical world far from politicians, philosophers, and the contentions of warring pedants.

He cleaned the tools and set them back in their place against the wall. He spread dust on the embers of the fire, then went inside to take a shower. He found a childish delight in the grouting he had done to the tile work and wished there were someone to whom he could demonstrate his handiwork.

He was still toweling himself when he heard the shrilling of his mobile phone. He hurried into the living room and answered in his usual laconic style.

"This is Luca."

The voice of the caller was familiar but rasping now with anxiety.

"This is Baldassare. Where are you?"

"An hour out of town. What can I do for you?

"Get back here as soon as possible."

"Why the rush?"

"We have a problem, Luca."

"Don't describe it. Just give me the code."

"Job and his comforters."

"Don't tell me Job has left so soon."

"That's the problem. He's very much with us and we're all sitting on the dunghill with him."

"I presume you've shut down communications?"

"As far as that's ever possible in this place. That's why we need you, Luca. You're good at this kind of thing."

"I wish I felt flattered. I'll be there as soon as I can."

When he switched off the phone, he burst out laughing. This was a moment of purest irony. He had survived the flaws in himself. He had survived with singular distinction the flawed system to which he had committed himself. Now he was summoned out of his private nowhere to lend strength and political skill to its most potent counselors—of whom, most surprisingly, he was one of the juniors.

The image of Job on his dunghill was a vivid one. The password signified much more than it said: that an irreversible event was taking place; that until it had been completed Job's comforters were themselves squatting on the dunghill; and if they failed to comport themselves with sufficient cunning, they themselves would be loaded with all Job's disasters.

Once again the scars on his back began to tingle, this time as if a small chill wind were blowing over them. Out of the past came the voice of one of his earliest physicians, a psychiatrist who specialized in the treatment of trauma victims.

"For a long time, my friend—how long I cannot tell you— you will find yourself looking backwards, worse still, wanting to live backwards. You will even find yourself using two mirrors, trying to look at the scars on your own back. You will seek redress, justice, retribution. You will never get full payment. You will declare a vendetta against the ungodly—and the godly who have collaborated with them. You will demand vengeance as of right. You will claim it even as a necessity for your personal survival."

"There's an old proverb among my people: 'Before you start a vendetta, make sure you dig two graves.' I'm not sure you can have both vengeance and survival."

"For a while, you may. The Nuremberg Trials disposed of certain war criminals. The Israelis caught Eichmann, tried him, and executed him. Nevertheless, the tally of atrocities has mounted over the decades. The Christian faith offered other solutions. The churches reconciled their criminals by demoting some of them and sending others into a penitential silence. There was a cost in that, too, but spread over a few centuries, no doubt it seemed reasonable."

"To the institution. Never to the victims."

"What do you expect me to say?" The doctor shrugged and spread his hands in a gesture of resignation. "I am not a miracle worker. I cannot rewrite your past. I cannot prescribe your future. You will make your own terms with life in your own time."

So, he had made a choice: to stay within the system, use it as a fortress from which to wage his private wars. The choice was highly dangerous. It involved another rift within his damaged self. He was now both victim and vindicator. By all the beliefs which he professed, vengeance was itself a crime. It preempted the rights of divinity. Nonetheless, he was committed to it. From the moment of that commitment, everything he did became a calculation and a contrivance. His public life was based upon a private lie. He could not surrender to uncertainty. The belief by which he lived had to be stronger than that to which he was bound by public profession. Very carefully, therefore, he sealed up the springs of compassion and the small seepages of doubt. He could not afford confusion. He could not afford illusion, either. He could work only by the clear light of his own reason. If that light proved in the end to be a darkness, so be it. There had been a moment when, spread-eagled on the cartwheel and waiting for each stroke of the lash, he had prayed for darkness as the last mercy.

He dressed quickly, put the food he had brought into a wooden bowl in the center of the table, scribbled a note on an envelope, stuffed the envelope with money for the custodian, and propped it against the bowl. He left, slamming the old studded gate behind him, then drove at speed through the gathering traffic toward the city. He switched on the car radio, listening intently for any news item that might indicate that security had been breached in the matter of Job and his comforters. When he heard nothing, he rehearsed in his mind the meaning of the parable.

Job was the code name of the Roman pontiff, aging, ill, and crotchety but still assertive. The comforters were the members of the Curia, the most ancient court in Europe. Mention of the biblical dunghill signified that the pontiff had been stricken with the illness which his physicians had predicted: a massive stroke involving severe brain damage. Already, there had been a series of minor preludes, ischemic episodes which, according to the doctors, presaged a major incident.

The man who had telephoned him was the cardinal camerlengo, chamberlain of the papal household, whose responsibility it was to consult with the physicians over treatment of the sick man, to run the papal household, and finally, when the pontiff died, to take over the interim government of the Church while a successor was elected. The camerlengo was a skillful man, but he was faced with a large and uncomfortable dilemma.

An ailing pontiff was one thing—a brain-damaged one was quite another. How did one dispose of him—if indeed *dispose* were not too colored a word? Toward the end of the nineties, rules had been promulgated to take care of the problems of aging among the high prelates of the Church and, indeed, of the pontiff himself. If he were incapacitated, either the secretary of state or a majority of the college of cardinals could declare him unfit for his office and discharge him, with all due charity, into retirement. This done, the camerlengo was free to declare that the See of Peter was vacant and to summon the electors to choose a successor.

The rules were less clear on what to do with the retired pontiff if he remained alive in a vegetable state. The worst-case decisions would be whether to place him on a life-support machine and, if he were so placed by error or misjudgment, whose hand would switch off the current. The presumption was that the pontiff would have expressed his own will in the matter of excessive prolongation of his life. However, if he had left no instruction, who would make the decision? Clearly, it could not be left only to the physician. It could not be left to family because, in theory at least, the pontiff had passed out of the circle of kinship. He belonged to God and to the Church of God. The prelates he had created were therefore the arbiters of his fate.

That, however, would be only the beginning. The press of the world would translate the Vatican dilemma into another chapter of the ongoing debate on euthanasia. As Rossini drove back to the city, this was the reading which he gave to the situation. If the pontiff had not been moved out of the confines of the Vatican, things were still under a measure of control. If, however, he were removed to his usual clinic, the Gemelli Hospital, outside the sovereign territory of the Vatican, the situation would change radically. Secrecy would be impossible. Medical bulletins would have to carry more than the mere color of truth. The media would suborn half the hospital staff to provide them with daily facts and salable fictions.

The cardinal camerlengo was an experienced administrator; yet one of his predecessors had made an egregious mistake by

trying to gloss over the details of the death of Pope John Paul I.
That mistake had released a torrent of political disinformation
and produced a world best-seller, in which it was claimed that
an American cardinal and an American bishop resident in the
Vatican, together with a mafioso criminal, Michele Sindona, had
conspired to murder the pontiff. The scandalous tale was still
current. The book was still in circulation. If the present affair
were handled badly, new rumors would spring up and grow
faster than the legendary beanstalk. This was another irony
which he pondered amid the tumult of horns and shouted im-
precations: Secrecy created and perpetuated the scandals it was
designed to prevent.

The homeward journey took an hour and three-quarters. By the
time he reached his apartment, he was convinced that the security still held. He locked the car in the garage, changed into his
clerical clothes, and telephoned his office to send a limousine
for him. Fifty minutes later, a guard at the Porta Angelica
saluted him and waved his vehicle into the parking place reserved for senior prelates. Luca Rossini—Cardinal Presbyter,
Gray Eminence of the Roman Curia—was back at work.

He hurried to the papal apartments, where a forlorn secretary sat guard in the pontiff's study, while the physician and the
camerlengo waited by his bedside. Pale and immobile, hooked
up to an oxygen supply and the portable monitors, which for
months now had become part of the furniture of the papal bedroom, he still had the look of an old lion dozing in the grass but
formidable to any intruder who might disturb his rest.

When Luca Rossini entered the room, the camerlengo and
the physician greeted him with obvious relief. He stood for a
moment staring down at the prone figure of his master.

"How is he?" he asked.

The doctor shrugged.

"As you see. Deep coma. We are administering oxygen. There is probably massive cerebral damage. No way to be certain, of course, unless we put him into the hospital for a CAT scan and twenty-four-hour monitoring."

"Is the damage reversible?"

"I would say not."

"So, at very best, there will be serious incapacity?"

"Yes."

"At worst, a vegetative existence?"

"If we put him on life support, yes."

"Which is the last thing he wants or deserves."

"I would have to agree." The physician hesitated a moment, then added a careful afterthought: "It would be helpful if His Holiness has left in writing some clear expression of his wishes."

"Did he ever express them to you, Doctor?"

"Only in the most equivocal terms."

"Such as?"

"We must wait and see what God has in store for me."

"Nothing more precise?"

"Nothing."

Rossini turned to the camerlengo.

"Does his secretary have anything?"

"He knows of no document expressing the pontiff's wishes in this matter. There is no relevant codicil to his will."

Luca Rossini looked from one man to the other. A small sardonic smile twitched at the corners of his mouth.

"I wonder what he expected: to exit like Elijah in a fiery chariot?"

The camerlengo frowned in distaste.

"I would remind you, Luca, His Holiness is still alive and with us. We have to decide what is best to be done for him and for the Church."

"Have you sought specialist advice, Doctor?"

"Cattaldo and Gheddo have both seen him."

"Their opinions?"

"Correspond with mine. There is irreversible damage. From a medical point of view, it would be simpler to have him in hospital care. However, we do understand . . ."

The camerlengo cut him off abruptly.

"There are certain consequences, very public ones. The pontiff will be outside the borders of Vatican City State. Those who treat him—though not the pontiff himself—will be under the jurisdiction of the Republic of Italy and the constant surveillance of the world media."

"If he dies," Luca Rossini laid down a series of bald propositions, "we have no problem. We bury him with pomp, elect a successor, and get on with business. If he survives but is grossly incapacitated, we have to retire him. There are provisions for that in recent amendments to the apostolic constitution. If, however, he survives in a vegetable state on life support, decisions will have to be made on when to terminate him and who will be the terminator of record."

The camerlengo challenged him formally.

"So, how do you answer your own questions, Luca?"

"Keep him here. Let him die with dignity in his own house. Do not attempt to prolong his life. Do not permit others to do so under any pretext. I will go on record that this was the desire expressed to me by the pontiff himself on various occasions during the last couple of years. You, Baldassare, can confirm that we have had a rather special relationship. It was hard to define sometimes, but yes, it was a very special relationship."

The camerlengo was silent for a moment. Then he nodded agreement.

"It makes sense."

"Eminent sense," said the physician with obvious relief.

Luca Rossini rounded on him.

"You still have a duty to perform, Doctor. We need an immediate bulletin for release by the press office of the Holy See. It needs a special tone, a certain emphasis. How far are you and your colleagues prepared to go in stating your prognosis?"

"I am not sure what you mean, Eminence."

"What words are you prepared to use? A massive cerebral incident? Beyond hope of recovery? Terminal? The end is expected hourly? What, Doctor?"

"Why are the words so important?"

"You know why." Luca Rossini was brusque. "So long as the pontiff is alive and in the care of his own household, the press will demand to know what kind of care he is getting and how long he may be expected to last. Baldassare here and the secretary of state will communicate with the senior hierarchy. The press office will deal with the media. It is not my business to frame the statements. I simply indicate the importance of their terms. Do I make myself clear?"

"As always, Luca." The camerlengo's tone was dry.

"And you, Doctor?"

"I'm sure we can come up with an appropriate text."

"Good." He looked from one to the other, studying their faces. His own face was set in a stone mask. "Now, with your permission, I should like to be alone with him for a little while."

The doctor and the camerlengo looked at each other. The doctor told him quietly:

"As you see, he is deeply comatose. He will see nothing, hear nothing. He will not feel even the touch of your hand."

"I want to be private with him." Luca Rossini was full of cold anger. "I have private things to say to him on the million-to-one chance that he may hear me. Can that do him any harm?"

"Of course not, Luca."

"Then indulge me, please!"

The camerlengo and the physician hesitated a moment. A glance passed between them. The camerlengo nodded his assent. The two men left the papal chamber, closing the door on Luca Rossini and his silent master.

As they waited in the adjacent room, the physician remarked:

"That man troubles me, Baldassare."

The camerlengo made a wry mouth.

"What in particular troubles you, my friend?"

"There are so many angers in him, so much arrogance. It is as if he has to master the whole world every day—with whips and scorpions!"

"The angers, I know." The camerlengo was a careful critic. "I have seen him face down senior colleagues in the presence of the pontiff himself. The arrogance is another matter. I see it as a defense. He is a man who has suffered much. He is still not fully healed."

"And that is a constant danger, is it not?" The physician put on his mask of clinical detachment. "The unhealed wound, the unresolved crisis of the spirit."

"Is that what you perceive in Luca Rossini?"

"Yes."

"I have to tell you, my friend, that he is superbly competent in everything he does. The Holy Father uses him as a personal emissary, and he is, as you know, a very exacting taskmaster."

"So what does that signify? The court favorite is always treated with indulgence. How do Rossini's colleagues feel about him? You, for instance?"

"I find him distant, but loyal always. He will confront you eye to eye and say what is in his mind."

"All of it?"

The camerlengo was beginning to be angry.

"How can I answer that? You heard him a few moments ago. He was saying things you and I had not had the courage to put into words."

The physician was instantly defensive.

"I have no authority here, Eminence. I am a physician, but I can only counsel, not prescribe, even for my distinguished patient."

"You have already agreed the treatment." The camerlengo corrected him swiftly. "But Luca Rossini is not your patient.

You should not offer an opinion on his medical condition or judgments about what you may see or hear in your privileged position."

The physician reddened with embarrassment and bowed his head.

"I am reproved, Eminence. Forgive me."

"There is nothing to forgive. At this moment we are both under stress. Luca Rossini is wrestling with his own dark angels."

He was sitting by the bed, one hand laid over the hand of the unconscious pontiff whose skin was cold, dry, and crepey like the skin of a reptile. There were tubes in his nostrils, and electrodes connected him to the monitors. Luca Rossini spoke into his ear in sharp staccato sentences, challenging him out of his silence.

"You hear me! I know you do! This time you listen! You were mistaken in me. You believed what they told you: that I was the hero, the young pastor spread-eagled on a cartwheel in a little town and publicly flogged to terrorize his people and teach them that there was no power but from God, and the colonels were God's voice in the land. . . . You ordered me brought here to shame the coward bishops of my country. You favored me. You pushed me forward and upward. You made me a high man. You could not believe that I was a flawed man, a vessel cracked and damaged. I accepted all you gave me. I was so full of guilts, so full of shame, I thought I was hearing the voice of God. Are you listening to me? It's the nearest I've ever come to a full and open confession, and you can't even raise your hand to give me the absolution I don't believe in! But let me tell you just this once that I loved you—not because you were my patron but because you made me pay for every trust you gave me. That's why I don't want you shamed now. I'd rather kill you with my own hands than see you rotting on the vine like a piece of fruit. But you can do it yourself. Just loosen your grip and slip away. Please, please go!"

He bent and kissed the forehead of the silent man. He pushed himself away from the bed. There were tears on his cheeks. He wiped them away, then composed his features once more into a mask, hostile and imperious.

Just before eight o'clock that evening a bulletin was issued by the *Sala Stampa,* the official press office of the Holy See.

At 1430 hours today His Holiness suffered a major cerebral hemorrhage which has left him paralyzed and deeply comatose. A series of minor ischemic episodes during the summer vacation at Castelgandolfo had alerted both the pontiff and his medical advisers to the possibility of a major incident.

Certain interventions had been discussed by the pontiff and his medical advisers. All were attended by high risk. His Holiness had steadfastly declined what he called the officious prolongation of his already long life by surgical means or by mechanical maintenance. He would go, he said, in God's time, and he would prefer to go from his own house, rather than from a hospital bed.

It is in response to these clear wishes that nursing care and appropriate neurological and vascular monitoring are being provided in the papal apartments. The pontiff's physician, Dr. Angelo Mottola, is assisted by two distinguished colleagues, Dr. Ernesto Cattaldo, a neurologist, and Dr. Piero Gheddo, a cardiovascular specialist.

All three hesitate to predict how long the pontiff may survive. They agree, however, that the cerebral damage is massive and the prognosis is negative.

The cardinal camerlengo begs the prayers of all the faithful that God may be pleased to call His good and faithful servant to Himself.

Further bulletins will be issued from this office daily, at 1200 hours and 1800 hours.

Background material will be available from Vatican Information Service (VIS) in English, Spanish, and French. The daily wire service from VIS will continue as usual.

"I wonder who cooked this soup?"

Stephanie Guillermin of *Le Monde* tapped the bulletin board with a scarlet fingernail and challenged her audience: half a dozen late drinkers at the bar of the Foreign Press Club in Rome.

"Who cares?" Fritz Ulrich of *Der Spiegel* waved away the question. He was into his third whisky and ready for an argument. "The man's been working himself to death for years now. Finally he's popped a blood vessel. What do you expect the *Sala Stampa* to say about it? They're saving the eloquence for his obituary."

"My point exactly, Fritz." Stephanie Guillermin was not easily rebuffed. "This text is completely out of character. It lacks the personal touch of Angel-Novalis. My guess is that it was put together in committee and handed to the press office for release."

"But who's the committee, Steffi, and why would they intervene?" Frank Colson of the *Daily Telegraph* knew the lady well enough to pay respect. She looked like a young Georges Sand and she wrote a clean, classic prose, with a fine edge of malice. She lived in some style with a very rich widow of an Italian banker, so her news sources were exotic but reliable. Her readings of people and events were subtle enough to have earned her the nickname of *la déchiffreuse*, the decoder. She was flattered by Colson's deference. She smiled and reached out to stroke his cheek.

"The committee? Figure it for yourself, Frank. It had to be at least a threesome—the camerlengo, the secretary of state, the physician, with maybe another curial cardinal. Jansen comes to mind or, perhaps that floating mystery, Rossini. The document had to be got out in a hurry and it had to represent at least a token consensus in the Curia."

"But why should they want to intervene in the composition of a simple document?"

"Because it isn't simple at all, Frank."

She had everyone's attention now. Fritz Ulrich's drink was suspended in midair. Enzo, the barman, laid down his napkin and leaned across the bar to listen. Colson prompted her out of the momentary silence.

"Go on, Steffi."

"What have we got here? Half a page of flat, banal prose; not at all in the usual style of the *Sala Stampa*. Nevertheless, it's very carefully contrived."

"To what end?" Ulrich was back on the attack.

"To answer awkward questions before people like us begin to ask them. Consider! They speak of a major cerebral hemorrhage, a massive incident. Why didn't they rush him into the hospital? We all know the monitor equipment in the papal chamber is basic stuff. They certainly don't have a CAT scanner. So, in spite of those three respectable names on the medical bulletin, what the old man is getting is basic bedside diagnosis, elementary monitoring, and home nursing."

"What more would he be getting in Gemelli Hospital?"

"Wrong question, Fritz." Guillermin was fast as a fencer on her feet. "When did you ever read a Vatican document that offered an explanation for any action—let alone an excuse for it?"

"Never in living memory!" Ulrich emptied his glass and pushed it across the bar for a refill. "So you are saying . . ."

"It was crafted to justify a very odd situation. It attributes to a stroke victim directions and dispositions which he could not have made after the event and which he seems to have addressed only in the most general terms before it."

"You still have not made your point," said Ulrich.

"They want him to die." Guillermin made an emphatic assertion. "They need him to die as quickly and quietly as possible. They are even appealing to the whole Church to pray for that event as a divine mercy. Why? Because if he doesn't die, they are left with a seriously damaged pontiff who must be formally retired and replaced to allow the life of the Church to continue."

"So, they kill him," said Colson softly. "They kill him by a conspiracy of benign neglect."

"That's one reading. The tabloids will certainly make headlines of it. However,"—Guillermin raised a cautionary hand—"the alternative is clearly stated in the bulletin. His Holiness is exercising his fundamental moral right to decline a prolongation of his life by officious and excessive intervention."

"Provided,"—Ulrich waved an admonitory finger under her nose—"provided always, the text we have is an authentic rendering of the pontiff's wishes! You will note that there is another departure from custom. There is no citation of a relevant authority—a letter, a will—not even a quotation from his encyclical on euthanasia."

"Fritz is right," said Colson. "That's something we could quite legitimately ask from the press office."

"I've got ten bucks to say they won't come up with a line." This from the UPI woman who had just drifted into the end of the talk. "Any takers?"

The others grinned and declined the bet. The UPI woman then made her own point.

"If they don't give us a citation, then we're free, are we not, to speculate? We have conflicting stories: a cabinet of concerned prelates nursing their ailing pontiff to a quiet end or, Frank Colson's version, conspiring to kill him by benign neglect."

"Either way," said Guillermin, "it makes part one of a great story."

"And what, pray, is part two?" Ulrich's tone was still provocative.

Steffi Guillermin, the code breaker, gave him a cryptic answer. "It begins with my first question, Fritz. Who's cooking this soup?"

"And you, of course, have the answer?"

"Not yet; but as always you will read it first in *Le Monde*! Then you can buy it from our syndication department. Excuse me now. I have to get home."

"Give my love to your Lucetta." Ulrich laughed. "That's one very pretty woman."

"And you're a pig, Fritz!" Guillermin was out the door while he was still groping for a retort.

There was a more muted hostility in the late-night meeting of cardinals summoned by the secretary of state. This was not a formal gathering but a convocation of those curial prelates residing in Rome and available at short notice.

These were all high men, firmly anchored to the rock of authority on Vatican Hill. Whether they were all as securely anchored in virtue was a moot question; but they understood the potency of protocol, the delicate balances of interest and influence, the awesome reserves of power that resided in the Petrine office. They knew how that power could be used to honor a man or hang him, high as Haman, on the slenderest thread of definition. For the moment, at least, the power was represented by the cardinal secretary of state. He came swiftly to the subject of the meeting.

"I understand that several of you are unhappy with the bulletin on the Holy Father's health which was issued this evening by the press office. Under the apostolic constitution of 28 June 1988, the press office is attached to the secretariat of state. I, therefore, must accept full responsibility for its actions. The text of the bulletin was drafted in consultation among the cardinal camerlengo, the papal physician, and myself. Members of the press office had no part in the composition. They simply distributed it through their normal channels."

"Then, with great respect, and in privacy among colleagues, let me register objection. This is a hasty and ill-considered document, which will, in my view, have serious negative consequences." The speaker was Gottfried Cardinal Gruber, prefect of the Congregation for the Doctrine of the Faith, watchdog of orthodoxy in the Church. A small silence followed his protest; then the secretary of state answered with studious restraint.

"The document was prepared in haste—because it was required in haste—to cover the unexpected event of the pontiff's illness."

"I would hardly call it *unexpected,* given the state of the Holy Father's health in recent times. I would accept that we were unprepared for the event. I submit that we might have been forewarned."

"We were forewarned, Gottfried, as was the Holy Father himself. However, he had his own mind on the matter. We could not move him."

"Did anyone try, seriously?"

"I tried, for one." Luca Rossini was cool and relaxed. "I tried many times in private talks. He would not change. He insisted that he would go when God called him. He wanted to die in his own bed."

"Did you never suggest that he leave some document expressing his wishes?"

"I suggested it several times; but you know better than I, Gottfried, how hard it was to get him to sign anything until he was ready to do so!"

A small ripple of amusement went round the assembly, and the tension relaxed a little. Gruber nodded a reluctant assent, but continued his complaint.

"I still say he should have been taken directly to the hospital."

"Against his published wishes?"

"He didn't publish them. We did."

"Are you suggesting"—the secretary of state was dangerously quiet—"that our colleague, Luca, is lying, or that the rest of us have conspired to fabricate a document?"

"No, of course not! But think a moment, we are on record now as praying for his death."

"I seem to remember," said the secretary of state, "that the traditional prayer for the seriously ill patient is that God will grant 'a speedy recovery or a happy death.' In the case of the Holy Father, there is no hope of recovery."

"But we cannot establish that with certainty except under full clinical conditions."

"Which, on the evidence, he has declined in advance as officious and unacceptable. We are all the family he has, Gottfried. What would you have us do?"

"I believe we should override the wishes of the Holy Father and put him immediately in complete clinical care."

"Do it, by all means," said Luca Rossini with weary indifference. "But remember his vital faculties are in decline. So, to protect themselves, the first thing they'll do at the hospital is put him on life support while they scan him. After that, if the present diagnosis is correct, you'll find yourselves tending a vegetable. Is that respect for life? Is that a moral imperative? If it's not, then I assume Gottfried here will volunteer to turn off the switch and the feeding tubes."

"That's enough, I think," said the secretary of state. "This is not a formal consistory. It has no canonical status, so I will not ask for your votes on the matter. I believe in good conscience that the Holy Father should have his wish. He will stay here in his own place."

"Then," Gruber asked the crucial question, "how long will you give him before you decide to depose him as incompetent and declare the See vacant?"

"I have trouble with the word depose." This time the prefect
of the Congregation for Bishops intervened. "It seems to me to
presume powers we may not possess."

For the first time, Baldassare Pontormo, the cardinal camerlengo, raised his voice.

"That's a problem which faces us all, in this meeting and
outside it. Let's ignore the drama of the Holy Father's collapse
and ask ourselves what we would do if the nature and circumstances of the illness were different—if he were dying of any
protracted disease, or were suffering from dementia. The Church
would go on. Its structures are strong, tested over the centuries,
and the Holy Spirit abides in it as our Lord Jesus Christ has
promised. For the rest, let us admit that we are not well organized to deal with one of the principal phenomena of our time,
longevity and the problems of aging, such as Alzheimer's disease. In the case of a stricken pontiff, it may not be possible—
it *is* not possible—to secure his explicit consent to resignation.
We may have to depend on implicit and circumstantial evidence of his will to do the best for the Church. So, we work in
prayerful prudence. We wait and watch and take counsel with
our medical advisers—and with one another! In spite of the
misgivings of certain of our colleagues, we are not subject to
outside opinion. The Vatican is a sovereign state. We hold our
stewardship of souls under God. We should deal with each other
in charity."

It was the longest speech Luca Rossini had ever heard him
make, and he was surprised at the eloquence and power of it. It
also made him wary, because it suggested that it might not be so
simple to depose an aging pontiff—even an incompetent one.
He led a small round of applause, which brought a smile to the
lips of the secretary of state and a nod of reluctant approval
from Gruber; but the old watchdog still had a growl in him.

"I agree with Baldassare, but only under caveat. The
Church can function without its pope. We know that. It has done
so in the past, it can do so again—but not for too long, not in

these troubled times! As for public opinion, we are not subject to it; but we have a duty to form it where we can, to accord it with the teaching of our Lord. I should like to propose that all future bulletins on the pontiff's health and treatment be submitted to a select committee of the Curia."

The secretary of state sat bolt upright in his chair. His knuckles were white against the dark fabric of his soutane. There was a rasp of anger in his voice.

"No! I will not consent to that. We are dealing here with facts and not with opinions on moral theology. My authority is clearly defined in the apostolic constitution of 1988. I will not, I cannot, delegate or abrogate it."

"As Your Eminence decides." Gruber bowed stiffly and sat down.

"The meeting is closed," said the secretary of state. "Thank you all for coming."

The secretary of state beckoned Luca Rossini to his side. He had a request and a commission.

"You said good words tonight, Luca. Now, if I may suggest, you should step back into silence: no arguments, no commentaries. You understand why?"

"Perfectly. There are issues and opinions here that could drag us all the way back to Constance in 1415: Papalists and Conciliarists at war with each other. That's an ancient mess; but part of it is still on our doorstep."

The secretary of state made a wry mouth. He fished in the breast pocket of his cassock and brought out a sealed envelope and held it out to Rossini. "I'd like you to read this at your leisure and send me a minute on it."

"What is it?"

"The Argentine ambassador to the Holy See is retiring soon. It's a patronage post, as you know. The government would like to make an early appointment. That's the dossier on their candidate. They want to be assured as soon as possible that we're happy with him."

"So, what has that to do with me?"

"Argentina is your home place. You have special insights into its people and its history. Your comment is important to me personally."

"Please! Don't involve me in this! Argentina, of course, is my home place; I do have special insights, but my judgments about it are skewed, as you know. You can find twenty better opinions in your own office. I beg you to dispense me."

"And I am begging you, Luca, to accept what is after all a very simple task. There is no hurry. We shall do nothing until our situation with His Holiness is resolved. Just toss the envelope on your desk and wait until you're in the mood to deal with it. Now, let's get to bed. This has been a brutal day for all of us!"

He thrust the envelope into Rossini's hands and clasped his palms together so that he was forced to retain it, then with a curt goodnight, he walked from the room.

For a long cataleptic moment Rossini stood staring after him, then he, too, hurried from the conference chamber. His day was ending as it had begun, in panic flight across a waste-land, filled with the wailing of yesterday's ghosts.

# 2

It was after midnight when Luca Rossini came home to his apartment in the Via del Governo Vecchio, a narrow thoroughfare lined with timeworn palaces built in the fifteenth century but converted long since into twentieth-century apartments. Once, this had been called the Papal Way because it led directly from the Lateran basilica to St. Peter's across the Tiber. Now, the ground floors were occupied by workshops and small traders, and the apartments inhabited by a population of middle-aged Roman bourgeoisie who cursed the pollution of the city but could not afford to move out of it.

Rossini's apartment occupied the fourth floor, to which one either climbed a stone staircase or ascended in an antique elevator. His household consisted of a Spanish couple—she a cook-housekeeper, he a valet and factotum—who had been recommended to him by an outgoing ambassador. They had their own living quarters. They were sober, quiet folk, drilled in the Castilian manners of the diplomatic service and protective of their taciturn master whose comings and goings were as mysterious as his past. They knew that he was an Eminencia at the Vatican. They knew that he spoke the Spanish of Argentina, where his father and mother had gone as migrants from Naples after the Second World War. They knew that he entertained exotic people of both sexes—Chinese, Indians, Ethiopians, Ukrainians, Indonesians, Africans.

Domestically, he was not an exacting man. He spoke to them quietly, and always with respect. His only demand was that they observe what he called "the privacy of the house." They should not discuss outside what they saw or heard in their daily service. They should not gossip about his guests. Rome was plagued by the threat of terrorist groups from more than one country. Lives could depend on their discretion, his own included. Did they understand that? They did. They kept his confidence, and he gave them a comfortable life within the means his office provided.

When he came home this night, dog weary, they were asleep; but, beside his armchair in the lounge, supper was laid out: a thermos of coffee, a decanter of brandy, sandwiches under a silver cover. Before he ate he went into the bedroom and changed into pajamas and dressing gown. The letter which the secretary of state had given him was still in his pocket. He did not bother to read it but took it with him into the lounge and locked it in his bureau drawer. The contents were already known to him. They were the cause of the unease that had plagued him since dawn. He switched on the computer and punched up the E-mail that he had received that morning from Isabel. Then he poured himself coffee and brandy and sat down to contemplate the text again.

Her letters came infrequently at irregular intervals, generally from New York, where her husband held a senior posting at the United Nations and she herself was a director of studies at the Hispanic American Institute. No matter how rarely they came, the fire and the passion in them never waned, and there was always a surprise and a smile to end them.

My dearest Luca,
    Even after all these years, I miss you. On one level my life is calm, well ordered, rewarding, as yours seems

to be. Buried deep below the surface, however, is a lava stream, flowing red hot, seeking always some crack or fissure in the thick crust of everyday existence to burst out and flood my life again.

One such crack appeared today. Raul told me that he has been recommended for the post of ambassador to the Holy See. This is a pre-retirement post, as you know—a reward for discreet service in the turbulent times, before and after our disastrous war with the British in the Malvina Islands.

For Raul it represents something much more, a final public absolution for things done and undone in his life as a vacillating careerist. I am not disposed to deny him this small, sterile triumph. He has been a good father to Luisa, and he has never attempted to deny me the freedom I demanded to survive the desert stretches of our marriage.

I could hardly object, therefore—though I did try to counsel him against it—when he insisted on including in his dossier an account of his part in getting you out of the country when the military put you on a list of those they wanted "disappeared" because of the witness you could mount against them. You and I know the real facts; but, each in our own way, we have consented to revise history at least enough to make our lives tolerable.

It was Raul's hope, I think, that I might intervene in some fashion on his behalf. I told him the truth, which is only half true: that you have been out of my life since you left my father's house, and I could not, in any case, solicit favors or recommendations from you.

Yet, that is exactly what I am doing now, my dearest Luca. I am doing it for myself and not for him. If Raul is appointed to Rome, Luisa and I will come with him. I want—I need—most desperately to see you again; and you, in your letters, confess the same need of me.

Love is like grief. One has to work through it. We have never been able to do that. I should like to think we could before the hidden fires are quenched and the ice age of indifference overtakes us. So, if you can, please write or say the word that may bring us to Rome, officially and without scandal.

I smile to myself when I think what a beautiful romantic comedy it would make if I, as the Senora Embajadora, could entertain Your Eminence in our embassy. Which raises another question: How and where would Your Eminence entertain me?

All my love, always,
Isabel

The symbols on the screen began to blur before his eyes. He deleted them. Then, because he was a punctual man, he typed in his reply.

Isabel, my dearest one,

My answer is yes. I will write and say the right words at the right time. I must tell you, however, that nothing will happen quickly. The pontiff is very ill and is likely to die soon. No diplomatic appointments will be made until his successor is elected. Inevitably, therefore, the comedy you hope to stage between the Eminence and the Lady will have to be postponed!

How right you are about the need to work through both grief and love! You seem to have done it much more successfully than I. I thought I could accomplish it like an athlete surfing on the adrenalin-rush of power games. I have become very good at that, as you know; but the disciplines are rigid, the diet is spartan, and the bed is lonely at night.

There's another cost, too, which mounts higher every day. I cannot call myself a believer anymore.

Ironic, isn't it? I am one of the hinge men of the Church. I am a potent figure in an ancient cult, whose rituals I practice but whose belief I no longer accept. Simple folk kneel to kiss my hand. For them, I still dispense a magic. For myself, there is no magic anymore. The inner shrine is dark and empty.

Strange as it may seem, there is a kind of liberation in this. There is no one who can suborn me or frighten me. Even so, I cower like a child from the vestigial nightmares, which still take me unawares. I use your name like a spell to rid myself of them. Perhaps when you come, you will help me to purge them forever. You ask where and how I shall entertain you. I have just the place. It is small and private, and every foot of soil, every plant and fruit, is mine. For me, it has been like the sacred island of Cos, a healing place. I shall be glad and grateful to welcome you into its peace.

It's late; the pope is dying. I have had a long day. There will be longer ones yet.

Good night, my dear, my very dear.

Luca

He waited a long moment before he decided to transmit the message. He knew that this was the most naked avowal he had ever made and that if it ever became public it would be a catastrophe. Yet, the need to say it was overpowering. So, drunk and reckless with the toxins of fatigue and stress, he entered the transmission code and let it go.

In the papal bedchamber, the pontiff still lay ashen and immobile. There were oxygen tubes in his nostrils, an intravenous drip in his arm. His eyes were blank and expressionless. Two Sisters of Mercy had just taken over the night watch, and Dr. Mottola was giving them instructions.

"You've both dealt with this sort of thing before, so you don't need a lecture on it. At the moment, he appears to be stable, though in fact, he is going downhill. All we're doing is administering oxygen and hydrating him with the drip. I don't expect any major change before morning. Of course, there will be a continuing buildup of mucous fluid in the lungs, because he can't clear it by coughing. There will also be an excess of carbon dioxide, which typically produces apnea and Cheyne-Stokes respiration. If that comes on, call me. I'll be here in ten minutes. Don't panic. You'll see nothing you haven't seen before. Even a pope gets no respite from mortality."

"What about coning?" the elder of the two nuns asked.

The doctor gave her an approving look.

"You do know your job, Sister. If coning occurs, he will be swiftly and visibly terminal, because the pressure of bleeding inside the skull will compress the brain and force cerebral tissue out of the skull case at the base. However, there are no significant indications that coning is imminent here. My hope is that you'll have a quiet night. Just look in on him every half hour or so—and make sure you write up the chart each time. It won't help the patient very much; but it will keep our professional reputations clean! Say a prayer for him—and for me."

"We'll do that, Doctor. Good night."

When he had gone, the two women settled themselves in the anteroom, from which they had a clear view of their patient. They were, as Mottola had acknowledged, experienced senior nurses, and they had kept a deathwatch many times. Even so, they were religious women, and there was a certain numinous quality about this event which would color the rest of their lives. The man, dying piecemeal before their eyes, was endowed with an awesome series of titles: Bishop of Rome, Vicar of Jesus Christ, Successor of the Prince of the Apostles, Supreme Pontiff of the Universal Church, Patriarch of the West, Primate of Italy, Archbishop and Metropolitan of the Roman Province, Sovereign of Vatican City State.

The titles were inflated by centuries of mythmaking, conflated with imperial histories, fortified by traditional Roman legalizations, sanctified by long memories of martyrdoms, buttressed by great edifices over whose lintels were carved in stone the legend: *Tu es* Petrus, "You are the Rock upon which the Kingdom of God is built." All of which was reduced to a single bleak irony: an old man dying in a small bedroom, attended by two women, gossiping softly in the antechamber.

There was a discreet knock at the door, and Claudio Stagni, valet to the pontiff, came in with a tray of coffee and food for their supper. He was a short man, ruddy and cheerful—the only one, according to court legend, who could make the pontiff laugh and lift him out of his crotchets and ill humours. In the small family circle they called Figaro because as he trotted about his tasks, he parodied himself with the Rossini melody, *"Figaro qua, Figaro la, Figaro su, Figaro giu!"* When the women thanked him for his service and apologized for keeping him up late, he grinned and shrugged.

"In this job, one has to be a night creature. His Holiness often works into the small hours. He needs coffee and sandwiches, and an occasional chat. He likes to try out his ideas on me because, he says, even a pope can't be a hero to his valet; but if he can get through to me, he has a reasonable chance of making sense to the rest of the Church!"

The younger nun asked him:

"What is he really like in private?"

Claudio made an eloquent gesture of deprecation.

"What's he like? *Boh!* How do you turn an epic into a sonnet? He's been a big man in his time—and it's been a long time, too! Some might say too long. But you can't measure him by what you see in the bed there."

"Would you say he was a saint?" This time it was the older nun who put the question.

"A saint?" The valet made an elaborate comedy of pondering the question. "My dear Sister, I'm not sure I know what a saint is. In lots of ways he's just as human as you and me. He's got a quick temper—and it hasn't got any sweeter these last years. He doesn't like people to contradict him, but he admires anyone who is prepared to face him in a knock-down fight. He likes gossip, which is why he likes to have me around; but he listens too readily to people who make him feel good, because it's lonely up here, as you can feel for yourselves. Any mistakes he makes are bound to be big ones, with big consequences. In spite of all that, he's a generous man. He'll listen to all sides of a case—provided, of course, the Curia lets him hear them, which doesn't always happen. Is he a saint? I'd say you'd have to be something of a saint just to stick out the life he's lived. He scoots around the world like a tenor on tour, handing out smiles and blessings, which the people lap up, and reading speeches that the local hierarchies have written and the people yawn over. He also prays a lot. He used to say he couldn't survive without God to lean on. And God is very real to him." He broke off, then gave the women a little conspiratorial grin.

"Tell you what, Sisters, why don't you two finish your coffee, while I go in and tell him good night. I'd like to do that. And I think I should just tidy his closet and leave out a change of nightclothes in case you want to freshen him up before morning. Besides, it will make me feel useful. There's precious little else I can do for him."

He left them then. They lost sight of him as he turned inside the door of the bedroom to reach the pontiff's clothes closet. A few moments later, they caught a glimpse of him bundling up a few items of laundry and setting down a small pile of clean nightclothes at the foot of the bed. Then he did a curious and touching thing. He took two white handkerchiefs from the pile of fresh linen and touched them to the brow of the silent pontiff. Then he brought them out and, with a rueful smile, presented one to each of the nuns.

"Here! We all know he's never going to need them again.

I'm sure he'd like to say thank you for what you're doing for him. If they make him a saint one day, these will be important relics, won't they? And don't feel bad about taking them. I'm his valet. I bought them for him. You can't imagine a pope going shopping for fine cambric in the Via Condotti, can you?"

The two women were deeply moved. They were still murmuring their thanks when he waved good night and stepped quietly out of the room with the bundle of laundry in his hands. They did not know—how could they?—that Claudio Stagni had just procured for himself a lifetime pension: three slim volumes of the most intimate diaries of the pontiff, which he had written up at the end of each day and kept concealed in a drawer in his closet.

Their existence was unknown to anyone except his faithful valet, confidant and court jester, who had often provided an audience for the brusque comments of a weary man as he set them on paper. When he died, these records would pass immediately into the custody of the cardinal camerlengo, who might well choose to bury them for a century or two in the secret archive. Better, far better, that Figaro, the happy ironist, the long-suffering body servant, should present them to the world, provide them with context and provenance, and, in due time, write his own biography of the pontiff. There were already profitable deals on offer from several media sources for any material he chose to provide about his life as body servant to the pope; but, with these texts in his possession, Figaro was certain he could double and redouble and double them again, and live rich and happy ever after.

The nightmare of Luca Cardinal Rossini never changed. It was as if a strip of old silent film had been looped inside his skull and set to roll at the coldest, darkest hour before dawn. The action began each time with the same frame: a tiny, sub-Andean town northwest of Tucumán.

There were a church and a priest's house, facing a small
colonnaded market square, where grain and livestock
and pottery and woven fabrics were traded for goods im-
ported from Buenos Aires. The local population was a
typical Argentine cocktail of the mid-seventies: Cre-
oles, legal and illegal migrants from Chile and Uruguay,
mestizos and the relics of Inca tribes fragmented by the
policies of old Imperial Spain.

The carts of the traders, heavy lumbering vehicles,
were lined around the square so that the dwellers above
the colonnades had a theatergoer's view of the small
dramas enacted on the cobbles below. This also was
Rossini's viewpoint for the film unrolling in his head.
He was watching himself, enacting himself on a silent
screen.

The action began with a military truck driving into
the square. The townsfolk froze at the sight of it. A
group of militiamen leaped out and formed themselves
in a line facing the entrance to the church. Their commander was a sergeant, a hulking fellow who looked like
a circus strongman. He stepped out of the cabin of the
truck and stood a long time—an ominous giant, survey-
ing the scene and slapping at his breeches with a riding
crop.

Then he began a slow circuit of the square while its
small population of men, women, and children huddled,
mute, around the carts. When he had completed the
circuit, he signaled with his riding crop to the waiting
troops.

Four men stepped out of the ranks, two on either
flank of the square, and moved around the stallholders,
demanding—always in dumb show—their identity papers. If there was any delay or hesitation, the trade
goods were smashed or trampled on the ground. Anyone

who protested was felled immediately with fist or rifle butt. Children were cuffed or kicked aside.

Halfway through this systematic intimidation, Luca Rossini came running out of the church. He was dressed in shirt, slacks, and sandals. The only symbol of his priestly office was a small silver crucifix hung about his neck. Even as witness of the dream, he was shocked to see how young he was. The terror was that he could not hear the words he shouted, nor restrain his fierce gestures of protest.

He noted, however, that his silent shouting had some effect. The militiamen halted in their tracks and looked to the sergeant for orders. The sergeant raised his hand to command a pause, then walked up slowly to confront Rossini, who was still expostulating with gestures and silent mouthings. The sergeant smiled benignly and slashed him twice across the face with the riding crop. He signaled again to the troops, and Rossini was overwhelmed by a rush of armed men.

They tore the shirt from his back and pulled his trousers down around his ankles so that his back and his buttocks were bare. They spread-eagled him against the big wooden wheel of a trader's cart and tied his wrists and ankles to the rim and the spokes. He could see nothing now, except a patch of cobbles between the spokes and a pile of spilled grain and the frightened face of a child, hiding under the cart.

Then, measuring and savoring each stroke, the sergeant began to beat him with the riding crop. At first he tried to remain silent, biting his lips; but finally the first soundless screams were torn from him, and the screams turned to moans and grunts as the blows continued to fall on his back and buttocks. The crowd in the square was silent. The watchers in the windows were dumb with fear and horror. From a quarter of a century away, in another dimension of time and space, Luca Cardinal Rossini watched the cold-blooded degradation of the young man he had been. Finally, the beating ended. The sergeant wiped blood and tissue from his riding crop, then he stepped back to survey his handiwork. He nodded, smiled, and turned to address his troops. This time, the words were audible. They were spoken in Lunfardo, the argot of the slums of Buenos Aires, which Rossini had learned in his childhood.

"There now, see! I've softened him up for you. He's wet and warm. Who'd like to fuck a priest?"

The screen went black, and Luca Cardinal Rossini struggled out of the nightmare to face a gray Roman dawn.

There were others in Vatican City stirring early that morning. Staff members of the *Sala Stampa* had been up all night monitoring media sources in Europe, the Americas, and Southeast Asia. Their director, Monsignor Domingo Angel-Novalis, was at his desk by five, summarizing the information for the secretary of state.

Angel-Novalis was Aragonese, educated in Madrid, and launched early—with family money—on a successful career as an international financier. He had married well. His wife, a pious woman, had encouraged him to join the lay wing of Opus Dei. When his wife and their infant son were killed, he was supported in his grief by the fellowship of the congregation. Their rigorism, their close-knit and elitist community life matched his needs. Their closed-circuit philosophy stilled all doubts, as the old battle cry of the crusaders had steeled them to battle: *ut deus vult!*, "As God wills it!" At the end of a year, he applied and was accepted as a candidate for the priesthood.

In any profession he would have been prime material. In

this one, with a marriage and a successful career behind him— a personal battle won—he was gem quality. He finished his studies in Rome and was ordained there. He was commended to the attention of the pontiff. His history and his manifest talents as a communicator brought him swift appointment to the *Sala Stampa,* where a certain cool irony about the world and its ways won him respect if not affection. His note to the secretary of state was touched with the same irony.

So far, we have not done too badly with the world media. Most editors were caught off balance by the timing of your first bulletin. They had little chance to assemble commentary material or strike a clear editorial line. However, we may be sure that such material will emerge in the next few days. Early indicators are the following:

*Daily Telegraph London:* "The pontiff's collapse was not an unexpected event. What was unexpected was the decision to treat him in his Vatican apartment, rather than in Gemelli Hospital where he has usually gone for treatment. One explanation current in Rome—though not yet advanced by any Vatican source—is that the pontiff is so severely brain damaged that no intervention is feasible or desirable. However, in his present condition, every medical act—the administration of oxygen, hydration by intravenous drip—represents a significant act of intervention."

*Le Monde Paris:* "The message of the bulletin is clear enough. His Holiness had at an earlier time expressed his desire that there should be no officious prolongation of his life. Someone in the Vatican is clearly prepared to give witness to that effect. What is not at all clear is whether, in the same context, the pontiff consented in advance to be relieved of his office if there were any

doubt about his competence to serve the Church. In the
absence of such consent, then other questions arise: Can
his wish be presumed? If the presumption is disputed,
who decides the issue? And, how and in what form will
he be removed to open the way for a successor?"

*New York Times:* "Vatican physicians and curial officials are now facing a tightrope walk on an issue that,
when it touches the ordinary faithful, they tend to dis-
miss with a trenchant theological proposition. It is said
that the pope has rejected in advance any prolongation
of his already long life. So far, no documentary evidence
has been offered. The pope can no longer express himself in any fashion at all. He certainly cannot function
in his office. Who decides for him: his physician or a
curial committee? And by what criteria will they judge:
a rigorist theology or a liberal one? Both are current in
today's church. The pontiff was, without doubt, a rigorist. He pushed the limits of infallibility as far as he
could stretch them without a schism. So now, *quis cus-
todiet ipsos custodes?* Who will guard the guardians at
the gates, and how will the faithful judge their actions?"

With great respect, Eminence, I suggest that from this
moment onward, we return to the customary order of
communication. The *Sala Stampa* drafts the bulletins,
submits them to you for approval, and issues them
through its normal channels. We are walking now through
a minefield, and we have yet to encounter the tabloid
press and the talking heads of television!

 I beg an urgent instruction from Your Eminence. I
should like to draft the next bulletin myself, as soon as
the physicians have made their morning report.

D. Angel-Novalis

At six-thirty in the morning, Dr. Mottola and his two specialist colleagues examined their patient. They had asked to be left alone with him. The nursing Sisters had gone to get coffee, while the secretary of state and a group of senior prelates, together with the papal secretary and Domingo Angel-Novalis, were waiting in the pontiff's study.

"So, gentlemen!" Dr. Mottola addressed his colleagues. "Diagnosis and prognosis. We have to be as plain as we can. The gentlemen in the other room are under the griller. They need us to turn the heat down. They've brought Angel-Novalis back into the loop. He'll fit the right words to what we tell him. You first, Ernesto."

Dr. Ernesto Cattaldo shrugged resignedly.

"What you see. Deep coma, fixed stare, no sensation. He can't swallow, his respiration is low and spasmodic, with moments of apnea, which will become more frequent. He can't cough to clear fluid from his lungs. I'd list him terminal."

"Piero?"

Gheddo, the cardiologist, nodded.

"I'd agree terminal, but the decline is more gradual than one had hoped. He could last a few days yet. I'd suggest that the *Sala Stampa* leave a little leeway in the prose: 'The Holy Father's life is ebbing peacefully to its close.' That sort of thing."

"So, prognosis negative. How do we describe the treatment?"

Dr. Gheddo shrugged.

"Tell them the truth but not necessarily all of it. We're administering oxygen, which still isn't enough to balance the carbon-dioxide levels in the blood. We're hydrating him enough to keep him from burning up. We're not nourishing him at all."

"We're walking on eggshells here." Dr. Mottola was dubious.

"No we're not." The neurologist was sharp. "We're carrying out normal ethical treatment. Our business is with our patient, not with the press or the Roman Curia."

"I think," said Dr. Mottola judiciously, "it's rather a question of helping them find the right words to fit both the circumstances and their consciences. I count on your support in there, gentlemen!"

"All they need," said Gheddo, "is a few well-rounded phrases: 'limited intervention,' 'studious care for the comfort and dignity of a dying man.' The gentlemen in there are even less disposed than we are to a debate on ethical principles."

"Are we ready then?" Dr. Mottola put the question.

"Ready as we'll ever be," said Dr. Gheddo with weary resignation. "Christians to the lions! Let's get it done!"

They were surprised to find how little was required of them. The half-dozen senior prelates assembled in the room gave them a subdued greeting. The camerlengo presented Monsignor Angel-Novalis, who would in due course seek any clarification of their medical reports for inclusion in his bulletins for the world media. He asked Dr. Mottola to deliver the report in simple, nonclinical terms. Dr. Mottola summed up concisely the conclusions he had reached with the assistance of his distinguished colleagues. Then he waited. The first response came from Domingo Angel-Novalis, who was no mean professional himself. He was good-humored, and he cut clean to the heart of the matter:

"Thank you, gentlemen. May I rehearse what you have told me, to make sure I have it right? First, the Holy Father is dying. The end is expected very soon. You are delivering oxygen and hydration. His body cannot deal with more than that, because its functions are deteriorating. Correct so far?"

"Correct," said Dr. Mottola.

"And your colleagues agree?"

"They do."

"Will they continue to attend the pontiff until his demise?"

"If the cardinal camerlengo so directs, of course."

"A question, then, for all of you, gentlemen. You have initiated the treatments you describe. You are continuing them at this moment?"

"Yes."

"Have you terminated any treatments for any reason?"

"No."

"Would you recommend any treatments which are not presently being given?"

"No."

"Have you had any invitations from the media to discuss this case?"

The three doctors looked at one another. Dr. Mottola hesitated a moment before he answered.

"I have been questioned, yes. I cannot answer for my colleagues."

Cattaldo and Gheddo nodded but did not speak. The quiet inquisitor continued.

"I am sure, gentlemen, your responses were respectful of the patient-doctor relationship and of the family-doctor relationship which subsists between you and all members of the papal household."

"That goes without saying," said Dr. Mottola.

"I wonder, therefore,"—Dr. Cattaldo was annoyed—"why it was necessary to say it at all!"

"Please!" Angel-Novalis was instantly the diplomat. "Please don't be offended. I am simply uttering a caution. My colleagues and I deal every day with media folk all round the world. They are adept at building headlines around the most fragmentary phrases. Your simplest answer to any question is that you cannot discuss the case."

"That can raise problems, too."

"I submit, my dear doctor, that we are better equipped than you are to preempt them and to solve them. I would not presume for one moment to trespass on your professional ground. In my own field, however, I am quite expert. I am sure, for instance, that in the next few days, you and your colleagues will be offered substantial sums of money by the media, either for press

statements or television interviews on the last days of His Holiness. When you refuse them, as I am sure you will, then you may
be invited to answer some innocent-seeming questions. I counsel you to decline."

A small murmur of agreement went round the assembled
prelates. They approved of this man. He did not mince words.
He waltzed lightly round the booby traps. Angel-Novalis picked
up his notes and left the room. The cardinal camerlengo made a
little face-saving speech.

"Before you leave, gentlemen, I should like to express on
my own behalf and on behalf of all the members of the Curia
our thanks for your care of the Holy Father. We know that you
will continue to support him to the end, which, we pray, may not
be long deferred."

He swept them to the door, shook hands with each one, and
was back in half a minute to face the assembly once more. He
looked like a man who had just eased a great weight off his
shoulders.

"So, my brothers, we are losing our Father. I do not think
any of us will grudge him relief from the burdens of his service
to the Church. It falls to me as head of his household to prepare
for his passing and then to assume the governance of the
Church while the See is vacant. There is much to do. I should
like your permission to begin work now. *Placetne fratres?* Do
you agree, my brothers?"

"*Placet.*"

The old-fashioned formula ran like a ripple through the assembly. To this they could all assent. Whatever their rivalries
and discords, the community of the people of God continued in
Christ.

Luca Rossini had dispensed himself from the early-morning
meeting at the Vatican. The secretary of state had counseled
him to silence. It was not easy to be silent in an assembly of cu-

rial cardinals who were keeping a deathwatch on their supreme pastor; preparing for his obsequies; waiting to elect his successor; wondering what would happen when, as custom demanded, they resigned their offices and waited for the new pontiff to redistribute them.

He had little to add to their discussions of protocol and procedure. They were the inner cabinet. He had always been a rider on the farther marches, an emissary to the outposts of Christendom. More than any of his eminent colleagues, he would be vulnerable to the sharp winds of change. He had strong adversaries and few advocates in the sacred college, and he lacked the patience to placate the hostile or cultivate those who favored him.

Soon his patron would be dead. The man who had used the power of his office to salvage a damaged body and spirit would absent himself forever. Luca Rossini would be alone then. They called him a cardinal, a hinge man—one upon whom the gateways to power swung. Soon he might be a hinge to a gate that opened into nowhere. He, too, would have to resign the shadowy office he held and swear fealty and obedience to a new bishop of Rome, a new successor to Peter the Apostle. Was he prepared to do that? Absent any questions of morality or ethics, was he prepared to accept the perquisites of office and use them without guilt or remorse for his own ends, however those ends might define themselves? Once, he had believed the definition was easy. His first medical counselor had given it to him: *You will seek redress, justice, retribution. You will never get full payment. You will declare vendetta against* the *ungodly—and the godly who have collaborated with them. You will demand vengeance as a right* . . .

At his first audience in Rome, the pontiff, who was to become his patron and protector, had offered another definition.

"You are scarred. You are bitter. You are angry. If I were in your place, I should feel the same. In a way, I am in your place, because I appointed some of the prelates who, by their silence

or their connivance, permitted these atrocities to happen. Because they were dumb, we here in Rome were rendered blind
and deaf. I'm ashamed of that. I am ashamed of the many bar-
barities we appear to condone, through culpable ignorance or
the false opportunism that induces us to make pacts with evil.
So, wear your scars with pride. Keep your anger but learn to forgive! Meditate every day on the words of our Savior at the
height of his agony: 'Father, forgive them. They know not what
they do.' Do not forget either that this was the same man who
strode through the precincts of the temple striking out with a
lash at the peddlers and money changers who defiled the house
of God. . . . You will not change the world or yourself overnight,
but you have to try. You have to practice every day; so I will give
you work to stretch your strength and enlarge your spirit."

He had accepted the counsel in good faith. He had discharged the tasks he had been given with energy and good
judgment. He had accepted promotions as they were offered because, though they healed no wounds, they put power into his
hands. He learned early to use it with restraint, mindful of its
misuse against himself. The last thing he wanted was to create
tyrannies of his own.

He was scrupulous to weigh all the evidence in a cause
against any cleric or clerical institution. He allowed the largest
tolerances common sense would permit; but a case once proven,
he was as ruthless and precise as a surgeon excising a malig-
nant tumor.

It was this draconian discipline—and the secrecy within
which he was permitted to exercise it—which had driven him
up the steep slopes of preferment. It was this same discipline
which had leached out of him, drop by drop, the last life-
sustaining dregs of passion, leaving him parched and empty, a
lost traveler walking in circles.

He had seen it happen to others, older and wiser than himself. Trapped in their careers, lacking the will or the inducement to break out of them, protected always, they declined all

risk and surrendered themselves to a sceptical conformity in creed and conduct. In his early angry days, he had mocked them. Now, he was faced with the choice they had been offered at some stage of their lives: If you can't stand the heat, get out of the kitchen; if you still want to wear the chef's hat, step back from the stove and content yourself with licking the spoons to test what real cooks have made. Now, he himself was confronted with the same bleak proposition: Stay without honor, until the mask you wear becomes your own face; or quit and walk out to become a no-man in a no-place.

The thought brought back the terrors of his nightmare. He thrust them away from him, rang for his morning coffee, then switched on his computer to download his overnight E-mail.

There were letters from Manila and Djakarta, from Taiwan and Thailand, from Shanghai and Bombay. All of them dealt with tinderbox issues in the lesser known bailiwicks of the Church, where he had been sent or called to mediate contentions or establish constructive dialogues. This was where his best work was done. His scars were his passport to the least friendly territories, even to old men in Beijing who had survived the cultural revolution. There was a curious freemasonry between political martyrs. There were perennial, unspoken bonds between the victims of the rack and the inquisitors who had put them there.

He toyed with this thought as he dealt with his correspondence. He remembered how Paul the Apostle described himself in his letter to the Ephesians: *Paul the prisoner of Jesus Christ . . . a prisoner in the Lord.* For Luca Rossini, the phrase carried a sour aftertaste. Unlike Paul, he had no zeal left, only a stale conviction that common decency required him to finish the work that lay to his hand.

Just as he was about to switch off the machine, Isabel's letter appeared on the screen. The superscription showed it had been sent from New York at 0215 hours. He looked at his watch. Rome time was 0820 hours. The transmission had been immediate. The tone of the letter itself was urgent, almost peremptory.

My dearest Luca,

As you see, it is very late for me, but at least I can be private and alone. My husband is spending two days in Washington. However, I telephoned him with the news that you are prepared to commend his appointment when the time is ripe. He was, of course, delighted, and he has asked me to convey his thanks to you. He will write personally to you in due course, but, prudent fellow that he is, he feels that any correspondence at this time would be inopportune!

I found it, however, an opportune moment to get his approval for Luisa and myself to leave immediately for Rome and to stay there long enough to show an unofficial family presence, with Argentine diplomats, at the obsequies of the present pontiff and the installation of a new one. I put it to Raul also that this would be a useful introduction for Luisa into diplomatic circles abroad. He thought that, too, was an excellent idea. Since he has maintained for a long time now a mistress in New York, he will not find himself too deprived of home comforts.

Why am I doing this? I am my father's daughter. You know how little taste I have for pomps and ceremonies.

I am coming to see you, Luca. I have been desperate with worry since I read your letter. I have known you in every mood. I have held you in my arms while you wept like a child. I have seen you murderous with rage. I, your Isabel, taught you to turn the rage into passion and spend it on my body in nights that I shall remember till I die. I reopened your heart to love. I cannot bear to see it locked again under this glacial calm which you display to the world.

The calm will not last. It cannot. Either the Luca I know will wither and die of the cold, or he will burst out like the volcanoes of Iceland and blow himself to fragments. So, like it or not, I am coming. In the morning I have to make final arrangements. I have to get there fast, before you go into conclave to elect a pope. What if they elect you and you never escape from your prison-house? That's a nightmare, isn't it?

Don't write again. I'll contact you as soon as we arrive. One special request: Please spare a little attention for my daughter. She is a beautiful young woman and much interested in this important man whom her mother and her grandfather had rescued from the brutal militia. Expect us very soon.

All my love always,

Isabel

He leaned back in his chair, sipped his coffee slowly, and contemplated the text on the screen. He smiled and shook his head, admonishing himself for his own self-deceit. This was the visitation he had dreamed often—and now, albeit subconsciously, had contrived.

There was nothing exaggerated in Isabel's memories of him, nor his of her. She was too open and forthright a woman to tolerate the half-truths which, as a celibate cleric in a high place, he used to assist his commerce in society. Everything she claimed to have done for him, she had done.

There was more still to be told. There were omissions even from the last story that had been told to him by Carlos Menéndez, Isabel's father:

"You know I'm running a big prospecting operation in the foothills for Petroleo Occidental. We have our base camp in the mountains, but I keep an apartment over the colonnades in the square. Sometimes Isabel comes in from Buenos Aires to stay with me. She's been married to Raul a little more than a year; but the honeymoon is long over. He's always been ambitious, always a snob. Isabel despises his lickspittle defense of the military, who, God knows, are a pretty shabby bunch. I've been a military engineer myself, rank of major. Then, I quit to join Petroleo Occidental. Still, I've remained on the reserve, and I keep a uniform handy. It pays when they send the bullyboys around to frighten the country folk. It happened that Isabel and I were both in the apartment when the militia hit the town. We saw you strung up. We saw the beating begin."

"And you let it happen?"

"We let part of it happen. I knew that sergeant, he was an ugly, sadistic brute. He was quite capable of ordering his men to open fire on the people in the square. I gave Isabel my rifle and told her to keep him covered while I climbed into my uniform and buckled on a sidearm. I knew you'd survive a beating, but no one survives a bullet in the head."

"But, for God's sake, Carlos, that beating went on for a long time."

"Long or short, by the time I was ready to intervene, it was over and the sergeant was challenging the boys to sodomize you."

"That's as far as I remember. I blacked out."

"Didn't Isabel tell you the rest of it?"

"She fed it to me in small doses like medicine. She said you'd give me the whole story later."

"I'm giving it now. The troops held back. The sergeant laughed and told them he'd show them how to do it. He started unbuttoning his breeches. I rushed down the stairs. When I hit the square, I saw him showing off his penis to the troops. Just as he turned to rape you, Isabel fired and blew the back of his head off. The troops were still standing flat-footed in shock when I fired two shots in the air and shouted to them to come to attention. When they saw the uniform, they obeyed. I ordered them to toss the sergeant's body into the truck and get the hell back to their barracks. As soon as they were gone, I cut you down. The townsfolk helped me carry you to the apartment. Isabel dressed your wounds as best she could. I called the military commandant at Tucumán. I told him he had big trouble on his hands, trouble with the junta and with the Church, whom the junta was wooing like a virgin bride. I had sent the troops back to him, with a body to bury. I told him to bury it fast and deep. Then, I made two calls, one to our base camp to send in a chopper with our camp doctor, the other to a friend of mine who has a big *estancia* north of Cordoba. We flew you there. Isabel stayed with you. I went back to San Miguel and then on to Buenos Aires to square things off with the junta and get the cardinal archbishop and the apostolic nuncio onside. My company helped, too, but God!—it was the roughest six weeks of my life. Isabel's husband was useless. In the end, we cut a deal. I would fly you into Buenos Aires and hand you over to the apostolic nuncio, who would have you flown out immediately to Rome. I would go back to my work. Isabel would return to her husband. No publicity. No comment. Case closed. Is there anything else you want to know before you leave Argentina?"

"How do you feel about Isabel and me?"

"She was good for you. You, in a strange way, were good for her. I was happy to see you enjoy each other. You're much better value than the clown she married."

"Why did she marry him?"

"He was a beautiful piece of merchandise: old family, well educated, good manners, rich, all the girls wanted him; so, Isabel had to have him. Well, she got him. An empty man who rattles like a gourd but still looks like sound fruit in the bowl."

"Why doesn't she leave him?"

"She's thought about it more than once. Now she can't—at least not for a while."

"Why not?"

"Use your brains, man! You don't know what it cost to bargain ourselves out of this mess. Isabel has to keep her head down. Her husband's not powerful in the junta but his father is, and he'd make a bad enemy . . . That's one very good reason why I want you gone and out of her life."

"Are there other reasons?"

"Several."

"Let me hear them!"

"You're a priest. She has no future in you."

"There's not much of the priest left."

"Something of the man may be lost, too. It takes a long time to recover from the experience of torture and the degradation that goes with it. That's why it's such a powerful tool in politics. It's too soon to know how you'll come out. If you want it plain, I'll give it to you. I don't want Isabel playing nursemaid to an emotional cripple. One of those is more than enough for any woman."

"What will happen to her now?"

"Nothing will happen. She's my daughter. She'll cut her life to her own pattern. Your folk came from Italy, didn't they?"

"Yes, why do you ask?"

"Because you'll understand what I mean when I tell you Isabel's a made woman now. I hope one day you'll be a made man."

"Does that mean I have to kill someone?"

"Someone, something. You'll know when the time
comes . . ."

Now it seemed the time was very near, the time against which
good Christian folk prayed every day. *Lead us not into temptation but deliver us from evil.* Luca Cardinal Rossini could not
pray. The gift of belief was gone from him. He could only wait,
alone in his desert, for the day of trial.

# 3

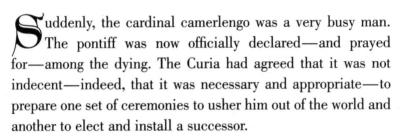

Suddenly, the cardinal camerlengo was a very busy man. The pontiff was now officially declared—and prayed for—among the dying. The Curia had agreed that it was not indecent—indeed, that it was necessary and appropriate—to prepare one set of ceremonies to usher him out of the world and another to elect and install a successor.

In each case, the presumptions of canon law were different. The pope was still alive; therefore, his wishes and intentions still prevailed—insofar as they were known or could be guessed. He was being cared for in his own house, with privacy and dignity; but now the embalmers were put on notice to come swiftly when he died. The three coffins—of cypress, lead, and oak—were already being made. The master of ceremonies was setting out the order of events that would take place at his lying in state, at his funeral Mass, and at his interment in the crypt of St. Peter's basilica.

The Council of State of Vatican City was already preparing the new currency and the new stamps which would be used during the vacancy of the See. The security force was making ready for a large influx of secular and clerical dignitaries who would attend the obsequies.

Vatican bureaucracy moved often slowly and cumbrously on creaking wheels; but in matters of life, death, and public image, it ran with wonderful smoothness. It performed most spectacularly in ceremonies, which also contributed to the aging and death of the most vigorous of pontiffs.

At this midmorning hour, however, the camerlengo was engaged, not in ceremony, but in a dialogue with Monsignor Victor Kovacs, private secretary to His Holiness.

"You understand, Victor, what happens when His Holiness dies?"

"More or less, Eminence. You have to verify the event, sign the death certificate with the physician, summon the embalmers, and consign the body into their hands."

"All that and a little more. I have to deface his personal seals and take possession of everything in his chambers, even down to his underwear. What I need from you now is a guided tour. I have to know where everything is kept: his will, his correspondence—both personal and official—his diaries. After the body has been removed, the rooms will be locked and sealed. It would help me a great deal if you could prepare an inventory as quickly as possible."

"I've already begun it, Eminence. Let me walk you around so that you see for yourself how everything is arranged. As I think you know, His Holiness was not—forgive me, *is* not—the most systematic of men. I've had to beg him not to rummage through files but ask me to find whatever he wants and let me put it back afterward. He always told me I was as fussy as an old woman. Even so, I confess I'll miss him . . . Let's do the desk drawers first and then the filing cabinets."

"Does His Holiness have a private repository of any sort?"

"There's a wall safe behind that picture."

"Who has the combination?"

"Only His Holiness and myself."

"You should give it to me also."

"Of course."

"And if you would, please demonstrate the opening and closing of the safe."

Monsignor Kovacs wrote out the combination on a card and handed it to the camerlengo. Then he showed him how the framed sepia sketch by Raffaello was hinged to the wall. When it swung back it revealed the wall safe. The secretary opened the safe, locked it immediately, and asked the camerlengo to repeat the routine. When he had done that successfully, the secretary swung the picture back into place. Neither man had attempted to take anything from the safe. This was the protocol. The pontiff was still alive. His writ still ran. The camerlengo and the secretary completed their circuit. The camerlengo asked:

"Is there anything of importance in his bedroom?"

"Not to my knowledge. He keeps a breviary and a bible on one bedside table; on the other, whatever other book he happens to be reading at the moment. When he's been ill at various times, he has had me bring him documents he needed. I always made sure that Figaro—excuse me, again!—Claudio Stagni returned them to the office. He, of course, would know what else is in the bedroom."

The camerlengo gave a small chuckle.

"Claudio Stagni knows everything—but never tells the half of it. Still, he's an amusing fellow. I'll talk with him now."

"It's strange, Eminence."

"What's strange, Victor?"

"His Holiness was always quite jealous of his personal privacy. Stagni was the only one who shared it with him. Now His Holiness just lies there with people coming in and out all the time. He would have hated that if he knew. He's so utterly dependent, like a newborn child, except he has no life at all ahead of him. May I ask you a question, Eminence?"

"Of course, Victor. What's troubling you?"

"When I said my Mass very early this morning, I offered it as a petition to God to release the Holy Father from this life—

which for him is not a life anymore. When I was reciting the creed, one phrase hit me like a blow: *descendit ad inferos,* 'He descended into the lower regions.' I asked myself whether it was just an archaic expression describing the mysterious time between Our Lord's death and His resurrection or whether it might also describe what has happened to the pontiff. Is he in some other region or state? Is he really with us still? Even you and I are acting as though he's long gone."

The man's distress was so real that the camerlengo himself was touched to a rare gentleness.

"I tell you truly, Victor. I don't know. Ask my colleague, Gruber, and I'm sure he'll read you a fine metaphysical lecture on the subject. But for my part, I confess ignorance, and I am content to remain ignorant. For me, the act of faith is an act of acceptance that we live and die in mystery. Hope is a trust that one day the mystery will be made as plain to us as God chooses to make it. And charity is the gift to love and be joyful in love. I know you're depressed; but be assured you served His Holiness well. He acknowledged that many times to me and to other members of the Curia. He could be difficult, I know, but he was fond of you."

"That's good to hear. Thank you."

"Now, I'll go talk to our friend Figaro. I'll inspect the bedchamber and say a prayer for our patient. You have work to do. I won't bother you any longer."

In the presence of the dying pontiff and the inquisitive camerlengo, Claudio Stagni gave a splendidly muted performance. He knelt by the bedside with the cardinal and the attendant Sisters and responded with grave emotion to the verse of the *De Profundis,* "Out of the depths I have cried to you, O Lord, hear the voice of my pleading." After the prayer, he led the cardinal around the chamber; opening every cupboard and every drawer; exhibiting the items they contained; pointing out, as the secretary had already done, that the pontiff, especially in his later years, was a hard man to keep tidy; he burrowed, he disarranged things, he put things down and forgot where he had left them.

"Of all the people in the world, His Holiness needed a valet. Monsignor Kovacs and myself worked out a little arrangement. No documents to be left lying around in the bedroom. His Holiness knew that he was being managed. He grumbled about it sometimes, but he was glad of it, really. Secret repositories? Strange you should ask that, Eminence. Here, let me show you something. This bureau drawer has a secret compartment. It is open, as you see, and empty. There is a key inside it, but in all the years I've served him, I've never known His Holiness to use it."

"And that's everything you can show me?"

"Everything, Eminence. But I do have a small confession to make."

"About what?"

"Last night, on an impulse, I gave each of the Sisters on night watch one of the handkerchiefs I had bought only a few days ago for His Holiness. They were so deeply touched, I was glad I had done it. Then, afterward, I began to think."

The camerlengo was not happy. His reproof was sharp and angry.

"That was a foolish and a reckless act, Claudio. That is the very thing I am appointed to prevent—any unauthorized traffic in relics and souvenirs after the pontiff dies. You've been here long enough to know better."

"I realized that afterward, Eminence. It was impulse only. If you want, I shall ask the Sisters to return the handkerchiefs."

"No, no! That would only compound the mistake. But understand, there must be no more of this! It could very easily grow into a scandal—or worse still, an absurdity! People peddling the pontifical underwear in the flea market at Porta Portese! Use your brains, man!"

"I am truly sorry, Eminence."

"We'll say no more of it, then. I'm finished here. You are excused."

"Thank you, Eminence."

He walked out, stoop shouldered and repentant as a schoolboy. The moment he was outside the papal apartment, he broke into a little jig step to the rhythm of his theme song: *Figaro qua, Figaro la, Figaro su, Figaro giu.*

Steffi Guillermin was a late riser. She liked to sit up in bed with Lucetta, sipping coffee while she read the morning papers and checked the various Eurovision channels for headline news. This morning's Vatican bulletin provoked an exclamation of surprise and a reluctant tribute to Angel-Novalis.

"He takes first prize, that one. He's clever and handsome as Lucifer. He's disarmed most of the land mines in the euthanasia argument and short-circuited his own right-wing theologians in Opus Dei. He makes no argument with them. They can have no quarrel with him, but he still creates a profound impression with a question he leaves unasked: What would you do if your own parent were stricken like this?"

"So, it's a clever piece of public relations. What else does it signify?"

"Possibly nothing; but think about this: His Holiness has been packing the hierarchy and the sacred college itself with men who are, by his standards, safe conservatives. In other words, he has tried to ensure, as far as he can, that his policies for the Church are continued after his death. He's always been a centralist and an interventionist; but both policies have already begun to backfire. So, there exists an interest group who wants to keep the old man alive as long as possible."

"But why?"

"The longer the election can be deferred, the better chance they have to consolidate their voting bloc. It's no secret that there has been much traveling of late by members of the sacred college—visits to colleagues around the world. In the old days, that wasn't possible. Now, it's easy, and much safer than correspondence."

"But now, you say, he's being nursed at home, and the conservatives may be thwarted by his early demise?"

"That's what I think, but I've always believed he was too smart to be outflanked even by death. My thought is that he must have kept notes, dossiers, observations for and against any future candidates for the succession."

"If such notes exist," Lucetta was dubious, "where are they now?"

"Probably not in the Vatican."

"Why do you say that?"

"It's common sense. His Holiness knows that when he dies, everything will pass into the hands of the cardinal camerlengo. I'm guessing that he would have made provision against that by giving the documents into safekeeping."

"Whose, for instance?"

"I don't know." Steffi pondered the thought for a few moments, then exclaimed, "My God, I'm a fool not to have thought of it before!"

"Thought of what?"

"Three days ago, my people in Paris told me they had been approached by a New York agent who suggested that a document written by the pontiff might be coming on the market after his death. They were asked whether they'd be interested in picking up French-language rights."

"And were they interested?"

"How could they not be?"

"Who else has been approached?"

"In Germany it has to be *Der Spiegel*—which might explain why Fritz Ulrich was being so obnoxious to me yesterday. Maybe also that was why Frank Colson was so supportive. The

*Telegraph* would not normally be the first target for a deal like that. The *Sunday Times* would be a more likely bidder."

"So, what's your next move?"

"Nose about. See if I can pick up the smell of money or rumor. Once the documents are demonstrated, then my people will expect me to check on provenance and authenticity before they pay out money. But by then the story won't be exclusive."

"Where can you start? You can't very well wander round Vatican City quizzing this prelate and that about contraband documents."

"I doubt Rome would be a good place to start, anyway. Whoever's offering this merchandise would be looking to make money far away from Italy—and wanting to keep it away."

"That still points to an original Vatican source for the documents, someone close to the pontiff, with ready access."

"In other words, a civilian, who has a readier exit than a cleric?"

"But how could you prove it?"

"Why would we want to prove anything? All we need to know is that whatever documents we're offered are genuine. Any more would be an embarrassment."

"Why should it be an embarrassment?"

"Because, my love, our prime interest is in the story. So long as its provenance is sound, nobody will care how it came into my hands. That's for other people to worry about."

Luca Cardinal Rossini was bidden to lunch with the secretary of state in his private apartment in the Apostolic Palace. He knew of old that it would be a spartan repast: soup, pasta, cheese, a small carafe of thin white wine, and strong black coffee to banish any thought of sleep during the Roman siesta time.

Cardinal Salvatore Pascarelli—Turi to his few intimates— was as tall and thin as a hay rake, and he deplored obesity in

clerics, which he said, with a certain sardonic wit, brought the
Church into disrepute. He was an industrious and subtle man
who had climbed the formidable ladder of training and educa-
tion in the secretariat from attaché second-class to attaché first-
class, to minute writer, counselor, office chief for general affairs,
substitute secretary, and finally to the award of a cardinal's hat
and the premier title in the Roman Curia.

He wore his rank lightly; but the cares of his office weighed
heavily on his bony shoulders. He claimed, with some reason,
that the only way to handle the political interests of a billion
professing believers on a very messy planet was to think of
them as a huge mosaic and to keep the loose pieces cemented,
however small or unimportant they might appear. If too many
loosened themselves at once, the whole picture could fall apart.
This attitude of mind made him often appear exacting; but his
sense of history, of how the past redisposed itself in the future,
was sound and sometimes prophetic. So, Luca Rossini judged
it prudent to have his minute on the ambassadorial candidate
written and delivered prior to the luncheon. The secretary of
state begged that it be read to him, apologizing for the eccen-
tricity with a disarming smile.

"I was taught in my youth that the test of a good document
was that the cadences fell rightly. The truth is, Luca, I like the
sound of your accent. Please read it to me."

"You're the host, Turi! You call the tune. It's a very short
text. I assume you didn't want a whole essay."

"Of course not. Go ahead."

" 'Minute on Raul Jaimé Ortega, proposed by the government of Argentina for appointment as Ambassador to the Holy
See. I have read the proposal. I have never met the candidate
personally, though I have some knowledge of his background. I
note that he claims an important role in securing my safe exit
from Argentina during the regime of the military junta. My information at the time was that his influence was minimal. The
real power was exercised by his father, General Jaimé Alfonso

Ortega, who was an important personage in the junta. On the other hand, Raul Ortega's wife, Isabel, nursed me back to health after the beating and sheltered me in secret while her father was negotiating for my safe conduct out of the country. Given Raul Ortega's eagerness to have this final posting at the Vatican, it is perhaps understandable that he should exaggerate his own role. I see no good reason to contest his version of the affair. I am sure he would make at least a competent ambassador, and by all accounts, an ornamental one. In short, I record a *nihil obstat*— no fundamental objection. I recommend, however, a minimal expectation of him in either good or harm to the Holy See.' "

The secretary of state leaned back in his chair and laughed.

"Beautifully read, Luca! Beautifully drafted! An elegant warrant for a bloodless execution!"

"Isn't that what you were expecting?"

"Let's say I was curious to know what you would say— given the special circumstances."

Luca Rossini chided him sharply.

"Don't play games with me, Turi! We've known each other too long."

"This is not a game, Luca, just the prelude to our lunchtime discussion. When you came to Rome all those years ago with the apostolic nuncio, a certain amount of rumor came with you. The nuncio discounted it in his report but pointed out that the junta would certainly use it against you if you attempted to speak out against them."

"The junta is long out of power. So the threat is irrelevant."

"True."

"But these rumors remain noted in your files."

"As a matter of record only."

"What do they say?"

"That during your rescue, a sergeant was shot and that while you were recovering in a secret hiding place, you had a love affair with Ortega's wife."

"The love affair was constructed as a rumor. It happened to

be a fact. I made this known to His Holiness when he first received me in Rome. I have never made any pretense or excuse
about what happened. On the other hand, I have never felt
obliged to broadcast it. To do so would have put Isabel at even
greater risk. She had killed a man to save me. She gave me a
love that restored my manhood."

"Were you never tempted to stay in Argentina and continue
the affair?"

"Of course, but that would have put both her and her father
at risk of their lives. My exile was the price of their safety."

"Did you love her, Luca?"

"I did. I do."

"And she loves you?"

"Yes. We still correspond. It doesn't heal the wounds, but it
makes them easier to bear. Why are you raising all this now,
Turi? It has been buried for more than twenty years!"

"Because I wondered how you would react to Ortega's posting as ambassador if he intended, as he obviously does, to bring
his wife and daughter with him."

"In point of fact, Turi, his wife and their daughter are coming to Rome for a private visit in the very near future."

"That's news to me!" The secretary of state was genuinely
surprised. "When did you hear this?"

"Only this morning. There was a message from Isabel on
my E-mail. I hope your people can reserve a couple of good
seats for them on the diplomatic fringes in St. Peter's, and in the
Piazza."

"Of course. I take it you'll be seeing them during their visit?"

"Isabel said she would contact me when she arrived in
Rome."

The secretary of state permitted himself a slow smile of approval. He said gently:

"I hope it's a pleasant experience for you both. You have
been given a special gift, Luca, the gift to survive in a solitude of
the heart. I've often wondered how you could be so bold in your

dealings, even with the Holy Father himself. You hide nothing. You face up to every question, as you have just done now. We're all going to need that gift very soon. Now, let's have lunch. There are large matters to discuss and we need nourishment."

The frugal meal was soon over. The wine was as thin as ever, but they lingered a long time over coffee. The secretary of state opened his heart to Luca Rossini as he had never done before.

"Our man is dying, Luca—the man who gave each of us the red hat and put me in this job. The press of the world is sitting in judgment on him. Before and during the conclave, you and I will be delivering our own judgments."

"And what will be yours, Turi?"

"We must abrogate many practices we have condoned too long, and many policies which our master has framed."

"And which you administered."

"Administered, enforced, or at the very least did not protest strongly enough. Even so, I shall feel like a traitor to his memory."

"Don't blame yourself too much, Turi. We are what we were trained to be: obedient in heart and mind and will."

"I'm not in the mood for mockery, Luca!"

"I'm not mocking you. God forbid! I, too, have wept over our pontiff. He gave me kindness when I needed it and dignity when I had none. I fought him, sometimes more bitterly than you know, because I saw behind him the shapes of old tyrannies, and before him the shadow of new ones."

"But you fought him. I didn't."

"You were always a good officer, Turi. You were incapable of mutiny. I've been on the verge of it many times."

"Where are you now, Luca?"

Luca Rossini frowned as he tried to frame his answer.

"I'm still in uniform. I live by the book. I draw my stipend. I do my job as best I can. Only my reasons have changed."

"How?"

"That's another question for another time. Tell me what's on your mind, Turi."

The secretary of state was silent for a moment. He seemed to be gathering his thoughts, sorting through words, debating whether or not to trust himself to Luca Rossini. Finally he began to talk, haltingly at first, then with passion and eloquence.

"You don't need me to read you a list of the ills of the Church. We have defied the reality of human experience; we have refused to listen to the people of God, men and women of goodwill. They have asked for the bread of life and we have offered them stones. So, they have turned away—men, women, and children, too. We, ministers of the Word, have become irrelevant to them. Sometimes of late, I have had a recurrent nightmare: His Holiness in full pontificals, standing on the battlements of a ruined castle, a lost crusader, shouting his rallying cry across a desert, empty of people . . ."

"When he topples off," Rossini supplied the coda, "we bury him and turn away to find another candidate for crucifixion. When that one's bled out, we let him, too, hang on the cross while the crows peck his eyes out."

"That's the beginning of the madness!" There was fire in Pascarelli's voice now. "We are twentieth-century people. God knows, we should have learned by now the diminishments and dangers of the aging process. Even for a pope, there is no insurance against dementia, or any other encroachment of age. Yet we elect our candidate for life, kneel in perpetual fealty, attribute to him an infallible discernment, and use every sophistry in theology to endow him with the numen of near divinity . . . Vicar of Christ! I've always found the title hard to swallow, though I've never had the courage to challenge it. Was Alexander VI a Vicar of Christ, or Julius II or Sergius III, who murdered his two predecessors? We can't blame ourselves for the past, but we are responsible for repeating it. You're right, my dear Luca, when you talk about electing a candidate for cruci-

fixion. We begin, indeed, by tempting him up to a high mountain and showing him literally all the kingdoms of the world at
one glance. I can do that little trick in my own office with a map
of the world and some flashing lights! Then we play on his crusader's ambition. The Word is the sword of the spirit. With swift
travel and instantaneous communication, the Word can be
made always and everywhere present, delivered by and in the
pontiff himself. That's heady wine, Luca—all those upturned
faces, those outstretched hands! The need they express is much
more seductive to a good man than all the gold and glitter and
lechery of Avignon or Renaissance Rome. So, when we ask him,
'Do you accept election?' he consents with appropriate gravity
and humility. Then he sets out, as Paul did, full of passion, zeal,
and certainty, to change the world." He broke off abruptly. "You
can finish the story, Luca. I need more coffee."

Luca Rossini picked up the narrative on a note of smiling
irony.

"He learns the hard way that jet lag and travel weariness
do impair the judgment, that those he leaves to keep house in
Rome have their own ambitions: to create their own dukedoms
inside the Kingdom of God. He learns what every politician
and every beautiful woman has to learn: that overexposure is a
danger, that the image becomes shopworn, the noblest phrases
sound like clichés, and the warmest welcome wears out in
time, because the guest and his entourage cost money to feed
and entertain."

"There's more yet, Luca." The secretary of state continued
the recital. "All this learning doesn't come at once. It comes in
a series of subdued shocks, like the tremors in an earthquake
zone. The tremors are unsettling. They create a sense of solitude, which creates in its turn a dependence upon the comfort
of counselors within an inner cabinet. So, the great traveler becomes a recluse, clinging to certainties within his own soul,
trusting a small cabal of intimate friends, losing the language of

the common folk from whom he sprang. We have a chance to change that, Luca—one chance."

"Define it for me, Turi."

"Let's find ourselves a pope who will agree to call a new general council, to write into the canons a statutory age for the retirement of a pope—just as it has been written for us—and a consent in advance to his own removal, should he become mentally incompetent."

"Let me ask you then, Turi, if you were elected, would you do such things? There's a catch here, you see. Once you're in office and endowed with all the absolute powers, who reminds you of your promise? Who exacts performance? You have to know the answer, Turi. You're a prime candidate."

"I shall not be a candidate. I shall so inform the electors."

"Why, Turi? Why are you telling me this?"

"To the first question: I'm a good diplomat because I can juggle endlessly with the possible. I work in private, not in public. I have no pastoral experience, nor any real wish to acquire it. Why am I telling you? I think there's at least an outside chance that you could be elected."

"Me?" Luca Rossini was shocked. He was no longer the sceptic and the ironist. "That's madness, Turi! I've always been an exotic here. Some of our colleagues used to call me 'the protected species.' That's what I was, the pseudohero, the young martyr miraculously preserved to do great things in the Church! Let me tell you, Turi, I was one of His Holiness's more notable mistakes! I'm not what you think I am. I'm not even . . ."

There was the muted shrilling of a telephone. The secretary of state held up his hand to silence Rossini. He fished in the pocket of his soutane and brought out his phone.

"This is Pascarelli." He listened in silence for a few moments, thanked the caller, and switched off. He turned to Rossini.

"His Holiness has just died."

"God rest him," said Luca Rossini, the unbeliever.

"Amen," said the secretary of state. "Now the See is vacant and we all have work to do."

Claudio Stagni had one last service to render to his master. He laid out the vestments in which the pontiff's body would be clothed by the embalmers for the lying in state and the entombment. Then he presented himself to the camerlengo.

"I have finished, Eminence. Is there anything more you need from me?"

"Thank you, Claudio. There is nothing."

"Will there be employment for me here after the election?"

"I'm sure there will be something, but not in the present post. A new pontiff will wish to make his own household arrangements. You are of pensionable age, yes?"

"I am. I also have several months accumulated leave."

"I suggest you take some of it now."

"Thank you, Eminence. I need to think what I shall do with my life."

"Of course. We are grateful for your long and faithful service, Claudio."

"It was my honor and always my pleasure to serve His Holiness. He was a great man."

"A great man," said the camerlengo absently. "Was there anything else, Claudio?"

"Just one thing, Eminence. I hope it will not seem disrespectful if I do not attend the funeral. I don't think I could face the crowds and the long ceremonies. My life with His Holiness was a very private one."

"You're a bachelor, I understand."

"That's right. His Holiness used to say sometimes we were just two old bachelors living in a house too big for them."

"That's one way of putting it." The camerlengo's tone was dry. "Have a good holiday."

"Thank you, Eminence."

His Eminence was already bent over his checklists. Figaro bowed himself out and walked sedately down to the paymaster's office to collect all the monies due him and file the application for his pension. Once outside Vatican City, he hailed a taxi to take him to his apartment in Trastevere, where he picked up his baggage: an overnight bag and a scuffed briefcase. From Trastevere he was driven to Fiumicino airport to embark on a six o'clock flight to Zurich.

On arrival in Zurich he checked into a suite in the Savoy Hotel. The tariff made him gasp, then he remembered what had brought him here and was cheerful again. He locked his briefcase in the room safe, called the desk clerk to tell her that he could be found in the grillroom, then went downstairs to order a dinner that even a self-indulgent cardinal might envy. He was sitting over his coffee and an excellent brandy when the waiter brought him the telephone. A woman's voice asked in Italian:

"Claudio Stagni?"

"Yes."

"This is Barbara Busoni from New York. We are downstairs in the lobby. May we come up?"

"The concierge will send someone to escort you to my suite."

"There will be three of us."

"So many?"

"A handwriting expert, an attorney, and myself."

"Good! I like tidy work. I, myself, am a very tidy man. I'll see you in a few minutes."

He called for the check, signed it with a flourish, drained the last drop of brandy, then walked jauntily to the elevator to face the inquisitors, whom he hoped to turn overnight into generous paymasters.

The woman was younger and more attractive than he had expected, with honey-colored skin, dark eyes, a Florentine accent, and russet hair cut in a pageboy style. She made the introductions quite formally.

"Mr. Stagni, I am Barbara Busoni. We have talked several times. I work with our agency on developmental projects. If we go ahead, I'll be your editor. This gentleman is Maury Rosenheim, our in-house attorney; and this is Sergei Malenkov, a recognized handwriting expert. This, gentlemen, is signor Claudio Stagni, formerly valet to His Holiness."

"Formerly or presently?"

"Formerly, Mr. Rosenheim. His Holiness died this morning."

"I didn't know. I've been flying for eight hours, sleeping for most of it. I take it you have already left your employment."

"Not at all. I am on holiday. The cardinal camerlengo— that's the chamberlain, in English—suggested I use up some of my accumulated leave before deciding whether I should seek other employment in the Vatican."

The lawyer frowned in puzzlement.

"This isn't the way it was represented to me, Barbara. I know I'm tired but . . ."

"Why don't you just hush up and listen, Maury. We're a long way from documents yet. It is my understanding that Mr. Stagni is offering us an intimate personal memoir of his years as valet to the pontiff, together with exclusive rights to certain private papers of the pontiff which have come legitimately into his possession. Mr. Stagni has agreed in principle that he would dictate his memoirs under my supervision and that I would edit them as we work, so that they could be ready for syndication before the conclave begins. The price we discussed was one million five in U.S. dollars for world rights in all media, payable half on the beginning of work and half on completion. Is that your understanding, Mr. Stagni?"

"I understood and accepted it as a starting point for negotiation. Circumstances have changed since then."

"In what respect, Mr. Stagni?"

"Much more material—intimate and exclusive material in the pontiff's own hand—has been made available to me. It is of such a nature that I believe it should be published first, and my memoir second, because that way great value would be added to both projects."

"You mean, Mr. Stagni, you're hiking the price?"

"On the one hand, yes. On the other, I'm offering you an enormously more valuable product."

"May we see some of it, please?" Barbara Busoni was testy now. "You must admit this is something of a surprise."

"Figaro was always full of surprises, wasn't he?"

"Figaro?"

"That was the nickname they gave me in Rome. I was the pope's valet, barber, costumier, whatever; but I was also one of the few people who could get a real laugh out of him. Here, let me show you what we're talking about." He opened his worn briefcase and took out a leather-bound missal. He opened it to a flyleaf and passed it to Malenkov, the handwriting expert.

"I presume, sir, you have studied some specimens of the late pontiff's handwriting; otherwise, you wouldn't be here?"

"That's true."

"And since this is a friendly discussion and not a court of law, I accept you as an expert. Now, would you be good enough to study the dedicatory inscription in this missal? In case you don't read Italian, I'll translate it for you.

To my faithful servant, Claudio Stagni:
My Figaro, who in some very dark hours offered
     me the gift of laughter.
On the occasion of his fiftieth birthday.

And that's followed by his signature. You have no problem identifying the handwriting or identifying the signature?"

"None at all."

"Now look at this. It is, as you see, a short letter from the pontiff, written on one of his memo cards. Again, I'll read the text.

My dear Figaro,

Five and a half centuries ago, one of my predecessors, Pope Pius II, Enea Silvio Piccolomini, dictated his
memoirs to his secretary, who later suppressed them for
fear of scandal. I did not dictate these pages to you, but
you were present in the late hours of many nights when
I composed them. In olden times, I might have been
able to enrich a faithful retainer like yourself. Soon I
shall die as a pope should, owning nothing.

These volumes are my legacy to you. Pray for me
sometimes.

Once again, you will recognize the signature. I ask you, again,
is the handwriting authentic?"

This time the expert took a little longer to scrutinize the
handwriting. He used a loupe and lingered over the details of
the calligraphy. Finally, he faced the small assembly.

"No doubt at all. It's authentic."

"So where does that lead us?" Maury Rosenheim put the
question.

"It leads us to this." Figaro put on a pair of white gloves,
took the three volumes from their tissue paper wrappings, spread
the wrappings on the table, and laid the volumes reverently upon
them. Then he made the climactic speech of the evening.

"I trust, ladies and gentlemen, you will not be disappointed.
Miss Busoni, you can read the texts and judge their editorial
value. Your expert has already authenticated the handwriting.
And you, Mr. Rosenheim, have seen proof of clean provenance.
Now, a very simple question. Do you want to start dealing?"

"Where do you suggest we start?" Maury Rosenheim was
leading with his chin, as he always did.

"We start at five million U.S. dollars," said Figaro calmly.
"That secures your right to handle the property in all media.
Then we talk about percentages and overriders."

Maury Rosenheim gaped at him in wonderment.

"Overriders? Where the hell did you learn about overriders?"

"I'm a quick study." Figaro gave his happiest smile. "If you want to sample the manuscript, if you want to confer, use the bedroom. If you want to call New York, please use the telephone or the fax. Just one detail, my friends. Please don't play bazaar games with me. My offer expires at eleven tonight, Zurich time. That's close of business in New York—and remember, it's cash against documents in Zurich tomorrow."

As the bedroom door closed on his three guests, Figaro breathed a long, silent sigh of relief. He had invested two thousand dollars in the best forger money could buy: an old counterfeiter who had served ten years on Lipari and had lived with his married daughter and her husband two alleys away from his apartment. Figaro had composed the text and supplied the necessary specimens of the pontiff's handwriting. The old forger had guaranteed his handiwork against any expert in the world. He was careful to point out that it was not poor handiwork which had put him in jail but a jealous woman who had found him in bed with her sister and denounced him to the carabinieri. Unfortunately, he could not guarantee himself against mortality. He had died of a heart attack two weeks after delivering his work.

Figaro had every intention of profiting from the event. The moment the funds were in his bank, he would be off and away to Brazil by a very roundabout route.

# 4

For two days after his death and embalming, the body of the pontiff lay in state in the Chapel of the Most Holy Sacrament in St. Peter's basilica. Tall candles burned about him. Officers of the Swiss Guard stood vigil while thousands of believers and nonbelievers—Romans and strangers alike—passed in slow procession by his open coffin.

His body was dressed in full pontificals. A veil was placed over his face, and a rosary in his hands. His breviary was laid upon his breast, with the silk marker set at the Office of the Day. Tucked into the casket were copies of the medals he had struck during his reign, and a small leather purse containing specimens of his coinage. These, so the reasoning went, would help to identify him if, after the cataclysms of another millennium, he were exhumed and reburied. The Romans, a sceptical people with a long history, had another explanation: The pope is human, too; he has to pay the ferryman like the rest of us.

On the third day, they entombed him in the crypt. The world media treated the obsequies and the interment with suitable gravity. The first editorials were couched in sonorous, panegyric prose. The first photographs emphasized architectural grandeur, ritual splendor, the worldwide reach and diversity of the Church—One

Holy Catholic and Apostolic. The television services delivered reverent rhetoric and self-indulgent visuals of the familiar and unfamiliar icons.

Then began the Novemdiales, the nine days of Masses, prayers, and public preaching by notable prelates in the major churches of the city. The sermons were not pious celebrations of a dear departed soul. They were intended as public expressions of the needs of the faithful, as signals to the electoral college about their duty to find a good pastor for the Romans and for the Church at large.

At the same time, the world media were playing in a different key. The florid prose was dropped. Pious platitudes became political barbs. The election of a new pontiff was a critical act whose consequences—for good or ill—would spill over the frontiers of nations and the barriers of race, creed, and custom. The world was in crisis, the Church was in disarray. The media reflected all their confusions. It was the *New York Times*, however, which pulled the pin from the grenade.

The late pontiff was a stubborn and courageous man who saw it as his pastoral task to mold human clay into a Christlike image. However, it seemed often as if he was trying to create a community as uniform and as passive as the entombed warriors of China. He alienated the women of the Church. He silenced or intimidated its boldest thinkers. He was always a centralist and an interventionist. The notion of collegial government was as alien to him as the idea of a priesthood of women. It was a not unexpected move when he appointed men of like views to vacant bishoprics and gave others the cardinal's hat. Clearly, he hoped that the college of cardinals would elect a pope who would continue his own policies.

Now, immediately after his death, there is a new surprise. It could be interpreted—and most certainly will be by many—as a posthumous attempt at intervention in the electoral process itself.

In our weekend edition, we shall be publishing, simultaneously with other major newspapers around the globe, an extraordinary document. The document consists of private diaries written each evening by the late pontiff. He kept them in a secret place in his dressing room, and finally gave them, as a personal legacy, into the hands of his longtime valet, Claudio Stagni, who often kept the pontiff company while he worked into the small hours.

The document has been fully authenticated by two handwriting specialists—one in Europe and one in the United States. The provenance is simple and direct— from the pontiff to Stagni. The title is beyond question: a letter of legacy written by His Holiness to Stagni in the last days of his life. All this evidence will be displayed in our publication.

The diaries contain revealing footnotes on Vatican policies and vividly penned portraits of high prelates all around the world, including those who are at this moment assembled in Rome to elect a new pontiff. The material will be published in full, except for a few passages which, on attorney's advice, might be considered libelous. . . .

There was more yet: a promise of backstairs gossip from Claudio Stagni himself under the title *The Little World of Figaro and His Papa*. The upshot of these announcements, and a rash of similar ones in various capital cities, forced the cardinal camerlengo to summon an emergency meeting of cardinals in the Apostolic Palace. They were aggrieved. He, himself, was hugely embarrassed, especially when the cardinal archbishop of New York tabled a proof copy of the offending material and distributed copies which had been run off that afternoon at the

Villa Stritch, where His Eminence was lodged. In his brusque
military style—the archbishop was Chaplain General to the
U.S. Armed Forces—he addressed the gallery.

"This was delivered to me this morning from the Roman bureau of the *New York Times*. They were quite courteous about it.
They said they had nothing to hide. They claimed their title was
unassailable, and from what I've read, the documents are authentic. What we all want to know is just how this could have
happened, and second, do we have at this late stage any hope of
enjoining the publication?"

"No hope at all, I'm afraid." The camerlengo was regretful
but firm. "I've discussed the matter with Monsignor Angel-
Novalis, and with our legal advisers, both lay and clerical. On
the face of it, Claudio Stagni has full title to the documents,
which the pontiff himself designates as a legacy. The buyers
and the literary agents who sold them around the world have
obviously conducted their own inquiries. Our advice is that
there are no grounds for injunction in any territory."

"But how could His Holiness have committed a folly like
this? You saw more of him than any of us, Baldassare. Was he
in his right mind?"

"I have no doubt of it—no doubt at all."

"Was there any possibility of undue influence by this Stagni
fellow?"

The camerlengo gave a small humorless smile.

"You know—we all know—how hard it was for any of us to
influence the late pontiff in these last years."

"Where is Stagni now?"

"He's on vacation."

"For which we are paying?"

"Naturally. He had accumulated quite a lot of leave, for
which he is entitled to be paid. He is also entitled to a pension,
to which he and we have contributed for a long time."

"Are we going to pay that, too?"

"Absent any evidence of criminal behavior, we are obliged to do so."

"Are we seeking such evidence?"

"We are at a loss where to begin. Consider a moment. Before His Holiness died, I made a full inspection of his study in the company of his secretary, and of his bedchamber and dressing room with the valet. There was no evidence of any of these documents."

"Did you see the secret hiding place?"

"It was shown to me. It was empty."

"And the valet made no mention of the documents?"

"No."

"In hindsight, at least, doesn't that look suspicious?"

"Not suspicious enough to go to the law about it, then or now. At worst, his silence could be characterized as an act of enlightened self-interest."

"Or a response to the wishes of the pontiff himself."

The interjection came from Luca Rossini, who stood up holding the text in his hand. There was a sudden shocked silence before the cardinal archbishop quizzed him sharply.

"Is that what our eminent colleague believes?"

"It's what this eminent newspaper suggests." Rossini was unruffled. "First it points out, quite correctly, that the late pontiff made certain appointments to the college of cardinals in the hope that the man whom the college elected would continue his existing policies. Then, it goes on as follows: 'Now, immediately after his death, there is a new surprise. It could be interpreted—and most certainly will be by many—as a posthumous attempt at intervention in the conclave itself.'"

Out of the silence that followed came the voice of the camerlengo.

"Is that what you believe, Luca?"

"I believe that such an interpretation will be made by many readers and many commentators."

"What is your own reading of this unfortunate incident? You were, after all, very close to His Holiness."

"I was close enough to know that, in his later years, he could be sometimes hasty in judgment and that sometimes he believed that he could, or should, preempt the future course of history. That, however, is a personal opinion. It gives us no grounds to take legal action against Claudio Stagni, or even to impugn his reputation."

"You mean we should do nothing?" The archbishop of New York was outraged. "The man's a thief!"

"Can we prove that?"

"Not yet. But we have to discredit him."

"We may end by discrediting ourselves. Let's reason a little here. The most powerful newspapers in the world will defend the authenticity of what they have bought. Most of us in this room recognize in the text echoes of remarks that the pontiff has made from time to time in public or in private. We can all attest, at the very least, that the handwriting closely resembles that of the pontiff. So, I think we'd look foolish if we tried to discredit the documents. Stagni's claim of ownership is another matter not easy to dispose of. He has a holograph document, a letter in the pontiff's handwriting, giving him the diaries as a legacy. Two handwriting experts have verified it as genuine. I submit that by the time we could offer contrary proof in court, we'd have spent millions—and we'd be handing our new pontiff a sackful of litigations in a dozen jurisdictions. Hardly a good beginning to a new reign!"

Rossini sat down. There was a long silence while the camerlengo looked about the room, waiting for another intervention. Finally, the secretary of state stood up.

"Our colleague, Luca, is right. Prima facie, the diaries are authentic. Our only real challenge—hard to mount and expensive to sustain—is to the validity of Stagni's title to the documents. Are they a valid legacy from the pontiff to his valet? The letter of gift is in the same handwriting as the diaries, which most of us here would accept at first glance as that of the pontiff himself. So what do we do? Mount a full-scale challenge or raise whatever legitimate doubts we can and hope that the affair will fizzle out like a Roman candle once the procedures of election begin?"

"Any more comments?" asked the camerlengo.

"Only one," said the man from Paris. "I hate the thought of that little *salaud* sunning himself in Rio, or some place like it, and living like a prince on his ill-gotten gains! Maybe he'll catch the plague."

"I wouldn't wish that on anyone," said the man from Rio. "My city is one of the pest-houses of the world."

"Not half as bad as mine," said the man from Kinshasa.

The camerlengo called the meeting to order.

"His Eminence the secretary of state has offered a motion: We make no challenge to the authenticity of the diaries. We announce that inquiries are being made as to the legitimacy of title."

"With respect," said Luca Rossini, "I suggest a small addendum. That Monsignor Angel-Novalis be given authority to conduct the inquiry and make whatever comments are possible to the press. The rest of us are going to have more important things to do."

"I accept the amendment," said the secretary of state.

"I second the amended motion," said the archbishop of New York.

"*Placetne fratres?*" The camerlengo put the ritual question. All hands were raised. All voices murmured agreement.

The archbishop of New York raised his hand with the rest, but being a testy fellow, he delivered a final unhappy protest to his neighbour, Gottfried Gruber.

"I still can't figure out the relationship between that little creep Stagni and the Holy Father."

"I can," said Gottfried Gruber moodily. "The Holy Father became such a public figure, he had no place to laugh or cry except in his own chambers. Even with us, his colleagues, he was often wary and withdrawn. His valet was the only person with whom he could relax and share a joke or the gossip of the day. We all knew that. Some of us were jealous of it."

"Do you really believe he gave his diaries to Stagni?"

"I'm sure he shared some of the entries as he wrote them."

"I could see that happening. I know what it feels like to be alone at the end of a rough day, with only God to talk to. He's a good listener, but a silent one. Sometimes it's hard to believe He's there at all."

"My point exactly," said Gruber. "No one has worked harder than I to keep the faith pure and defend the authority of the Roman pontiff as its arbiter and interpreter. But lately I have come to wonder—"

He broke off in midsentence. The archbishop prompted him sharply.

"You wonder what? Say it, man! We're all brothers here."

"I have come to wonder whether I have not helped to create a recipe for revolution."

"There's only one way to answer the question, Gottfried."

"Please, tell me!"

"Ask yourself what you would do if suddenly we sat you on the throne of Peter!"

The idea was proposed by Steffi Guillermin at the bar of the Foreign Press Club. Fritz Ulrich was loud in support. The vote in favor was unanimous. Monsignor Domingo Angel-Novalis should be invited to address the members of the club at lunch the next day, and answer questions afterward. Guillermin made the phone call and received a favorable answer. A shout of jubilation went up when she put down the receiver and gave the thumbs-up sign.

"He wants to do it. He's just got to clear it with the secretariat. He doesn't expect any problems."

"They'd be fools to refuse," said Ulrich. "It's the best chance they'll get to respond to our publication of the diaries."

"It could also be Angel-Novalis's last hour in the spotlight—and the Opus Dei people must be wondering how their role will change in a new pontificate."

"Angel-Novalis won't have to hedge as much as usual," Colson reminded them. "He'll give us answers in double space, so we can read between the lines."

"Provided we ask the right questions," said Guillermin, "and don't waste time duplicating them."

"A suggestion, then. Why don't we pool our questions and have them put by a single interrogator who can't be sidetracked and can move forward quickly? Our guest is very fast on his feet, as we all know."

"I nominate Steffi." Ulrich grinned at her. "She thought of the idea. She's fast on her feet, too. I've never known a man who could catch her!"

Guillermin ignored the jibe and refused the challenge.

"The questions should be asked in English, in which our guest is fluent. It makes for easier coverage and pooling both of questions and answers."

"Who chooses the final list of questions?" This from Colson.

"Bureau chiefs of those papers who bought the publication rights—and television services who contributed to the purchase. Does anybody have problems with that?"

"None from me," said the man from the *New York Times.*

"None from us," said the *Times* of London.

Guillermin had the final word.

"All questions to be handed to the barman by six this evening. We need a morning's work to set them in order and give ourselves the best chance at a first-rate story. I nominate Frank to put the questions. Even I can understand his English. One more thing—we're more interested in what is said than in camera angles. We'll allot positions for TV crews and still photographers. We can't have people popping off flashbulbs during the speech or the question time. And people who have paid for syndication rights get priority. Understood?"

Of course they understood! In Rome everyone understood everything, even before it was uttered; so no one took time to listen to anything. But Steffi Guillermin had lived long enough in the city to understand *arrangiarsi:* the art of arranging oneself. So, she gathered her own small group of conspirators to set a seating plan and edit the questions into English with Frank Colson.

At five in the afternoon, Angel-Novalis called. He had been granted permission to speak at the luncheon. There were, however, certain conditions. Guillermin was instantly in combat position.

"What conditions, Monsignor?"

"First, you must note in reports that I am speaking as a private individual and not as a Vatican representative."

"That's stretching the truth, isn't it?"

"It's expressing a canonical fact. The See of Peter is vacant. All the prescriptions of the recent pontiff are in force until a new pope is elected. I cannot comment on his policies or make prophecies about new ones. I can, however, express my private opinions, provided they are so designated."

"You understand that what we send from here may be changed or omitted by editors in our home offices?"

"Of course. I am, as you might say . . ."

"Covering your backside," said Steffi Guillermin. "We understand that, Monsignor. What's the next condition?"

"I will not express opinions on specific persons whose names are mentioned in the diaries. The risk of libel still exists for me and for you."

"But you won't back away from general inquiries about 'certain persons'?"

"I reserve always my right to refuse comment."

"We're comfortable with that. Anything else?"

"The subject of my address will be: past and future in an abiding Church."

"It doesn't sound like a lunchtime laugh show," said Guillermin, "but I'm sure you'll do a beautiful job. You may find this hard to believe, but you will be among friends."

"I never doubted it, Mademoiselle! Until tomorrow, then."

Guillermin hung up and gave a little yelp of delight. This man was bright—sometimes too bright for his own good—but he had enough self-esteem to guarantee a first-rate performance. This would be a classic courtroom piece with a very assured defendant and a very urbane prosecutor. At issue would be twenty-five years of centrist Church government and a vision—if such existed—of a new millennial epoch, each interpreted from the secret diaries of a dead man.

When Luca Rossini returned home at seven in the evening, there was a message from Isabel.

> Luisa and I leave New York at 1830 hours.
> We arrive Rome 0850 hours tomorrow morning and will be met by an attaché from the Argentine embassy. Raul has reserved a suite for us at the Grand Hotel. He insists that we "present ourselves with a proper style." After a long night flight, we shall both need a rest and some beauty treatment before we meet our very special Eminence! We shall expect you at eight for dinner in the suite. Please leave a message at the hotel to confirm that you will arrive—even if Attila is at the gates of Rome.
> All my love,
> Isabel

In spite of all the fantasies he had nourished, the impact of the news took his breath away. After a quarter of a century of separation and soul exile, they would be together in the same room. They would meet, eye to eye, lip to lip, body to body—and all the lost yesterdays would be forgotten.

Then a sudden panic seized him. This, too, was a fantasy. There would be a witness to the meeting, a young woman in her midtwenties, daughter of Isabel and Raul, granddaughter of that doughty old adventurer, Carlos Menéndez, who had bullied the junta and the Church to send him safely out of the country. Menéndez's grim warning still echoed in his memory: "It takes a long time to recover from the experience of torture . . . It's too soon to know how you'll come out . . . I hope one day you'll be a made man."

How would old Carlos judge him now—wherever he was lodged? He had died ten years ago, when his chopper went down in a remote Andean valley. Rossini asked himself also how the young woman would react to him. Most of all, he wondered how he would look to Isabel, who so many years ago had nursed him out of an obscene degradation into the image of a man.

He walked into the bedroom and stood a long time looking at himself in the mirror on his bureau. He saw a lean fifty-year-old fellow with the olive skin of a Mediterranean man, iron gray hair, and a mouth grim in repose, which could twitch into a rare smile when the lights were lit in his dark eyes. He was tall for a southerner, and he had wondered sometimes what tincture of corsair or raiding Norseman had given him his height and his long loping gait.

Suddenly he burst out laughing at the image in the mirror and the tally he was making of its good points, as if he were judging an animal. This was the root of his fear: that Isabel, the one woman he had loved, should find him ridiculous.

Which brought him by a round turn to a new series of questions. How would they greet each other? With a handshake or a kiss? And what sort of a kiss would be appropriate in the presence of her daughter? Isabel had given him no signals in any of her letters; yet she, too, must have dreamed the moment of their meeting. Whenever she mentioned her daughter, it was with pride and affection—and a genuine satisfaction that relations between the girl and her father were good. "She adores him, because he denies her nothing. She is his show pony, whom he delights to display—and he is very careful about whom among his friends, male or female, he introduces to her. She, on her part, has a generous and happy spirit, and we have become good companions."

So, another question—more foolish than any others: What should he wear to this three-cornered dinner party? He had several choices: a cassock, scarlet piped with scarlet cincture, highly formal and certain to create a stir in the lobby of the Grand Hotel; a standard clerical suit, with only a Roman collar and the purple stock to denote his rank; or the business suit with collar and tie, which he wore when he traveled to places where it was expedient to display a religious neutrality. He rejected that option instantly. It would take too long to explain. However, he promised himself that when he drove Isabel out to his retreat in the hills, he would wear his work clothes; and she, please God, would agree to come alone.

A shadow of resentment intruded into his musings. Why had Isabel arranged their first encounter like this? Had she already drawn some kind of line in the sand? Was she afraid of a sudden impulse of passion on his part, or her own? He was angry with himself even for entertaining the idea. She owed him nothing. He was the debtor. She had the right to set the terms of payment. Besides, her letters were the true testimony to her feelings for him—and, he had to admit, they were much more open than his to her. So, he rejected the untimely thought and exchanged a grin of self-mockery with the image in the mirror.

Nonetheless, he was left restless and uneasy. He did not want to face the evening alone. He told the staff he would be out for dinner. Then he dialed the number of a certain Monsignor Piers Paul Hallett, who worked as a paleographer in the Vatican library. Theirs was an unlikely friendship, which had flowered out of a chance meeting in the library just after Rossini's arrival in Rome. As soon as they had been introduced, Hallett had asked the languid question, "I say, dear boy, you wouldn't happen to know anything about Inca time numeration, would you?"

Hallett had a witty tongue, a gift for indolent scholarship, and a very English contempt for the excesses of clerical government. Was he free for dinner? Always, when the eminent were paying. Would he be happy with Antica Pesa? Of course. The place was splendidly discreet, and it would be even more comfortable if they could both wear civilian clothes.

"No offense to my eminent host, but Rome these days is suffering from a plague of prelates. All that red and purple! It's like a measles rash!"

The name Antica Pesa signified the Old Weigh-house, where carters' loads were checked and taxed before they went on up the Janiculum Hill. It was situated in an ancient tenement, the front doors of which opened onto the cobbled pavement of the Via Garibaldi, while at the rear it gave access to a small enclosed garden, a pleasant place for summer dining.

There was a chill in the air that night, so Rossini and his guest settled themselves in the glow of an olive-wood fire set in an inglenook large enough to roast an ox. They agreed on the menu: spaghetti *alla poverella* and *vitello arrosto*, with a flagon of red wine and a bottle of mineral water. Then, counting on a leisurely service, they began the ambling talk of old friends. Hallett, as always, put the opening questions.

"So tell me, eminent friend, what's the truth about these diaries? Are they authentic? Were they stolen? Why no public protest from the Vatican about their publication?"

Rossini shrugged and rattled off the answers.

"They're authentic, yes. The provenance seems simple. The Holy Father gave them to Stagni as a personal legacy. There's a manuscript letter to prove it."

"The man must have been in his dotage!"

"He's dead and buried, my friend. Let him rest in peace."

"What do you know about this valet?"

"Not much. He was already a fixture when I arrived in Rome. I've passed the time of day with him; but like everyone else, I've just taken him for granted. You've been here longer than I, what do you know?"

"I work in the library, which is a long way from the papal bedchamber, but I do take coffee every morning in the Nymphaeum across the garden. It's a lively place—for the Vatican at least! Stagni was there often."

"What was he like?"

"An agreeable gossip. People liked him. They called him Figaro; but you know that, of course."

"I know it."

"What you probably don't know is that he had been talking for a long time about writing a book when he retired. Obviously some Italian publisher had approached him, but he had larger ambitions. He was like a jackdaw, snatching up scraps of information about agents, publishers, and the media in different countries. I gave him an old copy of *Writers' and Artists' Yearbook* and suggested he get a similar publication for America. He was profusely grateful."

"Once he had the contacts," Rossini mused, "he would have been encouraged to extend the ideas."

"Exactly! Now here's another sidelight. This time I'm involved."

"You? How in God's name—"

"Patience, dear Eminence! Patience! In my line of work, the question of forgery crops up from time to time. It's an ancient trade: People have been forging artifacts and documents for centuries. We've done our share of it in the Church, too! Anyway, the question came up one morning at coffee time. Stagni was there. He claimed to know an old man who had done time on Lipari for forgery of identity documents, bank notes, and even—would you believe—phony patents of nobility. There was quite a trade in those just after the war."

"Do you remember this man's name?"

"I do, as a matter of fact. I got his address from Stagni and consulted with him on a disputed document. His name was Aldo Carrese. He's dead now."

"When did he die?"

"A few months ago."

"Was Stagni using him?"

"I suppose it's possible."

"Why would Stagni give you his name?"

"He could hardly refuse it. I told you he was a gossip. He had talked himself into a corner."

"Not that it helps us very much now. The man's dead. The diaries are already in publication. Stagni's home free and rich."

"That's a shame!"

"Still, we may be able to salvage something. Angel-Novalis is addressing the Foreign Press Club. I'll talk to him in the morning. I confess I can't care too much. This whole affair is a nine-day wonder."

"Is that meant to be a pun?"

"It is. We've just started the nine-day memorials—looking back, looking forward. The press will go into a feeding frenzy over the diaries, until we're locked into the conclave. After that, it will be a dead issue—a footnote to history."

"That touches a nerve!" Hallett was suddenly moody. He lapsed into silence. Rossini prompted him.

"Something's on your mind, Piers. We're friends. Tell me."

"I was just thinking," Hallett began slowly. "I've been dealing with footnotes all my life."

"I thought you were happy in your work."

"I was, until recently."

"Something's happened to change that?"

"Nothing's happened, exactly. I'm just going through a bad patch—boredom, accidie, vanity of vanities, all flesh is grass—that sort of thing."

"You probably need a holiday—or a change of job."

"The latter, more likely. It's the job itself that's getting to me. I used to love it; but now there's no taste in it anymore."

"Go on."

"It's simple enough. I'm a paleographer. I deal with ancient writings and inscriptions. It's one of the most arid fields of scholarship—one of the most lonely, too. Everything refers back to the past. The signposts all point down dead-end streets to crumbling temples and forgotten gods. My own self has become a very dusty habitat. That's why I was so delighted when you called and invited me to dinner tonight."

Before Rossini had time to respond, the waiter set down the heaped plates of pasta and chanted his litany.

"Cheese, gentlemen? Pepper? Good appetite!"

"I have the appetite," said Luca Rossini. "I could use a blessing."

Hallett made the sign of the cross over the food and pronounced the benediction.

"Bless us, O Lord, and the food we share in friendship."

"Amen!" said Luca Rossini. "I'm grateful for your company, too, Piers."

They ate steadily through the mountain of pasta; but halfway into the dish, Rossini was defeated. He picked up the thread of Hallett's talk.

"I understand what you say, Piers, about the solitude of specialist scholarship. The Hittites and the ancient Illyrians are hard to share over a breakfast table."

Hallett put down his fork with a clatter and looked up at Rossini. There was a fire of anger in his eyes.

"It's the breakfast table I'm missing, Luca! I'm withering in celibate solitude. I hit fifty next year, and what have I got to show in merit for myself or good for anyone else? I'm not a priest; I'm a pedant. More than that, Luca, I'm a wasted man!"

"Who's the girl, Piers?" It was only half a joke, a fly cast to catch a too difficult confession. Hallett rose to the lure.

"It's not a girl, Luca. It's a man."

Rossini hesitated for a split second only, then asked with studious neutrality:

"Do you want to tell me the rest of it?"

"He's a priest, like me. He's been working for the last six months over in the secret archive. He's British, like me, which adds a certain piquancy to the joke. Remember old Peyrefitte and the young French cleric who fed him material from the archive to build into his plots? Peyrefitte grew rich and famous on the novel, which, if memory serves me, was called *The Keys of St. Peter*. The cleric achieved fame as a character in his works."

"I never read the book," said Luca Rossini, "but I understand how you feel."

"I wonder if you do. This is the first time in love for me, Luca, and, God help me, it's the *coup de foudre!* I don't know how to handle it. I don't know what to do or say. Until now, all my fantasies and all my little lusts used to be safely hidden under my cassock. I had work I enjoyed. I prayed, as I was taught to do, against the noonday devil. I played by the rules. Now, I see no point in the game. I'm too vulnerable. The Church is too vulnerable to me."

"And your friend in the archive?"

"We meet, we talk, we find pleasure in each other's company. For the moment that's all—but it won't go on like that."

"What does he want to do?"

"I don't know. He hasn't had to declare himself, yet. I'm not sure, either, that I'm ready for it. All I know is that this is the wrong place for me."

"I'm sure we could find another appointment for you in a more congenial environment."

"You know that's not the answer."

"I know it, my friend—better than most. We carry our own devils on our backs, because often they're the only company we can endure. We're just friends talking through a difficult situation; even so, I am not sure how to advise you."

The waiter came back to clear the pasta dishes, carve the veal, and offer a second flask of wine.

"Can we manage it?" Rossini asked.

"I need it," said Hallett. "Perhaps we'll find wisdom in the bottom of the bottle."

"Better, I think, that wisdom be justified in her children." He said it with a laugh and then raised his glass to Hallett. "I'm honored that you've confided in me. I know how dangerous it is to be alone when a crisis hits."

"I believe you do," said Hallett. "The thing I fear most is that I could be so needy that I might enslave myself, utterly demean myself to a lover."

"In particular, the young man from the archive?"

"In a way, yes. He's like a young god, proud in his youth. I'm what? An aging cleric with the seven-year itch. Not a pretty picture, is it?"

"It's a sad picture, my friend. My heart weeps for you."

"I wish I could weep. I can't. I'm just so bloody ashamed of my own need. Do you have needs, Luca?"

"I do. Not the same needs as yours; but yes, I have them."

"How do you cope?"

"Not very well." Rossini smiled. Hallett persisted with the question.

"'This kind is not cast out except by prayer and fasting.' Is that what you're saying?"

"That hasn't been my experience." There was a sharp edge to his retort. Hallett apologized.

"I'm sorry. I stepped over the line. I should tell you I've been thinking of leaving the priesthood. It would be one less burden to bear, one fear less to carry. You know how exposed we are these days to scandal and litigation."

"I know very well. As a Church we have yet to learn how to cope with our own humanity. If you left, would you be able to sustain yourself professionally?"

"Without a doubt—even with the handicap of age. In my narrow field, I'm one of the best in the world."

"Then you should think calmly about it as a possible decision. There is a process to go through if you want a formal release

with all the seals in the right places. I'd try to shorten it for you if
I could; but God knows where I'll end up under a new pontiff. You
don't have to make a decision yet. You don't want a crisis situation
with your friend."

"He's not likely to create it. I am."

Rossini was silent for a moment, toying with a new thought,
then abruptly he put it to Hallett.

"First you need to cool off."

"What are you suggesting?"

"I was thinking of a retreat."

Hallett gaped at him in surprise and anger.

"Come on, Luca! Not from you of all people! Cold showers
and a hair shirt—and some solitary confinement!"

"Not at all! As a conclavist, I am entitled to bring with me a
minimal staff. I was thinking of taking someone from my office.
You can have the job if you want." His eyes lit up and his mouth
relaxed into a boyish grin. "At least it will keep you off the
streets and put you in the company of your elders and betters."

"That's uncommonly kind of you. You're right, it might provide a therapeutic shock to the system; but what happens
afterward?"

Rossini, still smiling, refused the challenge.

"One day at a time, Piers. That's all we're given; that's all
we can take, any of us. We invoke the Holy Spirit to guide us in
the conclave. Maybe the Spirit will speak to you."

"Are you expecting Him—or should it be Her?—to speak
to you, Luca? Give you a name for your voting card?"

"At this moment," said Luca Rossini lightly, "the Spirit and
I are out of touch with each other. You don't have to answer yet
about the conclave. Just think about it for a day or so. Pour me
some more wine like a good fellow!"

# 5

Early the next morning, Monsignor Angel-Novalis was summoned to a conference with the camerlengo, the secretary of state, Rossini, and three other cardinals. They were assembled for one of the Curial committee meetings which would take place every day until the conclave began. Rossini laid out a proposal for Angel-Novalis.

"You have accepted to speak today, as a private person, at the Foreign Press Club. As that same private person, we ask, but do not command, a service from you. If you agree, you will make few friends and some enemies in the high clergy. You will expose yourself to harassment and a possible lawsuit with big financial risks. We have explained the risks to your superior and assured him that we shall underwrite them. However, you will not be able to reveal that, now or later. If things go wrong, there may well be some damage to your public career in the Church. Are you prepared for that?"

"I am not a careerist, Eminence. My talents—such as they are—were placed long ago at the disposal of my superiors."

"Good. For this role, we need a very good actor."

"I'm a passable actor, Eminence. I'm not a good liar."

"You will not be asked to lie. You will be required to offer a

hypothesis to your audience. We should like you to offer it with
as much personal conviction as possible."

"Is it a reasonable hypothesis?"

"We believe it is."

"But you can't prove it?"

"At this moment, no."

"So you want me to see how it flies with the media?"

"Yes."

"Can you tell me what you are trying to achieve?"

"We want to throw the press a bone—a very big bone—
which they can gnaw over until the conclave begins. After that,
this unfortunate affair will fade into history."

"And I am to be the bone?"

"Exactly. How do you feel about that?"

"I'm prepared to hear you out. As you say, gentlemen, in this
I am a private person."

"Who may soon be very public." Rossini returned his smile.
"Here is what we propose."

Angel-Novalis heard him out in silence; then gave a thin
smile.

"Your evidence would be worthless in a court of law, Eminence. You know that."

"We are not asking you to present evidence, only to make a
public assertion of a private opinion."

"That's pure casuistry, Eminence."

"I know it is. You know it is. The press doesn't—and our
friend Figaro will assume we know a great deal more than you
are saying. Most importantly, you will have introduced into the
whole affair a useful element of doubt. Will you do it for us?"

"I will do it," said Angel-Novalis. "I shall try to compose
myself to total obedience—of mind, heart, and will. Now, if you
will excuse me, gentlemen."

"You are excused, Monsignor. We thank you for your
cooperation."

"*De nada,* Eminencia. In Spain we make fine swords and fine distinctions! By your leave, gentlemen!"

He bowed himself out of the meeting. As soon as he was gone, the camerlengo turned to Rossini.

"Now, my dear Luca, we have a commission for you, too."

"What is the commission?"

"Our eminent colleague, Aquino, would like to meet with you this afternoon. He feels that there are issues between you which need to be resolved. We are of the same opinion."

There was a long silence. Rossini looked from one member of the group to another. They did not meet his look. They sat, eyes downcast, their hands folded in their laps. Finally, Rossini asked:

"Has Aquino defined the issues between us?"

"He has," said the camerlengo. "And we'd be grateful if you would spare us the embarrassment of rehearsing them."

"Have you thought of the embarrassment to me?"

"We have, Luca. We believe you are a big enough man to wear it."

"In whose interest?"

"In the interest of the Church. Another scandal at this time— and on the eve of the conclave—would be highly embarrassing."

"We need more than embarrassment! We need to be shamed!" There was anger in Rossini's tone. "We have covered too many scandals. This one is already out. It is firmly planted in the newspapers. It has to be dealt with openly. I will not be party to any conspiracy of concealment."

There was another moment of silence, after which the secretary of state himself intervened.

"It is for that reason, Luca, that we think your meeting with Aquino is important. You can reason with him on a level different from ours. You may even find some ground of compassion which would encourage him to confront his accusers. You may, perhaps, break through to the real man behind all the enamel."

"If there is such a man," said Luca Rossini.

"You have to believe there is," said the secretary of state. "Will you please meet with him?"

"On whose ground, his or mine?"

"Mine," said the secretary of state. "Two-thirty in confer-ence room A."

"I shall be there. But understand, I make no promises on the outcome."

"We understand that. Thank you, Luca . . . Now, if we may pass on to the rest of the agenda."

When he stood at the lectern in the Foreign Press Club, facing an audience of media folk and a battery of television cameras, Angel-Novalis had the air of an ancient hidalgo, challenging all comers. When he began to speak, however, his tone was simple, almost humble.

"My dear colleagues, I speak to you today as a private man, caught, as you are, in a millennial moment in this ancient city. I have never explained myself to you before. As a Vatican offi-cial, I felt that would have been improper. As a private man, I can be open with you. You know that I am a member of the Priestly Society of the Holy Cross, better known to you as Opus Dei. Many people don't approve of us. They judge that we are elitists, rigorists, old-fashioned ascetics, dangerous dealers in secret works. I am not here either to defend our reputation or our practice of the religious life. I declare simply that when my world was falling about me, when my wife and children were killed, when I had neither wish nor will to survive, the society helped me to put my life and myself together again. I tell you this not to persuade you to join us. We wouldn't suit most of you—and most of you wouldn't be happy with us! However, there are larger fellowships, wider embraces, and broader fields where we can all meet in comfort, as we do today.

"The bishop of Rome is dead. Soon another will be elected

in his place because the Church abides and is continuous in Christ. In the memorial Masses, we pray for the departed: 'Enter not into judgment with your servant, O Lord.' Here, today, we are doing just that: entering into judgment on a dead man who can no longer answer for himself. On the other hand, it is your profession to report news and comment on it. I have no quarrel with that, provided you render true report and prudent judgment.

"This brings me at one stride to the subject of my small discourse: past and future in an abiding Church. The late pontiff represents the recent past—a large slice of this century. The man who is elected in his place is elected for the future but is commissioned also as a custodian of the past—that body of teaching, tradition, and revealed truth which we call the Deposit of Faith. Bear with me, I beg you, while we explore this notion together."

They were all professionals. They knew a good performer when they saw one. They gave him their full attention. They knew he was wooing them, softening them up with sedulous skill, trying to disarm them before question time. He was also making more concessions in his private role than he would ever have made in his public one.

"The Church has its own enormous inertia, its own glacial immobility . . .

"It is not, like truth, a seamless cloth, but it is almost as hard to unpick and reshape . . .

"The burden of office is laid like a leaden cope on the shoulders of a pontiff . . . It is not too long before he realizes that one day it will crush him . . .

"He knows, too, he can be destroyed by his own shortcomings—as Peter knew that he had betrayed his master three times at the jibing of a servant girl and Paul knew that he had stood in silence holding the cloaks of those who stoned Stephen to death. It has been my personal task to present the late pontiff to the world through the media with as much truth and as little blemish as possible. Now, in the diaries, he presents himself as

Everyman in pajamas and bedroom slippers. It's not always an edifying spectacle. *I* enter a personal plea: Pity him before you blame him!"

It was this final sentence that brought him generous applause: the simple admission of human frailty—and the implied confession of necessary mythmaking around the pope and his office. It also provided a standing-place for Frank Colson in his role as inquisitor.

"So you would agree, Monsignor, that your first task at the *Sala Stampa* is to protect the pontiff?"

"Our task is to convey official information and to convey it as clearly as possible. Others, like the congregations and the bishops, are the official interpreters."

"How did you feel—as a private person—when you heard of the publication of the papal diaries?"

"Saddened, angered."

"Angered by what?"

"The gross breach of privacy."

"But the pontiff must have been aware of that possibility when he made a formal deed of gift to his valet?"

"I know nothing of his intentions in the matter."

"There is a phrase in his letter which is interesting. I quote: 'In olden times, I might have been able to enrich a faithful retainer like yourself. These volumes are my legacy to you.' Do not those expressions indicate that the pontiff knew that his gift might be turned into money by his faithful retainer?"

"I have no brief as an interpreter, Mr. Colson. I must decline the question."

"Let me put it another way. Are you, as a private person, satisfied with the document of gift?"

"As a private person, no. I have certain reservations about it."

"Could you be more specific?"

"Not at this moment. Later, perhaps."

"Has any legal action been taken by any Vatican authority to challenge the document?"

"I have not been informed of any such action."

"Do you think it is likely?"

"I would venture to doubt it. The See of Peter is vacant. The camerlengo is only a caretaker."

"Given your doubts, would you recommend such action or inquiry?"

"My opinion will not be asked, Mr. Colson. In the normal order of things, I may soon be out of a job."

That raised a laugh, and some of the tension in the room relaxed. Frank Colson took a sip of water, straightened his papers, and glanced at the note which had just been handed to him. It was from Steffi Guillermin. It said: "He's pleased with himself. Move in. Cut him down." Colson gathered himself like a prosecutor for the next assault on his witness.

"It is clear, Monsignor, that whatever your private opinions, the Vatican is not prepared to challenge the authenticity of the diaries or the validity of the gift to Claudio Stagni."

"It would be more exact to say that, at this point, the Vatican has made no formal challenge."

"So, another scenario presents itself. The gift of the manuscript was valid. It was made by a pontiff in full possession of his faculties—fully aware of the use to which it might be put."

"That is pure speculation."

"But, you agree, at least an admissible hypothesis?"

"Improbable but, yes, admissible."

"Extending the thought a little, is it not equally admissible that certain members of the Curia, close counselors, suggested this stratagem to the pontiff and encouraged him in it?"

"That's too big a leap for me to make, Mr. Colson. I was counselor to the pontiff only on matters affecting the media."

"But surely this was a matter of prime concern to the media? It is the sole subject of our discussion here today."

"All I can say is that I was not consulted on the matter at any time."

"But you would concede that such discussion might have taken place with the most intimate and powerful counselors of the pontiff?"

"It's a possibility. I can say no more than that."

"The alternative is rather frightening, is it not?"

"What alternative, Mr. Colson?"

"That the Holy Father, a man charged with enormous responsibility, committed an egregious folly by giving a most private document into the hands of his valet."

"There may be other explanations."

"What, for instance, Monsignor?"

"Theft."

"Which would make us and our employers traders in stolen goods?"

"It could. Such things have happened before."

"Another alternative?"

"Forgery of the document of provenance. That, too, has happened."

"Either alternative leads to a very uncomfortable conclusion, does it not?"

"Tell me your conclusion, Mr. Colson."

"That the Holy Father kept in his close personal employ and shared his most intimate thoughts each day with a man who abused his trust, invaded his privacy, and committed or organized a series of criminal acts for personal gain."

"Precisely. And if your conclusion is right, Mr. Colson, then, you, your colleagues, and your corporations are all complicitous in crime."

"And the good judgment of a pontiff, charged with the universal care of souls, is sadly compromised."

"That, too, has happened many times in history, Mr. Colson. We are a pilgrim church. We are not a perfect society."

Colson let him take the point. He, himself, had won enough already. He started on a new line of questions.

"Let's look now at some of the most significant entries in the diary. You've more or less admitted that it's an authentic document. It will soon be a public one. It's a unique insight into the mind of a man whose titles are Vicar of Christ, Supreme Pastor of the Universal Church."

"He is also—in this document, at least—a private man, expressing intimate thoughts." Angel-Novalis was on the attack now. "He has laid aside the public role and is in discussion with himself and with God."

"Unless, as you have admitted to be possible, he is pursuing his public role through a postmortem testament."

"His role ceases with his death, Mr. Colson. His successor is not bound."

"But the electors may be influenced."

"Influenced by what?"

"Ambition, perhaps. The pressure from their peers, partisan loyalties. It is no secret that there are factions in the sacred college. I quote from the diaries: 'I am not blind to the ambitions of certain cardinals or their capacities for intrigue.'"

Angel-Novalis held up a hand to stay him.

"I think we should stop here, Mr. Colson. I am not prepared to offer a commentary on the secret papers of a dead man. I'll leave that to the historians. I think I've given you and your colleagues reasonable value for their lunch money."

"You have, indeed."

"May I then ask a small favor in return?"

"Of course."

"Thank you. I have a short formal statement which I should like you to report verbatim. Will you engage to do that?"

"With pleasure."

"This is a personal statement: I can say that the pontiff's private diaries are admitted as genuine. There is, however, some circumstantial evidence that they were stolen from his dressing room while he was in a coma, shortly before his death. The letter of donation from the pontiff is a forgery prepared by one Aldo Carrese, a convicted felon who died two months ago. I make this

statement as an open invitation to Claudio Stagni to answer
these charges or to sue me for defamation. I am aware that in
making it, I am exceeding my brief and exposing myself to censure. Nonetheless, I have a personal duty to protect the reputation of a man whom I admired and respected. What you or your
editors choose to do in the circumstances is up to you. Thank
you, ladies and gentlemen. I bid you good day."

As he strode from the rostrum, the storm of applause, led by
Steffi Guillermin, was breaking about him. He deserved every
hand clap. He had given them a week's worth of headlines.
They understood, too, however dimly, that he had put his career
on the line. The Vatican had a long memory and small patience
for turbulent priests.

While Angel-Novalis was tasting his sawdust triumph at the Foreign Press Club, the man who had set him up for it was waiting
in conference room A at the secretariat of state. His visitor, Cardinal Matteo Aquino, had telephoned to say that he had been
detained at another meeting and would be twenty minutes late.

As a former diplomat—he had served as nuncio in Buenos
Aires and in Washington—Aquino should have known better.
On the other hand, Rossini reflected, the man had never known
better. He had always been arrogant, proud of his soldier ancestry, his skills as a tennis player, a fencer, and a diplomat
who, to use his own words, "had special qualifications to treat
with military regimes."

He was seventy-five years old. He had already tendered his
resignation to the deceased pontiff; but he was still eligible to
vote in the conclave and—in theory, at least—was still a candidate for election. After a long reign, there was always the
chance that the electors might decide on a pontiff with a short
life expectancy.

Now suddenly, Aquino, that very soldierly fellow, was himself under siege. Those who threatened him were the Mothers of the Plaza de Mayo, a group of women who had exposed and ultimately destroyed the dictatorship in Argentina. They were the mothers, widows, sisters, and sweethearts of those thousands who had been "disappeared" under the regime of which Rossini himself had been a victim.

They had come to Rome with evidence, compiled over twenty years, on Aquino's alleged complicity in the reign of terror in acts of betrayal, kidnapping, torture, and execution, which the government tallied at nine thousand but the Mothers of the Plaza de Mayo declared to be nearer to thirty thousand. The purpose of their visit to Rome was to petition the pontiff to waive Aquino's immunity as a citizen of Vatican City State, and thus allow his indictment under the laws of the Republic of Italy. Many of the victims of the terror were migrants from Italy, and some, it appeared, had resident status only in Argentina, while remaining still Italian nationals. Now that the pontiff was dead, the women had announced their intention of waiting to present their formal petition to the new pontiff.

The substance of their material evidence was familiar to Rossini. The files of the secretariat of state were also open to him—one slim folder, chosen from many, lay before him on the table. For a brief span Aquino himself had been a familiar figure in his life: taciturn and withdrawn, an unwilling messenger delivering an unsavory package of damaged goods from Argentina to Rome. As Rossini rose in papal favor, they met rarely; and their greetings on formal occasions were brief and cold. Now Aquino was a suppliant for Rossini's public advocacy against the white-veiled furies of the Plaza de Mayo. For Rossini, he was a figure from the nightmare years and his shadow would lie over the meeting that same evening with Isabel.

There was a knock at the door, and in response to Rossini's summons, a young cleric ushered Aquino into the room. Rossini stood to greet him. He bowed but did not offer a handshake.

Aquino also bowed and made a brusque apology. Rossini motioned him to a chair. He sat, straight backed, unsmiling, until Rossini prompted him.

"You asked to see me, Eminence."

"Yes. I am, as you know, in a difficult situation."

"What is this difficult situation?"

"These women, the Mothers of the Plaza de Mayo. They have come here to mount a campaign against me. They want to bring me before a civil court in Rome. They want a waiver of my immunity as a citizen of Vatican City State. They propose to wait in Rome until a new pontiff is elected. It's all most embarrassing, most distressing."

"I imagine it must be," said Rossini mildly. "Of course, what these women suffered—what their sons, brothers, husbands suffered—was also very distressing."

"I know that."

"Of course. You had to know—it was your job. Though, on several occasions you did publicly disclaim that knowledge."

"That was a necessary diplomatic gambit."

"I've seen your reports." Rossini's manner was still mild. He tapped the file on his desk. "They belong to a very painful period of my life, which even now I find difficult to deal with. For that reason, I have been given other assignments in other areas. I am still too vulnerable to the traumas of twenty years ago. Still, in preparation for our meeting today, I did go through several key files. I note that your minutes were always judicious, carefully balanced, even on the most controversial subjects."

"Thank you. That is a diplomat's duty, never to exaggerate or overemphasize. He must penetrate to the root causes of events."

"Even when men and women are being tortured with cattle prods and stifled in shit buckets in the Navy school? Even when they are being flogged and sodomized with broom handles, and castrated and blinded, then tossed out of airplanes over the ocean?"

"I protested these things constantly."

"To whom? And how publicly?"

"Everything I knew was reported to the secretariat of state."

"But you still played tennis with the men who ordered atrocities. You still sought—what did you call it?" He lifted the cover of the manila folder and laid his fingers on a line. "Ah, yes, 'sound theological advice on the moral limits of torture which may be necessary to extract information from enemies of the State, and, in many cases, of the Church, as well.' You got your advice and you passed it along at tennis with the generals: 'Extreme measures may be used provided they do not exceed humane limits, have nonterminal consequences, noncrippling effects, and a duration not exceeding forty-eight hours in all.' Who wrote that garbage for you?"

"It was written by a reputable moral theologian."

"Reputable! God almighty!"

"To provide some basis of reconciliation for men in the armed services who were obliged by force majeure to undertake brutal tasks."

"And how did you propose to reconcile the families of the dead and the disappeared ones?"

"I did not come here to be abused!"

"This is not abuse. This is truth. Why did you come here? What did you expect from me? Silence? A gloss on all that filthy history?"

"Did it never occur to you," Aquino was still in control of himself, "that I might come to seek understanding and help?"

"If that's what you want, talk to the women! Plead for their understanding. Confess to them, beg their forgiveness. They will listen, I promise you! They are accustomed to silence. They waited every day, veiled in white, silent accusers outside the presidential palace. Their disappeared ones are silent forever."

"You know I can't confront them."

"Why not?"

"They would tear me to pieces."

"That would depend, would it not, on how you presented yourself to them?"

"That, too." A small humorless smile twitched at the corners of Aquino's lips. "What did you have in mind? A shirt of sackcloth, a halter round my neck?"

"You have another idea, perhaps?"

"I had hoped you might speak for me and with me, since you, too, were a victim."

Rossini let out a whispered blasphemy.

"Sweet suffering Jesus! What sort of man are you?"

"I'm a survivor," said Aquino calmly. "I need your help to survive this . . . this infamy!"

"What infamy?"

"These charges of conspiracy and collaboration."

"The best way to survive is to answer the charges!" In spite of himself Rossini was drawn into argument. "Look! Our late colleague, Bernardin in Chicago, was accused by a former seminarian of sexual abuse. He didn't hide behind the Church or his high office, he challenged his accuser to meet him in court. The charge was withdrawn. Bernardin met with the man and treated him with compassion and charity. Unfortunately, Bernardin did not survive, but he died with honor, and the people bless his memory."

"Everyone blesses a good pastor! Nobody blesses diplomats! You've seen what the Italian press has done already. Imagine what they'd do with a full court hearing! It's impossible!"

"Why impossible?"

"I refuse to be arraigned like a criminal. I helped many families of the victims. Now these women pursue me with unproven allegations."

"Then take them to court. Let the evidence be tabled and examined. If it's false, you will be vindicated. If it's true, then may God have mercy on your soul."

"You're playing a cruel game, Rossini. I came to you for

help as a colleague and a Christian. Remember, you owe me a debt. I got you out of Argentina."

"I know that. Thousands of others were not so fortunate. But I'm not playing a game. I'm trying to assess your situation and decide how and under what conditions I can help you."

"Conditions?"

"Of course. You're a diplomat. Conditions, terms, bargains, these are your stock-in-trade."

"Very well, let's have the deal on the table. What will you do to help me?"

"First, I will contact the women's delegation. I will engage to present you to them privately. I will ask them to give you, in my presence, a summary of their evidence. I will persuade them, if I can, to hear your rebuttal and at least discuss an arbitrated solution."

"And if arbitration is unsatisfactory to either party?"

"You will offer to waive your immunity and volunteer an appearance in court. If you do that, I will work with Angel-Novalis to secure the best possible interpretation of your situation by the world press."

"You ask too much, Rossini. You offer too little."

"It's the best I can do."

Aquino stared at him with cold and hostile eyes, then he stood up.

"You did better for Raul Ortega. You recommended him as ambassador to the Holy See so that you could bring your own mistress to Rome."

When Rossini did not answer, he added a contemptuous little postscript.

"You seem to have forgotten something. I need permission from the pontiff before I go to law on any matter. Therefore, I can do nothing until the new pope is elected. You, however, are free to intervene informally on my behalf. So, if you want to revise your offer of help, call me. There isn't much time left before the conclave. After that, as the Americans say, it will be a whole new ballgame."

It was then that the light dawned on Rossini. He let out a long exhalation of surprise, then shook his head in total incredulity.

"You're right, of course. I was a fool not to see it. You're not looking for a vindication. All you want is a reprieve—a truce!"

"Precisely. And you're the best man in Rome to negotiate it!"

"Suppose—just suppose—you were elected pontiff, what then?"

"Then, as I said, there's a whole new ballgame. The pontiff is head of a sovereign state. He is also the leader of a billion believers. He is not answerable to any court on earth. *Plenitudo potestatis.* The fullness of power. It's an old concept, but it's been growing again during this reign. There is much support for it in the electoral college. Think about it, Rossini. But don't delay. Time's running out."

He turned away and walked out of the room, closing the door behind him.

Ten minutes later, a very angry Rossini made his report to the secretary of state.

"It was a mistake, Turi! I should never have agreed to take the meeting. I can't stomach the man!"

"No matter." The secretary of state shrugged. "He asked for the meeting. We arranged it. You attended! *Basta!*"

"Do you think he could be elected—with his record?"

"The question's improper, Luca, but I'll answer it. His record is clean until he is convicted of misdeeds. He has a small faction of powerful supporters in the Curia. Yes, he could be elected, if only as a stopgap candidate. There are historic precedents for that. However, don't ask me to give you betting odds."

"Another question, Turi. How did Aquino know that I had given you a recommendation on the appointment of Raul Ortega?"

"I don't know. He didn't hear it from me. In fact, I haven't discussed it with anyone. I haven't shown it to anyone. It's still locked in my private file. Still, knowing that the Argentineans had made the recommendation, he could easily have guessed that I would refer it to you."

"So, he still has close ties in Argentina?"

"In Argentina, in Washington, wherever he has served. That's a merit in a diplomat."

"There was a threat in his remark about Isabel."

"And you will be wise to remember it, Luca, now that Senora Ortega is in town. I should tell you that Aquino is aware of her arrival."

"How the devil would he know that?"

"Again, from the embassy. He's been in constant touch with them over the Mothers of the Plaza de Mayo. He also suggested to me that there might be a connection between this group and the sudden arrival of Senora Ortega. Is there a connection?"

"I don't know. I'll certainly ask Isabel. We're dining together tonight, with her daughter."

"I trust you will have a pleasant evening."

"Thank you."

"I wish you nothing but good, Luca. You know that."

"I do."

"So, before you meet, calm down. Get rid of your anger. Enjoy your reunion."

"Thank you, Turi."

"Now, I have another job for you. Tomorrow I'd like you to attend a meeting with half a dozen elderly members of the college of cardinals who will not be able to vote because of their age. They want to communicate their views to you and other voting members."

"I'd like to be excused, Turi. I have reserved tomorrow for private business."

The secretary of state was annoyed. He demanded curtly: "More important than the service you owe here—at this time?"

"I believe it is, yes." Suddenly, he was a different man, open and passionate. "Listen to me, Turi. Try to understand! What our older colleagues want is what Paul VI denied them: a voice in the conclave, at least a hearing for their own lifetime's experience. I understand that. I believe they are entitled to it. But for me, Turi, it's another question altogether. I am in crisis, a desperate darkness. My meeting with Aquino plunged me deeper into it. I'm not sure that I should enter the conclave at all. I am tempted to resign before it begins."

"Why, Luca? Why?"

"Because I'm not sure I'm a believer anymore. Suddenly, I am bereft. The God I once believed in is a stranger to me. The Church in which I have spent my life—in which I hold, like you, high and honorable office—is a city of strangers. I'm not explaining myself very well, but you understand, I hope, why I need a small space of silence. I am what I was in the beginning: an empty man, a hollow man, with his head full of clear arctic light, and a lump of ice where his heart should be."

"Both excellent qualifications for a conclavist!" The secretary of state leaned back in his chair and toyed with a paper knife. "A clear head and a cold heart. I will not demean you with sympathy. If you decide to resign, I shall regret it, but I beg you to defer your decision until after the conclave. The judgment of an unbeliever, delivered without fear or favor, might help us all."

"How would that sit with your own conscience, Turi?"

"Perfectly well. I take what you have told me as a confessional confidence. I do not accept your present disposition as in any way final. The dark night of the soul is a familiar phenomenon in spiritual life—indeed, it is for some a necessary halting place on the road to sanctity. Absent a formal rejection of faith, I accept you still as a brother in Christ, a colleague in the government of the Church. Does that answer your question?"

"In part, at least. Thank you."

"Then may I suggest you suspend judgment on our colleague, Aquino. He, like you, has problems of conscience. We should not presume to adjudicate them."

Rossini bent his head respectfully under the rebuke. Then he grinned. "You're right, Turi. I'm sorry. Now, please may I have a free day tomorrow?"

"By all means. We have your mobile number. We'll try to leave you in peace. And, Luca?"

"Yes?"

"Walk warily. Aquino and his friends are a powerful group. Some unkind people call them the Emilian Mafia."

"What can they do to a man who has nothing to lose?"

"They can rob you of your power to do some good in the Church, which, in spite of your personal problems, is greater than you know. Enjoy your evening."

# 6

**H**e signed out from his office early that afternoon. The mood of black anger was still on him; he needed the open air and the press of heedless folk about him. He decided to walk home, across the Bridge of Sant' Angelo and through the old streets beyond Lungotevere Tor di Roma, where the bankers of another age had plied their trade.

As he walked, the cloud began to lift from his spirit and he felt a growing sense of liberation. The truth was out now. His confession to the secretary of state had been a necessary cleansing act. The secretary, good diplomat that he was, had noted it and had asked him to defer a final decision. He had even provided a convenient piece of casuistry to save face for Rossini and good conscience for himself. There was a charity in that, which Rossini prized the more because of its absence in men like Aquino.

Rossini wondered, not for the first time, why so many prelates, good liberal men in their youth, changed into tyrants when they were promoted to high office. It was as if suddenly they felt charged to upset the whole human order of things and replace it with a theological artifact instead of a new infusion of charity.

Halfway across the bridge, he stopped, leaned on the stone

balustrade, and stared down at the muddy waters of the Tiber. He remembered another confession, which he had made many years before, in his first interview with the late pontiff. The old man had pressed him hard, chivvying him, now from this side, now from that, like a sheepdog working a stray lamb into the pen.

"How do you feel about the man who flogged you?"

"He was a brute and a sadist. I am glad he is dead."

"Have you forgiven him?"

"I have not yet been given that grace, Holiness. I loathe everything that he represents in my country— the atrocities that are being planned and committed every day by high men and low ones. I hate—yes, I hate—the silence and the connivance of those who call themselves priests and bishops. I ask myself what Your Holiness thinks about all this, because we do not hear what you say about it."

"You forget yourself, young man."

"I lost my youth when they strung me up on the wheel."

"And your innocence, my son? When did you lose that?"

"Like many of my brother priests. I lost mine in the silence of our bishops and in the silence of Rome. There was torture and murder, Holiness—all done in silence. We didn't understand that. I still don't. That's another thing I find it hard to forgive. It was a woman who killed my tormentor. It took weeks of negotiation for the emissary of Your Holiness to intervene."

"Meantime, you had entered into an adulterous relationship with this same woman, Senora Ortega."

"A woman whom I remember with love and gratitude."

"You see nothing sinful in that?"

"My sins are my own, Holiness. I was a shattered man. Isabel put me together again, piece by piece. She put her life at risk to do it."

"She is out of your life now?"

"No. She will never be out of it. I remember her every day in my Mass."

"You are still a believer, then? You are still a priest?"

"I practice my priesthood in public. I pray for light in darkness. I wrestle all day and every day with my doubts about this church of ours."

"You're a very difficult young man."

"I have survived difficult times, Holiness. Others were not so lucky."

"Other people are afraid of me. You sit there like a young Lucifer and defy me."

"I do not defy you, Holiness; but I am not afraid of you. I find you easier to understand than many of those who speak with your authority. I know you're trying to be kind to me, but . . ."

"You're not making it easy for me, my son!"

"Please, Holiness! Try to understand. You sit here, an undisputed monarch in your own kingdom, supported by the loyalties of the faithful all round the world. I've just come from a battlefield where your ministers and your people, men and women, are down in the bloodied dust. Their stake is simple survival. The government's policy is total repression, 'woe to the conquered.' The gospel words that ring loudest are 'My God, why have You forsaken me?' It was a woman who answered for God to me, Holiness. I have left her, still at risk. I am shamed by the silence of those who claim to be defenders of the faith but will not raise voice or hand to protect the flock . . . I beg your pardon, Holiness. I am still angry. I have said too much. I beg your leave to go."

"Not yet, Luca! Let's bear with each other a while longer. I want to talk to you about your future."

The talk which had begun that day extended itself over years as the pontiff prepared him for higher office and drew him slowly into his personal confidence. Their relationship was a paradox, which the Vatican gossips embroidered with even more contradictions. While His Holiness, like his namesake, Paul, committed himself to spectacular global journeys, Rossini was put into tutelage at the secretariat of state and loaded with supplementary studies at the Biblicum, the Gregorian University, and Propaganda Fide. It was a harsh therapy that gave him no time to brood, if never quite enough to order his life to a free choice of a new vocation.

Slowly, at first, and then more swiftly the changes began. Now Rossini became the traveler, and the pontiff devoted more of his time to instruction and discipline within the Church. He gave more confidence and credence to rigorist theologians and hard-line disciplinarians in the Curia. At the same time, he turned to Rossini for private interpretations of a world which, as the years went on, was becoming less and less accessible to him, less and less welcoming.

Naturally enough, this gave rise to criticisms and jealousies, which Rossini studiously ignored. He had no talent for clubbishness, no taste for cabals and conspiracies. He had seen more than enough of those in his own country. If he was lonely, he never confessed it. He was his own man always, living at risk between the Almighty and Peter's successor and all the thrones, dominations, and principalities of the twentieth-century church.

The pontiff's speeches and writings were drafted by the most conservative theologians; and there was a concerted effort to extend their magisterial authority and stifle debate on their conclusions. There was small compassion in their juridical tone. They alienated, instead of uniting the pilgrim church. Expressions of dissent by the clergy were harshly repressed. Dissent by the laity was ignored so that, knowing themselves irrelevant to authority, they absented themselves from its bailiwick.

Rossini, on the other hand, minced no words with his patron. He stood like a rock against the waves of his anger, deferring only when he was forced to bow to a direct command. His argument was always the same.

"I know you want to be the Good Shepherd, and when you visit your people they love you; but when you write, you are like a judge delivering a verdict. One can almost hear the seal slamming on the parchment. 'There! That's the truth, pure and undefiled. Let them swallow it or choke on it!' Life doesn't work like that, Holiness. People aren't built like that. The best they can manage is a long way from perfection, and they need coaxing and gentling to get them even that far."

"Are you telling me I should dilute the truth?"

"I'm asking Your Holiness to consider how our Lord taught it: by tales and parables that took root and grew slowly in the minds and hearts of people. He called down woes only on the hypocrites and the overly righteous."

"Now you are presuming to teach the pope?"

"I'm a son of the house, Holiness. I claim the right to be heard in it—and that is another warning I keep repeating. The daughters of the house also have been ignored too long. They hold up the rafters of our world, and yet they have few voices and no votes at all in the assembly of the faithful. We are poor without their presence."

"This is old ground, Luca. I will not go over it again with you."

"It is ground you do not own, Holiness, though presently you claim to control it."

"And you give no ground at all, do you, Luca?"

"The small space I stand on was bought with blood.
Even for you, I will not surrender it."

Many times after such exchanges, he had expected to be exiled
to some outland on the fringes of Christendom. Many of his colleagues wanted him gone. His roving commissions kept him far
enough and often enough out of Rome so that the Curia could
tolerate his existence. Yet whenever he came back, the pontiff
welcomed him like a returning prodigal and spent much time
with him—time which others with some justice claimed as
their own due. A few days before his final collapse, he had
made a poignant confession.

"You have been a good son to me, Luca, though you
have often made me angry. I'm a stubborn old man.
From where I sit on Vatican Hill, I am supposed to see
the whole world and all God's plans for it, plain and
clear like a child's picture book. Yet you, my wayward
Luca, have shown me things I have never dreamed. You
have shown me the face of God, even in the temples of
the strangers."
    "I'm not sure what you mean, Holiness."
    "You, yourself, called it to my attention: On the sa-
cred island of Delos, where visitors came from all over
the Mediterranean to take part in the Delian games,
shrines were built in which each people could worship
its own gods in peace. I thought of that often when I
meditated on St. Paul's text about the unknown God. The
older I get, Luca, the more I regret all the time and all
the fierce effort I have spent trying to create a conform-
ing Church. I suppressed the liberal voices and the
questioning ones. I raised blind men to power and set
deaf ones to mediate the petitions of the people. In the
end, as you warned often, I have failed. The people were

tired of being berated, crushed with absolutes in a still unfinished universe. So, they simply gave up the argument and absented themselves from the family. They retreated to the God who still dwells within them—who, they know, instinctively still dwells even in the temples of the strangers. They will not come back in my time, Luca! I shall have much to answer for when I come to judgment."

"We pray every day that our trespasses will be forgiven, Holiness. We have to believe that our end will be a homecoming—not a session with the torturers!"

"Do you really believe that, Luca?"

"If I did not, Holiness, I think I could not endure the chaos of this bloody world or the presence of whatever monster called it into being."

"Until this moment, I have never understood why you were so angry with me. Forgive me, my son—and pray for me."

Rossini still remembered the wintry silence that fell between them and the bleak sadness of the final confidence they had shared.

He took one last look at the gray waters swirling about the foundations of the bridge, then resumed his homeward walk. The meaning of the stolen diaries was plainer to him now. They were the pillow-books of a sad and solitary old man whose time was running out, whose deeply divided family was spread around the planet, and whose bishopric would soon be voted to another.

A block from his apartment, Rossini treated himself to a small Roman indulgence, a visit to the barber for a haircut, shave, and manicure. It was a small sensual pleasure and a large concession to his male vanity. After all these years, he could not, would not, present himself to Isabel only half groomed. There

were other reasons, too. He still had time to kill, and he was
jumpy as a cat on hot tiles. The gossip of Dario, the barber,
would be a welcome diversion. It was delivered always in a
steady clattering flow. It covered the riverfront and the alleys
and the high life and the low life of the city, from Quirinal Hill to
Vatican Hill, and the latest crop of murders on the Via Salaria.
By the time the session was over, Rossini was fully sedated, and
his head was bursting with Roman trivia. Home at last, he
bathed and dressed in street clothes, then took himself by taxi to
the Grand Hotel.

He had just entered the foyer when he was stopped by a
young woman whose appearance was vaguely familiar.

"Excuse me, Eminence, are you not Cardinal Rossini?"

"I am."

"I'm Steffi Guillermin, Rome correspondent of *Le Monde*.
I've just been interviewing one of your colleagues, Cardinal
Molyneux, from Montreal. I recognized you from the photograph
in my files."

"I'm flattered, Mademoiselle. Just now the city is full of
people like me."

"Well, like all journalists, I'm an opportunist. I'd like to
arrange an interview with you."

"Another time, perhaps."

"How do I contact you?"

"Call the secretariat of state. They'll connect you to my
office."

"I'd like an hour of your time, if that's possible."

"My office will let you know what time I have available."

"Thank you, Eminence."

"Excuse me now, Mademoiselle."

She watched him as he moved briskly to the concierge
desk. She saw the concierge lift the telephone, speak briefly,
then direct Rossini to the elevator. When the door closed on
him, Steffi Guillermin took his place at the desk and slid a

fifty-thousand-lire note under the blotter. She had found a lot of good stories here in her time. She had kept the natives friendly. They told her that the eminent person was dining on the third floor, in suite number thirty-eight, with an Argentinian lady, Senora Isabel Ortega.

He had a moment of panic when he rang the doorbell of her suite. There was a long pause before Isabel opened the door and drew him into the salon. The next moment, she was in his arms, and time stopped while they embraced and kissed and held to each other and wept quietly in wordless wonder. Time started again when he held her at arm's length and said simply:

"I'd forgotten how beautiful you are."

"And you, my Luca, you've become so grand!"

It was only then that he thought to ask:

"Where's Luisa?"

"In her bedroom. I'll call her when we're ready."

"I kept wondering how it would be when we came face-to-face again."

"I knew exactly how it would be." She kissed him again and wiped a smear of lipstick from his mouth. "Luisa will join us for a drink, then a very presentable young man from the Embassy is taking her out to dinner."

"I asked myself how you were going to arrange that."

"Did I ever disappoint you?"

"Never. I was afraid I might disappoint you."

"Pour yourself a drink. I'll call Luisa. She has her own room down the corridor. She needs her privacy as much as I do mine."

When she left him, he crossed to the bar, poured himself a brandy and soda, and made a silent toast to the dark-eyed, passionate beauty whom the years had touched so lightly, dusting the raven hair with gray, leaving still the fire in her eyes and the laughter lines about her lips. The simplicity of their encounter after so many years had an air of miracle about it, even though

Isabel had happily confessed to her contrivances. For himself, it was like the rising of a new moon: For this night, at least, all fears were laid to rest, all mysteries swept aside; tomorrow could take care of itself. He had another surprise when Isabel came back with her daughter. Luisa Ortega was a startling replica of the young Isabel whom he had seen for the first time when he woke after his beating in the village square. He looked from one to the other, groping for words.

"I can't believe this, you are so like your mother. I'm happy to meet you, Luisa."

He offered her his hand. She bowed her head and made to kiss it in the old-fashioned style.

"I am honored, Eminence."

He declined the gesture and drew her to her feet with a smile.

"Tonight, young lady, I am not an Eminence. I am Luca, your mother's old friend."

"I hope you will be mine, too."

"How could we not be friends!"

"What do I call you, then?"

"Unless your mother has any objections, why not Luca?"

"But only in private," said Isabel. "In company he is always Eminencia."

"Mother! You can be so stuffy!"

"Your father can be even worse, as you know. May I have a glass of white wine, Luca?"

"And for me, a Campari and soda, please."

Rossini poured and passed the drinks, then offered a toast.

"To the friends of my heart, absent too long!"

They touched glasses and drank. Luisa challenged him, smiling.

"One of these days, Luca, I want to hear your version of how you and my mother met. Everyone seems to be using a different text. I really am quite confused."

"It's a long story—we'll keep it for another day. Your young man will be here any moment. Who is he, by the way?"

"I haven't met him yet. His name is Miguel Alamino. Mother set him up to get me out of the way while you're here. His father is first secretary at the Argentinian embassy, a friend of Papa."

"Where is he taking you?"

"A place called Piccolo Mondo. Do you know it?"

"I do. I can't afford to eat there very often, but you'll enjoy it."

"I thought all cardinals were rich. Aren't they called Princes of the Church?"

She was beginning to tease him, and he was happy to play the little game.

"Very few of them are rich in this day and age. As for being princes, that's an old-fashioned notion; but a few still cling to it."

"Do you?"

"Do I look like a prince, Luisa?"

"Mother thinks you do."

"And what do you think?"

"I'm reserving judgment till I know you better. So far I'm impressed."

"And I'm impressed, too. You're a very beautiful young woman. Your mother and father must be very proud of you."

"Father is very proud. Mother keeps trying to turn me into a scholar and a lady. I want to be a painter. I go to art school in New York, but Mother is reassured because I'm also working as a restorer at the Metropolitan. She wants me to be an independent woman."

"She was always an independent woman herself."

"Do you think I could see how the restorers work in the Vatican museum?"

"I'm sure I can arrange it; and you should also go to Florence."

The telephone rang. Luisa answered it. A moment later she announced:

"My date is waiting in the foyer. Don't wait up for me, Mother. And you, Luca, don't keep her up too late. She hasn't been well lately, and the Atlantic flight didn't help."

She kissed her mother and surprised Rossini with a hurried embrace and a flattering request.

"I hope you can find some time for me, too, while we're in Rome."

"With pleasure. I may not have too much free time before the conclave, but certainly after it."

"Good! I'll hold you to that. Now wish me luck. I hate blind dates, but a girl has to start somewhere in a big city. And remember I'm doing this for you both."

When the door closed behind her, Isabel laughed.

"Well! You've made another conquest. I'm glad. I had no idea at all how it would go between you. Would you pour me another drink, please, then let's relax for a while. I've ordered the meal to be served at nine. I chose a simple menu, so we wouldn't have waiters skipping in and out."

"I'm so happy that you're here." He handed her the wine and sat facing her across a low coffee table. "I'm as awkward as a schoolboy. I don't know how or where to begin."

"Remember the game we used to play when you were sick: Past, Present, or Future?"

"I remember it very well. Let's get the past out of the way first."

The phrase seemed to disturb her. Her smile faded. She shook her head.

"That's not quite as easy as you think, my love."

"Forgive me. It was a clumsy expression."

"You're forgiven; we've both been traveling a long time, with oceans dividing us. There's an awful lot of baggage to be dealt with—most of it mine!"

"So, let's deal with it. Your marriage seems to have lasted."

"For what it was, when and where it was, it has lasted very well. It got us all through some dangerous times. I was an impulsive, greedy young woman, who demanded all life's good things as soon as I saw them. Raul was a weak, handsome man with small talents, big family money, and a powerful father clever enough to survive his brother generals, the disasters of the Malvinas, and even the aftermath of the atrocities. In Argentina we stayed together because we were safe together. By the time we were posted to the United States, Raul had learned enough from his father to make himself a useful nonentity among the bureaucrats. I taught him enough to maintain a diplomatic ménage and provide a civilized upbringing for Luisa. I was able to develop a career for myself in American Hispanic studies and maintain the friendships that kept me—what can I say?—emotionally stable. It was a marriage of convenience, that somehow worked. My father was a great help in all this. He was an old-fashioned cynic who taught me never to expect too much of human relationships. You, my love, were the one indulgence he approved, and when he watched your star rising in Rome, he took it as a compliment to his own good judgment. It was he who helped me with Luisa while Raul was catting around in New York and Washington and Paris."

"She's a beautiful and impressive young woman. You should be very proud of her."

"I am. Now tell me about yourself. Your letters were landmarks in my life—yet they told me nothing that I did not know already: You loved me, I loved you. Don't forget, we didn't start corresponding until I moved to New York with Raul. In the bad times in Argentina, letter writing was dangerous."

"And even when the good times came, I never had the right words." He gave a small embarrassed smile. "They don't teach you to write love lyrics in the secretariat of state. My minutes, on the other hand, are highly praised for brevity and accuracy!"

"Even so, I've kept all your letters."

"Is that wise?"

"When have I ever been wise, Luca?"

"Then I can confess that I have kept yours."

"Now tell me how it was when first you came to Rome."

"That was another Luca Rossini, the one with stripes on his back and the taste of wormwood in his mouth. I had been a good

priest—a simple one, but a good one. I thought I had heard the
call, and I had answered it. I cared for my people—I tried to
protect them, but I failed. Afterward, when I realized how
deeply we had all been betrayed, I was enraged enough to kill.
There were moments when I think I was a little mad."

"I remember those moments. I nursed you through some
very bad ones."

"You did more than that. You kept another Luca alive, the
simpler one who still had cobwebs of dreams in his head. You
put your imprint on him: your taste, your touch, your perfume
that smelled like citrus blossom. When that Luca was separated
from you and taken to Rome, he was fragile, powerless, uncertain as a hurt animal in a jungle of exotic predators. The other
Luca was in control then. He began a vendetta against all those
whom he saw involved in the conspiracies of oppression—and
there are too many of those still in the Church. He was not yet
armed for open warfare, so he campaigned by obstructions, impediment, challenge. Because he was still a little mad, and because he did not fully understand what was happening to him,
he survived. He was patronized by the pontiff himself. Because
he did not seek the patronage and refused to bargain for it, he
was respected—and sometimes feared."

"And the other Luca, the one with my imprint on him?"

"At first he was like a pale ghost, living on fading memories:
the memory of a lover's bed, of long-dead parents, of neighbor-
hood loyalties, of early trusts. Sometimes when I looked in my
mirror, I would see this Luca and mourn him, and lust after the
love I had lost."

"But I was never there with Luca the avenger?"

"Oh yes, you were! You were the Isabel who taught him
never to waste a bullet in a fight or a word in argument. You
taught him to bow his head and say softly: As Your Eminence
pleases! You taught him the usances of power. You gave him the
gift of silence. You convinced him that he should never let his
peace reside in the mouths of others."

"Were there no other women in your life, Luca?"

"Neither before you nor after you. My only regret is that I wasn't bold enough to carry you off and join the guerrillas." He grinned and spread his hands in a comic gesture of defeat. "Just as well I didn't try it. I'm sure I would have bungled it, and we'd both be long dead."

"You'd probably be better at it now."

It was a provocative remark, but he chose to sidestep it.

"We'll talk about that tomorrow."

"What's happening tomorrow?"

"I'm taking you out for the day, to my own private place."

"The one you mentioned in your letter?"

"The same. You'll dress in country clothes. You'll take a taxi from here and come to my apartment, then I'll drive you into the country and we'll spend the day pottering in my garden. We'll drink wine. I'll cook you lunch; and nobody in the world will know where we are. I'll drive you back before the traffic gets too bad. How does that sound?"

"It sounds wonderful; but what about Luisa?"

"Give me two minutes, and I'll have her happily arranged for the day." He picked up the telephone and dialed the home number of Piers Hallett.

"Piers? Luca Rossini."

"My eminent friend. I tried to call you a couple of times, but you were out. I wanted to say thank you for the dinner, thank you for your invitation to devil for you in the conclave. I'm happy to accept. I'll wait on your instructions."

"Good! Now I'd like you to do something special for me."

"Anything, my friend."

"Call the Grand Hotel first thing in the morning. Ask for the Senorita Luisa Ortega. Tell her you've been designated by me to show her round the Vatican museum and especially the section where the restorers work. After that, buy her lunch at a cheerful place in Trastevere, hire a *carrozza*, and deliver her back to the Grand in good order."

"All of this, I hope, on your expense account."

"Of course. If you're short of cash, call my office, ask for Roderigo, and have him advance the cash on my authority."

"Please! I was joking. I'm flush with cash at the moment— a check at last from *The Connoisseur.* What time do you suggest I call the lady?"

"Eight o'clock, no later; and make your own arrangements for the pickup. If she wants to bring a friend, take care of him, too. If she cries off, try not to be too hurt."

"Where will you be?"

"In the country with her mother."

"Enjoy, Eminence, enjoy! Who knows what plagues may strike after the conclave. Ciao!"

Rossini put down the receiver and turned back to Isabel.

"There now. All arranged."

"And who is Piers?"

"Piers Hallett, a Monsignor, no less; an Englishman; a scholar who works in the Vatican library and who will, I promise you, prove a most amusing and instructive tour guide for your Luisa. Before I leave, I'll write a small note of explanation, which the concierge will give her tonight when she picks up her key. If she's made other arrangements, like falling madly in love with Miguel what's-his-name, then she can take him with her, or cancel Hallett. It makes no matter."

"It seems to me," Isabel mocked him gently, "that you, too, did some careful thinking about this visit."

"I had to. The secretary of state had me listed for a meeting with a group of elderly cardinals who are not entitled to vote but want their views made plain to the conclavists."

"And what excuse did you offer to the secretary of state?"

"The truth. He knows you're in town. He knows I want desperately to spend time with you. He gave me a free day tomorrow."

Isabel frowned and shook her head.

"If this means what I think it does, then you and I are an open secret in Rome."

"We have been for many years, my love. Ever since my return, in fact. I was brought back, if you remember, by the apostolic nuncio who is now Cardinal Aquino. He worked hand-in-glove with the junta. He made sure that every suspicious circumstance about me was noted, every guess inflated into a known fact. I was questioned by the pontiff himself."

"And you told him about us?"

"No! He told me."

"And what did you say?"

"That you saved my life; that we were lovers; and that I would love you all the days of my life."

"So, he made you a high person, to purge your demons on a mountaintop."

"Rather the contrary, I think. He used me to purge his own devils."

"You know what this tells me, Luca?"

"What?"

"You and I are still pawns in this game of silences."

"Will you answer one question for me?"

"If I can."

"My colleague, Aquino, confronted me with it. He suggested you were connected in some way with the Mothers of the Plaza de Mayo, who are here in Rome now trying to bring an indictment against him."

"And what did you tell him?"

"I told him I would ask you."

"Then, when you see him again,"—there was resentment in her dark eyes—"tell him to go to hell!"

"With very great pleasure, Senora."

The doorbell rang. Rossini stood up to answer it. A waiter and a butler came in with a trolley to lay out the meal and serve the wine. Isabel went into the bedroom, while Rossini waited in the salon, chatting with the butler about the food, the talents of the chef who had prepared it, and the virtues of the wine from a very noble reserve near Montepulciano.

Finally, they were seated at the table, alone, with the hot dishes simmering in the chafing dishes and the wine ruby red in the goblets. Isabel was calm again, and Rossini was sedulous to divert her.

"The wine you'll be drinking tomorrow is a lot rougher than this one—but it goes well with my home cooking."

"Are you a good cook, Luca?"

"Within limits, yes. Soup, pasta, salads, paella, ragout, a charcoal grill; that sort of thing."

"Do you entertain much in your country house?"

"You'll be my first visitor since I built it."

She gave him an odd, searching look and an uncertain smile.

"Should I be honored or afraid?"

"I hope you'll feel welcome and comfortable. Understand something, my love. This is my hermitage, the foxhole where I hide from the wars of the world. No one comes except the local farmer and his wife who keep it tidy for me."

"The way you put it, I could be invading a shrine."

"No. You have always been there. I have lived without you all these years, yet I have worn you, sleeping and waking, like my own skin."

"I had no idea my Luca was a poet." She said it lightly, as if she were fearful of lending too much importance to the words. He answered in the same easy fashion.

"Not really. The songs I sing for you are all borrowed, but in my hermitage garden they sound sweet."

"I'm proud that you love me so much, Luca. I am more happy than I can tell you in my love for you. It is your loneliness that frightens me, I think."

"It should not, believe me. My exterior life is busy and varied. In my secret life I have had some bad times, but since I have known you would be coming, I have reached a strange, calm place. The air is cold, but there is no wind, and the sea is flat under the moon. I feel it is a gift I have been given to help me reflect on my future, to make a decision about it."

"What decision, Luca?"

"To stay in the Church, or leave it."

"Luca! You can't mean it." There was a note of panic in her voice. She set down her fork with a clatter. "That's an enormous decision for a man like you. I pray God that I am not part of it!"

"You are part of everything I am, everything I do. That is something both of us know and neither of us can escape. But this experience is personal to me. I have to decide whether, here and now, or next week, or the next month, I am truly a believer. I feel curiously relaxed about what may be, in the end, a devastating loss. Piers Hallett tells me the English have a saying: 'God tempers the wind to the shorn lamb.' I can't even pray about it. I just wait."

"I'll pray for you, my love."

"You are still a believer, in spite of everything?"

"Because of everything, probably. I fight like an old conquistador hacking my way through to what I want, but always with the Church to clear up after me. You're different. You swallow all the bile and wait . . ."

"As you taught me."

"Or as you read my lessons. Who knows? In any case, there are things I have to tell you. I wasn't going to do it tonight; but why carry them into tomorrow? I want to enjoy your hermitage."

"You can tell me anything you want—and in your own time."

"That's the problem. There isn't too much time. You're going into conclave. I can't stay in Rome indefinitely. And yes, I have work to do for the Mothers of the Plaza de Mayo. There is evidence that most of the files on the 'disappeared ones' were shipped out to Spain to keep them out of the hands of future investigators. Some, however, were copied by friendly hands and sent to Switzerland. While you're in conclave, I'll be flying to Lugano with two of the women to verify them. Since I was a protected person in the bad times, I feel it's one way I can pay off my debt. There's another thing also, but it can wait." Abruptly she changed the subject. "Let me serve the second course. We shouldn't let the food spoil."

"It's very good food." Rossini matched her changed mood. "You'll make a splendid Embajadora."

"Tell me frankly, Luca. Do you think Raul has a chance of appointment? Will the Vatican accept his nomination?"

"That is a decision for the next pontiff."

"What did you say about Raul?"

"I gave him a qualified approval. He couldn't do much harm. We shouldn't depend too much on him, either."

"You weren't tempted to make it better, for me?"

"A little tempted, yes, but cynical enough to know that stratagems like that never work for very long."

She laid his plate in front of him and took her place at the table again. They ate for a while in silence. Then Isabel said:

"Even if Raul got the appointment, I should not be coming with him."

"But you said in your letter—"

"I wrote it while I was waiting for the specialist's report on the CAT scan he had ordered for me. I have bone cancer, Luca, a serious invasion. When I go back, they want me to go into the hospital for therapy, but they warn me the prognosis is negative."

For a moment he stared at her, dumb with shock; then the only words he could find were banality.

"O God! I'm so sorry."

"Don't be, Luca. Like you, I have come to a certain place; and your love is there, too."

His grief threatened to choke him. Isabel reached across the table and imprisoned his hands in her own, holding him until his emotions subsided and he surrendered to quiet tears. Finally, he asked:

"Does your husband know?"

"Yes. He's accommodating to the idea in his own fashion.

He will be generous in everything except personal involvement. He will tailor his life as he always does."

"And Luisa?"

"She doesn't know it all, yet. She thinks I'm going into the hospital for more tests. I've tried to spare her the worst so she can enjoy her holiday."

"Is there any way I can help? I feel so useless to you."

"Never think that! In a strange way, we have completed each other. And there is something, perhaps, that you can do for Luisa."

"Anything in my power. You know that."

"I do, but we'll talk about it after dinner. Now, I want you to finish this meal, which I ordered so carefully. We'll talk about Luisa over coffee. So for the moment, no more of my affairs. Talk to me about the conclave and what you think will happen there."

Once again, though his heart was breaking for her and for himself, he bent to her wishes and talked about what would happen when the hinge men met to elect a new pontiff.

It was nearly half past ten when the waiter wheeled out the trolley and they were alone. Isabel looked suddenly weary. Rossini told her he would leave in fifteen minutes. She would not hear of it.

"Please, Luca! I know that look of yours. You are closing yourself to me."

"Not to you, my love! Never believe that. My life has been lived so long behind a facade, I lack the words of common speech. I am not sure of the moment when my hand's touch may become an intrusion instead of a comfort. But please believe I am not—I never have been—closed to you."

"But you must let me talk. I have other things to tell you."

"I am listening."

She set down her cup, folded her hands in her lap, took a

deep breath to steady herself, then she told him, "Luisa is your child, Luca."

It was then that she saw what the spartan years had done to him. There was the faintest flicker of surprise in his eyes, but his lean features were frozen into the predator's mask. When he spoke, his voice was soft as the rustling of silk.

"Well! This is a gift I didn't expect!"

"Is it truly a gift, Luca? Some men in your position would find it a poisoned cup."

He stared at her in silence for a long moment. Then, in the same subdued fashion, he explained himself.

"I don't think I have ever said this to you before, but my hardest moments as a young priest were when I held a baby in my arms at the baptismal font and knew that I had renounced forever the right to fatherhood. I am telling you the truth: You have given me a gift. My problem is I am handling it very awkwardly. Does Luisa know I'm her father?"

"No."

"Does Raul know?"

"No."

"So, let's pause here. Tonight I visit you, an old-time lover, yes, but a constant one, remembering happiness, celebrating the bonds that have held us together. Suddenly, you open a box, and these big secrets pop out. You have a mortal illness. I have a child who is a grown woman."

"I debated a long time before I decided to tell you."

"Thank you for trusting me," said Luca Rossini. "Yet I would never have thought to find myself so poor in words or in resources. I am a man in bondage. What can I offer you but a helpless love? What can I offer to Luisa? She won't thank me for invading her life, nor will she thank you for rocking the foundations of it. Am I missing something here?"

"I wondered for years whether I should tell her. I respected your right, and hers, to live in ignorance."

"But now you think differently?"

"That happens when they read you the death sentence. My courage failed me. I couldn't any longer carry the secret alone. That's why I'm putting the question to you now: Should Luisa be told?"

"I don't know," said Luca Rossini. "I truly don't know. However, I'm sure of one thing. If she is to be told, you and I should tell her together."

Suddenly he laughed, a dry humorless chuckle of self-mockery. Then he stretched out a hand to touch her cheek and told her, "Now, why don't you start again and explain this old-fashioned opera about which you have told me nothing all these years."

"I think a drink might help."

"Pour one for me, too, please; but only mineral water. I need to be very sober for this performance. And please sit opposite me so I can see your eyes."

"Why? Don't you believe me?"

"Oh yes, I believe you; but I want to read your face as you tell me. Don't you understand? You've just endowed me with a love child. It's a strange experience. It would have been easier in olden times when prelates bred quite large families and endowed them with wealthy livings or arranged noble marriages for them."

His taut features relaxed into a grin. Isabel gave him an uncertain smile.

"Luisa is quite well endowed—from my father's estate. She will also inherit from Raul. What I don't want to risk is Raul trading her off into a marriage of convenience."

"What happens if he tries: Luca comes riding in like Julius II in full armor crying, 'Stop! Stop! Unhand the girl!'? Isabel, you're telling yourself fairy tales! Please, pass me my drink and sit down."

She huddled herself in the big armchair, facing him, as he had directed. She gagged a little on her first mouthful of brandy, mopped her mouth with a paper napkin, and then started slowly with her story.

"You've probably forgotten some of this, but I remember it by days and even by hours. When Papa went into Buenos Aires to bargain for your life—and, indeed, for mine—we were left together on his friend's *estancia* near Cordoba. We lived in the guest house, and for everybody's sake, we kept away from the workers. For the first ten days, you were very sick. You were also in great pain from the wounds of the beating and the infection. It was not until the fourth week, just after my period had finished, that we began to make love. Figure it then, our honeymoon lasted a few more weeks. I thought I was being careful; but I wasn't careful enough. At the end, you were spirited away to fly back to Rome with the nuncio. Papa, according to the agreement, took me back to my home in Buenos Aires. Fortunately—or so I thought—Raul was away on business in Chile and Peru. I was home nearly five weeks before he returned. Meantime, I had missed my period. When Raul came back, I gave my usual performance as a loving wife until, as usual, Raul got bored. Then I missed another period, after which I went to a doctor—not just any doctor but one recommended by my Aunt Amelia, my father's sister—a tough old lady, wise in the ways of male society in Argentina. When my pregnancy was diagnosed—and remember, Luca, you were thousands of miles away, back in the warm bosom of mother Church!—Aunt Amelia gave me wise counsel: 'Think ahead, Isabel! Your father has told me everything that happened. You shot a militiaman and slept with a priest. If your husband—or your husband's family—ever turned nasty, you'd be in deep trouble. What you don't want to happen is to pop your baby six weeks early and then have to explain it. So, think ahead. We'll find you a good physician in New York and a good medical excuse to visit him. Then you'll set a date for a cesarean birth in his hospital—a date that fits the facts and creates the convenient fiction. The cesarean won't hurt the baby, and it will save you a lot of trouble.' Well, that's exactly what I did, with help from Papa and Aunt Amelia. Even Raul was happy with the idea. He was able to build his contact list in New York and romp in some old playgrounds. When Luisa finally arrived, beautiful and healthy, he was enchanted. His father and mother showered her with gifts and attention. The fairy story was complete . . ."

"But not for you?"

"No. I was in total confusion. During all the celebrations, I was living a lie. I was deceiving Raul. I was making a mockery of his real joy. If the truth ever came out, it would be a devastating shame for him. On the other hand, it was your child I had borne. I was happy about that, but the happiness turned sour because I could not share it. For a while, I lapsed into deep depression; but I recovered and began to count my blessings."

"And Raul never asked a single question about my sojourn with you?"

"Not one, not ever. I doubt he could ever perceive a country priest as a rival. Besides, all the papers were in order, my medical history in order, too. So, what misgivings could he have?"

"So, I ask again,"—Luca Rossini was suddenly another man, an imperious inquisitor—"why did you have to raise the question with me after all these years?"

She did not flinch but thrust herself forward in the chair to confront him.

"Because I wanted you to know! I wanted to share her with you, to have you see what we made together in that country bed in Cordoba. I didn't expect you to acknowledge her. I still don't, but yes, yes, yes, I wanted you to know. I hoped you might find some happiness in the secret—the last, probably, we shall be able to share."

"I can understand that." Rossini's tone was carefully neutral. "That takes care of you and me. What did you plan for Luisa?"

"I hoped—God knows why I hoped—that you might be a gift for her, too. When I saw and heard you together this evening, I knew you would be good for each other."

"That's a guess, a gamble. You have no right to take it with your daughter's life!"

"She's your daughter, too, Luca. Or don't you believe what I've told you?"

"Oh yes! I believe Luisa is my daughter. But she's mine by nature; by nurture, she's yours and Raul's. There's a precarious balance here. If you tip it the wrong way, who knows what damage you may do? I have to think about this. We'll talk about it again tomorrow."

"Do you still want to take me to your hermitage?"

"I do."

He stood up and stretched out his hands. He drew her close and held her to his breast, his lips brushing her hair.

"I love you. Nothing changes that. I shall love you from now until doomsday. But I'm sad, too, because you're suffering and there's nothing I can do about that—except pray, and my praying isn't very good these days. Then there's Luisa. I'm sad about her, too, in another way. There was a spark between us, wasn't there?"

"There was."

"Then let's push the gamble a little further."

"What do you mean?" She drew away from him so that she could look into his face. He was smiling again.

"I was thinking about tomorrow. These days there are few graces in my life, but my little country place is one of them. I wanted desperately to share it with you. Now—"

He broke off, hesitating over the next phrase.

"Now what, Luca?"

"Now, much to his own surprise, Luca Rossini, Cardinal Presbyter, is a family man! I'm suggesting we invite our daughter to join us on our picnic."

"You mean you're going to tell her?" There was a note of alarm in Isabel's voice.

"I have no idea—except that I'm going to take her into the kitchen to prepare lunch with me, while you sun yourself in the garden. We'll talk and see where the talk takes us. How do you feel about that?"

"What can I say? The grace of your garden may touch us all."

"Good! Now I'd better call Piers Hallett and cancel the pickup arrangement. He'll be very disappointed."

"Have you thought what we'll do if Luisa doesn't want to come?"

"So be it. Let her do what she wants. There will be other times and other seasons."

"Don't count on that, my love," said Isabel somberly. "Remember I'm on call for the last act of this opera."

They parted that night in the shadows of mutual griefs. The passion of their long-awaited encounter had spent itself, like a firework, in a fine dazzle of emotion. Now they clung together in a dark landscape under a moonless sky, bereft of all but the most primitive physical comfort— hands' touch and brief body-warmth—and the trailing of yesterday's dreams. It was Isabel who found the few words that needed to be said.

"I know what you're thinking, Luca, my love. We should lock the door and shut out the world and sleep together until morning. But we can't; and even if we could, we'd wake and feel ridiculous when the sun came up."

"To me, you are the most beautiful thing in the world. You always will be."

"Go home now please, Luca."

"You have my address, my telephone number."

"Everything. We'll see you at ten. Good night, my love!"

It took him more than an hour to walk home through the city sinking slowly into sleep but still turbulent with traffic and night noises, still fetid with the smog that lay along the Tiber and coiled like a lethal snake through the ant heaps that covered the ancient hills.

For all his iron self-control, he was still in shock. Isabel was the rock upon which his ravaged manhood had been rebuilt. Now the rock was crumbling, like a sandcastle in an encroaching tide. He could do nothing but watch helplessly while the foundation of his fragile inner life was swept away. Luisa was another kind of grief: a daughter whom he could not acknowledge, whose childhood he had never shared, whose future he might well put at risk. The anguish rose in him again; anguish for the illusions he himself had nurtured and which now lay scattered at his feet like the petals of last week's roses.

He walked fast but heedlessly, head down, shoulders hunched, bearing vaguely in the direction of his house but caring not at all when he arrived there. Lovers embracing in doorways ignored him. A drunk jostled him. A motorcyclist with a girl riding pillion roared past him with an eloquent Roman curse. A pale Madonna, imprisoned in a little glass shrine with an oil lamp guttering in front of her, gazed at him with blank, plaster eyes.

The sight of her woke childhood memories of a Neapolitan household in the slums of Buenos Aires, with a picture of the Dolorous Virgin over the matrimonial bed and, tacked over his own, a First Communion card representing the mythical Virgin Martyr Philomena, for whom his mother was named.

The passing years had made him more and more sceptical of the mythography of the Church, yet more and more conscious of its potency and the deep human need for mystery and miracle which sustained it. The irony was that while rejecting one set of myths, he had adopted another: the myth of the ideal lover, enshrined in memory, endowed with heroic virtue, immune from the risks of mortality. This was a creature he could dream without guilt, desire without remorse, because she was set beyond his reach like the street-corner virgin behind the dusty glass.

He had been warned, of course, a thousand times. His earliest teachers in the spiritual life had cautioned him against attachments to perishable things and perishable people. They had tried vainly to cauterize his emotions—and the cautery had lasted until a brute with a whip had stripped the hide from his back and left the raw tissue exposed.

Tonight had been another kind of exposure: to the pain of the beloved, now perilously mortal, to whom he could offer neither healing nor heartsease, not even company beyond a few short hours. Even if he quit the Church and took the long road to nowhere to maintain his own precarious identity, what could he offer Isabel? She was stronger than he. The love she gave and the love she took carried no price tags. She had accepted, like the she-wolf, to live and die in her own place, in her own skin.

And where did that leave Luca Rossini? In love. He could not—would not—ask for more than had been given him. He understood the obsessive element in his own nature. His sense of the ridiculous—his refusal to compromise the personal dignity for which, as he saw it, he had paid in blood—had kept him safe from folly, if not from questions about what might have been.

One thing, at least, the evening had done for him. It had separated Isabel from the question of his relations with the Church as a baptized believer. The question was now radical and simple. Was he still a believer? If so, he must renew his assent and serve in that office to which he was called. If not, he must withdraw with dignity and make no scandal for others. He could not see himself as a seedy renegade, piping his protest in the forecourt of the temple; neither could he beg the charity of the faithful or their pity for his reduced estate.

By the time he had wrestled his confusions into this elementary order, he was home again. There was a notice pinned to the elevator *FUORI SERVIZIO*, which meant he had to trudge up the long stone staircase to reach his apartment. Then, because custom and ritual were the last fragile armor against fear and grief, he opened his breviary and read the compline of the day.

" 'Hear, O Lord, my prayer and let my cry reach you . . . My life has vanished like smoke, I am alone like a pelican in the wilderness.' "

# 7

It was Rossini's custom to say his early-morning Mass in the chapel of a small convent a few blocks from his apartment. The convent was the property of a community of women who called themselves the Sisters of Redemption. They devoted themselves to charitable works, one of which was based in the convent itself: a halfway house for women who had served prison time or were released on conditional bail.

The community was small, and funds were low; so in traditional Italian fashion, two nuns went out each day—professional mendicants—begging alms from local residents and shopkeepers. It was a thankless task. The community was aging, and few young women offered themselves for service, but the Sisters themselves managed to preserve a wry Roman humor, which matched the often anarchic wit of their jailbirds.

Rossini had met them first on one of his bad days when, dressed as a layman, he was preparing to set off for his hermitage. He gave them a donation, then fell into talk with them. A slum child himself, born to an emigrant Neapolitan family, he had a traditional respect for beggars and a deep-seated hate for the indifferent who despised beggary but accepted it as a social imperative.

In the course of his dialogue with the Sisters, he revealed his identity and offered a continuing subvention in cash and his occasional service as celebrant to the community. Many times later he was to regret the impulse, as he found himself drawn more and more into the position of confessor, counselor, and friend-of-last-resort to the community and those whom it protected. He was coolheaded enough to recognize the system for what it was: old-fashioned ecclesiastical charity, no substitute at all for an overdue but impossible reform in the Italian social system.

So the women in the convent became for him a small private constituency where he could function as he had done years before in his upland parish in Argentina. The nuns trusted him. The other women were cautious at first. He understood that they could hardly be otherwise. They knew the harshness of life around the campfires on the Annulare, where the truck drivers pulled in for a quick tumble on a greasy blanket. They had suffered the violence of pimps and the bullying of police and prison staff.

In the end, however, the older ones spread the word that this was a man to be trusted. He gave no lectures. He understood the words and the facts of life on their side of the street. He understood how it could be with the police. They knew that his gifts made life a little easier for them all. There was nothing furtive about him, either. He spoke gently, but he knew the difference between *merda* and macaroni; and he'd tell you straight if you tried to play games. He let it be known discreetly that he, too, had been embroiled with the police in his own country and that he understood their reticence. There was no compulsion to come to his Mass, and at first only a few came. But after a while, when they knew he was coming, the chapel was usually full.

This morning he was reluctant to move from his house, but he would not disappoint them. The nuns were a special breed, a diminishing but still courageous tribe. The women in their care were, like himself, outlanders, exiles, proscribed, *avanze di galera*, remnants of a jail system to which some would almost inevitably return. It was to these he addressed his own poignant petition.

"My friends, I have a favor to ask you. A very dear and close friend of mine has just been told she has an incurable cancer. Many years ago, this woman risked her life to save mine. I beg you to pray for her this morning. I am offering the Mass not to ask for a miracle cure but that courage may be granted to her, and a speedy respite from pain. I wish I knew why she, of all people in the world, should be so stricken; but that's the mystery we all face, isn't it? As I came here this morning, I kept asking why she? Why not me instead? I feel like a blind man, groping in sudden darkness. Then I remind myself that Our Lord and Savior was stricken with this same darkness, just before he died. Pray for me, too. You are all my sisters. Pray for me." His voice cracked. He stood for a moment recovering himself, then he stepped to the altar to begin mass.

When the Mass was over, he lingered just long enough to drink a coffee and exchange courtesies with the mother superior. Then as he was leaving the building, one of the women—a sturdy veteran of the roadside—stopped him and thrust into his hand a small medallion of the Virgin, on a flimsy silver chain. She told him, "Here! Give this to your friend. It saved me from a lot of trouble on the street. Maybe it will do something for her." Then she was gone, clattering down the paved corridor on her wooden pattens. Rossini, touched again with emotion, shoved the gift into his breast pocket and hurried out of the building.

Back at his apartment, he checked the screen for his E-mail. There were three messages. The first two were from his office. The interview requested by Steffi Guillermin of *Le Monde* was scheduled for ten o'clock the following morning at the *Sala Stampa*. Monsignor Angel-Novalis was prepared to attend and to record the conversation, if His Eminence wished. A moment's reflection convinced Rossini that this was wise insurance. The next message was from the secretary of state: "I have reset your meeting with the nonvoting cardinals for eleven-thirty. This gives you a half-hour break after your meeting with the press. Angel-Novalis may need some support, and you may expect some rough words from the press over the pontiff's diaries. They resent the notion that they may have been trafficking in stolen material. So, they are establishing a defense line. Our colleague, Aquino, gave me his version of your conversation. When I told him you'd be talking to the press, he asked, rather more meekly than usual, whether I could arrange another brief talk with you—'More brief and more friendly' was the way he put it. I suggest you call him. You may be able to dispose of the matter with more grace and civility. Have a pleasant day in the country."

Rossini glanced at his watch. There was still an hour and twenty minutes before Isabel arrived—with or without Luisa. He picked up the phone and dialed Aquino's number. When His Eminence answered, Rossini was carefully bland.

"I have a message from the secretary of state. He asked me to get in touch with you."

"That was kind of him. Good of you to respond so promptly. I've been troubled. I felt our talk went astray. My fault, I'm sure. If it's possible, I'd like to make amends, repair the damage, so to speak."

"We were both revisiting old battlefields," said Rossini calmly. "There's always the danger of stepping on a land mine. What would you like me to do?"

"I'd like to accept your offer of intervention with the women. I'd like to see whether an arbitrated situation is possible. I'd be happy to use Angel-Novalis to handle the press. However . . ."

There was a momentary silence. Rossini prompted him.

"I'm listening."

"However, I felt, I still feel, that the condition you made—that I should offer myself for a court appearance—is too much to ask; and besides, it is canonically impossible."

"I thought about that, too," said Rossini mildly. "It was a condition I had no right to make; but there is still a condition, as far as I am concerned."

"Which is?"

"Open response, open discussion. There is much anger. I don't want yours—or mine—added to it."

"How do we handle matters of secrecy?"

"We don't. If you have the answers, you give them freely and openly. If you do not have the answers, say so. If there is a real impediment to disclosure, you admit at least the impediment. But there is one thing that you should know. In addition to the evidence collected by the women, there are documents lodged for secrecy in Spain. Some of these have been copied and deposited in Switzerland. The women will be inspecting them while we are in conclave."

"You're sure of this?"

"Yes—though I have no knowledge of the documents themselves."

"But the source of your information . . . ?"

"Is impeccable."

"I shall have to think a little more about this. There are certain complications, not least of which is any clerical involvement in the transactions. I'm sure you take my meaning."

"Not all of it," said Rossini, "but I should prefer not to embarrass Angel-Novalis, who will be doing us both a service."

"I'll keep that in mind. Expect a call from me very soon; and thank you for your courtesy, Rossini."

"It's good that we understand each other better."

"Very good, very good indeed. Thank you."

When he put down the phone, Rossini was smiling. Aquino's words were cordial enough, but he sounded as though he were sucking a very sour lemon while he spoke them. He glanced at his watch. There was still time for a call to Turi at the secretariat of state to brief him on the conversation with Aquino. His response was warm.

"Thanks, Luca. I appreciate it. The less friction we have at this stage, the better. By the way, where did you get your information on the Spanish and Swiss documents?"

"From Senora Ortega. She is going to Switzerland to help authenticate those which are held there. It's a matter of conscience for her. That's confidential to you, Turi."

"Of course. You had a pleasant evening, I trust?"

"Pleasant but sad. Isabel won't be with us very long, I fear. She tells me she is very ill—and the prognosis isn't good."

"I'm very sorry, Luca—for her and for you. I'll say my Mass for her."

"Thank you."

"You're spending today in the country?"

"Yes, her daughter's coming with us. She's a beautiful girl, the image of her mother."

"You'll be working tomorrow?"

"As promised, Turi. I meet the elders of the college at eleven-thirty, before that I have an interview with a woman from *Le Monde*. Angel-Novalis will be there to hold my hand."

"A word of caution, Luca. You, yourself, are mentioned in the pontiff's diaries. The piece will be coming up soon. You may be questioned on it."

"I wonder if the Guillermin woman will raise it tomorrow."

"Who knows? If she does, you'll have to handle it as best you can."

"I'm not too worried, Turi. I don't want scandal for the Church any more than you do; but for myself, I'm a stripped-down man. There's nothing they can take from me that I shall miss very much."

"I'm glad to hear that. The weather's beautiful. Enjoy the day, my friend."

But when he put down the receiver, the secretary of state was pensive. He dealt with crisis somewhere in the world every day. Men and women were made martyrs while he brokered deals with their executioners to protect the remnant faithful. He was a man of disciplined appetite and cool judgments, but he cherished a deep friendship with Luca Rossini. He knew very well that what had kept Luca sane and stable was not the ancient faith. It was the private and potent cultus of a personified Madonna of Perpetual Help, represented by Isabel Ortega. He preferred not to speculate what might happen to Rossini if she were taken from him and he were left a worshipper at an empty shrine in a wasteland of abandoned beliefs.

The elevator was still out of service. There was a promise that it would be fixed by midday: Midday today or one fine tomorrow was always a moot question. So Rossini decided to spare Isabella the long trudge up the staircase. He waited in the street by his car, a twelve-year-old Mercedes, which he had bought cheaply from an American colleague transferred back to the United States. It had been lovingly cared for; and now it stood, solid and gleaming, on the cobbles outside the entrance, while Rossini waited, lounging against it like any Roman driver on guard against cruising youths who might scrape it with a coin, or wrench off the radiator symbol. He prized these moments of complete anonymity, when he was absolved from his past, detached from his present estate, and accountable for neither.

Isabel was late. The arrangement had been clear. They would meet at ten. It was now ten-thirty. Roman times were flexible, but Rossini was irritated, because with the shadow of coming loss hanging over them like a storm cloud, he was jealous of the few hours they could spend together. He called the hotel on his mobile phone. There was no answer from the Senora's room. According to the doorman, she had just left in a taxi with her daughter. If the Signore would like to leave a message? No, thank you.

It was another ten minutes before the taxi pulled up with a squeal of brakes and decanted the two women onto the pavement. Both were voluble with excuses, talking over and against each other: Luisa had come in late and had overslept; Raul had called from New York, which meant a long conversation with both Isabel and Luisa; then Miguel had called to make another date for this evening, which Luisa wasn't sure she wanted; and, finally, when they were just about to step into the taxi, Isabel was called back for a very long conversation with the woman with whom she would be traveling to Switzerland.

"And that, my dear Luca, ends our litany of excuses. We're sorry! Now, will you please give us absolution and get us the hell out of here!"

"Kiss the woman, for God's sake," Luisa commanded. "She's wound up tight like a fiddle string. That's not good for her—or for me!"

Rossini did as he was bidden. He kissed Isabel and laid a comforting hand on her shoulder as he settled her into the car.

"Now you may kiss me, Luca."

"Luisa, please!"

"Why not, Mama? He's out of uniform, isn't he?"

Rossini leaned into the back seat, gave her a hurried peck on the cheek, then climbed into the driver's seat and pulled out.

"My place is tucked away in a fold of the Sabine Hills a few miles south of Tivoli. If you like, we can go by way of Tivoli— you can see Hadrian's Villa, and the Villa d'Este—then go on to my place for lunch. I should warn you, however, it's a popular tour, so there'll be lot of groups in buses."

"If you don't mind, Luca, I'd be happier to spend a quiet day with you."

"I'm all for a quiet day." Luisa was prompt to support her mother. "I had a very late night. Miguel was attentive, but he did it all by the book: dinner, a club, then the whole Rome-by-night scene with bells and whistles!"

"That's settled then. No tourism. We'll take the back road to my place. We'll stop in the village to buy food, which you, Luisa, will help me cook while your mother takes her ease. Agreed?"

"Agreed."

"We'll both help," said Isabel firmly. "I'm not yet an invalid! What did you do with yourself after you left me last night?"

"I suppose you could call it my own version of Rome by night. I walked home. I lost myself a few times, because I had a lot to think about. I remember looking up and seeing through a lighted window a most wonderful frescoed ceiling. I was almost run down while I was staring at it. When I got home, I read the last of my breviary and went to bed. I had to be up early today to say Mass for a community of Sisters, and make phone calls. So, here I am. A free man today with a loaded calendar tomorrow!"

Dressed in country clothes, behind the wheel of his own car, Rossini was a changed man—a throwback to the Neapolitan street urchin. He drove with skill and verve. He responded with enthusiasm to horn blowing and personal abuse. As a tour guide, he was less than informative; as a commentator on the racetrack tactics of Roman drivers, he was eloquent, entertaining, and theatrically abusive in Lunfardo. The two women were laughing one moment, gasping the next, and deeply grateful when they turned off the Via Tiburtina and wound their way through a series of country byways toward Rossini's hermitage. They stopped in a small village to buy food; and watching him in easy talk with the shopkeeper, Isabel was overwhelmed by a rush of memories, of another Rossini, youthful pastor of another village tucked away in the sub-Andean foothills.

Finally, Rossini unlocked the heavy gate and drove into his kingdom. He helped the women out of the car and left them standing while he walked back to close the gate. When he rejoined them, Isabel smiled and laid a hand on his arm.

"I remember in one of your letters you told me you wanted to have *un huerto abigarrado,* a dappled garden. Now I see what you mean."

"You are both welcome. My house is your house."

Inside there was a chill, but the fire was set with kindling and logs. He set a match to it and switched on the CD player. The flames were rising and the *Haffner Symphony* was filling the room as he took them on their tour of his small retreat.

"I did most of the alterations myself." His pride in his handiwork was beguiling. "You can see where I started—and how the work improved as I got better at it. I like to have tools in my hands."

"Did you design it yourself?" Luisa was already testing the faucets, opening drawers and cupboards, checking cutlery and crockery.

"Yes, I did. For the plumbing I had some local help; but the rest of it is mine. You two finish looking around. I'll bring in the box of food."

When he stepped out the door, the two women looked at each other. Luisa shook her head incredulously.

"He's so happy with so little."

Isabel challenged her sharply.

"Are we happier because we have so much more?"

"Mother, please! You've been snappish all morning."

"I'm sorry. I had a restless night. You were touring Rome. I was touring my yesterdays and looking at the future. It's not a pretty landscape."

"Luca has his own past to cope with, and you're part of it. No! Don't turn away, please! When his face is in repose, it's tight and closed. When he looks at you, it changes completely. I don't see where he fits in your future, but I hope I can find a man who will look at me like that."

"I found him and then I lost him."

"You never lost him, Mother."

Rossini came in at that moment and dumped the food box on the table.

"Leave these now and let me walk you round the garden. The house will be warmer when we get back."

As they walked, they held hands, a family trio comfortable with each other, yet separate, each preoccupied with a private question. Luisa asked:

"Don't you ever feel shut in here? Nobody can look in, but you can't see over your own fence either."

"That's the way I like it, but you have to understand I spend most of my life meeting people, engaged with them always in discussion or negotiation. I come back empty as a clay pitcher. Here, I am filled again."

"But don't you ever get lonely?"

"The celibate life is a lonely road, Luisa."

"But Mother has never been celibate, and she's been lonely, too, though she hates to talk about it."

"I don't talk about it either." Rossini was gentle with her. "In one way or another, we all have to cope with the essential solitude of being human, whether we're celibate or married."

"If you're a good person, doesn't God fill your loneliness?"

"He fills it, I think, with a divine discontent."

Isabel seized on the phrase with an intensity that surprised them both.

"It's the discontent that keeps us alive. When the last desire is stilled, we've already crossed the river."

"Then you and Luca have a long way to go yet."

"Meaning what?"

"Please, Mother! A blind man could see that you two love each other. I'm happy for you both, but I don't understand why you've made it so hard for yourselves."

This time it was Rossini who reproved her.

"You're treading on private ground, young lady!"

Luisa refused to be silenced. "You told me this house was my house, too. So if there's ground I can't tread on, point it out to me. I don't know the whole story about you and Mother—because nobody's thought I had a right to know it. But I'm here with you both in this garden. That needs some explaining, doesn't it? It's no secret that Mother and Father live separate lives; and Mother, too, has had lovers from time to time." .

"Luisa, please!" Isabel was angry. "Now you're really over the line."

"Let her finish," said Rossini quietly. "She's right. I gave her the freedom of the house. Please say whatever you want, Luisa."

"I don't blame Mother or Father. I've had love and care from both of them—a different love, a different care from each. So I have no complaints, Mother. But Luca has been part of my life also: a legend, a mysterious figure whom Grandfather

Menéndez used to talk about sometimes. It was only yesterday that he became real. So you can't shut me out anymore, either of you."

Isabel was about to intervene again. Rossini cut her off with a gesture.

"Here's what we do. Let's all prepare the meal together. While we work, we talk. If you have questions, I'll try to answer them. Your mother can speak or be silent as she chooses. Does that sound fair?"

"Yes, it's fair, provided neither of you patronizes me."

He steered them back into the house, talking as he went, pausing to pluck ripe pears from the laden tree.

"Understand something from the beginning. Some of what you'll hear happened before you were born. Some of it happened when you were a very little girl and Argentina and its people were bitterly and brutally divided. No matter what side you were on, there was enmity and suffering. You were spared a lot of that, so try not to judge anyone too harshly. One more word before we start. I do love your mother. I'll love her till the day I die. She loves me, too. We have corresponded for years. But in the circumstances of the times, each of us was a mortal threat to the other. In a way, we still are . . ." He turned to Isabel and asked, "May I show her?"

"If you can bear it, so can I."

As Luisa watched, Rossini unbuttoned his shirt and took off his undershirt so that he stood naked to the waist. Then Isabel turned him about so Luisa could see the crisscross of scars and welts on his back. Luisa gasped in horror.

Isabel said calmly, "That's where the story starts for both of us. Raul was away in Chile and Peru. I was staying with your Grandfather Menéndez. Our apartment looked down on the square and the church where Luca was pastor."

After that first brutal moment of revelation, the rest of the story seemed to fall naturally in rhythm as now one, now the other, picked up the cadence of the narrative, while Luisa worked silently at the kitchen bench with them, asking no questions, offering no verdict, until the narrative ended with Rossini's return to Rome and Isabel's return to Raul.

"So, now you know," said Rossini.

"Thank you both for telling me." Luisa was subdued. "Now, may we eat? I'm very hungry."

Rossini poured wine while the women served the pasta. Then he invoked a blessing on the food and on the company. After the first mouthfuls, Isabel raised her glass.

"Compliments to the chef!"

"And the chef thanks his sous-chefs!"

"This sous-chef was working under a certain stress," Luisa admonished them both gently. "That was high drama you were giving me."

Isabel laid a hand on her cheek.

"I'm sorry you had to wait so long. Luca told me there was a grace in this house."

"There is love in it this day," said Rossini.

"And what was there before, Luca?"

"Some faith, some hope, a memory of love only. But this is our *ágape*, the meal at which we celebrate love together."

"And what about tomorrow?" Luisa's question hung between them like a drop of clear water ready to fall into a dark pool. Isabel sat silent, with downcast eyes. It was left to Rossini to offer an answer.

"There's an old adage among diplomats: Deal with the hard questions between the pear and the cheese. Why don't we do that? Let's enjoy the meal and the moment, and talk afterwards."

"Promise you won't put me off?"

He looked at Isabel. She nodded. He answered Luisa.

"We promise, both of us."

He got up to clear the first platters from the table, but Luisa pushed him back into his chair.

"Leave these to me! Mother and I are serving the meal. You look after the wine and try to look like a prince of the Church!"

It was a cheerful and chatty hour before the fruit and cheese were laid on the table and the coffee was ready to be served. Their talk trailed off as Rossini made a small ceremony of slicing a pear and offering "the first taste of the fruit of my garden." When they had approved the offering, he turned to Isabel.

"Now, my love, we have a promise to keep. Let's talk about the future."

"Not yet." Luisa stayed him with a gesture. "We haven't finished with the past."

"I thought we had," said Isabel. "When Luca came back to Rome, I resumed my life with your father. Luca and I have corresponded, but last night was our first meeting in—"

"In twenty-five years," said Luisa. "I know that; but while we've been talking, I've been doing some simple arithmetic. I know when I was born, where I was baptized. I know you had a cesarean in New York. So I ask myself whether there's any possibility I might be Luca's child."

"You were born, registered, and baptized Luisa Amelia Isabel Ortega."

"That doesn't answer my question, Mother."

"Why do you ask it now?"

"Because this is the first time I've seen you and Luca together—and it's the first time I've seen two middle-aged people so desperately in love it breaks my heart."

"I think you should tell her," said Luca Rossini. "Tell her exactly what you told me last night. It's your story. She can interpret it as she chooses. I'll do a little work in the garden. Call me when you want me."

He left them then, stripped off his shirt, and began hoeing the rows of vegetables, trying to slow down his whirligig thoughts to the pace of the mattock strokes as they broke the dry crust of the soil. It was the most primitive and most effective remedy he knew against the manic conflicts of ideas and arguments, of high matters and low ones, of interests and prejudices and claims and counterclaims which pressed for his attention every day.

Whatever argument or discussion Isabel and Luisa were pursuing inside the house would spill over on him. But their destinies were ultimately beyond his control. The question of his acknowledgment of Luisa as his natural daughter was a minor one, already settled. Her acknowledgment of him was another matter, far beyond the simple dispensation of affection. Soon her mother would be gone from her life; but the going could be long, painful, and destructive. What could he offer to Isabel to ease her passing, what to Luisa to make up for her loss?

Which brought him by a round turn to a question he had debated many times with the pontiff and discussed with his curial colleagues: the abiding problems of a celibate clergy in the Roman discipline of Christianity. Each age in the life of a celibate cleric brought its own crop of problems. In the training period, their sexual instincts were suppressed, their expressions of affection inhibited, their language purged of passion, so that when they encountered it again—if they ever did—in the writings of the great mystics, it was always with a sense of shock. In the middle years of pastoral life, companionship or shared ambition provided a partial support, but in the later years, illness or ennui or simple loneliness changed the landscape of their lives into a gray despair. And they had lost too long the simple skills of companionship with women and other men. What angered Rossini often was the element of hypocrisy in the discussions at every level—and that, also, was a very Latin skill: to add the color of virtue to the least convincing argument, as the forgers of antiquities aged their bronzes and marbles in dunghills and cesspits.

This much-chewed argument brought him to the end of his bean rows, and he was just scraping off his mattock when Isabel came out of the house, hand in hand with Luisa. He waited, dusty and sweating, as they approached.

Isabel stopped a few paces away. Luisa halted just out of his reach. He leaned on the handle of the mattock and waited.

Suddenly Luisa looked small and vulnerable, a lost child alone on an empty beach. Yet he could find no words either to comfort her or to explain himself. Her first words put him completely off balance.

"How are we supposed to feel about this, Luca?"

"I don't know. Luisa. I can only tell you how I feel."

"Then tell me, please!"

"I'm glad the truth is out at last. I was upset that I'd been kept so long in ignorance. I'm sad to think of the years that are lost to me. That's pure selfishness, I know. I'm glad you've seen your mother and me together. I think you understand the love that has bound us together all these years. I hope you understand that you are truly a love child and that you will let me spend some love on you. I confess I don't know how, but I know the love is there to spend. How do you feel?"

"Confused but not unhappy. I feel as though I've been born again and all the landmarks in my life have changed suddenly."

"For better or for worse?"

"When Mother goes—and I know how ill she is!—it will be for the worse. But now that I've seen you both together, I know how important your love has been in her life. That still leaves me with a lot of puzzles to solve."

"Like what?"

"How do I cope with two fathers in my life? Nothing will change with Raul. I know it can't. I know it mustn't. How can I live with so big a secret—because I know I'll have to? How can I get to know you better—because I want that, too? Then there's the problem of how I should feel about you."

"How would you like to feel?"

"At ease, even loved a little—but for myself, not for Mother.

I'd like you to hold me in your arms and kiss me and tell me I'm as welcome in your life as Mother is."

He straightened up and tossed the mattock away and held out his arms to her. She came in a single leap and he held her to him, murmuring over and over, "Welcome, my daughter, welcome." Then Isabel joined them, and they embraced in silence until Luisa herself broke the cobweb that bound them. She said lightly:

"Mother was right. Look at us! Three graces in a garden! You need a shower, Luca, and afterwards I think we should all have a drink to celebrate."

"Well, we're dealing with country matters," said Isabel.

"And what, pray, are country matters?" Rossini asked.

"My Aunt Amelia taught me the phrase. She learned it from the British who made themselves very rich in Argentina. Country matters are anything to do with sex and reproduction on either side of the blanket."

"I never knew Aunt Amelia," said Luisa. "But she certainly played an important role in my life. I think I would have liked her."

The rest of the afternoon should have played itself out as an agreeable epilogue to the drama of revelations. Instead, Rossini found himself witness to the sudden eruption of a quarrel between mother and daughter. It was triggered by an apparently casual remark from Luisa.

"Now that you've sorted my life out so neatly, Mother, let's talk about yours."

"There's nothing to talk about. As soon as we get back to New York, I have another series of tests. What happens after that depends on the results. It's simple. One day at a time."

"It isn't that simple and you know it. Father has told me how seriously ill you are."

"Then he shouldn't have! It's my life."

"And he's your husband and I'm your daughter and now Luca comes into the frame as well."

"My life is still mine. I'll make my own decisions about it, as long as I can."

"And when you can't?"

"Then your father can take over for whatever time remains. I won't have you wasting your life nursing a terminal case. Raul can well afford any nursing I may need."

"I know that, Mother. Father isn't a monster. He's kind and generous but a fool with women."

"That's enough!"

"No, Mother, it's not enough! What I want is that you should face whatever's in store for you with calm and contentment—"

"I can't do that if everyone's badgering me about how I arrange what's left of my life. Give me time to work it out. I need privacy. I need personal space. You try to explain it to her, Luca!"

It was then he remembered the medallion which the woman had given him at Mass that morning. He picked up his jacket from the bed and took from the pocket the small tissue-wrapped object. He carried it back to the table and laid it in front of Isabel.

"What's this?"

"Before you open it, let me tell you about it. This morning I said my Mass in a convent where the Sisters run a halfway house for women on release from the jail system. They've all had tough lives, but they've learned to trust me. I asked them to offer their prayers for you because, as Luisa does, I feel help-less to change the future for you, helpless even to support you toward it. After the Mass, this woman came up to me. She's in her early fifties, I'd say, and she's spent a large part of her life as a campfire girl flagging down truck drivers on the highways leading into Rome. It's a rough game, as you may imagine, ped-dling yourself winter and summer in a roadside ditch. I was just walking out when she hurried after me and pushed her gift into my hand. She said, 'Give this to your friend. It saved me from a lot of trouble on the street. Maybe it will do something for her.' That's the end of the story. Look at it one way, it's a social outcast and a not very good cleric invading your privacy. Look at it again, and it's an act of love and care."

Isabel opened the package and brought out the medallion on its fragile chain. She asked Luisa, "Would you put it on for me, please?"

As Luisa adjusted the pendant, Isabel reached up to touch her hands.

"Forgive me! I don't mean to snap. When I'm frightened, I get angry. When I'm angry, I have to hit out at someone. Luca should be glad he didn't marry me!"

Rossini was swift to answer.

"Married or not, we're all bound to each other. So let me say my little piece in my own house. My whole life has been an act of gratitude for what you did for me and what you gave to me: dignity and manhood! I can't make any judgments on your husband. I know only what you've told me. However, you must leave him the chance to give you what he can, to be what he can for you in this last term of your life. You can't refuse that to Luisa, either. We all need the chance to redeem ourselves by giving. Do you understand?"

"I understand; but no more lectures please, Luca!"

"My God!" said Luisa with a grin. "He sounds just like the Grand Inquisitor, doesn't he? I'm glad he's on our side!"

"Come and help me do the dishes, young lady. Isabel, why don't you put on some Haydn. I feel we need some nice orderly music in our very disorderly lives!"

As they worked together at the kitchen sink, Luisa asked, "Are we likely to see you again before the conclave?"

"It's unlikely. We could probably make a dinner at my place, but all of us in the college are under heavy pressure for the next few days. After the conclave, it will be much easier."

"Unless you're elected pope?"

"That, dear daughter, would be the outside bet of all time. What's much more likely is that I'll be exiled to some very obscure office in the Vatican."

"Is there any chance you could come to New York to see Mother—before the end? That's what she's hoping, though she's too proud to admit it."

"I'll move heaven and earth to be there. That's a promise. But I need a promise from you, too. I'll have to depend on you for regular news of your mother's condition. Send it E-mail."

"Count on it. I'll keep you informed."

"Good! Now we should think of heading back to Rome."

"Not yet, please. Mother needs some time alone with you. I'll go talk to the birds in the garden."

Then, swiftly, she was gone, and he was alone with Isabel, sitting side by side on the battered sofa, his arm around her, her head resting on his breast, savoring the silence.

After a long time, Isabel murmured drowsily:

"Luca, my love, I think this has been the longest day of my life."

"Has it been happy?"

"Happy, yes; but after all, each of us will sleep alone tonight—and all the nights after. I'm scared, Luca—and cold inside, as if I were already locked in my burial chamber."

He drew her close, murmuring words of comfort and hope which, even as he spoke them, sounded dry and hollow. Isabel, however, seemed to brighten a little. She began to finger the tarnished little medallion, which lay in the cleft of her breasts. Finally, she spoke again, in the same drowsy, detached fashion.

"Imagine all the things this little virgin saw by the light of the roadside fires. I hope the woman who gave her to me isn't lonely without her. Will you do something for me, my love?"

"Anything. You know that."

"Buy another medal, a gold one with a gold chain, have it

blessed by the new pope and send it to her with a note from both of us."

"What shall I say?"

"Tell her the gift was very important to me and already her little virgin is looking after me, and most of all, I feel I have a new sister. Can you remember all that?"

"How could I forget it?"

"Too easily, my love. I know this black spirit that haunts you. Whatever you decide to do with your life, don't do it in haste or anger. Above all, don't do it for me, because I shan't be here to share anything with you."

"Please, my love, please—"

"No! Let me finish. If you find in the end you can't believe, I'll believe for you. If you can't hope, I'll hope for you. If that sounds foolish, remember that we both have love and that's stronger than death, stronger than despair. Kiss me now. Hold me a moment, then take me back to Rome with our daughter."

# 8

To prepare for his interview with Steffi Guillermin, Rossini had arranged a half-hour briefing session with Angel-Novalis at the *Sala Stampa*. He was an ideal mentor: crisp, lucid, dispassionate. He offered first a portrait.

"She's a stylish woman, with a clear mind. She will come prepared in her subject and its vocabulary. She has no interest in men as sexual partners; but she demands that they acknowledge both her brains and her style. You may rely on accurate quotations of what you say, some acid descriptions of your attitudes under questioning, and some insight that may surprise you. She will not accept anything off the record. Her attitude is that you have accepted the rules of the game. Subjects? Certainly she will refer to the pontiff's personal relations with you. Certainly she will want to discuss the drama of your rescue from the soldiery and your eventual exit from Argentina. My guess is that she will have more information than you may be expecting. It is common knowledge now that the husband of Senora Ortega has been proposed as the next Argentine ambassador to the Vatican . . ."

"Which leads directly to the Mothers of the Plaza de Mayo."

"Yes."

"And since you will be present at the interview, that will certainly raise the question of the participation or involvement of members of Opus Dei in the dirty war in Argentina. Do you have any briefing for me in that area?"

"Guillermin is too practiced to address any questions to me. This is your interview, Eminence. I shall simply be a fly on the wall. My counsel would be to give your own answers and not try to guess what her commentary will be or attempt to instruct her in the faith. Some of your eminent colleagues have already fallen into that snare. You'll inevitably get two general questions: What is the present state of the Church, and what kind of a pope do we need? Each one of those has its own built-in bear trap. If the Church is in a bad way, who's to blame? If the Church needs repairs, who's the man to fix it? And your answer to that one could have you in trouble with the whole electoral college. Any more questions, Eminence?"

"Let's get back to the one you haven't answered," said Rossini. "What is your personal response to the actions of certain members of Opus Dei in my country during the dirty war?"

The question took him completely by surprise. He blushed crimson. He opened his mouth and closed it again. Then he sat in silence, staring down at the backs of his hands. Finally, he lifted his head to face Rossini. His voice was steady and his answer studiously formal.

"You are not my confessor, Eminence. So, I am not obliged to answer that question."

"I understand that."

"So, why does your Eminence ask?"

"Because, in my personal life first, and now in my collegial life as a cardinal, the matter assumes a special importance. A few moments ago, when I raised the question, you declined to give me any directions at all as to how—if at all—it might be answered for the press. So, I put it again to you in confidence. There is evidence, clear evidence, that members of Opus Dei were involved directly or indirectly in the repressive activities of the military in Argentina, that they helped to suppress proof of crimes committed in the dirty war. I know you as an upright and honorable man. It would help me to know how you come to terms with these anomalies. I, too, have questions of conscience to solve, and I'd like to have a very clear head when I face my inquisitor!"

"Then the answer will have to be in shorthand, Eminence."

"I accept that."

"Let's start with this proposition: Opus Dei is not a popular or populist group. It is elitist. It is secretive. It does deal with power groups in the law, in money, in politics. It endeavors, not always successfully, to apply Christian principles to the mechanics of social order. Its origins, like those of the Jesuits, are Hispanic. Its asceticism is, if you like, Hispanic, too. For my part, I have to acknowledge that its training enabled me to survive a most difficult period of my life. But, as we both know, power is a dangerous and corrupting game—especially when you have God and Christ's vicar on your side! Our society constitutes a very strong pressure group in the Iberian and the South American churches. Areas in which, let me say it, the power game has been played most brutally. Ask me for evidence of our involvement, I cannot give it. It is too deeply buried. I have chosen not to dig any deeper than I am obliged to do. Like you, Eminence, I have lived and worked under the close personal patronage of the late pontiff, who gave our society a special place in his plans. His Holiness was a potent influence in the downfall of Communist regimes in Eastern Europe. In politics, and in the Church, he leaned more to the right than to the left. Thus, living so close to the seat of power, it has been easy to dissociate myself from its abuses, to pull the cowl over my head like an ancient monk, and tell myself that God and the Holy Father know what is best for the world. Now I'm not so sure! What to do about it? I'm not sure either, especially with all the changes that a new man will bring. So, I wait. I wrestle with my conscience and pray for light enough and strength enough one day to cleanse my own corner of the house of God!" He broke off. His fine-boned features relaxed into a smile, and his voice took on its habitual tone of irony. "You see how easy it is to forget the disciplines and lapse into excessive emotion."

"Your excess was a gift to me," said Luca Rossini. "The light dawns slowly, doesn't it?"

"Too slowly sometimes. But let me repeat my warning, Eminence. Steffi Guillermin is a seductive interviewer. She has much intelligence and she likes to display it. Just remember, she's got ice water in her veins and acid in her pen!"

The interview took place in a room, in the press office. Guillermin and Rossini sat facing each other, with a small table between them. Angel-Novalis sat apart, out of their line of vision. His tape recorder sat beside Guillermin's on the tabletop. She began without preamble.

"You're a busy man, Eminence. I thank you for consenting to this interview. Let's deal with the big questions first. What's wrong with the Church?"

"The same things that have been wrong with it for two thousand years: people! Men, and women and children, too, who make up the family of believers. This isn't a community of the pure and the perfect. They're good, bad, and indifferent. They're ambitious, greedy, fearful, lustful, a rabble of pilgrims held together by faith and hope—and the difficult experience of love."

"Let's be more specific, then: The institution of which you are a key official, how would you describe its present condition?"

"Sometimes it's called the 'barque of Peter.' It's a good metaphor. It's a ship—a very old ship riding in stormy waters. It's been well built—its essential structures are sound—but its timbers creak. Some of them are worm eaten and have to be replaced. The rigging is frayed, the sails have been patched and repatched. It wallows in the troughs and lurches over the crests of big seas. But it's still afloat and the crew is still manning her—even though they, too, look a motley bunch sometimes."

"And now, of course, the captain is dead. You are one of the people, the very few people, who have to elect a new one. What special talents do you bring to that electoral task?"

"Fewer than you might think. I know how bureaucracy works, though I have little taste and less talent for it. However, the electoral process is a play of forces and interests within a small body of highly diverse individuals. Sometimes an oddity, like myself, may tip the vote in one direction or another—at least that's what I am told by those who have attended a conclave. This will be my first."

"His Holiness had a very long reign. Is that a good thing or a bad thing?"

"Good or bad, it's a fact which produces certain consequences."

"Could you be more specific, Eminence?"

"There's no mystery about it. The process of aging produces certain inevitable consequences. The catalog is familiar. The arteries get clogged. The joints stiffen. The brain functions may change radically. There are psychological changes as well. The aged can become fearful, paranoid, even tyrannous. In human societies under a long regime, there are analogous changes."

"Does this not suggest that changes in the traditional system may be necessary? A compulsory retiring age for a pontiff—a revision of the rules for retirement or deposition on the grounds of incapacity?"

"These are all matters of proper concern for the whole Church. Yes."

"But in the end, as things stand, they can be determined by one man, the reigning pontiff?"

"That's true."

"And in the normal course of events, what pontiff is going to provide for his own execution?"

Rossini threw back his head and laughed.

"You have a point!"

"The secret diaries of the late pontiff emphasize the point. An accusation has been made that they were stolen by the pope's valet and that we, along with other media, are publishing them illegally. You're aware of that?"

"I'm aware of it, yes."

"Are the diaries authentic?"

"To the best of my knowledge, they are."

"Were they stolen?"

"There is strong presumption that they were."

"One of the passages in the diaries reads as follows: 'There are those in the Curia who think my advancement of Luca Rossini is a mistake. They claim that he is secretive, arrogant, and too readily dismissive of opinions that run contrary to his own. I know what these critics mean. I have often had to reprove him for overemphatic argument. But I know what he has been through. I know how tenaciously he has fought to maintain the integrity of his tormented spirit. He has confessed to me his deep and abiding affection for the woman who saved his life. I believe this experience has given a special value and character to his service to the Church. I cannot protect him from scandal, calumny, or hostile rumor. He would consider it beneath his dignity to seek such protection. His reasoning is very simple. He told me once: "Holiness, I have been stripped naked in front of my own church, and flogged into a bloody pulp. I was about to be raped. My assailant was shot just before he penetrated me. What can rumors do to me?" This thought was in my mind when I named him cardinal. It was my fantasy to think how he might act if he sat on Peter's throne. But then I thought of others who survived torture and were considered *papabili:* Beran, Slipyi, Mindszenty. All were maimed in some fashion.' Do you have any comment on that, Eminence?"

"None."

"Are you a deeply tormented spirit?"

"Let's say I limp, like Jacob after his wrestle with the angel."

"How do you see your future?"

"Each day is new to me. I take it as it comes."

"Do the pontiff's remarks embarrass you?"

"I am embarrassed that his privacy has been invaded by their publication."

"This woman for whom you have this deep and abiding affection. What can you tell me about her?"

"I owe her my life. That says it all, I think."

"According to my information, her name is Isabel Ortega, born Menéndez. She is married to an Argentine diplomat, whose family protected her during the dirty war. She has a twenty-five-year-old daughter."

"You're very well informed, Mademoiselle. So, let me say now, I have no intention of pursuing the subject with you."

"The episode is closed, then?"

"Please, Mademoiselle, don't play games with me. We are talking not of episodes and incidents, but of my abiding gratitude. When I first went to Japan on a private mission for the Holy Father, I was given some instruction on the habits and customs in that country. I was warned, among other things, not to intervene in any way in a street accident, but to leave the victim to the care of others. If I intervened, I risked a lifetime relationship of duty to the victim—a relationship I could not possibly sustain."

"And the moral of that story, Eminence?"

"I could not, would not, and did not lay any burden of continuing relationship on the woman who saved my life. Now, let's address whatever other questions you have."

"Before we do, Eminence, please let me say something. I cannot avoid discussing this matter in the context of the diaries—and of the election itself. It has in fact been raised with me by certain of your colleagues."

"I will not ask you who these colleagues are."

"Better you don't. I understand from my interview with Car-

dinal Aquino that you had agreed to mediate a discussion between him and the Mothers of the Plaza de Mayo."

"Hold a moment! You say you have interviewed Cardinal
Aquino?"

"Among others, yes."

"And he volunteered this information?"

"Yes."

"When did you have this interview?"

"About this time yesterday. Why? Is something wrong?"

"No. Nothing's wrong. I did have such a discussion with
him. I find it strange that he should reveal such a delicate matter in a press interview."

"How delicate is the matter, Eminence?"

"Very."

"I ask myself, therefore, why you have consented to be advocate for Aquino?"

"Once again, Mademoiselle, your language is loose and in-
accurate. I have not consented to be Aquino's advocate, only to
mediate a discussion on the accusations which the women are
laying against him."

"That could be interpreted as a very effective plea for his
defense—or the defense of the policies of Rome and of the
local church."

"It would be a false interpretation."

"So, how do you describe what happened in your country,
Eminence?"

"Too many of our people sold their souls to the devil."

"For what, Eminence?"

"An illusion of order, stability, prosperity. An illusion, old
as history, that you can wipe out ideas by guns and the instru-
ments of torture."

"Why then would you agree even to give comfort to Aquino,
who, on his own admission, gave at least some comfort to the
regime?"

"Because, first, he has a right to my presumption of his

innocence and, second, I am bound as a Christian to find forgiveness in my heart for those who have injured me."

"Have you succeeded in doing that, Eminence?"

"I work at it." Rossini made a wry mouth. "I have not succeeded yet."

"Can you explain why?"

"Yes. As the late pontiff rightly says, I am still a flawed
man, conscious of my own capacity for evil."

"Are you afraid of that capacity?"

"Oh yes, I am. The prevalence of evil is the darkest and
most frightening mystery of the universe."

"So, how do you see the role of the Church in the fight
against evil?"

"As a community of believers, formed in faith and hope,
supported and enriched by charity, spreading the good news of
redemption. But the community has to renew itself every day."

"Let's talk about the role of leadership in that renewal."

Rossini smiled and shook his head.

"That's a very big can of beans. There's no way either of us
can digest it in a short interview."

"Let me put it another way, then. In a few days' time, you'll
be going into conclave with a hundred or more members of the
electoral college to choose a new pontiff. What sort of man will
you be looking for?"

"I can speak only for myself, as a single elector."

"Yet you share a common interest: the good of the people of
God."

"But being human, we are divided on how that interest
should be served."

"It is claimed, is it not, that the Holy Spirit is present in the
conclave?"

"We invoke the Spirit." Rossini's tone was cool. "There's no
guarantee that all of us, or any of us, is open to its promptings."

"And the man you elect, will he be filled with the Spirit?"

"We pray he may, but he, too, will be subject to the daily

temptations of power, which, as a great Englishman once wrote, tends always to corrupt."

"'And Satan took him up onto a high mountain,'" Steffi Guillermin quoted the familiar text, "'and showed him all the kingdoms of the world and the glory thereof.' So truly, Eminence, you and your colleagues are embarked on a high-risk enterprise. And the risk is doubled, is it not, by the dogma of infallibility, which of late has been given some very wide interpretations?"

"I would express it otherwise," said Luca Rossini. "I believe that the Church is best served when infallibility is not invoked but charity is most abundantly dispensed."

"Let's talk about charity, then—divine love and human love."

"Two sides of the same coin."

"And the sexual act is an expression of that love."

"It should be. It is not always. Sometimes it is an invasion, sometimes a debasement. As, for example, sexual abuse by clerics or religious teachers."

"And you, of all people, must find such abuse intolerable."

"I do and I find that its concealment by authorities within the Church compounds the crime."

"What about the perpetrators?"

"We have to admit that some of our training systems have contributed to their delinquency. We cannot keep them in hidden circulation through the pastoral or educational systems."

"Forgive them?"

"They, like all of us, must have the chance to change and seek forgiveness."

"The ordination of women: Where do you stand on that?"

"I stand where the late pontiff ordered us to stand: against the idea. Unless and until a later wisdom changes the order, and so long as I hold an official position in the Church, I will not speak against it."

"Is there any possibility that either position could change: a papal decision, your own position within the Church?"

"In spite of rumor and pressure to the contrary, I believe the papal position could change. My own position? Like everyone else in the Curia, I resign automatically and wait, at the disposition of the new man."

"How do you feel about partnerships between gay or lesbian couples? Should they be given marital status?"

"I think not. On the other hand, they should be given a civil recognition as partnerships with mutual rights and obligations."

"And what about the physical and emotional side of their lives?"

"The Church proclaims a Christian ideal of chastity. It cannot, and should not, intervene in the commerce of the double bed."

"That sounds rather cynical."

"It is not meant to be. Men and women are very complex creatures. I repeat, they need love more than they need legal prescription."

"And moral prescription?"

"The Church points out the road. We are free to choose or refuse it. If we choose the wrong road, the Church holds out its hand to help us back to the right one. That's what a family is for, is it not?"

"Do you have any thoughts on where you'd like to be, what you would like to do, at this stage of your life?"

"I'm not sure I can answer that question. The words that keep running through my head these days are those of Goethe on his deathbed: *mehr Licht,* 'more light.'"

"We're out of time, Mademoiselle," said Angel-Novalis from the sidelines.

"We're finished." Steffi Guillermin switched off her tape recorder. She stood up and held out her hand. "Thank you for your time and trouble, Eminence. I hope I can do you justice."

"When do you expect to publish?"

"Two days before the conclave begins."

"Then you send me like Daniel into the lions' den." He said it with a laugh and Guillermin laughed with him.

"If I were a lion, Eminence, I'd try very hard to make friends with you."

As he ushered her out of the room, Angel-Novalis added his own postscript.

"I warned you. He's a hard nut to crack."

"He made me work for every damned line. He's a formidable fellow. Just for the hell of it, I might have a small bet on him in the election stakes at the press club!"

Rossini's next appointment was more daunting: a midmorning coffee session with six of the most senior members of the college of cardinals, whose collective ages totaled half a millennium. They were all Italian, all veterans of pastoral or curial appointments, but still active enough and ambitious enough to lobby the electors before they went into conclave.

They were also openly resentful. In 1975 Pope Paul VI had excluded as electors all cardinals over the age of eighty. The move was planned to stop the growth in the Church of a gerontocracy, a government of old men, stubborn and jealous in their hold on power. Logically, it should have dealt with the tenure of the papal office itself. It made no sense that the pontiff alone should be elected for the term of his natural life, throwing the Church into possible disorder if he were crippled by age, infirmity, or even dementia. However, the radically indecisive nature of Paul VI had caused him to draw back, leaving this essential anomaly still to be confronted.

This deputation to Rossini was a lobby group of elders, pointedly addressing a junior with a clear complaint and a firm request. They were led by a sturdy eighty-five-year-old, the archbishop emeritus of a major Italian city.

"We are all brothers in the same family, but we are disfranchised by the apostolic constitution of 1975. Whatever we possess of wisdom and experience is denied to the Church. We need you—and other colleagues—to convey our views to the voters in the conclave."

"I've never been in a conclave." Rossini was mild and accommodating. "So I'm rather at a disadvantage."

"You'll learn! Keep your eyes and ears open. Weigh your words and watch your back. Things can get rough in there."

"'Rough.' I'm not sure I understand."

"Sibling jealousy!" The old man broke into a wheezing laughter. "We're all brothers in the Lord; but when we're all locked up together, we're like a sackful of cats, mewling and scratching. The longer the conclave goes on, the worse it gets."

"Tell me, then, exactly what you do expect of me?"

"A voice to express our opinions."

"An approving voice?"

"Not necessarily. We'd be content with an honest messenger."

"Why me?"

"Oh, you're not the only one we're talking to; but you have a special interest for us. On the one hand, you're a foreigner. On the other, your origins are here in Italy. We believe you have—how shall we call it?—a sympathetic position, a certain neutrality."

"I'm not a neutral man," said Rossini. "And with what or with whom am I deemed to be sympathetic?"

"With the notion of an Italian pontiff."

"There are certain merits in the idea."

"How would you define them?"

"I would rather you defined them for me," said Rossini mildly.

"Let me try, then, my friend." This was a new and emphatic voice. Rossini glanced down at his list to identify an eighty-three-year-old, former chancellor of the Lateran University. "We start with a proposition, clearly stated by the Second Vatican Council, that the Church is a community always in need of reform, 'ecclesia semper reformanda.' The process is sometimes slow, sometimes fast, but it does and it must continue. For some time now, the pace of reform has slowed almost to stasis, in spite

of the fact that we have had all these years a globe-trotting pontiff with a personal mission to unify and centralize the Church.
He has succeeded to an astonishing degree. Radio, television,
the Internet, and fast travel have brought the world to Rome and
Rome to the world in a fashion never even dreamed before!
What we have now is a new imperial church, united but deeply
divided, policed by Vatican congregations, monitored by Vatican
nuncios and delegates, doctrinally censored in secret by today's
version of the Inquisition, the Congregation for the Doctrine of
the Faith."

Rossini burst into laughter.

"I value your frankness, Eminence. So how do you propose
to change this imperial image?"

"I think we need an Italian pope and a total review by an
ecumenical council of the role and the office."

"How do you get the two things in one package?" Rossini's
puzzlement was genuine. "A pontiff who is prepared to commit
hara-kiri and an ecumenical council which will forge the weapons to help him do it."

"Simple! Muster enough votes for the right man, and he'll
agree to it."

"Why should he? You know that no preelection promise is
binding in law, and even simony itself does not invalidate an
election. One more question: Why does an Italian candidate
offer you better prospects for change than a non-Italian?"

"It's a question of attitude."

"Can you explain that, please?"

"Easily. The biggest problem we've had during the recent
pontificate has been old-fashioned absolutism, the fear of
'moral relativism.' It was and always has been the talent of the
Italians to arrive at a workable concordance between the two
notions: We make horrendous laws about everything. We accept
that the principle of law is immutable and its perfect practice
impossible. That's where *tolleranza* comes in. That's where we
differ from the Germans and the Anglo-Saxons . . ."

In principle Rossini *was* sympathetic to the idea. The Italians had a singular talent for dealing with impossible situations and somehow coexisting with the perennial criminalities of human nature. Their family life was firmly rooted in the matriarchal system, in which—provided she could survive infidelity, male tyrannies, and multiple childbearing—every woman must arrive at sovereignty, the respect of the whole tribal family, with whom her word was law. It was one of the great strategic errors of his late master that he had alienated the women of the world. Faced with the ill-fated decision of his predecessor to rule against artificial birth control, he had mitigated nothing of woman's burden, and in a hungry and overpopulated world, he had opened the gates to more grievous problems yet, while closing the door to open discussion of them by Catholic theologians.

Rossini had no illusions about the complexity of the issues involved in the primitive process of survival. He understood also that most individual human decisions were made in moments of crisis and often without support or counsel. He had learned painfully in his own life that to preach against sin was one thing, to offer compassion and forgiveness to the sinner was quite another. His answer was simple and pragmatic.

"I agree that we have to elect a pontiff who will embrace a mission of reconciliation. That's the heart of the matter. Whom do you have in mind?"

This time the answer came from a cardinal who had in former times headed the Congregation for Bishops. He was frail and white haired, but clearly this was his brief and he was ready to speak to it.

"We have three candidates. Two are pastors of important Italian cities, one is a curial prefect with long diplomatic experience."

Rossini waited in silence for the rest of it. This was the old Roman treatment: Keep the man in suspense; dole out information like pearls. Finally, it was delivered.

"Our first candidate is the cardinal archbishop of Genoa. You know him, I believe?"

"We've met, yes."

"No other comment?"

"For the moment, no."

"The second candidate is the cardinal archbishop of Milan."

"I know him also, a little better than Genoa."

"The third is your curial colleague, Aquino."

"He is well known to me."

"Would you be prepared to give your vote to any or all of these?"

"I'd be prepared to consider each one on his merits—and in the changing climate of each ballot, presuming that multiple ballots are required."

"Is there anyone you would reject out of hand?"

"You mean here and now, outside the frame of the electoral process?"

"Here and now, yes."

"I don't think it would be appropriate to preempt the electoral situation."

"As you wish, of course."

"Did you have any advice to the contrary?"

"We were led to believe by our colleague, Aquino, that you were a man with positive opinions."

"Did he give any examples of my opinions?"

"Not specifically. In fact, it seemed to me he was paying you a compliment. He said 'Talk to Rossini. He gets about a lot. He knows how to read the wind. If I were pontiff, I'd make sure to keep him very close to me.'"

"That was most kind of him," said Rossini. "Did either of the others offer a comment?"

"Let me think now. Genoa simply shrugged and said you were a good man who kept his own counsel and probably would make little impact on the conclave."

"And Milan?"

"That one's a Jesuit, of course, and a biblical scholar of high reputation. Both are, or could be, handicaps for a pontiff.

How did he describe you? Oh, yes. He said, 'Rossini? Interesting fellow. I'd like to think we could learn from each other.' So, there you see! If you helped to elect him, he'd probably become a good patron. Two prospects in one batch. That isn't bad, is it?"

It was a bad joke and it fell flat. An awkward moment followed. Rossini sat tight-lipped and silent. The others in the meeting studied the backs of their hands. Then the Angelus bells began to toll all over the city. Like the well-drilled soldiers they were, the old men stood and looked to Rossini as the host to make the ritual prayer: "*Angelus Domini nuntiavit Mariae.*" Their old voices responded in a ragged chorus: "*Et concepit de Spiritu Sancto.*" When the prayer ended, there was a moment's silence as each one remembered that this day, and for more days yet, there would be no familiar white-clad figure at the window of the papal apartment, reciting the Angelus with the pilgrims in the square. The See of Peter was vacant. Those who stood together in Rossini's office were members of a trusteeship whose powers were limited by the decree of a dead man. Rossini seemed suddenly withdrawn. Out of the silence, the archbishop emeritus prompted him tactfully.

"It would help greatly if you could give us some immediate reaction to the ideas we have proposed to you."

Rossini was momentarily nonplussed, but his answer was firm.

"To be frank, they puzzle me. Your trio of candidates is interesting, but I can't believe it's exhaustive. Your policy—if it can be so described—lacks substance and detail. I should have expected a more reasoned exposition of the needs of the Church."

"We presumed that you were aware of them. We hoped you had already some remedies in mind."

"I fear, gentlemen, that you are asking too much of me. Let me speak plainly. My service as a pastor was very short. It was given in a primitive corner of South America. It ended abruptly. For the rest of the time—by the personal disposition of the late pontiff—I was trained, if you like to express it so, to a vagrant mission. I reported from places as far apart as Tokyo and Tulsa. His Holiness saw, or thought he saw, a certain value in my reviews of local situations, in my contacts with politicians and with leaders of other religions who would not, or could not, have received me formally and openly. I used to think often that what I was seeing was the underside of a carpet and what I was losing was the grand design on the other side. I developed insights, yes. I had friends and acquaintances who could give me backstairs access to people in power; but remember, my reports were delivered on the basis of that fragmentary knowledge and my instinctive reaction to unexpected circumstances. My judgments acquired value because of the man to whom they were delivered. He gave me confidence. He added his own insights to mine. Now, I have to tell you, I am much less confident. I am not at all sure that my opinions have any value for you."

"Be assured, Rossini, they do; and whether our opinions are right or wrong, we need your voice to offer them to the voters in conclave. We are old and only sometimes wise, but we have been rendered dumb by decree."

Rossini made a gesture of resignation.

"So be it, then. I promised you an honest voice in the conclave. You shall have it. Now, do you all have transport? If not, it will be my pleasure to arrange it."

And so it was done, if not successfully, at least in traditional style. Soundings had been taken. Plans had been drawn in a fine Italian hand, then magically erased as if they had never existed. There had even been the muffled chink of those most precious currencies of all: position, preferment, patronage, none of which was truly the gift of those offering it. And yet, Rossini knew there were kernels of truth among the husks of fallacy.

In the last decades of the twentieth century, the office of the Roman papacy had been inflated beyond any one man's capacity to fill it. The late pontiff had traveled the world with the Good News in his briefcase—even though half of it was rewritten for him by local advisers. Modern media had given him a pervasive presence, a degree of exposure unthinkable in olden times. The aura which surrounded him now was no longer of mystery but of familiarity and idiosyncrasy. Too many of his texts were written by other hands. They had begun to smell of the lamp, of stale incense and stale argument.

No man—even one filled with the Spirit—was large enough, wise enough, durable enough to bring off the illusion of universality: a universal pastor of a universal church. There was much more reason—much more appeal, perhaps—in the image of a Roman pontiff, bishop of his own See, subsuming in himself, as indeed his city did, the long history of Christendom, the fundamental unity of its sacraments and beliefs. His primacy would be one of millennial tradition among the churches. He would be the final arbiter of their disputes, the ultimate censor of their conduct. He would rule not by the devious exercise of bureaucratic power but by collegial consent to a common gospel and a common apostolic tradition.

This, too, perhaps was an illusion, because power once gained was not readily relinquished; yet the notion of authority based on service, validated by apostolic tradition, was, in the end, the only authentic one. This was the true mustard tree of the parable, sprung from a single root, spreading its branches so that all the birds of the air could rest therein. If the Good News of a universal gospel was to be heard above the babble of tongues and the clangor of discordant temple bells, it must be delivered with the simplicity of morning birdsong: "Love your enemies. Do good to those who do harm to you."

It was the easiest of all prescriptions to preach, the hardest to practice. Rossini was coming painfully to understand that this was the core of his own problem. Ever since he had come to Rome, he had been building a fortress for his fragmented self. The fortress was founded not on firm, level ground but on a granite outcrop of anger and resentment. At the heart of it was a shrine where a silent God dwelled but where a lamp burned always to a miraculous image of an absent woman, Isabel Menéndez. It was she who mediated between him and the silent God, whose existence he acknowledged with all formality but who, in his subconscious mind, was always associated with the harshest presumption of magistracy. *There is no power but from God—and the powers that be are ordained by God.*

It was the visible lover who had kept him alive and sane. After her, he had lived celibate, he had refrained from acts of retribution or revenge; yet the very punctuality of his service was an act of exclusion against the memories of abuse. *I don't expect you to love me, gentlemen, but respect me you will!* Now, Isabel was here in Rome. He had kissed her and held her in his arms. She had displayed to him the fruit of their love, a girl child grown into a woman. He had embraced his child, and she had embraced him. All three had found a measure of joy in the encounter.

But the silent God had presented them with an exquisite irony. Isabel was under a death sentence. It might be deferred, but it could not be rescinded. He, himself, was one of two fathers to Luisa—the one who could offer her least in terms of love, care, and heritage. The silent God had hidden his face, perhaps forever, so that the public liturgies he offered, the duties he performed in high and public places, became a sterile mockery. Soon, the shrine would be empty. The foundations of his fortress were cracking. The walls were crumbling about him. One fine day, he would be standing amid ruins, staring up at an empty sky, deprived even of the gift of tears.

And that was the final irony of the silent God: There would be no one with whom he could share his desolation. Isabel would be gone. Luisa, grieving but secure in the love of two fathers, would in the end dispense with both of them and find her own man.

In spite of the impending ruin about him, he could not surrender without a fight. He would not involve Isabel or Luisa in his private war. If love meant anything, it meant the last steps had to be made to support the beloved. The last prayer had to be shared, even if it had no meaning for himself, but only for the other. After that, what? One last great horn-blast, like Roland's at Roncesvalles, to challenge the mute God to make himself heard once more in the desert silence?

Luca Cardinal Rossini was an ironist himself. He could still raise a thin smile at his own conceits. Too much talk and too much caffeine on an empty stomach were bad medicine. The black devils were beginning to crowd in on him again. He needed food and company. He reached for the phone and dialed the number of Monsignor Piers Hallett at the Vatican library. Mercifully, the man was still at his desk.

"Piers, we need to talk. If you're free, I'll feed you lunch at my house. Pick me up here in twenty minutes."

"Eminence, you've saved my life. I'm facing a stale ham sandwich and a page of a sixth-century gospel text in Greek. My problem is that it's owned by a rather irascible prelate from middle America. He isn't going to be very happy when I tell him it's a poor fake and the original text is held in Rossano in the custody of the archbishop!"

# 9

Isabel and Luisa had spent the morning in an orgy of shopping. They had wandered into every gilded trap between the Via Condotti and the Corso and had fetched up, footsore and poorer, in Babington's Tea-Rooms at the foot of the Spanish Steps. They found themselves a discreet corner, kicked off their shoes under the table, and ordered Earl Grey tea, with cucumber and smoked-salmon sandwiches.

"Just like a pair of Anglos," said Luisa, with a grin.

"Don't mock, young lady," Isabel admonished her lightly. "This place has a lot of happy memories for me. My father and mother brought me here when I was sixteen years old. That was back in the late fifties, when Argentina was rich and Italy was very cheap to visit. We came by ship, a return trip on one of the big liners that were bringing Italian migrants from Naples to Buenos Aires."

"And this place was here then?"

"This place has been here, if I remember rightly, since 1894. It was founded by a Miss Anna Babington, who was British, and Miss Isabel Cargill, who came from New Zealand. I remember her because her name was the same as mine, Isabel. There's a lot more to the story, but I won't bore you with it."

"No, please! You're not boring me. I love it when you share memories with me. It doesn't happen often enough these days."

"One loses the habit," said Isabel. "I'm told one needs grandchildren to bring it back."

The waitress came, laid out the sandwiches, poured the tea, wished them good appetite, and left.

"Please," Luisa begged her. "Please finish the story."

"It's strange how things arrange themselves in your mind. Babington's I remember as my mother's place. The Anglo part of it appealed to her, and the history fascinated her. Anna Babington was descended from one Anthony Babington, who was hanged, drawn, and quartered for treason against Queen Elizabeth I of England. Her friend Isabel Cargill was descended from a Covenanter who preached against Charles II, accusing him of tyranny and lechery. He was executed in Edinburgh. When times were bad in Argentina and Luca and I were at risk, I used to dream about this place. Your grandfather Menéndez, on the other hand, was never comfortable here. He preferred the Caffe Greco just across the square on the Via Condotti. All the great romantics went there: Byron, Liszt, Wagner . . . And my father was a romantic—but he had the heart of a lion. When we were in hiding, after I'd shot the sergeant, he went alone to Buenos Aires and bargained for our lives. He never told me what happened. But when he died in the chopper crash, I wondered if it was a final payback from someone whom he had threatened. It was reported as an accident; but who knows? We have buried so many secrets over the past twenty years. Still, here we are, you and I, drinking tea and eating cucumber sandwiches at Babington's on the Piazza di Spagna!"

"While your Luca—my new father—is a cardinal with a red cap and could even be our new pope."

"How do you feel about him now?"

"I don't know. You've had twenty-five years to get used to him. I've only had twenty-four hours. Don't you understand how confusing that is? It's as though a figure has stepped out of a picture and is now pacing about the most private room in my life. You have to help me! You have to explain him. Where has Luca fitted in your life all this time? Where does he fit in your future?"

"The future? That's easy. I'll go home without him. I'll die loving him."

"My God, you can be brutal sometimes, Mother!"

"I killed a man, remember. That's a brutal act. I lived through brutal times. Forgive me! You asked me to explain. I'm trying. But this love for Luca doesn't explain itself in easy words. I was young then. I adored my father, who was everything Raul was not. He was strong, adventurous, decisive. He had himself seconded out of the army because he hated what was happening in the forces. I was still learning that Raul was what he would always be, a spoiled boy, an agreeable charmer, and a dead loss when you had to depend on him. He traveled a lot. He played when he traveled. When he was absent, I used to visit my father wherever he was working. That's how I came to be in Luca's parish that morning. I'd seen him a couple of times in the village, long enough to say good morning, to notice that he was a good-looking young man, and to wonder why he was content to bury himself in a no-place like that. The day the soldiers came, everything changed."

"Please, Mother, I don't want to hear that part again. How did Luca behave?"

"You have to understand, nobody 'behaves' after a beating like that. He just hung on the wheel, moaning and twitching, with the sergeant's riding crop stuck into his backside, while the sergeant unbuttoned his breeches and prepared to sodomize him."

"My God!"

"Luca has blocked that part out completely. In all the weeks we were together, he never mentioned it. The doctor said he might suppress it till he died, if his reason survived that long. The internal injury was not serious; but the damage to his psyche was, as the doctor put it, 'inadmissible.'"

"So, you pitied him and fell in love with him?"

"No! Quite the reverse. I fell in love with the anger he still had, the curses he could still summon up, the defiant soul of him. I wasn't seeing him as a victim but as a man tormented yet unbroken in spirit. He was my prize. I had killed for him. I, too, might be killed in the end; but this man was mine."

"But you couldn't keep him?"

"No! I healed him. I nursed him through fevers and nightmares. I used every trick I had ever learned to stir his passion and restore the ravages to his pride and his manhood. My God, Luisa! If ever there was a love child in the world, you were that child."

"So, why did you let Luca go? Why did you stay with Raul?"

"Because that was the deal my father had to make with the generals, and with the Church."

"And if he hadn't made it?"

"All three of us would have ended among the disappeared ones."

"How much of this does Raul know?"

"I can't say. We have never discussed the matter."

"I can't believe that."

"It's true. As soon as Grandfather Menéndez confronted the generals—and remember Raul's father was one of them!—they all saw the danger of the situation. There had been massacres and killings and disappearances in the past. This could be one too many. A little up-country priest—he was a cipher! But the daughter-in-law of a general, wife of a well-known international playboy, daughter of a well-known engineer in the oil business? Enough, they said! Get the woman home to her husband. Get the priest out of the country. Let the apostolic nuncio deliver him, gift wrapped, to Rome. But in silence. One word out of place and you'll never guess how bad it can get! We were all hostages to silence!"

"Why didn't you and Luca run away together?"

"Where could we have run? Peru, Chile? And don't forget

there were other hostages, too—my father, Raul and his family. There was no way we could better the deal we had. We both knew that."

"How did Luca react?"

"I have never seen him so enraged. Our last lovemaking was wild and desperate and wonderful—but our good-bye was calm and quiet. We stood in the shade and watched the helicopter land. We didn't kiss. We didn't embrace. We had decided there should be no witnesses—no official ones, at least—to our love for each other. Two people got out of the helicopter: a cleric and an army major. Luca's eyes were like dark stones. His face looked like carved wood. I remembered what he had said to me in the first hour of the false dawn: 'I love you. I will always love you. There will never be another woman in my life.' He walked away, proud and silent between the two men, without a backward glance. I don't know whether he waved to me or not when they lifted off. I was blind with tears."

"But you still went home and made love to my father; and you had other lovers. How did you feel when you were with them?"

"They were the toys I played with. They were my revenge for what Raul was doing to me."

"But Luca, too, was part of your revenge."

"No! He was my man."

"You said he was your prize. Did you truly own him?"

"Not all of him."

"Do you own him now?"

"No. Nobody owns him. His love is a free gift from a free man."

"I'm sorry, Mother, but I'm trying to understand. Do you think Luca kept his promise about other women?"

"I'm sure of it."

"How can you be? Did he feel so guilty about you that he lost all taste for women?"

"On the contrary. He refused to see me as a guilt in his life. He called me 'a saving gift,' and he was right."

"But he's not saved yet, not altogether. He's wrapped the Church around him like a cloak of invisibility. That hermitage of his tells another side of the story. He's still in flight. He still needs a refuge. He won't admit it. He's too proud to do that, but you are still the lodestone which gives direction to his life. What will he do when you're not here?"

"Is that what you're afraid of, Luisa: that he will try in some fashion to lean on you?"

"It's possible."

"It's impossible, and it won't happen. When Luca and I surrendered ourselves to the inevitable, that chapter of our lives was closed. The affair was over. Neither of us was prepared to accept a self-inflicted torture. Love was something else, a treasure—secret to both of us. We didn't even begin to write to each other until your father and I moved to New York and I was working at the institute, with an office of my own. I was the one who began the correspondence. So, never think Luca will intrude in your life!"

"But, like you, I can't ever shut him out of it."

"That's true. So, why not welcome him?"

"And thank him for acknowledging me as his daughter?"

"That, too, if you want."

"It would make a big mess of his career if that news got out!"

"I doubt it." Isabel signaled to the waitress to bring the check.

"How can you say that, Mother?"

"Because I think he may be on the verge of leaving the Church."

Luisa gaped at her mother in surprise.

"To do what?"

"I don't know, and I don't think he knows either."

"But why would he want to resign? Unless they make him pope, he's climbed as high as any man can go in Rome."

"I don't think he sees it that way."

"How, then?"

"He's come to a crisis of belief. It may be that this is the form in which the unresolved trauma in his life will work itself out. The beating, the violation, our love for each other, the conspiracy of silence between the Church and the State in which, to save our lives, we both consented to be joined. It's a lot to wear, my dear daughter. So try not to judge either of us too unkindly. By the way, what are you doing with your afternoon?"

"I'll take our packages back to the hotel, then I'll write some cards and letters. What about you?"

"I have a meeting at two-thirty with the leader of the Mothers of the Plaza de Mayo. She's staying with the Missionary Sisters of Nazareth over on Monte Oppio. After the meeting, I'll pass by Luca's house and spend a little time with him, provided he's home and will receive me."

"Remember we're booked for dinner at the embassy tonight. They're sending a car for us. You should leave enough time for a rest before we go."

"What time are we due?"

"Eight for eight-thirty. Oh, and since we're still in mourning for the pope, dress is informal."

"That's a blessing," said Isabel. "Let's move. We'll pay at the desk."

"Before we go, Mother . . . I know I sound like a bitch sometimes, but I do love you and I do know it's very special to be your love child, as well as your legal one."

"Do you know why?"

"Tell me!"

"Aunt Amelia used to say 'Love children are lucky when they're welcomed. They have better care, and generally better manners than the rest of the family!'"

On his small rooftop terrace in the Via del Governo Vecchio, Rossini was pouring coffee for Monsignor Piers Hallett. He was also delivering a short information piece on the conclave arrangements.

"This time, all the conclavists and their attendant staff will be lodged in Saint Martha's House. It isn't exactly the Grand Hotel, but it's an all-new building with a hundred and eight suites and twenty-three single rooms, together with dining and lounge areas. The present tenants will be moved out to accommodate the conclavists. We're not sure yet how many cardinals will be present, but let's say anywhere between a hundred and ten and the top limit of a hundred and twenty. That doesn't leave too much room for attendant staff. Each of us has been asked to specify the personal staff we need and to justify their presence in an accompanying memorandum to the camerlengo. Quite apart from questions of space, the move is to cut down on the number of clerical flunkies, who used to be trotting between various factions of electors. So I've decided, my dear Piers, to present you as my personal confessor."

Hallett burst out laughing.

"That's rich! Piers Hallett, paleographer, pedant, library mouse, now private confessor to an eminence. They'll never buy it. They'll run me out of the place by the scruff of my neck!"

"No, they won't," Rossini told him. "I've already made it clear that I have a personal problem and that I hope to sort it out during the conclave, during which we are commanded to act 'having God alone always before our eyes.' So, in fact, I do need a confessor—and I'm nominating you."

"You still have to be joking."

"No, I'm not. You're a priest, yes?"

"Of course. But look, friend to friend, I'm not a spiritual man. I'm a scholar in a dog collar. What counsel can I offer a man like you?"

"But you asked counsel of me, about a very spiritual matter, your own identity, your own moral life. I hope I can help you; I'm sure you can help me."

"How, for God's sake?"

"By listening, by hauling me through the bramble patches

into open country. All our talk will be under the seal. We're free, either of us, to grant or refuse forgiveness at the end."

"This is pure formalism." Hallett was genuinely surprised. "I never expected to hear you talk like this."

"I know," said Rossini. "But it's all I have left at this moment. You see, what I have to decide—with your assistance, I hope—is whether or no I am still a believer, whether or no I should resign quietly and go into the desert for a while."

"Where would you go?"

"That was Peter's question: 'Lord, to whom shall we go?'"

"But Peter answered it for himself: 'You have the words of eternal life.'"

"Exactly; but Peter already had the answer. I'm not sure I have any longer."

"And I'm not sure, either." Hallett was suddenly moody. "I'm not sure where I fit in this pluperfect world of the moral absolutists. Perhaps we'll make some discoveries together while we watch the raree-show of Peter's Successor!"

Luca Rossini was puzzled by the reference. He asked: "What was it you said?"

"'The raree-show of Peter's Successor.' It's a quotation from the English poet Robert Browning."

"But what, please, is a raree-show?"

"Oh dear! In Italian or Spanish, I guess the nearest word would be *carnival*, although the expression in English suggests a fairground with jugglers, sword-swallowers, bearded ladies, and other freaks."

"With some comic ecclesiastics thrown in—a cardinal or two, or a skeleton from the vaults of the Franciscans."

"Now you've got the idea," said Hallett happily. "It's an old-fashioned word, but it might raise some ghosts in Vatican City!"

Rossini was still chuckling over the image when his mobile rang. He answered brusquely; then his whole expression changed. One moment he was eager, the next dubious and concerned.

Finally, he said, "Very well. I'll see her with you. I'll have my man drive her back afterward. I need to talk with you alone for a while. No, not at all. I have a visitor with me, that's all." He switched off and turned to Hallett.

"I have people to see in about twenty minutes, so I'll have to throw you out. Are we agreed, then? You will enter the conclave as my personal confessor. All our personal transactions henceforth are under the confessional seal."

"We're agreed. And thank you for the trust you're showing me."

"Come to think if it," said Rossini with a grin, "we're both putting a lot of trust in each other. If either, or both of us, becomes a nonbeliever, none of the rules makes sense, except as tools for the conduct of the institution."

"Which is why most of them were invented down the centuries," said Piers Hallett. "A well-ordered society is a splendid thing to see. It's like a hothouse. You can grow anything in it, but not everything will survive the rough weather outside. That's the real terror of the world for me, Luca. All us humans—and so many are so bloody lonely!"

In the lounge of the Foreign Press Club, Fritz Ulrich, well primed with a heavy lunch and two brandies, was dispensing wisdom and irony to a group of newcomers from the Bavarian Catholic press.

"This is the smallest and most exclusive electoral college in the world: a hundred and twenty male celibates appointed to choose an absolute ruler for the largest religious constituency on the planet. Think about that! They, themselves, are not elected. They are appointed by a reigning pontiff. Whom, truly, do they represent? Certainly not the vast mass of the faithful. What are they charged to do? Find a universal man for a universal church. Impossible! In theory, they can elect any baptized male, and make him priest, bishop, and pope in one ceremony. In fact, they'll choose one of themselves: one out of a hundred and twenty—if they all turn up!—to hold the keys of the kingdom for a billion believers and all the other benighted souls whom they claim a mandate to convert."

"You're talking very loudly, Fritz!" Steffi Guillermin called to him across the room. "Some of us are trying to work."

"I apologize! I will try to be more quiet. Anyway, I have said my piece. These good people will make up their own minds."

"Thank you, Fritz."

Now that they were both under pressure to report a millennial event, now that they were involved in pooling and syndication deals, their relations were less abrasive. Ulrich dismissed his audience, heaved himself out of his chair, and crossed to her table. She frowned and waved him away.

"Not now, please, Fritz. I'm working."

"A few moments only, Steffi. Home office has sent me a query."

"On what?"

"Your Aquino interview. You know we bought the German-language rights to all those portrait pieces of yours."

"So, what's their problem?"

"You discuss the accusations brought against him by the Mothers of the Plaza de Mayo. My people ask do you have any notes on another aspect of the situation: the involvement of former German nationals in the dirty war, suspected war criminals and the like?"

"No, I don't, Fritz. That's old ground. I didn't want to walk over it again. Why do they need that sort of stuff, anyway?"

"They're trying to build a background piece on candidates who may have black marks against them for political or other reasons. Italians who have lived in the pockets of the Christian Democrats, South Americans who turned too far left or too far right, that sort of thing. I told them I'd send some brief notes; but I didn't want to waste time on it. It's filler material—pure speculation."

"Well, tell them I'm sorry I can't help. Now, if you don't mind . . ."

"Just one more thing, then I'll leave you in peace. What do you know about the Janissaries?"

"The who?"

"Janissaries!" He was happy to have surprised her, happy to be launched on a new monologue. "Shock troops of the old Ottoman Empire, founded in the fourteenth century, they garrisoned all the Balkan outposts of the Ottoman Turks."

Steffi Guillermin stared at him blankly.

"And what the hell have they got to do with a papal election? Are you sure you're sober, Fritz?"

"No, I'm not sure. I need another drink. One more would prove it one way or the other. You wouldn't like to join me, would you?"

"No way! And you shouldn't have one either. Now, what's this garbage about Janissaries?"

"Analogy." He stumbled over the word, then took a run at it. "Important historical analogy. They recruited captive Christian boy children. They enslaved them to Turkish families, where they learned the language and embraced Islam. After that, they were enlisted in the army as an elite corps. They trained in special barracks; they were celibate; they were debarred from trade or commerce; their obedience was absolute. Their badges of honor were the old slave-names: pot cleaner, woodcutter, cook. But they were a feared and formidable force. Now, my dear Steffi, do you see where my little analogy is leading me? All the prelates who are assembling in this city are like the Janissaries—shock troops of a religious empire."

"It's an interesting thought, Fritz. But what are you going to make of it?"

"A panel piece, perhaps. Would your people be interested in picking it up?

"I doubt it, but I'm willing to try for you when it's done. The problem we've all got is an overdose of information and not enough educated readers to deal with it. Now, get the hell out of my hair. I've got a deadline to meet."

"I'm going! I'm going!" He scrambled awkwardly to his feet before delivering his exit line. "The Janissaries did well so long as they had a regular supply of slave boys. But once the fighting stopped, the breeding had to begin; so they tossed celibacy out the window. There's a lesson in that, Steffi—a lesson for the Church. A lesson for you, too, come to think of it."

"Thank God I'm not a breeder, Fritz; otherwise I could be stuck with a child like you!"

As he wandered away laughing, Frank Colson came to the table. Before he opened his mouth, Guillermin appealed to him:

"Why do I always fall for it? I'm an intelligent woman, yet every time he talks to me I fly off my perch like a demented parrot."

"Fall for what, Steffi?"

"Fritz Ulrich's bad jokes! He's such a tasteless oaf."

"He knows you too well. You always rise to the same lure. Now, I have a little news for your ears only."

"Good news, bad news, what?"

"The London tabloids are floating a story about the morals of the senior clergy—old stuff, most of it: one Austrian cardinal, a couple of stalwarts in the Curia. They're just trawling muddy waters; but one of the names that came up was Luca Rossini's. You interviewed him the other day. You called him the mystery man."

"I know. I'm revising the story now, and I still don't like the phrase. I'd like to find a better one before I file. Anyway, what are the London tabloids saying?"

"They're sailing very close to the wind. They're talking about a mysterious crime with which Rossini was connected, a horrendous beating, a statement that he had been sodomized, a secret arrangement to smuggle him out of the country—and they're making smoke signals about a love affair and the birth of a child after he had left the country."

"My God! They're taking a hell of a risk!"

"Of what, a lawsuit? He can't sue, except by permission of the pontiff—whom we don't have at the moment. And besides, what would it matter? So far as election chances are concerned, Rossini will be dead in the water."

"So, who loaded the cannon and fired the shot?"

"Good question, Steffi! What's your answer?"

"There are two. First, the Argentines have had this information for a long time. The one thing they'd never want to see is one of the victims of their dirty war enthroned in the Vatican—scars and all. The second guess, which I don't like half as much, is someone inside the Vatican who has access to the records and the motive to leak them against Rossini."

"Cleric or layman?"

"Cleric. It would have to be."

"Motive?"

"Jealousy or malice; either or both."

"So now I need your advice. My office has asked me to advise whether we should investigate the story or drop it cold and let someone else do the autopsy."

Steffi Guillermin considered the question in silence for a few moments before she answered.

"First of all, Frank, there's nothing there except the sodomy and the illegitimate child which wasn't implicit in the pontiff's diaries. The love affair is mentioned, if not described. The child? A birth certificate would settle that question out of hand."

"You're right, of course. I hate rummaging in dirty linen. I guess I'm looking for a good excuse to cry off."

"You know, Frank, that whatever advice one gives in a case like this is bound to be wrong. You turn down a dirty story, it turns into tomorrow's headlines. You chase it, and you're giving aid and comfort to the bastards who floated it in the first place. I'm keyed in to both Aquino and Rossini—and it wouldn't be too hard to prize some comment out of the Argentinians. But as a friend, I'd say don't touch it. You've got an easy out, anyway.

You're bureau chief. You advise that any attempt to play up such a story on the eve of an election could be construed as an attempt by an Anglo-Saxon Protestant country to interfere in an election."

"That wouldn't wash, Steffi."

"So, invoke your conscience. Tell him you refuse to be party to scurrilous rumormongering at this crucial time."

"The plea might just appeal to him. He has a taste for well-rounded phrases. I owe you a drink. Ciao!"

Which left Steffi Guillermin face-to-face with her own dilemma: How much treachery to a colleague would be involved if she took another look at her story before she filed it, and perhaps—only perhaps—floated some smoke of her own. It took her at least two minutes to make her decision. She telephoned Rossini's office and asked that her call be transferred to him wherever he might be. Yes, the matter was quite urgent. She needed to check a key passage in her interview text before she filed it for publication. There was a longish wait before the answer was relayed to her. His Eminence had a very busy afternoon, but he would make time to see her at his apartment at five-thirty in the evening. He hoped she would not be offended if she were kept waiting a short time. Of course not. Please convey Mademoiselle Guillermin's thanks to His Eminence!

The woman Isabel presented to him that afternoon was more than seventy years old. Her name was Rosalia Lodano. She was the leader of the Mothers of the Plaza de Mayo, sojourning in Rome.

Her hair was snow white, her skin like old ivory, seamed and scored by time and bitter experience. There was a strange sibylline calm about her, a formidable gravity beyond the reach of fear or malice. Her eyes were dark, hooded, and implacable. With Isabel at her side, she sat, bolt upright, her clothing loose about her thin figure, her hands lying flat and immobile on a thick folder of documents. Her first utterance was a surprise: a curt, imperious statement.

"I know your history, Eminence. I know Senora Ortega. I am prepared to trust you."

"You understand I make no promises; but those I do make, I keep."

"You know why my friends and I are in Rome?"

"I believe so; but I want you to tell me, simply and clearly."

"In 1976, I lost a son and a daughter. My daughter was arrested, questioned, tortured, raped, and finally killed. My son was arrested. We know he was taken to ESMA, the school of mechanical engineering. After that, no trace. There are thousands like him: the disappeared ones. We know they are dead. We do not know where or how they died. There is a torture in not knowing, a torture that never ends! We need to know—and once we know, perhaps we can bring the killers to justice. But knowing is the first step. You understand?"

"I do."

"Understand something more. At home, the regime has changed, yes. However, our president has blocked all roads to the justice we seek. He has granted amnesty to the senior officers who were responsible for the years of terror. He will not authorize the taking of testimonies and depositions against them or other offenders in Argentina. Vital records have been sent out of the country—we believe to Spain. As Senora Ortega has told you, we hope to lay hands on some of them in Switzerland."

"But you have come to Rome. Why?"

"We want to bring this whole dirty business to the International Court in the Hague. As individuals, we cannot do that. The petition must be made by a country, through its legal government. Our own country refuses to act. So, we address ourselves to Italy. You and I, Eminence, are of Italian origin, but we are not citizens. Again, we have no voice. However, hundreds of the disappeared ones were Italian citizens, holders of Italian passports, legally resident in Argentina. They have no voice, because they do not exist anymore. So, we turn to an Italian who knows what happened: the pope's man, the apostolic nuncio, Archbishop Aquino."

"But you discover you can't touch him, either, because he is a citizen of Vatican City?"

"Precisely! We beg him to abdicate that position so we may lay charges against him in an Italian court and there expose witnesses and testimonies which may force the Italian government to bring the matter to the International Court. The archbishop—he is now a cardinal—declines. He claims we have no evidence. He says he should not be asked to convict himself. Besides, he needs the consent of the Holy Father to present himself in a civil court. Now the Holy Father is dead; and whatever hopes we had, died with him. I mean no disrespect. You have received me in your house, but I have to say I have no faith in the Church anymore. In Argentina, too many of the hierarchy made a pact of silence with evil men. It seems we shall have to wait to argue the matter with God!"

"If you are looking for justice, Senora," said Luca Rossini, "that's the only place you'll find it. I should be a liar if I told you differently. Listening to you, I myself feel guilty. I suffered, as you know. Senora Ortega took a mortal risk to save me; but in the end we owed our lives to that same conspiracy of silence. A bargain was made. If we broke the bargain, others would suffer."

"But why are you still silent now that things have changed? Are you still afraid?"

"I can answer only for myself," said Rossini. "I have nothing to fear."

"I have something to fear," said Isabel. "I have a husband, a daughter. I cannot play dice with their lives."

"I understand," said the old woman. "I know very well what fear means. So, my brave Eminence, what do you think you can do for us?"

"Let's talk a little more, Senora. We get one chance at this; we cannot afford any mistakes. I want to hear your whole case against Aquino—and remember, it's against him, not against the local church."

"I have the documents here . . ."

For more than forty minutes they sat huddled together at the desk while Rosalia Lodano displayed the contents of her dossier and Rossini questioned her closely on their authenticity and their provenance. Finally, he broke off the conversation.

"I have seen enough. I'll have Juan bring you tea or coffee. I need to be private for a few minutes."

He rang for the servant, ordered refreshments for the women, then retired to his bedroom, where he made a telephone call to Aquino. He began abruptly.

"This is Rossini. I am at my house. With me is a woman from Argentina, Rosalia Lodano, with whom you have been in correspondence. I have just gone through the documents in her dossier against you."

"This is outrageous! You have no right to intrude in this fashion."

"Be quiet, please. Just listen. I did not intrude; you asked for my help. Today, this woman came to me with the same request. A couple of days ago, you gave a rather mischievous interview to a journalist from *Le Monde* in which you revealed our private conversations about the Mothers of the Plaza de Mayo."

"I would hardly call it a revelation. I thought it a good opportunity to prepare the ground for any discussions we might have with the women—create an atmosphere of goodwill. I saw nothing objectionable in that."

"I found it gravely objectionable. You represented me as your advocate and defender."

"I did not."

"The lady said otherwise."

"Come now, Rossini. Be fair. You know how exposed one is to misinterpretations, especially in a relaxed interview."

"And you know it, too! You're an experienced diplomat.

You've been weighing words all your life. You weighed these, too, before you spoke them."

"That's ridiculous—utterly paranoid!"

"Is it? Let me put it in context for you. I consent privately to mediate a discussion—not arbitrate, not adjudicate—just mediate. The Guillermin woman is very intelligent; an accurate reporter. You give her a version of our agreement that immediately and irrevocably compromises me and absolves you: The victim himself is pleading the innocence of the accused. That does everything you need. You don't have to answer any accusation. You walk into the conclave a clean-skin candidate for an interim papacy. And that's another thing—please don't recommend me to anyone."

"What are you talking about?"

"Another meeting, with a deputation of our colleagues. You were quoted: 'Rossini gets about a lot. He knows how to read the wind. If I were pontiff, I'd make sure to keep him near me.'"

"It was a compliment."

"It was conveyed to me as an inducement."

"And you were appropriately insulted!"

"Yes, I was."

"Then I suggest you cool off before we finish our business together."

"We can finish it this afternoon, if you wish. Rosalie Lodano is still here. Mademoiselle Guillermin will be here at five-thirty. I have all the dossier material I need to take an intelligent role in the discussion."

"To what end?"

"To give you the chance to state your case openly to the press—to a woman with whom you were obviously comfortable. To give the Mothers of the Plaza de Mayo a chance to be heard in an open forum. To give me a chance to do what you asked in the first place—mediate a position of minimal risk for you and for the Church."

"And if I decline?"

"Then I shall take the meeting and do the best I can."

"I can't decide immediately on this. I need time—"

"You have none." He quoted ironically: "'Now is the acceptable time. Now is the day of salvation.'"

"Can you at least limit the scope of—"

"I believe I can limit the damage and still leave you some vestige of reputation. Tell me now, Eminence, yes or no?"

"Have you told the secretary of state about this?"

"I remind you that it was he who arranged our first meeting at your request. I quote him verbatim: 'You may even find some ground of compassion which would encourage him to confront his accusers. You may, perhaps, break through to the real man behind the enamel.'"

There was a longish silence on the line. Then, Aquino asked, "How will you arrange this?"

"Rosalia Lodano is here. You should speak with her first. Then we should all meet Mademoiselle Guillermin."

"Who else will be there?"

"Senora Ortega. It was she who put me in touch with Rosalia Lodano."

"What is her standing in all this?"

"Rather like mine, a friend of the court. Well, what do you say?"

"I'll be there as soon as I can."

"I think that's a wise decision," said Luca Rossini. "Very wise."

When he went back to report the conversation to the two women, he found Rosalia Lodano quite hostile.

"The more I think of this, the less I like it, a private talk in a private room. Afterward, everyone has a different version. This is what happens always, here and at home: soft words, careful phrases, a promise to study the matter further—then nothing."

"We shall record the talks," said Rossini calmly. "You shall have the original tape. Much more important, however, is what you will get out of the meeting."

"We have to get him into court!"

"No, Senora." Rossini was curt. "You will never do it. I have seen your documents. You will bleed yourselves of money and of life; but you do not have a case to bring to court."

"How can you say that?"

"Because it's a fact, clear from your own files. In any legal sense, Aquino is not a criminal; on what I have read in your dossier, you will never get an indictment against him either in Italy or the Hague."

"So why am I wasting time here?"

"Because this afternoon you have the chance to bring the story once again to world attention, implant it more deeply in world memory—so that the shadow of guilt hangs always over the perpetrators. As for Aquino, his previous silence may yet be a powerful witness in your cause. If you can get him to admit to moral guilts, then you will have won a great victory."

"Can you guarantee he will admit anything?"

"I believe he can be brought to it, yes. His consent to this afternoon's meeting puts him halfway along the road."

"And the rest of the journey?"

"I believe I can coax him further."

The two women stared at him in astonishment. Isabel uttered a warning.

"You've arranged the meeting, Luca. Already that's a great deal. Is it wise for you to conduct the discussion?"

"I'm not sure. That is, in any case, a choice for Senora Lodano. The fact is that I can use words and arguments which she would find too bitter in her mouth. I can judge the impact of those words on Aquino. In their own context they may prove more potent than any reproaches pronounced upon him in the name of the absent ones. However, I am equally prepared to be mute and let her conduct her own dialogue."

The old woman sat in silence for a few moments, then she said abruptly, "Why do you think you can plead our case better than we can?"

"I cannot plead it better. I may deliver you a quicker result and perhaps a better one than you will otherwise get."

"Convince me of that, Eminence. Convince me that we should trust you so far!"

# 10

There was a sudden winter chill in the air when Aquino entered the room. Rossini introduced the two women. Aquino acknowledged them with a bow but, fearing a rebuff, did not offer his hand. Rossini seated him on the opposite side of his desk, then he took his own chair and laid the folder of documents before him. The women sat together, a pace away from the desk. A third chair was set beside them for Steffi Guillermin, who was due to arrive within the hour.

Rossini was carefully formal. He announced, "I propose that we record our conversation so that there can be no doubt about what is said here. If either party wishes to speak off the record, then I shall simply stop the machine. Are we all agreed?"

They nodded assent. Rossini switched on the machine and dictated the time, date, location and names of those attending the meeting. Then he began.

"This conference is being held in the hope of settling certain problems outstanding between the Mothers of the Plaza de Mayo and His Eminence Cardinal Aquino, formerly Apostolic Nuncio to Argentina. Let me make it clear that some days ago Cardinal Aquino had asked me to mediate such a discussion. The secretary of state approved the idea. Senora Lodano, leader of a delegation of the Mothers of the Plaza de Mayo, presently in

Rome, had been trying to arrange a meeting for some time.
Nevertheless, all the discussions are without prejudice to the
position of either party, and they have no formal character. My
role is that of mediator only. I am not called upon to make judgments, only to facilitate discussions. My role does not exclude
a certain advocacy for either party, if such advocacy helps to
bring about a solution. Unfortunately, some solutions are beyond our reach. We cannot bring back the dead. We cannot—
for this moment, at least—say where or how the disappeared
ones met their ends. Justice for them—redress for their sorrow-
ing relatives—is beyond our reach.

"Let me also say that it is not possible to render full justice
to Cardinal Aquino, who, as a diplomatic representative of the
Vatican, served in Argentina during a terrible period of its history. Documents he sent directly to His late Holiness are now
held in the Secret Archive. Others, held by the secretariat of
state, cannot be released until a new pontiff is elected. Conflicting claims are made about the actions of His Eminence in
the context of the period. It is not my function to adjudicate
those claims but simply to elicit those facts upon which both
parties can agree at this time. Eminence, are you prepared to
stipulate that during your service as apostolic nuncio in Argentina, there was a large-scale campaign of terror by the State
against certain classes of its citizens, and that this campaign
resulted in the arrest, torture, and death of many thousands,
and the total disappearance of many others whose fate is still
unknown?"

"Yes. I do not have an exact number for the victims, but I
can stipulate that the numbers were in the thousands. The government itself admits to ten, I believe."

"Now, let us see if we can arrive at an accurate, if not all-
embracing, description of your functions as apostolic nuncio.
Please be as clear as you can. This is very important for Senora
Lodano and the colleagues whom she represents here."

"The function is a double one. A nuncio is a legate of the

Holy See, a permanent diplomatic agent of the pope, who is sovereign of Vatican City State. He carries the rank of ambassador. His second duty, separate from the first, is to watch over the welfare of the Church in the country of his mission."

"And what is his rank in the local church?"

"He outranks all local clergy except a cardinal archbishop. He is responsible only to the Holy See."

"Can he direct the local clergy?"

"At the request of the Holy See, yes."

"But he does render regular advice to Rome on the state of the local church—and, even if he doesn't use them, he has wide powers of intervention."

"Yes, but he is expected to use those powers with prudence and discretion."

Rossini turned to the two women.

"Any questions so far?"

"Only one," said Rosalia Lodano. "It seems we have a watchdog with two heads. Which one was supposed to bark when our people were being arrested, tortured, and killed?"

"Would you care to respond to that, Eminence?" asked Rossini.

"I admit that neither one made enough noise." Aquino was surprisingly subdued. "An ambassador can only work within certain protocols. Normally, his exchanges with governments— his own government and that to which he is accredited—are made in secret. Much of his influence depends upon the tactful handling of difficult situations."

"One understands that." Rosalie Lodano was ominously cool. "One asks how tactful one must be about a young woman, a student, picked off the street, imprisoned, tortured, raped, and then murdered. That's what happened to my daughter. My son? We don't know what happened to him after his arrest. How do you come to terms with that?"

"I heard many such stories during my term as nuncio. It was not possible to determine whether they were fact or rumor."

"But you were very close to the generals. No one was in a better position to ask for facts."

"I'm not sure what you mean, Senora."

"I think this is what she's talking about." Rossini leafed through the dossier and brought out three glossy photographs of a much younger Aquino dressed in tennis clothes, with a group of officers similarly dressed. Aquino glanced at them and waved them away.

"That, in hindsight, was an indiscretion. On the other hand, I was a diplomat. One does not conduct diplomacy from an office chair. One tries to make friends, cultivate people. I did that. I was able on several important occasions to make deals for the release of prisoners who might otherwise have disappeared."

"We have a record of at least one such deal." Rossini leafed through the file again. "You were offered—what was it?—forty detainees, who had just been sent to Buenos Aires from other areas. The local commander did not want to handle them. You were told that if you could arrange to get them out of the country, they would be spared some very unpleasant experiences ending in death or disappearance. You did that. You managed to persuade the Venezuelan government to receive them. These documents confirm it."

"Yes, I did. It wasn't enough, but it was something."

"You did something special for me, too. You gave me safe conduct out of the country after my own experience."

"Again, it was a question of doing what one could in difficult times."

"But there is an anomaly here, is there not?"

"What kind of anomaly?"

"Before and after these events, in public interviews with the press, you denied any knowledge of what was being done under the system of State terror."

"When one is walking a tightrope, one slips sometimes. It was, I confess, a diplomatic lie."

"But the quesiton arises, does it not: You knew and you were silent?"

"I explained to you, as a diplomat, I had to work in silence."

"Did it never occur to you, Eminence?" Rosalie Lodano was implacable. "Did you never ask yourself what might have happened if you had shouted the truth just once to the world?"

"I asked myself that question many times."

"Did you seek advice from your supervisors in Rome?"

"I did. The answer was always the same. I was the man on the spot. They had to rely on my judgment and the judgment of the local church."

"Again," Rosalia Lodano challenged him harshly, "again, two dogs' heads, but neither barks!"

"No, Senora!" Rossini rounded on her swiftly. "Not true. There were many others who barked and shouted and fought, too. There were many good pastors killed. There were nuns and monks among the disappeared ones."

"But their leaders were silent! They are still silent now. They play with words, trying to construct documents that will say yes and no at the same time."

"Again, Senora, not all." He leafed again through the dossier and came up with a passage, which he read slowly. "'We, the members of the Church of Argentina, have many reasons to confess our sins and to beg forgiveness for our insensibilities, our cowardice, our omissions, our complicities . . .'" He broke off and turned to Aquino. "You know the man who wrote this, Eminence?"

"I do. He was—he is a good bishop—but that is his testimony and the testimony of the clergy of his diocese. His statement was not welcomed by all the clergy. They still do not welcome it."

"Why not?"

Aquino did not answer immediately. He sat, hands clasped, head bowed, staring at the desk, searching for words. Then he pieced out the answer with painful deliberation.

"It's the oldest and saddest story in the world. Too little and too late. Evil bloats itself on silence. Good people are seduced by comfort into indifference. Men of God flatter themselves that they are empowered by the Church behind them. They go out to sup with the devil, confident that they will convert him in the end. They are always shocked when they see blood in the soup. A few of them, very few, thank God, seem to develop a taste for it." He turned to Rosalia Lodano and said with somber pathos, "That's the best I can do for you, I'm afraid. We could go on for hours. The rest would be more of the same. I wish I could bring back your lost ones, Senora. I can only beg your forgiveness."

Rossini switched off the recorder and the room was filled with silence. Then, on a rising note of anger, Rosalia Lodano attacked again.

"This still stinks of conspiracy! Both of you wear the same uniform, say the same bland words. You are both protected by the same institution. Have either of you ever borne a child, nurtured that child in love, and then had it brutalized and killed? Have you?"

"Enough!" Isabel's voice sounded like the crack of a bullet. "Now, Senora, you will be silent and listen to me."

She reached for her handbag, opened it, and took out a small leather-bound folder the size of a passport. She opened it and thrust it at Rosalia Lodano.

"Look at that and tell me what you see."

The woman stared at it for a few moments, then asked, "Why do you show me this?"

"You talked about conspiracy, protection, bland words. Do these images spell conspiracy to you? Please pass it to His Eminence."

Aquino held up his hand to decline.

"Thank you. I've already seen it. I have my own copies."

Rossini asked, "May I see it, please?"

Rosalia Lodano handed him the folder. He opened it and found himself staring at a series of plastic-covered photographs of himself, naked, spread-eagled on the wheel like a flayed animal, with the sergeant's riding crop dangling like a tail from his backside. The sergeant was shown in each shot in a different position, now opening his breeches, now displaying his penis, and finally lying on the ground with his head exploded like a melon.

Rossini turned to Isabel. He was pale as death. His voice seemed to curdle in his gullet.

"Why have I never seen these?"

"Because my father took them with him to Buenos Aires. They were his bargaining card with the generals and with His Eminence here."

"But I spoke with him before I left the country. I asked him why he had let the beating go on so long. He didn't say he was taking pictures! Why didn't he show them to me then?"

"Because he thought you weren't ready. The doctor agreed with him. So did I. This was something you had blocked out completely. We thought you might have been unconscious when it happened."

"So, tell me the rest of it, for God's sake."

"He took the pictures as fast as he could, but carefully, too. Then he tossed the camera onto the bed, handed me the rifle, and told me: 'As soon as you see me hit the square, kill the son of a bitch and take a picture of him dead.' That's what I did. I killed him and took the last shot. You know the rest."

"I look like an animal." Rossini was still staring at the photographs. "They skinned me like a beast in a slaughter yard and raped me with a riding whip."

He tossed the folder onto the desk and fled the room. The next moment, they heard him retching his heart out in the toilet. Isabel was on her feet instantly; but the old woman held her wrist in an iron grip.

"No! Better he deals with his own devils." She turned to Aquino. "Even with those pictures in your hands, you did not speak out?"

"There were lives at stake. That was the deal I had to make."

"That was the blood in the soup," said the old woman. "How does it taste now?"

"Be quiet, Grandmother!" There was vast weariness in Isabel's voice. "There's no profit in anger anymore. Better you ask His Eminence to say Mass to quiet the dead and give some peace to the living!"

Fifteen minutes later, Rossini emerged from his bedroom. He had taken off his clerical garb and put on a clean white shirt. He was pale but composed. He walked straight to Isabel, laid his hands on her shoulders, and said plainly for all to hear, "Thank you, my love, for the photographs. They were the missing piece of myself I did not dare to look for, did not want to find."

He touched his lips to her hair. Aquino averted his eyes from the intimate gesture and began toying with the paper knife. The old woman's face was unreadable. Isabel reached up to touch Rossini's fingers with her own. Then he withdrew from her and sat down at his desk again, turning to Aquino first and then to Rosalia Lodano. He said:

"Mademoiselle Guillermin will be here shortly. I should like to spare both of you any more interrogation. I propose, therefore, that we let her hear the tape and then address any questions to me. You need intervene only if you feel my answers are inadequate."

"I understand what you are doing," said Aquino, "and I thank you for your consideration. But you may be opening yourself to a great deal of criticism from our colleagues once this interview is published."

"After the deluge, what does one do? Wait for the dove with an olive twig in its beak? How do you feel, Senora Lodano?"

"I'm an old woman with bitterness in my mouth. I'm sorry for some of the things I said—not all, but some. If this woman wants more information, then I will give it to her directly, but not here. We have all had enough emotion for one day."

A few moments later, Steffi Guillermin was announced. She was clearly surprised by the group which confronted her. Her comment was addressed to Rossini.

"Two Eminences and two distinguished ladies. That's quite a catch for a journalist like me."

"And you will be appropriately grateful." Rossini said it with a smile, but she was instantly wary.

"And how am I expected to show my gratitude?"

"In our previous interview, I accepted to play by your ground rules: everything on the record. Today, you are in my house. I am giving you an exclusive release on an important story. Certain other subjects may arise which will be off the record. You have a high reputation as an honest journalist. If you can't accept that condition, then we should go no further. Do you agree?"

"I have no choice, do I?"

"You do have a choice. You can give me your word and then find some plausible excuse to break it. Or you can give me your promise and keep it."

She made him wait a few seconds for the answer.

"You have my promise."

"Thank you. Please sit down. I'm going to play you a tape made this afternoon in this room. You may copy it on your own machine. Cardinal Aquino will decline to make any further comment. Senora Lodano is prepared, if you wish it, to make another appointment with you for further discussion."

"And you, Eminence?"

"I'm reserving my position until I hear the questions. Shall we begin?"

The playback held them all speechless. It was only when it was finished that they realized how far Aquino had committed himself and how adroitly Rossini had led him into the confession. Even Rosalia Lodano offered a reluctant compliment.

"I see now what you meant. If this is published, it may well save us money and grief."

"It will be published," said Guillermin. "We will originate and syndicate the material. We need a document of authority and a quitclaim."

"If everyone else is agreed, you can prepare them and send them to me for execution," said Rossini.

The others made no objection. Guillermin pressed on:

"Now, Eminence, may we dispose of the questions which brought me here in the first place. They relate to the interview I had with you and to the material I have just heard."

"What are the questions?"

"A tabloid in England is floating material, which is still vague but which may balloon into something more substantive. It refers to a violent crime connected with your escape from Argentina, a sexual assault on your person, a love affair, and an illegitimate child born after you left Argentina."

"We are now off the record," said Rossini.

"As we agreed," said Guillermin.

"I advise most strongly against any disclosures on this subject." Aquino, at one stride, had put himself center stage. "They are not opportune. No matter what Mademoiselle Guillermin promises, rumors multiply. You can never control them all."

"The deal stands," said Luca Rossini. "Are we off the record, Mademoiselle?"

"We are."

Rossini picked up the folder of photographs and handed it to Guillermin. She, too, paled at the sight of the pictures. She closed the folder and handed it back. Rossini said flatly:

"The man on the wheel is me. The photographs were taken by Senora Ortega's father before he ran down into the square to rescue me."

"Who shot the sergeant?"

"I did," said Isabel. "My father took control of the troops, ordered them back to the barracks, and sent us both into hiding while he negotiated amnesty for me and safe conduct for Luca."

"And you became lovers?"

"For those weeks only," said Rossini. "Now, we have only love."

"But you, Senora Ortega, have a daughter, yes?"

"I do. She was born in Doctors' Hospital, New York City. She was baptized Luisa Amelia Isabel Ortega in the Church of St. Vincent Ferrer in New York."

Guillermin turned to Aquino.

"I have some questions for you, Eminence."

"We are still off the record, I trust?"

"We are. First question. How much did you know about Luca Rossini before you brought him to Rome?"

"Everything. I, too, was given copies of the photographs. I gave them to the Holy Father when I presented my report."

"And you also told him of the association between Luca Rossini, an ordained priest, and Isabel Ortega, a married woman?"

"I did."

"Yet, in spite of that, the Holy Father took him into his confidence and promoted him steadily over the years. Can you explain that?"

"It would be a presumption to try. In such matters, the Holy Father acted on his own absolute discretion. May I ask why you are pursuing this line of questioning with me?"

"Because two days before the conclave, we shall be publishing my interview with Cardinal Rossini and the final section of the papal diaries. There is a significant reference in the diaries which only now makes sense to me. The pontiff wrote: 'I have never learned the tenderness or the terror of love. Rossini paid a high price for that knowledge. In the end, I think he is more fortunate than I.'"

She turned to Isabel and offered an unexpected tribute of admiration.

"When I was a girl in convent school, I always admired the valiant women of the Bible: Ruth, Esther, Judith. I think you've earned your place among them."

Isabel acknowledged the compliment with a smile and a shrug.

"You flatter me, Mademoiselle. Killing is very easy. The real art is to stay alive." To Luca Rossini she said, "I should be leaving now. Luisa and I have a dinner engagement. Will you call me in the morning?"

"Of course. Juan will drive you to the hotel and take Senora Lodano on to Monte Oppio."

"She could come with me." Steffi Guillermin never missed a move. "We could talk on the way."

"Thank you. There is much more to say than we have covered here. Nonetheless, I am grateful to Cardinal Rossini for what he has done, and for the good offices of Senora Ortega. Neither do I forget that it has cost Cardinal Aquino some pains to be here today."

At this moment, Rossini thought it prudent to intervene.

"Does Your Eminence have transport? If not, Juan can take you with Senora Ortega."

"My own driver will come for me when I telephone; but I'd like to have a private word with you before I leave."

Which was how, after the three women had left, Rossini found himself entertaining his former adversary over a decanter of brandy. Aquino made the first toast.

"*Salud!* You gave me a rough ride. But you're a bigger man than I ever believed, Luca Rossini."

"I'm glad, for both our sakes, it's over."

"It will never be over," said Aquino somberly. "But now, at least it's in the open. I'll still be looking at the same man in the mirror, but I won't have to keep the door closed."

"You said you needed to talk with me," Rossini reminded him. "I don't want to seem inhospitable but I think I'm suffering from some kind of delayed shock. The sight of those photographs was like a punch in the belly."

"I don't understand why she brought them to Rome in the first place."

"Unfinished business," said Rossini simply. "We haven't seen each other for a quarter of a century."

"I could see you were shocked. I thought you recovered very quickly."

"I knew what she was trying to do. When we met for the first time, I was like a shattered vase. Shards of me were scattered everywhere." Rossini seemed to be musing aloud. "Day by day, piece by piece, she put me together again. When we parted and I came to Rome, there were pieces still missing. You were with me. You remember how I was."

"I remember very well."

"Those photographs were the missing pieces. I couldn't admit the horror of the violation. Isabel knew I would finally have to face it."

"And you can now?"

"Yes, I feel I am whole; but please don't shake me too much before the glue sets."

"I have to confess something to you."

"What?"

"When I brought you out of Buenos Aires and back to Rome, I made a report to the Holy Father. I told him that I thought you were a very fragile case and that there were elements of scandal in your situation. Before I went back to Argentina, he summoned me again. He told me he had thought much about the young man I had brought him. He gave me a discourse about St. Paul's letter to Timothy: 'In a great house there are vessels of gold and silver, some also of wood and earth.' I didn't know quite where he was leading me until he said, 'Our son, Luca, he's a damaged vessel, but he will one day be a vessel of honor, for the master's use.' It has taken me a long time to see what he meant." He broke off and then put a question to Rossini.

"Do you have any plans for this evening? Would you consider

dining with me? The rector of the Angelicum is entertaining a few of us electors to dinner. I'm sure he would be delighted to welcome you. You're much talked about but little known. In a few days, we're all going to be locked into St. Martha's House. It wouldn't hurt to condition yourself a little. I'll drop you home afterward."

There was a refusal on the tip of his tongue, but he did not utter it. The prospect of a solitary evening was too daunting. He hesitated only for a second and then said, "It's a kind thought. I'd like to come."

"Good! Let me call the rector and alert my driver. Then, we can make ourselves comfortable for a while . . . This is an excellent brandy. And later, if I can borrow a razor, I'll make myself presentable for our colleagues."

The dinner party was good for him. It wrenched him out of his isolation and forced him to assume the collegial function implicit in his office. It did more. It required him to match himself with a tightly knit group of Italian prelates, most of them graduates of the institution which was entertaining them.

It was not only language and scholastic tradition which bound them together. Italians were now a beleaguered minority in the electoral college. They held only 17 percent of the votes. Certain key positions in the Curia had been taken over by non-Italians, so that they now depended for their power upon a curious little oligarchy of highly political men, who were called the "grand electors" and sometimes the "night fishermen."

Their nets were cast wide, even in the least promising waters. They trawled patiently in intricate patterns, ignoring the minnows in the surface stream, waiting for the big fish who must, sooner or later, swim into their traps.

In the old days, not so long past, a candidate needed two-thirds plus one of the votes to be elected pope. Basically, that meant that even a popular candidate could fail if one-third of the voters refused him. However, since 1996, a further provision had been in force. If more than thirty normal ballots had failed, then a simple majority would suffice for election. This meant that, if the balloting went on long enough, a candidate could scrape by with a bare majority of one. This was not a matter of debate at the rector's dinner. It was, like so much else in Rome, taken as read and filed for reference until the moment came to invoke it. However, it did provide a subtext for Aquino's invitation. In terms of nationality, Luca Rossini was an outlander, a cultural hybrid. In terms of the coming event, he was a collegial voter and a long-odds candidate for office. To the "grand electors" he was a disposable but potentially useful piece in the chess game that would begin in a few days.

So, they courted him with small respects and flattering curiosities about his missions. They also tested him with subtle allusions to matters with which a new pontiff must deal: a married clergy, how it might be addressed, how would it be received in this country or that, how, in any case, could it be financed; the powers of the dicasteries, should they be limited or increased; a third Vatican Council, should it complete the work of Vatican II or not be held at all.

They did not expect a textbook answer every time; they judged him by his skill in fielding the questions, by the good humor he displayed when he saw the snares they had laid for him. They wanted to know how he would react in a crisis—could he be bullied, seduced, or blackmailed into conformity with a powerful group like the "grand electors?" There was one question to which a peculiar emphasis seemed to attach itself. It was framed like a conundrum.

"You travel much, Luca. How do you see the Church: as one or many? What shall we become in the new millennium?"

Rossini, rendered less wary than usual by fatigue and fraternity and the rector's Frascati, rose to the bait.

"Of all the men in this room, I am the least equipped to answer that question. I have traveled widely enough to know the diversity of the world. I have lived long enough in Rome to understand both the truth and the fallacy of the claim that where Peter is, there is the Church. I think that's one of the historic notions which we accept without examination. There is a much older statement made by Jesus Himself: 'Where two or three are gathered together in my name, there am I in the midst of them.' In that sense, many churches, one in faith, yes. It depends, does it not, on whose sign is over the lintel of the door? 'By this shall men know that you are my disciples if you have love, one for another.' But what am I saying? You didn't invite me here to debate Petrine primacy." He raised his glass in a toast: "To the brotherhood we share, to the future we hope to shape together!"

They drank. They gave him a good round of applause. Some of them laughed over his choice of the word *fratellanza* for brotherhood, because that was a word colored by many associations, good and bad. However, after all, Rossini was an exotic and was not expected to understand all the nuances of the mother tongue.

As they were driving home to Rossini's apartment, Aquino told him, "You made quite an impression there tonight, Luca. They gave you more than the usual roasting, but you came up smiling like Saint Lawrence on his gridiron. That last little homily went down well, also, because it was the last thing they were expecting."

"I hope I passed the test."

"Oh, you did, with high marks! It will all help."

"Help what?"

The driver was just drawing up at Rossini's house when Aquino answered.

"I fear you may be in for another roasting in Guillermin's article. She's not going to forgive you too easily for keeping the best part of the story off the record. Not that she won't give you a fair run, but she'll plant a few pics in your hide!"

"She could come straight over the horns for a kill." Rossini was bone weary. "I wouldn't feel a thing. Thank you for the dinner and the company."

"I wish you golden dreams," said Aquino. "Good night."

At five in the morning, he was wakened from a dead sleep by the shrilling of his telephone. He groped in the darkness to find the light switch and the instrument. Luisa was on the line. She was obviously in distress.

"I know it's an ungodly hour, Luca, but Mother's sick. I wanted to call the hotel doctor. She refused to have him. She told me to wait until morning and call you. She said you'd be able to recommend a good doctor."

"How is she now?"

"The vomiting has stopped. She still has a high fever. She's drifting in and out of sleep."

"Has this happened before?"

"Yes, but the intervals are getting shorter. In spite of medication, this was the worst attack I've seen."

"Where are you calling from?"

"I'm in the salon of her suite."

"She told me she carried a copy of her medical records."

"They're in her briefcase."

"I'll be with you as soon as I can. Meantime, I'll get a doctor and have him meet me at the hotel."

"I'm worried. Whatever happened yesterday left her very stressed. She held up well during the dinner; but by the time we got back to the hotel, she was in a state of collapse."

"But the medication helped?"

"Yes. It always does. One more thing, Luca. I really don't want her to go to Switzerland. I know it's in a good cause, but she does not have too much energy to spend. Could you talk to her?"

"I will. Now, order up some breakfast for yourself and some tea for your mother. I have to get busy. I'll be with you as soon as I can."

He rang off and then went into his study to find the private number of Dr. Ernesto Mottola, physician to the late pontiff. The good doctor was less than happy to be wakened, but he also had a healthy respect for this odd, peremptory alien who seemed to command spirits in high places, as well as his own private demons.

He listened attentively as Rossini sketched what Isabel had told him of her illness, then he said, "I will examine her, of course. It helps that she has her medical records. I'm not a specialist in oncology, as you know. I can, of course, bring in a specialist; but even without seeing her, I would recommend an immediate return to New York, where they have much better facilities than we do. If she remained here, I would have to recommend treatment in Milan rather than in Rome. Does she have next of kin here?"

"An adult daughter; the husband is in New York but within easy contact."

"Then shall we say eight this morning at the hotel?"

"Thank you, Doctor. I'm very grateful."

"May I ask what is Your Eminence's connection with Senora Ortega?"

"She's a distinguished compatriot," said Rossini. "A quarter of a century ago, she saved my life."

"That makes her a special patient." Dr. Mottola was a very practiced courtier. "Thank you for recommending her to me. Until later, Eminence."

# 11

Dr. Angelo Mottola had come and gone. He had read the medical reports. He had examined the patient carefully. His advice, which had cost two hundred dollars, was simple. "There is nothing I can do for you, dear lady, beyond what your own physician has prescribed. Your condition will continue to deteriorate. The remissions will be shorter. You should go home immediately and put yourself under proper clinical care with your own doctor."

To which, as Luisa put it, there was only one sensible answer: Pay the man and get the hell back to New York. Isabel protested. Luisa refused to listen.

"I've already made the arrangements, Mother!"

"What arrangements?"

"I've called Senora Lodano and told her you can't go to Switzerland. She regrets that you are ill. She thanks you for your help yesterday. She tells you to go with God back to New York. I've rearranged our travel. We leave tomorrow midday on a Delta flight to Kennedy. The concierge has done the ticketing. I'll do your packing. I've called Father. He'll pick us up at JFK."

Isabel was furious.

"I swore I'd never let this happen. I refuse to surrender

control of my own life. You understand what I'm saying, Luca. Tell her!"

Rossini laid a soothing hand on her wrist. She jerked away from his touch. He reasoned with her quietly.

"My love, your own body is telling you that it's time to surrender. You know that. Dr. Mottola explained to me and to Luisa that even if you did stay on, you'd have to go to Milan for treatment, and it would be no way comparable to the treatment you would get in New York. Please believe me!"

"I was counting on doing so much with Luisa. I made so many plans."

"Mother, I'll settle for having you safe and cared for at home."

Isabel beat on the coverlet with clenched fists.

"You can't settle for anything! This is my life! Let me spend it the way I want!"

"Please listen, my love." Rossini was persuasive but firm. "Do you remember what you used to say when you were nursing me at the *estancia*? 'Save your angers. Live on the strength others will lend you. Fight from friendly territory.' To stay here will only deplete your strength. Even among the kindest people, the traveler is always a stranger. If I could be with you, it might be easier, but I have nothing to offer you. I'm in bondage. Even if I break the bonds—which I well may—what am I? A man in his fifties with no prospects. What can I offer you?"

Isabel closed her eyes and lay back exhausted on the pillow. Luisa drew the covers about her, kissed her, and moved toward the door of the bedroom. Rossini followed, closing the door behind him.

"That was the saddest thing I have ever heard, Luca," Luisa said.

"I had to say it."

"I know. Can you stay a while longer?"

"Of course. I'll talk to my office from here. You should try to get some sleep. Hang out the DO NOT DISTURB sign."

"Promise you'll wake me before you leave the hotel. We have to talk, too. This is our last chance."

"I promise. Go!"

When she had left, Rossini called his office. The only urgent message was from the secretary of state. When he phoned in, the secretary asked, "Where are you now?"

"At the Grand Hotel. Senora Ortega was taken ill last night. I called Dr. Mottola to see her. He recommends her immediate return to the United States. She leaves with her daughter in the morning."

"I'm sorry to hear that. When do you expect to be free?"

"About noon."

"Let's have coffee and a sandwich in my office at one o'clock. There are things we need to discuss. Aquino called me this morning. He told me about your meeting yesterday with Senora Lodano. Apparently it came off well."

"Better than I expected; but, as always, there's a price tag."

"Ah yes, the presence of the press! A pity you didn't let me know in advance. I should have counseled against that."

"Then you would still have had the war on your hands, Turi. This way, at least you have a truce—and you can always blame me for any backlash."

"In the circumstances, I wonder why you didn't ask Angel-Novalis to monitor the meeting."

"Because their documents—and ours, Turi—cast certain shadows on the conduct of Opus Dei. Angel-Novalis is a good man. I preferred not to embarrass him—or ourselves."

"You were probably right. I'm told also you made a guest appearance at the Angelicum last night."

"News travels fast in this town!"

"And there's a lot of it floating around just now. We have a note from our nuncio in Brazil. Claudio Stagni has surfaced in Rio. He's living in a rented apartment in a certain style. He's accompanied everywhere by a bodyguard."

"That does argue a certain style." Rossini laughed. "I wonder who guards the bodyguard. I'm told there are some very rough players in Rio. Is there anything else, Turi?"

"The rest can wait until we meet. I'm sorry to hear about the Senora Ortega, but I'm sure it's wise that she get home as soon as possible. Rome is fast becoming unlivable. Until later, then."

When Rossini went back into the bedroom, he found Isabel awake and out of bed. She had put on a robe, brushed her hair, and smelled of lemon flowers. She kissed him but winced when he touched her. He withdrew instantly. She explained.

"I'm better now; but my joints ache, and my skin is very sensitive. I'm sorry I behaved so badly. Where's Luisa?"

"Resting in her room. She wants to talk to me before I leave."

"I'm sorry, Luca." She led him out to the salon. "This was meant to be a happy time. Now look at us. We're smothering you with trouble."

"Please, my love. My problem is that I'm working with one hand tied behind my back. I'm on call at all hours—I have no practice in family life."

Then, without warning, she cracked. The words came out in a tumbling rush.

"I'm scared, Luca! I can't face going home! All those hours in an aircraft, all that waiting in line for passport check, all that jostling for luggage. My body hurts most of the time now, somewhere or other. The pain is not intolerable but it never leaves me. When we get home, Raul will be there. He'll be charming and solicitous. The house will be full of flowers. The staff will be careful of me." She gave a small shaky laugh. "I tell you, my love, the Ortegas run a very classy hotel! But that's what it is, a hotel in which we all have separate rooms. Mine will have to be turned into a clinic—until they ship me out for terminal care. And yet, come right down to it, what do I have to complain of? Nothing, really! Ever since I was young, I grabbed the tree of life and shook it and gorged myself on the fruits that fell into my hands. Now, very soon, it will be time to go . . . What was the little Latin verse you taught me, 'Satis something'?"

"*Satis bibisti, satis ludisti tempus est abire.*"

"That's it! 'The drinking's over, the playing's over, it's time to leave.' That frightens me most of all, Luca. Leave for what? And who will be waiting for me on the other side of the river?"

And there it lay, clear and unblinking as the eye of Horus, a question from the loved one in terror of the final parting. He would not lie to her, yet he could not cheat her of the consolation of the Word, of which he, Luca Cardinal Rossini, was still a professing and accredited servant. She reached for his hands and held them as he talked softly and persuasively.

"Nobody knows what happens after death, my love. We have only symbols and parables to express our desires, our hopes, and our beliefs. It is not only the unknown which frightens us, but the loss of the known—the things to which we cling, as though they were given to us in perpetuity instead of as temporary support. When we are born, strange but loving hands receive us into a strange new world. When we die, we believe— though we do not know—that we shall be received with love in another world altogether. When he was dying, our Lord cried out in agony and despair, 'My God, my God, why have you forsaken me!' When he died, it was with relief, commending himself into the hands of his Father!"

"I'm not Jesus Christ." There was a weary mockery in her voice. "More like Mary Magdalen."

"To whom many sins were forgiven, because she had loved much."

"Will you hear my confession please, Luca?"

The request surprised him more than the declaration of her fears. It put him to a more stringent test. From the winter of doubt in which he dwelled, he was thrust back into the formalism of which Piers Hallett had accused him. Yet, once again, he could not refuse her.

"If you're sure that's what you want, yes. But you should not tax yourself with a long recitation. Say simply what you think you have done wrong. Express your sorrow, your desire to change. Then I'll give you absolution."

Isabel frowned and shook her head.

"I know you want to make everything easy for me, Luca, but I have no intention of reciting a list for you: how many lusts, how many rages, how many lies. I want to tell you the real truths: what I am to myself, what I have been to Raul and Luisa—yes, even to you who are dearer to me than anything in the world. Will you listen, please? I don't want ever to go through this again. I couldn't . . ."

"You won't have to." Again, the ritual intonation colored his own voice. "Each absolution is a new beginning." He disengaged his hands from her grasp, reached for the pectoral cross under his jacket, and held it up to her view like a rood screen between their past and their present relationship. "Tell me what's troubling you."

This time, there was no panic rush of words, but a slow piecemeal recitation, as if the tale tasted bitter on her tongue.

"As long as I can remember, I have always wanted to be a winner. Whatever I did, I had to be the best and the cleverest. If I couldn't be that, then I lost interest in the game. No, that's not quite true. If I couldn't win today, I would wait until tomorrow or the next day, until the moment when everyone else thought I had lost interest. Then, I would step up to the mark again and carry off the prize. Looking back, I realize that, like the old brigands and gangsters, I traveled always armed and dangerous. It wasn't malice, I think. I had nothing to be malicious about. It was the jungle thrill: Kill or be killed. That's why my father and I were so close. He was a daring man. When he tossed me the rifle that day and told me to kill the sergeant, he put his life and the lives of all the villagers in my hands; but he knew I could do it! That's not a boast. It's part of the truth. I've said a lot of bad things about Raul, and all of them are true.

The one thing I haven't said, which is also true, is that he wouldn't play the game I was playing, so I could never beat him. Because I couldn't beat him, I could never forgive him. The terrible thing was that there were moments, months even, when I knew that with a little generosity on my part, we could have come closer together. Even when I discovered that I was very ill, I was too proud to plead for a truce, too angry to give one more inch of ground. You asked me the other day, did he know about you and me. He knew about the killing. For the rest, he seemed ready to accept that you were a broken man for whom I had been caring. He said simply, 'That was the least you could do for the poor devil like that. Let's talk no more of it!' And we never did, which was another bitter pill to swallow. You were important to me; but you were not important to him. I was furious when he loitered away, like a duelist refusing to engage an opponent whom he thought unworthy."

"If you were so desperate for revenge," said Luca Rossini, "I wonder why you didn't tell him about Luisa? You said you always traveled armed and dangerous. Why did you surrender that weapon?"

"I knew that if I used it, I could lose both her and you. I couldn't face that."

Rossini made no comment. He was still the minister conducting a ritual. The rest of him had retreated into a camouflage. He asked, "You are telling me, are you not, that you refused any reconciliation with your husband?"

"Yes."

"How can you, therefore, ask to be reconciled with God?"

"That's why I need your help."

"Are you sorry for what you have done?"

"I am sincerely sorry."

"Do you remember the Act of Contrition?"

"It's a long time since I said it."

"Say it now, please."

She recited the words as formally as he had prompted them.

"O my God, I am sorry with all my heart for the offenses I have committed . . ." When the brief prayer was over, Rossini admonished her again.

"You must try now to mend, if you can, the damage you have done. You are required to do penance."

"I don't have too much time to do either."

"One act will suffice for both. When you go home, tell your husband what you have found the words to tell me."

"And beg him to forgive me?"

"Why not put it another way? Can we at least forgive each other—please?"

"That's the hardest part, isn't it? One word: *please.* Can you explain me to Luisa?"

"No. You must do that, too. My guess is that she already understands most of it."

"I'll try. Now, please will you tell me I'm forgiven."

He raised his hand, made the sign of the cross, and pronounced the words of absolution. "'I absolve you for your sins, in the name of the Father and the Son and the Holy Spirit. Amen.'"

Isabel stood up. Her face was drawn and pale. Her eyes were moist with unshed tears, but her voice was steady.

"Thank you; but haven't you forgotten something?"

"I don't think so."

"Shouldn't you say 'Go in peace?' We both know this is good-bye."

"There are no good-byes," said Luca Rossini softly. "Love is the only thing we carry with us across the river. We've done this before. Remember what you said to me: 'Let's do it in style, Luca. Heads high, no tears, and no looking back.'"

"Hold me gently when you kiss me, my love. I hurt all over."

He found Luisa sitting at the desk in her bedroom writing postcards. There were suitcases open on the bed. He had to clear a space so that he could perch himself on a corner of the mattress. Luisa shifted her chair so that she could face him; but she made no move to come closer.

"How's Mother?" she asked.

"She's calm now. She's ready to go home. She just needed some help and reassurance."

"Thank you for giving it to her."

"She needs help from you, too. She wants desperately to be reconciled with Raul before she dies."

"Reconciled?" Luisa seemed shocked. "What exactly does she expect?'

"She wants to say she's sorry. Her problem will be to find the moment and the words."

"That's my problem, too, Luca. I can't find the words I need to say to you."

"Perhaps I can help." This was not ritual anymore. There was no formula to recite. He answered with a grin. "You don't know how to cope with me. I'm the pebble in your shoe that hurts when you walk. Am I right?'

"Yes."

"And you love Raul, who is more of a father to you than I can ever be, and soon there will be grief in the house when your mother goes. So, there's no time now to build anything between you and me."

"All of that, yes! But it seems such a waste. I like you, Luca. I think I could begin to love you. I suppose I should read some history and find out how Renaissance prelates got along with their sons and daughters."

Rossini laughed. "They enriched their sons and made important marriages for their daughters. It doesn't work like that anymore. Times have changed."

"But I don't have any time. There's not enough for me! And you're owned by that, that great big sprawling monster of a Church."

"It commands my services." There was an edge to his reply. "It doesn't own me."

"I'm sorry. I didn't mean that."

"I know what you mean. I'm like the centurion in the Gospel. They say to me, 'Come,' and I come, 'Go,' and I go. But there's something else, more important. You have your own life to make. If you want to be a good artist, you'll need to travel, meet the old masters and the new ones. You'll need to travel light. A cardinal for a father is too much baggage to carry—but here or some other place, you may find him useful."

"Please, Luca! I don't want you to write me out of your life altogether."

"How could I possibly do that? You are my daughter. I am written into you forever. When you have children, I'll be written into them, too. There'll always be a genetic inscription that reads 'Luca Rossini—his mark!' Quite awesome when you come to think of it! Now, may I kiss my daughter good-bye?"

"You've had a rough morning, Luca." It was an observation, not a question, from the secretary of state.

"You might call it that, Turi. I had hoped Isabel and I would have some time together after the conclave; but we shan't have it. We've said our good-byes. I have a favor to ask you."

"Ask it, please."

"I know we're held incommunicado during the conclave. I know also that there's an open channel of communication from the Sacred Penitentiary and the vicar-general of St. Peter's. I'd like to be able to receive news of Isabel. Her daughter has agreed to keep me informed. Can you arrange a reliable inter-mediary to pass messages? Dr. Mottola warned me that the final collapse could occur quite soon. I'd like to give Luisa the con-tact details before she leaves in the morning."

"Leave it with me, Luca. I'll make arrangements and call you this evening."

"You're a good friend, Turi."

"Is this likely to be a painful exit for her?"

"It can be, even with the best of palliative care. We're back to the old questions, aren't we? When does palliation become positive intervention; and does the Almighty demand death by crucifixion?"

"We all have a lot of questions to face during the conclave, Luca. That's why I've asked you here." Swiftly, as he had acknowledged the subject, he was off it again. "Coffee or tea? And I've finally taught them in the kitchen to make English sandwiches. They're very good."

"I'll take tea, Turi. But you won't play parlor games with me, will you? I'm not in the mood."

The secretary of state moved briskly to the text of his agenda.

"You've already begun to see the electoral factions defining themselves, Luca. They'll shift, of course, during the conclave, and they may shift quite dramatically, because no one is accountable, except to God or his own self-interest, for any change of allegiance during the voting processes."

"I've noted it." Luca gave him a crooked grin. "Our friend Aquino is a master of the art of solicitation. He reminds me of the pickpockets in Sri Lanka—the ones they call 'finger dancers' because they surround you and distract you by dancing their fingers all around your body without ever touching you. You never know where they're coming from until your wallet's gone and they're away with it."

"That's our good diplomatic training!" The secretary of state laughed. "At least you know the game . . . But to be serious, this election can be—in my view, has to be—a new beginning for the Church. Our late pontiff—God rest him!—has tried to pack the college and the episcopate with men who, he thought, would continue his own policies like faithful disciples. If they vote that way, they'll go for an interim candidate—one with a low life-expectancy but enough experience to hold the boat steady on course. Personally, I don't think we can afford that time. We are losing congregations too fast. There are too many closed

issues, too many undebated questions. Rome is losing rele-
vance, because the people are not being heard. I was invited
last night to a small dinner at the English college. The speaker
was an elderly Benedictine. His text was a quotation from the
English Puritan poet, Milton: 'The hungry sheep look up and
are not fed.' His treatment of the text was surprisingly frank.
'They are being fed,' he said, 'but we are feeding them paper instead of the bread of life!' "

"So," said Rossini, quizzically, "you bring me here to feed
me tea and English sandwiches. Come to the point, Turi."

"The point is this: We won't get the right candidate from
wrangling and dissension among partisan groups. The dissension can arise, as it has done in the past. Even though the present system is designed to prevent a prolonged conclave, a point
may come where a simple majority of voters will decide the election. That's the danger: a divided college, a divided church, run
by a compromise candidate. Am I making myself clear, Luca?"

"Admirably, my friend, and the tea and sandwiches are excellent; but tell me what you expect of me."

"Please! Be patient, Luca! It's customary, as you know, at
the beginning of the conclave, to offer the electors an overview
of the whole Church: 'Here we stand, who is the best man to
lead us?' By custom, the secretary of state delivers a statement
on the political situation as it affects the Church in every country. Then, there is the keynote speech, a meditation on the
Church as the City of God, witness of the Word to the World.
That is supposed to set the mood of the electors, remind them of
their duty to find the best pontiff to lead the people of God. The
camerlengo offered a choice of speakers to a committee of the
sacred college. The committee has chosen you."

"This is a joke, Turi!"

"On the contrary, it's a heavy responsibility: to set the mood
of a historic moment, to open the minds of the electors to the
promptings of the Spirit."

"Turi, my friend, you know I hate to be manipulated. You

know I've had more than one dose of it in the last few days. So, please, not another!"

"Calm down, Luca! I'll tell you what our friend Baldassare told me. Your request to have Monsignor Hallett attend you as a personal confessor during the conclave was not kindly received. Certain members of the Curia felt it smacked of privilege. Space in St. Martha's House is at a premium. There are already confessors rostered for duty in the conclave. However, Baldassare thought he could stretch a point if you were willing to preach. You know the way it goes, Luca." The secretary of state was savoring his own dry humor. "In the eyes of God, we're all equal—but some have to work harder to stay equal!"

"You're blackmailing me, Turi."

"It's called a nice balancing of interests. That's what diplomacy is all about."

"I have nothing to offer, Turi." Rossini was seized with sudden passion. "I'm the wrong man at the wrong time. I'm flawed. You know that. I'm going through a crisis of belief, which I can only describe as a night journey under a storm cloud in a world from which God has removed himself. The woman I have loved all these years is being taken from me—and I can't even blame God for it, because he isn't there. This morning, she asked me to hear her confession and give her absolution. I could not refuse; yet I went through the motions like a stage magician, knowing that the illusion would hold good for the audience but that I couldn't deceive myself. That's why I want Hallett with me. He's got problems of his own with which I am trying to help him, but he's also a sceptic with whom I can talk without dissimulation, and perhaps—just perhaps, Turi—find myself in daylight again. And there's one more thing. I have bled for this Church. It has nurtured me and promoted me far beyond my personal worth. I do not wish to divide it by anything I might say or do. There is much, very much, that I disapprove in its politics and procedures. If I cannot in conscience accept to live in the house, I shall leave quietly after the conclave. In all the

flurry of a new pontificate, no one will be interested in the early
retirement of Luca Rossini. But this sermon you want me to
make is another matter altogether. I cannot talk platitudes. I
will not. I am prepared to be silent; but if you call me to speak,
you must accept the risk of what I say, just as I must accept the
risk of saying it."

There was a long silence during which the secretary of state
poured himself another cup of coffee, sugared it, stirred it
slowly, and then with elaborate care, inspected the meat in the
last sandwich before he bit into it. Rossini watched and waited.
He was tempted to offer applause for Pascarelli's familiar but
beautifully timed performance. One of the junior wits in the
secretariat had nicknamed him Fabius Cunctator—Fabius the
Delayer—because of his talent for avoiding awkward con-
frontations. Finally, he finished his sandwich, took a sip of coffee, dabbed at his lips, and delivered judgment.

"Let us distinguish here, Luca. I am not your confessor. I do
not wish to enter the forum of your private conscience. I pray for
you in my Mass, that you may be given the light you need. For
the rest, you are attached to the secretariat. I am your legitimate
senior in office. I could, if I chose, direct you to this service. I
seek rather to persuade you that your speech may not be as
divisive as you fear. If it raises contention, so much the better.
A papal election is no time for nuances and carefully edited
proclamations. Your personal credit with your peers is much
higher than you think. You were in the confidence of the late
pontiff, and you never betrayed it. On the contrary, you fought
for colleagues whom you deemed to have suffered injustice—
and for causes which were considered unpopular. Your personal
character is another matter. There is a large black mark against
you: your adultery with Senora Ortega. Your stoutest defender
was the late Holy Father. But it makes no matter who is for you
or against you. You speak always with your own voice, Luca, out
of an understanding heart."

"I speak out of a darkness of desolation, Turi. My heart is breaking, yet I cannot even weep. What do you expect me to say to my brothers in the conclave?"

"Just that, perhaps," said the secretary of state. "Just that: I am Luca, your brother. Let me talk to you about the news we are charged to deliver." He made a small dismissive gesture and ended with a wry smile. "You do not need me or anyone else to write your sermon, Luca. It will be enough that you speak from the heart."

Luca Rossini was not so easily moved.

"You're a very persuasive fellow, Turi. Imagine what you could do with a rack and thumbscrews! But please, think a little further down the road. I make this eloquent appeal. Then one fine day, while you are all basking in the light of a new apostolic age, I am not there. I have found myself a retreat and become . . . whatever I have become; then you, my dear Turi, are stuck with a whole line of new scandal about the hypocrite preacher, the traitor at the supper of the brethren. You're offering me a poisoned cup. Why are you urging it on me so strongly?"

"Because what you call poison, Luca, may well be the physic that cures the sickness from which you are suffering so acutely. When you stand to speak, you will confront your brethren from all over the world. You will read yourself in their faces. You will reason with yourself, as you are reasoning with them."

"Turi, you still don't understand! This is not a crisis of reason! If it were, I could argue Gottfried Gruber and his whole team of assessors and inquisitors into the ground, and myself into instant serenity. This is something else. I am imprisoned in darkness, the darkness of an empty house. One day, Turi, His Holiness asked me did I never regret my exile from my homeland. I told him, no, I carried the coals from my hearth fire with me. I had only to blow on them and they would blaze again. He knew I was telling him only half the truth. He smiled and asked me what would happen when finally the coals burned

down to ashes. I couldn't answer him. I can now. The house
gets very, very cold."

"So, you have to build a new fire. You pray for the spark that
will set it blazing again . . . But I have to know now, will you address the conclave?"

Now it was Rossini's turn to play the delaying game. There
was more to this situation than the presentation of a homily to
open the hearts and minds of a hundred or more electors, all of
whom were high men, settled in their opinions, each jealous of
his own principality. He knew that he was being palmed off to
them as a prophet of a new age, who could be as easily dismissed with contempt as welcomed with respect. Either way,
one faction or another of the electors would be served; or all
could be served at once by uniting in a single condemnation of
an upstart. So, he asked an apparently flippant question.

"When we call on the Holy Spirit to inspire us in conclave,
does he endow us automatically with the gift of tongues?"

"Regrettably, he doesn't, Luca. And a lot of our prelates
have lost their skill in Latinity. Whatever language you use,
you'll lose some of the conclave. It's rather like an opera.
They'll share the melody—and struggle with the words."

"So, what's the point of the exercise?"

"The point is that we'll provide a polyglot text. That's one of
the things we do well here, as you know. That way, they get the
music and the words. You have six days, Luca—and I need
three of those for our translating and printing."

"Which gives me three days to prepare my text?"

"Two and a half. I need a morning to read and discuss your
draft with you."

It was then that the full light of revelation dawned. Already
the puppeteer was pulling the strings that moved the mari-
onettes. Rossini leaned back in his chair and laughed.

"Turi, you are quite shameless. There will be no drafts, no
discussions. There will be no interpolations, no nuances, no
marginal comments. I've agreed to speak. This may be the last

testimony I offer in the assembly of our brethren. I insist that it be my own utterance. If they accept it, good! If they reject it, then put it through the shredder. Simple. Either way, no one outside the conclave will ever know. We're all under the oath of secrecy, are we not?"

"We are, of course," said the secretary of state, "which makes one wonder how so many columns of information leak out of the conclave. I concede the point. You give your own sermon."

"And I get Piers Hallett, and my link with New York."

"Now, I think you're blackmailing me, Luca!"

"On the contrary, I think we've just arrived at a nice balance of interests."

"I'd feel a lot happier, Luca, if you would discuss your text with me. That way, I won't feel quite such a fool when the roof falls in."

At that moment, the telephone rang. The secretary of state answered it. A moment later, Angel-Novalis was ushered into the room by a young cleric who carried out the remains of the meal. After a brief exchange of greetings, Angel-Novalis explained the reason for his visit. He laid on the desk facsimile clippings of two pieces from the *New York Times*.

"We're six hours ahead of New York. These two items appeared in this morning's edition. I've shown them to the camerlengo, and he recommended that I discuss them immediately with you. The first one is the final installment of the pontiff's diaries."

Rossini leaned over the shoulder of the secretary of state to read it.

I am not well tonight. I am plagued by a headache and by that strange malaise, which in the past has signaled the onset of a small cerebral incident. I try not to let myself exaggerate the possibilities, but I have been warned several times that this is how death may come for me. I carry a time bomb in my head and one day it will burst and kill me. Still, I must work on "because the night cometh when no man can work."

Living thus, in the shadow of judgment, I am forced to judge myself most stringently. I am still vested with authority, but the power to use it is slipping from my hands. For a long time now, I have been forced to delegate more and more to men whom I have appointed, yet in the end, it is I who am responsible for what they do. What troubles me most in these gray hours is the use of my power over the consciences of men and women, the power of binding and loosing, which over the centuries we have inflated too often into tyrannies.

What I, myself, have thought to justify as a rightful exercise of authority, I see now as a harsh and often opportunistic intervention. I have acted more as a general deploying armies under command than as a pastor watching his scattered sheep grazing over vast hillsides, exposed to the incursions of predators. I have condemned brave minds to silence. I have chosen to crush, rather than persuade, rebellious spirits. I have refused the counsel of our Lord, to let weeds and wheat grow together until harvesttime. Instead, I have sent rough gardeners to root out the weeds—and good grain has been torn out with them.

In all this, I have invoked the counsel of men whom I, myself, appointed, so it was always my own voice I heard. To justify my decisions, I have counted upon the tolerance of loyal Christians and upon the sheer ignorance of the vast flock grazing in the distant pastures. Why have I succumbed to this most subtle betrayal? Because I saw it as a means to continue my policies for the Church long after my reign is ended. There is an ingrained fear in all who govern, that to respect dissent is to foment rebellion. So, be our edicts good or bad, we let them hang upon the walls of the city until the rain of centuries washes them away. So long as they are there, they can be invoked against the incautious and the unwary.

It is easy to find collaborators in this continuance of power, because I am seen to be their guarantor, their justification against all attainder. More, their power will continue after mine has dropped from my hands. Custom will only confirm it. Challenge will only make its exercise more rigorous.

The terror that invades me now is this: I am too old to change anything. I count my life like a child: by sleeping and waking, by bedtime prayers and thanks for each new day. What shall I answer to the God in whose name I govern, to the Lord Jesus Christ whose vicar I claim to be . . ."

There was a long quiet between the three men, as each finished his own silent reading of the text. Then, Luca Rossini gave a long exhalation which ended in a whispered regret.

"Dear God! That is what he was trying to say to me for weeks, but he could never bring himself to utter the words. The poor, lonely man."

"The cat is out of the bag," said the secretary of state baldly.

"I think you should read the editorial," said Angel-Novalis respectfully. "There will be many others like it."

They read it in silence, Rossini leaning over the shoulder of the secretary of state.

Although the provenance of the papal diaries is still clouded, there appears to be no serious challenge to their textual authenticity.

These passages, written the night before he collapsed into a final silence, constitute a document of singular importance. It is the confession of an old and

powerful man at the end of a long reign. There is a great
sadness in it: a sense of guilt, a recognition that the
clocks are never turned back for any of us.

Too often, especially in this age of instant information, Vatican authorities make themselves ridiculous
and bring the faith into disrepute by tardy reversals of
decisions that should have been scrapped centuries
ago. The Galileo affair is one notorious example. Less
evident, though perhaps more dangerous, are the exac-
tions of new professions of faith from teachers in
Catholic universities, professions which go far beyond
the traditional propositions of the Nicene Creed. It is
not enough to leave the cure of error or exaggeration to
the simple lapse of time. The poignant record of the dis-
quiet of the late pontiff under the threat of death ac-
knowledges that souls must be served in the here and
now, because for them, too, time runs out swiftly.

One hopes, however, that the electors, assembling
now in Rome, will read this final document and reflect
on it while they consider their candidate. Their decision, too, will soon become irreversible.

The secretary of state leaned back in his chair, locked his
hands behind his head, and surveyed his visitors in silence.
Angel-Novalis was the first to speak.

"I shall be asked for comment. Do you gentlemen have any?"

"None from me," said the secretary of state. "The man is
dead and buried. Comments are yesterday's snowflakes on the
grave."

"*Requiescat,*" said Luca Rossini. "Let him rest in peace."

"With great respect," said Angel-Novalis, "I need more
help than you seem prepared to give me."

"Perhaps,"—the secretary of state was deceptively mild—
"perhaps we have missed a point here."

"Then permit me to clarify it, Eminence. In a private diary entry, written just before his death, the pontiff has recanted— or at least cast grave doubts upon—policies that took him two decades to set in place. We understand his state of mind as he wrote. He was an aged and overworked man trying to cast up the accounts of his life before the final audit. You will remember that I addressed this question in a public statement at the Foreign Press Club. I voiced my personal opinion that the diaries were, in fact, stolen property. I did that, if you remember, at your formal request. This final extract is the strongest piece of internal evidence to support that contention. I, for one, cannot believe His Holiness would have conspired with his valet to destroy his own life's work. I think that comment has to be made and made strongly. Otherwise, those who, in good faith, have executed the policies of the pontiff will be left without recourse in their congregations. More, there will be a colorable suspicion that the publication is condoned. That is a gift in hand to the liberals, a weapon against those of more conservative views. To let it pass without Vatican comment smacks of opportunism. A crime is left without constant challenge because it conduces to a change of policy."

The secretary of state toyed with the paper knife on his desk. Rossini made a flat statement.

"If you want to emphasize the theft, you need more evidence against Stagni. If you want to salvage any of the policies of His late Holiness, you won't do it by polarizing the electors. The whole Church is in stasis at the moment. The See is vacant. We're all sitting under that symbolic umbrella, waiting for a new sun to rise upon us."

"Something has to be done." Angel-Novalis was a man secure in his own convictions. "I shall be asked for comment. I cannot refuse to give it."

"Then, you work within the conventions of your office," said the secretary of state. "You are already on record with a personal and public statement at the press club. Repeat it, by all means; but remember, you're playing entr'acte music here until the curtain goes up on the big act, the election of a new pope. That act hasn't been written yet. It would be a great mistake if you, in your zeal for an impossible justice, tried to meddle with the script."

"Let me be sure I understand, Eminence. You are instructing me to work within the discretions of my office?"

"Precisely."

"Then, I had best be about my business. By your leave, Eminences."

When the door had closed behind him, Rossini offered a mild protest.

"You gave him a rough ride, Turi."

"He has a good seat on a horse." The secretary of state allowed himself a grim smile. "But he was trained in the Spanish riding school: It's a wonderful style for dressage, but it's not best for a long cross-country steeplechase."

It was late in the afternoon when Rossini left his office, walked out of Vatican City by the Angelic Gate, and headed down the Borgo Sant' Angelo toward the river. It had been a long day. Now, a black depression settled over him. He was haunted by the childhood fairy tale of the boy who lost his shadow. He had no point of reference anymore. He was an empty man going nowhere.

It seemed an age, though it was only six hours, since he had said his farewells to Isabel and Luisa. They were still in the hotel. They would be there until the morning. He was consumed with desire to see them again, but it was better not to revisit so soon the scene of their mutual grief. Their farewells had been said. There was nothing to add to the last halting words of tenderness. The embraces that were meant for solace had now become painful for Isabel. He cherished the hope, however faint, that he might visit her in New York after the conclave. For the moment, he would walk silent and alone in his own darkness and wait for sunrise, if indeed sunrise would ever come again.

Then he remembered, he had at least to contact Luisa and give the instructions, which the secretary of state had provided, for contact with him during the conclave. He had proposed to fax them to her at the hotel, but the secretary had demurred. Security was involved. Hotel message desks were places of notorious risk.

So, when finally he reached the river and stepped onto the Bridge of Sant' Angelo, he dialed the number of the hotel and asked to be put through to Luisa's room. He was relieved but embarrassed when she answered. He hurried to explain.

"I've managed to set up a communication link which you can use while we're in conclave. It's quite official, but it depends on accurate use of the time difference and direct access to the named person. So, I want you to copy it carefully as I dictate, then read it back to me, then make sure you have it always with you. The Vatican's a big place; soon it's going to be a very crowded place. Until the conclave is over, this is the only link I'll have with you. Understood?"

"Understood. I'm sitting here with pen and paper ready."

He dictated the information slowly, spelling out each word, repeating each number. Then, he had her call it back to him, making sure her spelling and pronunciation were accurate. It was only when it was all done that he felt free to ask her:

"How is your mother?"

"She had a bad hour after you left, but she's better now. I've just been in to see her. She's sleeping. Later, I'll take her up to the restaurant for dinner. All the packing's done. We won't have to scramble in the morning."

"Would you like me to come and see her this evening?"

"Better not, I think. Why put yourselves through it again?"

"You're right, of course. Just tell her I called and give her all my love."

"I'd like a small share of it for myself."

"You have it. You will have it always."

"And how are you holding up, Luca?"

"I'm marching forward—even though I'm not sure where I am going."

"I'm not either. It is just beginning to dawn on me what losing a mother means."

Instantly, he was filled with tenderness for her plight. The loss of a parent was like the cutting of a taproot. The flow of nourishment from the past ceased abruptly. The future became an uncertainty.

"My dear girl, nobody is ever ready for anything. The moment comes; you deal with it. That's the sojourn tax we all pay for being human. And let me tell you something else, which your mother has learned and I am still trying to learn. There are moments for all of us from which God seems absent and we are left in darkness and terribly alone. We work our way forward like the blind, tapping the way before us with a stick, hoping the ground remains firm and that whatever creatures we encounter will be friendly. There are no guarantees, ever. We keep ourselves open to love, because without it we become feral beasts."

There was silence on the line, so that he thought he had lost her. Then, in an odd strained voice, she asked, "Do you pray, Luca?"

"I say the words. I do not know who hears."

"Will you say them for us—for me and for Mother?"

"Of course."

"And we'll pray for you. I'll be in touch from New York." There was another brief silence before she demanded: "Tell me you love me, please!"

"I love you, my daughter."

"I love you, Papa."

The connection was broken. He put his mobile back in his pocket, then leaned against the stone balustrade, staring through a mist of tears at the gray water.

# 12

onsignor Domingo Angel-Novalis was a punctilious
man. He was also an angry man. There was no heat in
his anger, only a frosty calculation. Things were amiss; they
must be set right. Ideas were muddled; they must be made clear.
Time was running out: There remained less than a week before
the cardinal electors went into conclave. After that, the words
and deeds of a dead pontiff would be yesterday's news, fit only
for pulping. Therefore, the record must be set straight immediately. So from the moment he left the office of the secretary of
state, Angel-Novalis had been very busy.

First he called a colleague in Rio de Janeiro, one of those
laymen who in Opus Dei were called "Numeraries." His name
was Eduardo da Souza and he was the editor of a large conservative newspaper. Angel-Novalis asked him to call up from his
files every available piece of information on the lately arrived
Claudio Stagni. He would like the information in three hours.
Possible? Of course, according to the Blessed Founder, nothing
was impossible if the cause was good and God was on your side.

His next call was more difficult, because he was a proud
man and he hated to be indebted to anyone. The proper order of
things was that the media came to him for news. He never had
to beg for space or attention. Today he was ready, if not to beg,

at least to call in some favors. His most likely target was Frank
Colson of the *Daily Telegraph,* who had been his interlocutor at
the Foreign Press Club. The *Telegraph* had missed out on the
bidding for the papal diaries. Colson might well be disposed to
file a final story before the forthcoming election blanked out the
immediate past. Colson was open to the idea. They arranged to
meet at the Caffe Greco at five-thirty.

Angel-Novalis spent the next two hours in his office putting
together a tersely reasoned story on the suspect provenance of
the papal diaries and the possibility that the texts would be
used to change radically the disciplinary policies of the late
pontiff. It was nearly five o'clock when the E-mail answer came
from Rio:

> Claudio Stagni has taken a three-year lease on an
> expensive apartment in a high-security block on the
> Rua Lisboa. His household staff consists of a cook, a
> maid, and a chauffeur-bodyguard, hired through a
> bonded agency. Given the moral tolerances of this city,
> there is nothing to excite comment on Stagni's lifestyle.
> He has a fondness for handsome young men, readily
> available in this city, and is said to be seeking acquain-
> tances in literary and artistic circles. He has begun to
> frequent local art galleries and has been entertained by
> a couple of local publishers who are interested in the
> work in progress dealing with his life in the service of
> the late pontiff. He seems acutely aware of the risks of
> a too public or too dissipated a life in this city. He pre-
> sents the discreetly low profile of a literary gentleman of
> substantial means. On the other hand, he does not ne-
> glect the company of women—provided they are of a
> certain age and addicted to fashionable gossip. In short,
> he is a very cool customer who knows exactly what he
> wants and is very clever at getting it.
>
> There are, however, a couple of useful footnotes.

Brazil is on the verge of signing extradition treaties with certain countries, like Great Britain. Stagni has consulted a well-known lawyer, with whom we have connections, to advise whether he is at risk in any matter. I do not believe that Italy or Vatican City are listed as treaty prospects, but I can inquire; and it would do no harm to begin a small campaign of harassment to unsettle him.

This is a common game in this country, which produced some sinister by-products, such as the "Squadrons of Death" and other forms of violent vigilantism. I do not for a moment suggest you could contemplate such methods to achieve your aims. However, there are simpler ways of unsettling an undesirable resident. If I get any good ideas, I'll let you know. Meantime, I'll keep digging.

Fraternally yours,

Eduardo da Souza

It wasn't much; but it provided a text for his discussion with Frank Colson. He printed it out, shoved it into his briefcase with his own material, then tapped out a reply to da Souza:

Many thanks for your time and trouble. Stagni seems to have built himself a solid bunker. One can only hope that one day he may be flushed out. There is no way one could condone violent harassment, but a buzzing of insects can create an unease.

Fraternally yours,

Domingo Angel-Novalis

When the message had been transmitted, he switched off the machine and hurried out to his appointment at the Caffe Greco.

Colson sipped his coffee and read carefully through the documents. Then he shook his head.

"There's nothing new here—certainly nothing to warrant a story of any size."

"You're missing the point, Frank! Stagni has always been suspect, as a thief of the pontiff's diaries, as an utterer of forged supporting documents."

"Suspect, yes; but never accused, because there's zero evidence on either count."

"But obviously he's scared of something; else why would he consult a lawyer in Brazil?"

"And why would that lawyer be ready to breach a client's confidence?"

"He's a friend of friends. He was stretching a point to do us a favor."

"God preserve us from such lawyers! And you, Monsignor, should be careful of such friends."

"You are still missing the point, Frank: the internal evidence of the text; the pontiff recanting his policies. I've worked for him for a long time. I can't imagine his colluding with a valet on a project of destruction."

"He wrote the text!" Colson was testy. "Why? Surely not to have it buried for centuries in the Secret Archive? We all write to communicate to someone. The valet was the last human being he spoke to at night. He was the most natural mediator between the pontiff and whatever constituency he wanted to reach!"

"If you're saying that constituency is the Church at large, you're mistaken! All his efforts have been to confirm the authority of the hierarchy and reduce the intervention of the laity. Why would he set out to damage his own lifework?"

"Because, in the end, he didn't like it! Sculptors destroy their works. Painters slash their canvases. To me, this reads like a warning confession: 'The structure I have built is faulty. Don't put too much more stress on it. Extend in other directions. Look to the foundations.'"

"I don't read it that way, Frank!"

"How, then?"

"A sudden failure of nerve on the part of a very old man and overworked man. In panic, he confessed a private fear. What he wrote fell into the hands of a thief. Now it can be used to subvert the spiritual life of the Church."

"Subvert? That's a strong, active word. You are saying that the pontiff, himself, wrote the formula for subversion."

"I don't believe he intended it to be so used."

"The text is clear. If that doesn't hold good, who is to interpret his intention?"

"The new pontiff. Nothing changes while the See is vacant."

Colson could not restrain a smile.

"That, my dear Monsignor, is pure myth and fairy tale. Of course things change! Views, policies, colorations, they all change as we speak, as the prelates gather in religious institutes all over the city. The world doesn't wait for a new resident in the papal apartments; it just keeps spinning and we, poor devils, hang on to it by the skin of our teeth."

"I'm sorry you feel that way, Frank. I had hoped—"

"Relax, my friend. You'll get your story. I'll have to rejigger it a little, use some of the things we've just been talking about; but, yes, we'll give the subject a good airing."

"Thank you. At least I can feel that I have performed a piety for him. I shan't forget this service, Frank."

"I've never seen you eager to plant a story."

"I am furious. A wrong has been done. I want to see it righted."

"The best way to do that is to replay the event in the center of the stage and let the audience make up its mind. Do you mind if I leave now? I've got to get this written and on its way to London."

"Will it make tomorrow's edition?"

"I hope so. I asked them to reserve space."

"But I thought you said there was nothing new in it?"

"An old trick, Monsignor: Make the narrator justify his plotline. Your text was good. Your performance was much more eloquent."

Monsignor Angel-Novalis ordered himself another cup of coffee and a piece of chocolate cake. He was too intelligent a man not to know that he had been jockeyed into an indiscretion. He was no longer relaying official Vatican opinion but adding personal commentary. On the other hand, what did it matter? His time in office was running out. Under a new pontiff, Opus Dei itself might well be due for a sojourn in the deserts of official disfavor. That was the nature of life in an imperial church. Religious institutes were the duchies and baronies, and marquisates and corporations of the commons, where property and money, man- and womanpower were assembled at the disposition of a pontiff for the people of God. Sometimes they stood high in favor. Sometimes they fell from both grace and favor. It was rare, however, that their official patents were rescinded. It required a big blot on the escutcheon to have it withdrawn altogether.

So calm and patience, Domingo! You have tried to protect the honor of a man whom you served with honor. If you stumbled in this final service and spilled wine on the carpet, apologize and mop it up and retire with as much dignity as you can muster. If God grants it, there will be a new day tomorrow.

Now that his own story was safely bedded down, Angel-Novalis thought he might make a detour to the Foreign Press Club and see what other stories were being floated around the globe and how the betting list on the new pontiff was beginning to shape itself. He checked his wallet to see that he had cash enough for a couple of rounds of drinks at the bar. He, himself, drank only mineral water, but he believed that a salaried cleric should pay his score like the rest of humanity. He noted with amusement that Frank Colson had left him to pick up the check for the coffee. He paid it and headed out into the rumorous autumn evening.

At the press club, Fritz Ulrich was jubilant over the editorial presentation of his piece on the Janissaries of the Ottoman Empire. An astute editor had spotted the possibilities of the article and had inflated it into a two-page spread with illustrations by a noted satirical cartoonist, Georg Albrecht Kirchner.

Ulrich's simple analogy between the Janissaries—captive Christian boys turned into fierce soldiers of the Islam—and the celibate clergy of the Roman Church—diminished in numbers, plagued by sex scandals and large damage suits arising from them—had been interpreted into the context of a global confrontation between Christianity and a resurgent fundamentalist Islam. It was a powerful piece, and there was much praise for it. Steffi Guillermin was generous in tribute.

"I confess, Fritz, I didn't give it enough attention when you talked about it. But with this display, and with the cartoons underlining the allegory, it's great. There'll be lots of discussion points: Algeria, Serbia, Indonesia, Pakistan—"

"I am proud of it." Ulrich was delighted as a schoolboy. "And Kirchner is so clever. See how simple he makes it look: Switch the miters for turbans, then emphasize the vestments on the one side and the panoply of the Ottoman troops on the other. Presto! The theme is clear, and my text makes the argument! How is your own piece coming—the portrait of Cardinal Rossini?"

"I'm not sure. Some of it is good, but there are shadowy areas in the man I haven't reached yet. Time's run out. I have to file no later than tomorrow morning."

"Do you mind if I take a look? We're doing the piece in German, as you know."

"Be my guest."

She punched it up on the screen of her laptop. As Ulrich sat down to read it, Angel-Novalis came to the table and nodded a greeting to them both. He asked whether he was interrupting anything. Guillermin assured him he was not and explained what she was doing.

"It's a final review of my portrait piece on Cardinal Rossini."

"Would you mind if I read over your shoulder? I was there,

remember, monitoring the interview. I'd love to see what you have made of it."

"You may be able to help me tidy it."

Angel-Novalis took up his position behind them and read the text as it was scrolled up on the screen. Guillermin sipped her drink and waited. Whatever Angel-Novalis said might be valuable or irrelevant. Ulrich, however, was a professional, and his people in Germany had paid good money for the rights. He had a clear interest in the final text. His first comment was a compliment.

"It's a good portrait, Steffi—even though you had to chisel it out of a very tough stone. But one question you haven't answered."

"Tell me."

"His late Holiness was a black-and-white man. 'Intrinsically good, intrinsically evil.' Those two phrases keep popping up all over the documents of his reign. So why would he patronize a damaged man like Rossini? Why would he offer him the red hat? Why would he send him as his personal legate on missions of confidence all around the world?"

"I think I've answered that quite clearly," said Guillermin. "If you go back to paragraph three, you'll find it in the text. Since his return to Rome all those years ago, Rossini has lived a blameless life. He has refused to deny his debt to the woman who saved his life, or his affection for her. The late pontiff respected that. How could he not? That's what Christianity is about: reconciliation, growth, progress on the pilgrim road— and always love!"

This was the moment at which Angel-Novalis chose to intervene in the discussion. He asked, "What is your final reading on Rossini?"

Guillermin frowned over her own admission.

"That's my problem. I have no final reading. You were present at the interview. You saw what happened. He never refused a question. He answered everything I asked. But he explained

nothing, least of all himself. I understand it in part. I've seen
evidence of what was done to him all those years ago. It was a
terrible violation."

"Twenty-five years ago," said Ulrich. "How long does any
man need to heal?"

Guillermin rounded on him in sudden anger.

"Sometimes a lifetime isn't enough!"

"And how would you know that?"

"Because I had a brute for a father," said Guillermin curtly.
"He turned me off men for life."

"I'm sorry," said Ulrich. "I'm sorry for all my bad jokes. I
am truly sorry."

"For the love of God, Fritz! Go back to your cursed Janissaries and leave me in peace."

Ulrich got up without another word and shambled toward
the bar. Angel-Novalis swung the talk swiftly to another subject.

"I understand the problem you have to define this Rossini.
For more than a quarter of a century now, he has tried to make
himself invulnerable. He has become—how shall I say it?—
like a great iceberg at the heart of which a fire burns. You can
see the fire, but you cannot get close enough to feel the heat.
You ask yourself whether one day the fire will melt the ice or the
ice freeze out the fire."

"Would you like to hazard a guess, Monsignor? After all,
you described your own experience after the loss of your wife.
You found salvation, or at least a safe harbor, in a religious fraternity. Would you say the Church has filled that need for Cardinal Rossini?"

"I would say it probably has not—at least not to this point
in his life."

"Why not?"

"Because he has never trusted himself completely to the
Church, which he saw in his own country all too often as a con-
spirator with military governments. It had its martyrs, to be sure.
Rossini, himself, suffered for the faith; but its martyrs were what

martyrs generally are, outsiders who become heroes and hero-
ines after their deaths. In spite of his rise to power—and he
does exercise power—Rossini's surviving self was built around
the woman who truly was the tangible savior, the restorer of the
shattered vessel. You knew she was here in Rome?"

"I knew it. I tried to arrange an interview. She declined. I
hear from the hotel that she has been taken ill and is leaving tomorrow for New York with her daughter."

"She is, in fact, mortally ill," said Angel-Novalis. "Rossini
called the papal physician, Dr. Mottola, to attend her."

"So what will happen when she is gone from him altogether?"

"I don't know. I've sometimes asked myself what would
have happened to me if all my supports had failed me. Sometimes I've wondered whether I might have been a wiser man, a
better man in the end, if I had been forced into another pattern
of growth. Other times I've thought . . ."

"Thought what, Monsignor?"

"About the parable of the empty house, all swept and gar-
nished, and the seven devils who moved in to live there."

"And you think Rossini has devils in his house?"

"We all have, but you're going to have to put your own
names to Rossini's demons."

Even as he uttered the words, he remembered that there
was one mischievous imp tapping at the window of his own soul.
His fraternal colleague in Rio had introduced the small devil
not as a serious tenant but rather as a jester in the house. It was
amusing to contemplate Claudio Stagni, secure in his exile and
his new wealth, suddenly pestered by gadflies and stinging
wasps. Then, because he was a man with a finely honed conscience, Angel-Novalis understood that this was no jesting imp
but a very gentleman of a devil, demonstrating with clear reason
how the perversions of power might serve the cause of justice.
He gave a small involuntary shiver. Steffi Guillermin cast him
an inquiring look.

"Is there something the matter?"

Angel-Novalis grinned in embarrassment.

"An untimely thought. We were talking about devils. I just caught a glimpse of one out of the corner of my eye."

"Now, there's a thought!" Guillermin turned back to her screen. "Perhaps that's the key to him. Rossini is a man who has seen the naked face of evil, and he can't look past it to any vision of goodness. Belief in a beneficent creator is hard to sustain. I understand that very well."

"Have you ever read *Don Quixote?*"

"Years ago. Why do you ask?"

"There's a sentence that sticks in my mind. '*Tras la cruz esta el Diablo.*' Behind the cross stands the devil."

"I don't remember it. But it makes sense. Let me play with this for a while. Buy me a drink, will you please—a gin and tonic—and offer one to Fritz Ulrich with my compliments. He was trying to be nice and I snarled at him. But, for God's sake, don't bring him back here!"

She turned back to the screen and tapped in a new introductory sentence: "Luca Cardinal Rossini, who is slowly emerging as a possible papal candidate, is a complex man, not easily deciphered."

In the privacy of his own office, Frank Colson was putting together his version of Angel-Novalis's subversion theory. He knew that the provenance and authenticity of the documents were dead issues, soon to be buried under an avalanche of speculation over the election, and picture journalism on the new incumbent of the See of Peter. He had two reasons for picking up the tag end of the story: Angel-Novalis himself and the future of Opus Dei under a new pontificate.

Angel-Novalis was adequately explained by his own personal history. A bereaved man, he had committed to the point of obsession to a fraternity which had given meaning and direction to his life. He had been trained in a bankers' world, where every item in an audit must be sedulously noted. Opus Dei, therefore, presented itself as the last and safest refuge of orthodoxy in a world going rapidly to hell in a basket. The perilous notion of a remnant Church, faithful amid universal decay, was etched into their thinking. The emphasis on the highly colored word *subversion* seemed to be the key to large areas of their thinking, and to the sense of outrage in Angel-Novalis himself. Colson began, as he usually did, by jotting down a lead line.

The papal diaries, believed to be stolen and published with forged provenance, may well be something more: a blueprint for subversion of the spiritual life and discipline of the Church.

This was the personal view clearly expressed today by Monsignor Domingo Angel-Novalis, head of the Vatican press office and its official spokesman. It should be said clearly that this comment was not solicited by us. Monsignor Angel-Novalis asked that his personal point of view be published. He came to us because we were not one of the publishers of the diaries.

Challenged by this writer on his use of the word "subversion," Angel-Novalis insisted that it was accurate. He claimed that the diary entry made by the late pontiff the night before his collapse was a panic confession, "a sudden failure of nerve on the part of a very old and overworked man." He expressed the fear that this momentary loss of confidence might be used to destroy the pontiff's own policies and disciplines.

It was pointed out to him that there was an inherent contradiction in the argument, namely that the words were those of the pontiff himself. Angel-Novalis immediately took refuge in a legalism: The See of Peter is vacant. All existing determinations hold good until a new pontiff changes them. He went further, asserting again that the documents had been stolen, were in fact private utterances with no canonical validity.

Pressed further, Angel-Novalis admitted that no evidence had been brought against the seller of the documents, Claudio Stagni, now living in some luxury in Rio de Janeiro. Clearly, such evidence had been sought, at least unofficially, by a colleague of Angel-Novalis in Brazil.

For this correspondent, the most curious features of this situation are the apparent indifference of Vatican authorities, who seem resigned to writing off the diaries as an unfortunate incident that will be forgotten in time, and the sudden burst of anger and zeal on the part of Angel-Novalis himself.

His personal loyalty to the late pontiff is well known. His demeanor has always been one of cool detachment from controversy and a purist precision in the statement of Vatican views.

One asks whether he has become suddenly sensitive to the inevitable partisanry of the *sede vacante* period, or has he, too, become partisan enough to invent labels for those who disagree with the prevailing policies and seek change through the electoral process? My own view is that, having founded his life on the fraternity of Opus Dei, he is disturbed by any challenge to its rigid conditioning. Those who live close to the seat of power grow restive when the power is in abeyance or when it begins to pass into other hands . . ."

The more he wrote, the more eloquent Colson became. By the time he had closed the story, he realized that what he had written was the obituary of a loyal servant who had put his career at risk to defend a position which his late master had already abdicated. Still, Colson felt very little remorse. This was the name of the news game. Everyone was playing to win. Someone had to lose.

He reread the piece and decided he would recant nothing of what he had written. This was, after all, the standard practice of the Vatican itself. *"Quod scripsi, scripsi."* What I have written, I have written. A change might be considered, but it would take centuries to get around to it—unless a new pontiff intervened; but even his name was still secret in the mind of God.

Frank Colson signed off on the piece and sent it to London.

Luca Cardinal Rossini came early to his house that evening. The black winter mood was still on him, the sense of desolation and fruitless endeavor. He knew from long experience that the only remedy against it was routine, a drudgery of habit with no expectation of relief.

He greeted his staff, asked that a light supper be prepared for him, then retired to his bedroom to bathe and change into pajamas and dressing gown. Next, he read the last hours of his breviary: vespers and compline. The cadences of the psalms were familiar on his tongue, soothing to the ear; but it was as if they were spoken by another. They were incantations, not prayers. It was almost as though his will stiffened itself against them, as it might against pounding drums and clashing cymbals in the temple of unfamiliar gods.

He ate his supper to the sound of music, Haydn's *Oxford Symphony* played by the Vienna Philharmonic. The music did for him what the psalms could not. It laid the chattering ghosts to rest. It silenced argument and imposed the structured unreason of pure sound on the convoluted reasonings of theologians and philosophers, and the obdurate legalisms of canonists.

When the music ended and his meal was finished, he carried his tray out to the kitchen, said good night to his staff, and settled himself back at his desk with pen and paper in front of him. Normally he would have used his word processor, but the task on which he was now embarked was an intimate and private venture in which the machine became suddenly an intruder. He did not stumble or hesitate over the beginning but set down the words the secretary of state had suggested: "I am Luca, your brother . . ."

Even as he wrote them, he knew they would not be acceptable to all in his audience. At second glance, it was perhaps not so good a beginning. Brotherhood and sisterhood were loaded words, even in the millennial Church. The taint of populism still hung about them. Orders and hierarchies were a more stable and more recognizable currency. Even in the electoral college itself, there were grades and degrees: cardinal archbishops, cardinal bishops, cardinal priests, cardinal deacons—and not so long ago, laymen, too, carried the title and the benefices of the rank. In the electoral college all men were equal—but in the order of being, some were more equal than others. So he changed the phrase a little: "I am Luca, your brother. Like you, I am a servant of the Word."

What next? What of value could he say to this assembly of hinge men that they had not heard and preached a thousand times over? What could he, the doubter in darkness, offer them of light and energy to direct their choice of the Servant of the Servants of God? So, begin again. "I am Luca, your brother. Like you, I am a servant of the Word. I want to open my heart to you. I am not here to teach you anything. You know it all better than I. Allow me simply to declare my thoughts to you as a brother in that huge family of the faithful who do not know even our names, who would not recognize us if they bumped into us in the street."

He paused there. He asked himself again what he was trying to do in this address. He wanted them to feel vulnerable, responsible, self-doubting, self-searching. They had lived so long under the protection of the institution that many were afraid or unwilling to venture beyond it. For these, the formal obediences were like the old Roman *testudo*: a canopy of shields under which they retreated from dangerous or threatening decisions.

So long as one remained in obedience, one lived safely and meritoriously under the system. Protest it, however, and one was marked, or thought oneself to be marked, as a disturber of the peace. Subtle penalties were exacted. Direct access to the pontiff was curtailed. Visits to him were difficult to arrange and reduced, in any case, to formal exchanges. The Vatican was still a court, and if one did not learn the manners of the court, one should expect to be disadvantaged. So, forget the brotherhood then. Think your way again through the maze. Prepare yourself for blind alleys and water tricks.

He wrestled with the text for a long time, filling his waste-basket with crumpled sheets of rejections. Finally, the humor of the situation dawned on him. The secretary of state, his good friend Turi Pascarelli, had presented him with the spiky end of a pineapple—an unsympathetic role in the most boring stretch of ritual drama.

Turi himself had the easiest part: to demonstrate the demography, the geography, and the geopolitics of a millennial Church. He had all the facts in his head and in his files. He could—on his own confession—demonstrate them with a globe and colored lights.

But the mind of the pilgrim assembly, the disposition of all the churches everywhere, their loyalties, their griefs, their angers, these were not easy to grasp. They were most damnably difficult to communicate to this polyglot group of electors, each jealous of his own corner of the vineyard and the quality of the wine it produced.

There was more, much more, to the joke, however. In this celibate assembly, there was no voice for women, who held up more than half the sky. There was no one to speak their language, express their growing concerns, their relationship to God, who was expressed only in masculine gender. Luca Rossini, laconic and stumbling to express the passion of his own life, would have to remind them of their duties and shortcomings. He, the doubter in darkness, was nominated lamp bearer to this assembly of electors who would appoint a *pontifex,* a bridge builder to span the vast gap between the sexes. And for a final dash of vinegar in the joke, Turi Pascarelli had given him two days to come up with a text.

It would certainly not be written tonight. He poured himself a glass of mineral water, switched on the CD player and surrendered himself to Mozart's oboe concerto. The piece was almost ended when Isabel called from the hotel. His heart lurched at the sound of her voice. He stammered like a schoolboy.

"I wanted to see you; but Luisa thought I shouldn't—"

"She was right. I was very fragile after you left; but I'm calm now. I wanted you to know that I've spoken to Raul. I told him I blamed myself for much of our unhappiness, that I wanted us to live in peace for whatever time I have left. I told him I didn't expect him to change his life, just to keep our part of it in a separate compartment. He was grave and quiet and tender—which proved your confessional advice was right. Also, it makes the homecoming easier for me and for Luisa. How are you, my love?"

"I'm sitting here listening to Mozart and trying to make sense of an assignment that's been handed to me. It's a real poison cup. I, of all people, have to address the electors at the beginning of the conclave and direct their thinking to the consequences of their choice. My wastebasket is full of my failures. I've given up for this evening."

"Why did you take it on?"

"I was pressed into it."

"Forgive me, Luca my love, but you were never pressed into anything—except your flight from Argentina."

"And you would never let me lie, even a little. Very well, then! I was willing to speak. For a short while there were things I thought I wanted to say. Now they've all flown away like pigeons from a bell tower."

"That means it's time to stop thinking and let your heart speak."

"I have to write the words. The translators need a text."

"Then, go back to your desk and write what we thought and said and argued in those few weeks we had together in the countryside near Cordoba, when we tossed our caps in the air and let the pampas wind whirl them away. You were so angry then, so passionate. I remember one thing you said: 'We have to summon Christ back out of his nowhere and have him talk and walk among us again. If he doesn't, we're all lost beasts lowing in a slaughter yard, waiting for the butchers.' That was the first night we made love . . . You were a boy priest then. Now you are an Eminence. Does His Eminence remember?"

"I remember," said Luca Rossini.

"Then tell it! Tell it as your heart remembers. Tell it for me."

"But you will be gone."

"I shall never be gone from you, nor you from me. Pick up your pen and write!"

# 13

Now Isabel was gone, and Luisa with her. The labor she had enforced on him—to write the experience of their love into a passionate plea for change—had cushioned, for a while at least, the impact of loss, and the fear of a future devoid of her presence. While he was grateful for the brief mercy, he knew that the agony would follow as surely as night followed day.

At ten in the morning, dog tired but bathed and shaved and spruce as a guardsman on parade, he presented himself to the secretary of state and laid the manuscript on his desk. The secretary acknowledged it with careful respect.

"Punctual as always, Luca! Thank you. I'll read it later, if you don't mind. Have you timed it?"

"Fifteen minutes—give or take thirty seconds. I hope the roof doesn't fall in while I'm delivering it."

It was a small joke, but the secretary chose to take it seriously. He frowned and shook his head.

"They'll be a hard audience, Luca. You'll be addressing them in your mother tongue. The Nordics are sceptical of Latin eloquence; so they'll be reading the text in translation. Don't be too discouraged if their reaction seems tepid. There is much uneasiness, much discontent with the workings of the curial bureaucracy of which you and I are a part."

"And of which certain ambitious members will try to maintain control."

"As the list looks at the moment, they may well succeed." The secretary of state was somber. "We have arrived, my dear Luca, at a critical moment in history: the end of a very long papal reign, the end of a century, the beginning of a new millennium. It is idle to pretend that such events do not affect people. They do, most profoundly. They affect us also, much more than we are prepared to admit. We are the mandarins of the bureaucracy, but we are just as vulnerable as the lowliest peasant to the changes of times and of manners."

"It would help me, Turi, to have your reading of the conclave as it is now constituted."

"Well!" The secretary of state took time to order his thoughts. "First we shall be a deeply divided assembly. It is not easy to label the divisions because they are not all based on religious belief or disciplinary policy. Some are based on pure self-interest. Not all of us are good men. Not all of us are halfway good. A few of us are secret villains who have made their own pacts with greedy and tyrannous men. You know that. We all know it, even if we can't confess it. Most of the men of goodwill admit that change is necessary. They all face two basic questions: What change and at what speed? The larger the ship, the harder and the slower it is to alter course. Our late pontiff tried—though he would never admit it—to reverse the course set by the Second Vatican Council toward a collegial government and a compassionate assembly. He almost succeeded; but he put the ship in stays, stalled its progress so that, at this moment, it sits dead in the water. The crew is discouraged; there are murmurs of mutiny between decks. The officers—you, me, and all the thousands of others—try to maintain good order and discipline and confidence in our celestial navigation. Many of us have found ourselves changed into officials, sceptical of our own priesthood. The people, too, are sceptical of the ministry we offer. We are commanded to silence on too many questions which should be open for active discussion. You and I can talk ourselves through a whole catalog of other questions clamoring for attention: celibacy of the clergy, an imperial Church or a collegial one, the theology of sex and marriage, the persistence of inquisitorial practices within the church, the imposition of new oaths and professions of faith on educators in our schools and universities. Suppression of debate is an untenable position in today's world. The people ask for light. We condemn them to darkness. They cry for warmth. We who claim to be the keepers of fire offer them a penitential cold. Sitting where I do, Luca, I am probably the least-constrained man in the Church—but, God forgive me, I have felt the straps of the straitjacket tightening every year!"

"Suppose," Luca Rossini challenged him quietly, "just suppose, you found yourself in my position—not from frustration, but from the slow erosion of belief itself—what would you do, Turi?"

"I have no idea, Luca, because I have no idea how the problem presents itself to you. Mine is an unexamined faith. I wear it as I wear my own skin. I accept it as I accept my own genetic identity. I claim no merit in that. It is a comfort I have done nothing to deserve."

"What I am experiencing,"—Luca Rossini chose the words with great care—"what I have experienced for some time is like the threat of blindness. I know that I may wake one morning and see nothing of what I see now. Will it be dark for me then, or light? I have no means of knowing. What sense will I make of the world—the same world, Turi—when all the intricate apparatus of reason and revelation and myth and beautiful legend, familial continuity even, has been dismantled, made to disappear by a single magic phrase *non credo*, I don't believe, I can't accept to believe anymore?"

"I don't know, my friend. I don't know. I suspect, however,

that it might make life a little easier if one were absolved from all the burdens of belief. One could pursue any path one chose, adapt oneself in any possible fashion to an accidental universe. I could see certain advantages, for instance, in a sceptic pope, an opportunistic secretary of state. We have had some of each down the centuries." The slow smile belied the irony of the utterance. The afterthought took the edge off the irony. "I am not mocking you. I read your suffering in your eyes. Your Isabel is gone. You fear you may never see her again. Yet you will not ask me to share your mourning. You deliver what I ordered—fifteen minutes of homily, carefully timed. I admire that. I envy you—understand me well, Luca!—I envy you the experience of love, which I have never known but you have had with Isabel. I cannot guess how you have managed to live, as I know you have lived, all these celibate years without her. I understand, or think I understand, the emptiness you fear after she dies. Belief, like sight, is a gift that may be taken away. But love will not fail you, as Isabel did not fail you in the time of terror."

"I hope you're right. I dare not think too far beyond today. I have never asked you this before; I had too much pride, I suppose. How much do you know of those early events in Argentina?"

"Most of it is in our files and those of the Holy Father, which are consigned to the Secret Archive. Our friend Aquino is a careful recorder, if a self-protective interpreter. The Argentine government was also sedulous to report its side of the story—including the birth of a daughter to Isabel Ortega, by cesarean section in a New York hospital."

"You should know, in fact, Luisa is my daugher," said Luca Rossini. "Isabel had never told me before this visit. Luisa did not know. As you may imagine, our first encounter was somewhat dramatic."

"And how does Luisa feel about it?"

"Confused, I think, but she is kindly disposed to me. More importantly, she has seen her mother and me together. Our love is open to her. She understands and approves it. I may be able to offer her some support when her mother is gone. It's too early to tell."

"And Raul Ortega?"

"My understanding is that he loves her and accepts her as his child. I did not ask any more questions."

"I ask," said the secretary of state calmly, "because, given this new knowledge, you may like to revise your somewhat tepid recommendation of Ortega as ambassador to the Holy See. The letter is still in my hands. It has not yet been filed in the dossier. If he were appointed, it might make you and your daughter a little more accessible to each other."

"You're a kind man, Turi." His voice was unsteady, and there were tears pricking at his eyelids. "But I couldn't let you do it. My daughter and I will find each other in due time."

"I'm sure you will." The secretary of state was suddenly brusque. "Now, I need your help on a couple of matters. First, I received this message from our nuncio in Brazil." He pushed the text across the desk.

At a social gathering last night, I spoke with a promi-nent editor, Eduardo da Souza, whom I know to be a nu-merary of Opus Dei. He talked in guarded fashion about a communication from a Roman colleague on the sub-ject of Claudio Stagni and the disturbing effect of the papal diaries inside the hierarchy and outside it. Ap-parently, there was a suggestion that what he called "a discreet harassment" of Stagni might be the first step toward discrediting the provenance of the documents themselves. I told him I had no knowledge of such a suggestion and would counsel strongly against it. Da Souza declined to reveal his Roman source. I recom-mend an inquiry at your end.

Rossini was still frowning over the document when the secre-tary of state pushed a second one toward him.

"This piece was faxed to me from London this morning. It was published in the *Daily Telegraph* and is attributed to their Roman correspondent, Frank Colson."

Rossini read the piece carefully and then asked, "Do you have a problem with this, Turi?"

"Don't you?"

"At first glance, no. I was here when you instructed him. You told him he was free to 'work within the discretion of his office'—your exact words, Turi. It seems to me he's done just that."

"No, he hasn't. I questioned him closely just before you arrived. He admits that he sought evidence on Stagni from a colleague in Rio de Janeiro. He admits that he had no brief to conduct investigative procedures. Secondly, he ascribes motives and states of mind to the late pontiff: 'panic utterances, an old and overworked man.' Already, this is too much. Finally, he lays special emphasis on a highly colored word, 'subversion.' That reflects on all of us!"

"You should remember, Turi, this is a reporter's version. It does not purport to be a verbatim interview."

"It was an occasion sought by Angel-Novalis to state his personal convictions. That is outside his official brief. He claims he had a moral obligation to defend the reputation of the pontiff and to defend the Church from damage arising out of the misuse of private documents. He had grace enough to apologize for what he called the 'taint of anger' in his actions."

"I think you were too hard on him, Turi. He's like a thoroughbred racehorse. He runs best when he's wearing blinkers."

The secretary ruminated on that thought for a while and then nodded a cautious agreement.

"You could be right, Luca. I was angry with him. He remained in control of himself. He offered me his immediate resignation."

"Did you accept it?"

"No. I told him that, as he had been appointed by the late pontiff, he should follow the common practice and offer his resignation to the new man."

"A wise decision on your part, Turi."

"I'm glad you think so, Luca," said the secretary of state in his direct fashion. "I have also told him that the last thing we need is any involvement with his colleagues in Buenos Aires, or any involvement by them in the Stagni affair."

"One has to presume Angel-Novalis has enough influence to prevent it."

"Who knows?" The secretary of state shrugged in resignation. "We create our own sacred monsters in the Church, both individuals and organizations. The monsters create their own agenda and stamp the documents with their own seal of godliness or perversity. There are great saints, great institutions of piety, learning, and charity. There are also witch-hunters, murderous crusaders, Jew-baiters, inquisitors who will condemn a thinking mind to silence and solitude. And now, my dear Luca, having delivered myself of all these indiscretions, I have to put you to the question. The camerlengo would like to see us both in his office."

"About anything in particular?"

"I would guess your interview with *Le Monde* would at least be mentioned."

"I haven't seen it, Turi."

"A lot of other people have."

"Do you have a copy?"

"I do." He gathered up the other papers from the desk and offered Rossini the article, clipped inside a folder. He also offered a cautionary comment. "Take enough time to read it carefully, while I look over your text. Then we'll stroll across to see Baldassare."

"What else does he want to talk about?"

"He hasn't told me. The See of Peter is vacant. We are

simply invited to sit under the chamberlain's umbrella and drink
morning coffee. I'll tell him to expect us in fifteen minutes!"

Steffi Guillermin's piece was much longer than he had expected. It had been laid out with great care, divided into two
distinct sections, with key portions of the text boldly boxed. It
was headed: "Inquiry into an Eminent Person." The subhead-
ing read simply: "Portrait of a papal candidate." The introduction was deceptively prosaic.

This portrait was composed during two sessions with
the subject, Luca Cardinal Rossini, Italian by ancestry,
Argentinian by birth and nurture, who has lived in distinguished exile for a quarter of a century and was promoted steadily by the late pontiff to curial rank.

The first session was a formal one, supervised by
the chief of the Vatican press office, Monsignor Domingo Angel-Novalis. The conditions were agreed in
advance. I was free to ask any questions I chose. His
Eminence might decline to answer, but everything that
was said during the interview was on the record. It is
printed here in full and without comment.

The second session was much less formal. It took
place in the private apartment of His Eminence in
Rome. Present were His Eminence Cardinal Aquino,
former nuncio apostolic in Argentina; Senora Isabel Ortega; and the leader of the Mothers of the Plaza de Mayo,
Senora Rosalia Lodano. The conditions were changed,
also. I agreed in advance that certain subjects would be
discussed off the record. I consented to this arrangement, and I have observed it. However, certain information embargoed during the discussion was available to
me from other quarters. This, I have not scrupled to use.
What I hope to have captured is the public and private

faces of a complex man, who, though he is little known to the Church at large, will not fail to impress himself on his colleagues in conclave.

The public man is easy to depict. He is a presence in any company. He is tall, lean, and handsome, with aquiline features and dark, observant eyes. When he smiles, his face lights up, and he radiates an eager interest. When he is displeased, his features harden into an unreadable mask. He is always courteous; but, as I discovered at my first meeting, he is impatient of tricks and professional ruses. I learned quickly to deal from the top of the deck. In professional terms I found him grave, occasionally humorous, and always precise. He appreciated the fact that I had come well prepared and that I knew how to spell the words. He returned the compliment with the well-turned answers you will read on this page.

The private man revealed himself by indirection. He was engaged in a delicate diplomatic enterprise. The Mothers of the Plaza de Mayo want to bring Cardinal Aquino before an Italian court on charges of complicity and collaboration with the Argentine military dictatorship in the death and disappearance of Italian nationals—both lay folk and those in religious professions—who were tortured, murdered, or simply disappeared during the dirty war. To accomplish this, they need a waiver of immunities by Vatican City. This, one guesses, would be unlikely to be granted. So, enter Cardinal Rossini, himself a victim of the dirty war: As a young priest, he was flogged and violated in front of his own church. He was rescued from further horror by Senora Ortega and her father.

While her father went on to Buenos Aires to negotiate a deal for Rossini's safe-conduct out of Argentina, Senora Ortega fled with Rossini to a country estate and nursed him back to health.

I saw photographic evidence—which I have agreed not to describe in these pages—of what was done to Rossini.

I perceived then, very clearly, how Rossini achieved a personal salvation through a woman. I was privileged to see them together under circumstances of extreme paradox. Both are now in their fifties. They had not seen each other for a quarter of a century. Even so, there was no doubt in my mind that once, for however brief a time, they had been lovers and that the love endured in them both. It lit up the sparse bachelor room in the cardinal's residence. One read it in every glance and gesture. It lent a special character to Rossini's plea for a truce, if not a settlement, between Aquino and the women who were his accusers.

Isabel Ortega is married. Her husband is a serving diplomat at the United Nations. She, herself, has pursued a successful career as a specialist in Hispanic American relations. Their daughter is an artist, working on restorations at the Metropolitan Museum of Art.

Cardinal Rossini, on the other hand, stood high in favor with the late pontiff, who sent him on many missions abroad. It is clear that papal favor brought its own penalties. Some of his colleagues envy him. Others are prone to gossip about his early history, carefully planted from the earliest days by the military dictatorship through its Roman embassy. But, not even his most hostile judges have ever been able to challenge the integrity and fidelity of his clerical life in Rome.

There is a size and stature about Rossini which impresses one instantly. This, one knows, is a man who has paid his dues. This is a man whom I would believe if he talked or preached about love. I would guess that he unlocks his heart very rarely, but when he opens it, one sees the glowing coals inside. I know for a fact that

he is now facing another tragedy. Senora Ortega is returning immediately to the United States for treatment
of an illness already diagnosed as terminal.

How will Rossini be regarded in the conclave? He
will perhaps be better known than he expects. He is
recognized as a man who travels light, moves fast, sees
and reports clearly. Such a one tends to underrate the
impression he makes, because he does not concentrate
on himself but on the matters in hand.

I have heard both sides of the Aquino story—from
the cardinal himself, whom I interviewed for this jour-
nal, and from the Mothers of the Plaza de Mayo. There
is no love lost between Aquino and Rossini, who are
as different as chalk and cheese. They are curial colleagues but certainly not friends. I would say that Cardinal Aquino was fortunate to have found an advocate
as strong—and let me say it—as generous as his colleague Rossini.

The affair of the disappeared ones, and of all the
other thousands whose fate is known, will not go away.
No silence is deep enough to engulf so many accusers.
It will not go away for Cardinal Aquino. My guess is that
the new pontiff, whoever he may be, will not hand him
over to a civil court—though more and more clerics are
being handed to civil courts for criminal abuse of the
young, a tragedy much smaller in scale than the brutal-
ities of the dirty war. However, Aquino will still have
to reckon with his own conscience, as Luca Cardinal
Rossini will have to carry for the rest of his life the scars
on his back and in his psyche.

Now comes the new paradox. Both Aquino and
Rossini will enter the conclave to elect a new pope.
Both are, by definition, candidates for office. Given the
climate of reaction that is already closing in, neither
can be too readily dismissed. Aquino is mature timber,

seasoned—some believe stained—by long diplomatic
and curial service. Rossini, on the other hand, is the
lone wolf, familiar with the outlands and uplands, nursing his love and slowly transmuting his griefs into service. Of the two, I prefer him as an outside bet for
election. Why? Because I believe he could keep the
coals of love alive, even if he were elected and the great
freeze of absolute power came upon him.

There was more yet; but Rossini had read enough to know that
his attachment to Isabel was no longer a secret. It would be
picked up in some form or other by all the world media. He was
glad that Isabel had made peace with her husband and that he
had helped toward their reconciliation. The revelation of her illness to the media was an unexpected shock; but he had to admit
that, by and large, Steffi Guillermin had kept her promise and
that her commentary had been less critical than he expected.
He wondered what comments the camerlengo would have on
the matter. He was still musing on the possible fallout from the
article when the secretary of state looked up from his own reading and spoke.

"I hope my translators can give a decent rendition of your
text, Luca. There is much more passion in it than I anticipated."

"Is that a bad thing, Turi?"

"No, I think it fits well with Mademoiselle Guillermin's portrait of you as a very passionate man."

"Does that trouble you?"

"Not at all! If there is no passion in this election, the chance
of change will be lost. If we don't vote ourselves the right man,
we're all in trouble. This is our one opportunity to make the
barque of Peter shipshape for a millennial journey."

"I've always liked that metaphor," said Rossini simply. "I
used it in my interview with Guillermin."

"I know. Your words impressed me, too. As you know, my father was a sea captain," said the secretary of state. "He could

read the stars and he loved the sea. I am told his crews always respected him because he ran a safe ship and cared for his men."

"Is he still alive?"

"No. He died in the early fifties. My mother brought up two girls and two boys in her widowhood. I entered the Church. My brother became head of the family. He's an executive with *Italcable*. Both my sisters are married. My mother is a *nonna* six times over . . ." He gave one of his rare smiles and made a gesture of surrender. "There! You have finally coaxed me into family talk. Anything else you'd like to know?"

"Yes. Why this meeting with the camerlengo? I hate walking blind into a conference. Your father would have understood that, I think."

"He would have understood very well. He used to say to me: 'The wise men were given a star to lead them to the Christ child. Every sailor has to know the stars that lead him home.' Let's go, shall we? Baldassare hates to be kept waiting, and just now he's carrying the whole Church on his shoulders. It makes him just a little irritable."

The gathering in the camerlengo's office was larger than either man had expected. The archbishop of Los Angeles was there, as were the prefect of the Congregation for the Doctrine of the Faith; the Maronite patriarch of Antioch; the archbishops of Tokyo and Bangkok; and the archbishop of Ernakulam in India, who was of the Syro Malabar rite. Aquino was also there, with the Archbishop of Seoul. There were eleven people in all. Rossini wondered why and to what special pattern they had been coopted. The camerlengo explained with his usual blandness.

"It was not possible—or even desirable—to have a full consistory of cardinals before the conclave. This is the last of a long series of small gatherings, at which talks have taken place and our senior brethren, excluded from the conclave, have been able to share their views and their experiences with us. Tomorrow between four and five in the afternoon, you will repair to Saint Martha's House where you will be lodged, I hope more comfortably than conclavists in other times. On your arrival, your rooms will be allocated, and you will be provided with all necessary documents: the timetables, the orders of rituals, the oaths of secrecy, the rules of the conclave, the names of the various persons who will be there to assist you: secretaries, confessors, a doctor, a surgeon, nursing orders, and so on. If any of you have special dietary problems, the kitchen staff will do their best to accommodate you. There will be room-to-room communication by telephone but no outside contacts at all, except in cases of extreme urgency, and then, only with permission of the marshal of the conclave. There is, however, one matter on which a special briefing seemed necessary. Certain of our brothers have requested me to make known, quite formally, that, if by any chance they were elected, they would decline the honor. They made the point that by abdicating the candidacy in advance, they could save the electors time and trouble. I have pointed out to them, of course, that all electors must be free to cast their votes as they choose, even if they know the candidate has abdicated in advance. This may suggest an imperfection in the system. However, the electors are free to use the system in any way they choose to bring about the valid election of their own candidate. I raise the matter now, informally, because when you enter the conclave, you will find a final complete list, which falls under the oath of secrecy and which applies to all conclavists. However, certain of our brethren have already made their intentions plain and public. Our brother from Westminster has already announced his intention of retiring to his monastery to go fishing. Matteo Aquino, who is here with us this morning, has abdicated his candidacy so that there may be no fallout in the new pontificate from long ago events in Argentina."

"One asks,"—the intervention was made by Gottfried Gruber—"one is compelled to ask whether, in the same context and for the same good reason, our eminent colleague, Rossini, might consider a public withdrawal of his candidacy?"

There was a sudden deathly silence in the room. Rossini rose slowly in his place. Ignoring Gruber, he turned to face the camerlengo. Very quietly, very deliberately, he asked, "We have known each other a long time, Baldassare. Did you have any knowledge that this challenge was to be put to me in this meeting?"

"No, Luca."

He waited for more. The camerlengo did not offer another word.

Rossini turned to Aquino. "And you, Matteo, did you prompt the question?"

Aquino shrugged off the challenge.

"In a manner of speaking, I suppose I did. After I had read the report of your interview in *Le Monde* I made a jocular remark to Gruber here, something to the effect that we lived in less tolerant and more scandalous times, and the press dominated our lives much more than we are prepared to admit. On the other hand, I said that you had survived the scandal better than I."

"What scandal?"

"Your relationship, brief as it was, with Senora Ortega: a priest with a married woman. That's what it was, that's what it will become again. Once we are in the history books, we can't step off the pages."

Rossini turned slowly to face Gruber.

"And you, Gottfried? You're the watchdog of the Church, master of the hounds of God. You feel I should make a public abdication of my candidacy because of this episode in my young life?"

"In today's climate, yes."

"And you, Turi, you are my immediate superior. What do you have to say?"

"I have no comment," said the secretary of state.

Rossini turned away from him and addressed himself once more to the camerlengo.

"With your permission, Baldassare, and with the consent of our brethren, I should like to deal with this matter now."

The camerlengo frowned but put the formal question: "*Placetne fratres?*"

The answer was unanimous: "*Placet.*"

Rossini stood for a long moment in silence, gathering himself, settling his turbulent emotions, searching for the appropriate words.

"My brothers. We have all met before. Sometimes I came to you as personal emissary of His late Holiness. Sometimes I received you in Rome, in my own house. We have celebrated the Eucharist together. Now you sit silent while I am urged to abdicate rights and privileges conferred upon me by our late pontiff. Why so? Am I on trial here? Or simply under challenge? I will not defend myself to you because I have nothing to defend. I will not plead with you because I have no cause to justify. I did not plead when they strung me up on a cartwheel and flayed me and violated me with a riding crop in front of my own church and my own people. I screamed, I shouted, I prayed—and yes, I cursed my tormentors. But I did not plead. When Isabel Ortega killed a man to save me, then took me into her care and fled with me into hiding, *then* I pleaded! I pleaded man-child to mother, man to woman—whom I had renounced unknowingly—make me whole! Make a man out of this wreckage. She did that. She did it by the gift of herself and all her womanhood. She did it in daily risk of capture, torture, and death. Do you find this scandalous? I have never been able to see it as anything but an act of love and of healing.

"How my brother Gottfried Gruber judges me, how his assessors might rate my acts and my attitudes, is irrelevant to me. I came to Rome under no pretense. I was brought here under a deal made by our brother Aquino with the military dictatorship in Argentina. I was delivered, a package of damaged goods, to the pontiff. There was a price tag attached to the package, and the price was silence. Isabel Ortega and her family were held hostage to that silence. I was held, too, a bonded servant to Mother Church, whom I have served, not always with joy or love, but with fidelity and punctuality until this day. I have made myself a public advocate for our brother Aquino, who is still vulnerable to the consequences of his service in Argentina. The Mothers of the Plaza de Mayo have a case against him. I have tried to mitigate their rage against him, although he now sits silent.

"His late Holiness befriended me. I made my first confession in this city to him personally. I told him I repented whatever guilts resided in my own acts, that I would accept whatever penance he chose to lay upon me, but I could not accept his absolution if it involved a condemnation or a censure of the love and gratitude which I bore, and still bear, for Isabel Ortega. He did not exact that. But the penance he gave me was harsh enough: a lifetime separation—in honorable exile, yes, but as a hostage nonetheless. I have performed the penance. I have paid the debt. Isabel Ortega came to Rome for a few days to bid me good-bye. She is terminally ill. Her presence helped you also, Matteo. It softened the attitude of the Mothers of the Plaza de Mayo in your regard. I trust you will remember her in your prayers. Now let me ask you all: Are we still crying scandal here? I will not tolerate it from you, my brothers! If you want a Church of the perfect, I see no place in it for me. Peter betrayed his master; Paul raised no hand or voice at the execution of Stephen, the first martyr; Mary of Magdala was beloved of the Master because she had loved much; Augustine was both a libertine and heretic before he came to belief. Tertullian separated himself because he could not forgive those who had quailed under persecution.

"At this moment, you are custodians of this our Church. You do not own it. You are responsible to God for the people of God. Finally, I answer our brother Gottfried here. The office I hold was conferred upon me legally, with all its rights and privileges. I will surrender none of them to a false charge of scandal. God forbid you should think of making me pope! God forbid that any here should abridge my right of candidacy. I thank you, Eminences, for your patient hearing. I beg you to excuse me."

He was halfway to the door when the camerlengo called him back.

"Wait, Luca! Please resume your seat. We have more business to transact."

Rossini hesitated for a second, then turned back to the camerlengo, bowed, and sat down. The camerlengo looked around at his audience and asked formally, "Does anyone wish to comment on the remarks of our brother, Luca?"

No one answered. Rossini knew he had won a victory: He had faced down the grand electors, but the taste of triumph was like gall in his gullet. Aquino he could understand, and Gottfried Gruber. But Baldassare the chamberlain and Turi, these were his friends; yet they would not raise a voice to defend him. Then the camerlengo gave the floor to the cardinal archbishop of Tokyo, a small, smooth man, who looked younger than his sixty-eight years. He spoke perfect Italian, colored only by the Japanese lilt to the phrases. His tone was deprecating and gentle.

"I have to say that I am troubled by what I have heard here this morning and by what I have heard in other gatherings since my arrival. There is a friction between brethren, which I find alien and upsetting. There is pressure to impose viewpoints and disciplines as if we were an army and not a family joined in love. Let me try to explain something. We Christians in Asia live as exotics in huge communities who have their own beliefs, much older than ours; but they are still our people, our friends, our relatives. We are forced, therefore, to carry out our mission of spreading the gospel with humility, discretion, and great charity. To use the words of Pope John XXIII: 'We seek always that which unites us instead of that which divides.' This means that in our teaching, we have to work through a large number of semantic barriers. We have to cast our Christian thinking in the terms of other languages and other cultures. We have to examine, with an open mind, the religious propositions of other great religions, always in the conviction that whatever is true by whomsoever said is an authentic revelation of the Spirit. We need great care and great discernment to put ourselves in this attitude of mind. We have to concede emotionally what we admit intellectually, that even the most refined perceptions of theologians, the most precise prescriptions of canon law, will be a barrier to religious understanding if they are not expressed in the language of the heart. The knowledge of God and of the truths of salvation is offered to all; therefore it must be available in all the modes of human communication.

"There is a great mystery here: the mystery of God's own secret, wordless working in every human life, which the Divinity itself sustains in being. It is always a dangerous enterprise to impose a verbal definition on this mystery, or to condemn those who seek to explore it with new tools or by unfamiliar paths. Our faith is not a series of propositions which we impose on people as a kind of entry fee into the Kingdom. Faith is an illumination which lights everything and every happening in the world. It is like a candle in a room full of mirrors, repeating and reflecting itself to infinity. We do not define Christ in our creeds. We proclaim him 'Light from light, true God from true God, begotten, not made, of one substance with the Father.' That proclamation was put together by Mediterranean people. How do I, a Japanese Christian, explain it to my people? I do it the only way I can, by making myself the mirror which reflects the light, however imperfectly. We are met here to elect ourselves a bishop of Rome. He will, by tradition, become the successor of Peter the Fisherman, who was the first to deny his master but who was named by him as the foundation stone

upon which he would build his church. We have to find ourselves another Peter, sensible of his own frailty, sensible of the
needs of a vast, scattered flock. We must not create myths
about him. We must not claim that all creation will be made
plain to him the moment he is elected. We must choose a man
careful of his people, open to them, not seeking always to direct them in all the acts of their lives, not using against them
the powerful bureaucracies of the Church, but trying to learn
from them, through the daily parables of their human experience. Once we elect him, we cannot depose him. We should
not, therefore, indulge in personal jealousies, but seek that one
among us whom we can trust to guide the flock toward new and
more open pastures."

"Amen." Luca Rossini's assent was strong, but, even as he
uttered the word, he wondered whether his own belief would
survive the outcome.

The meeting went on for another half hour. When it was
over, he offered formal courtesies, pleaded another pressing engagement, and left in haste.

He wandered down the Street of Conciliation and turned into
a shop selling pieties to the tourists. He idled away a half hour
buying a gold medallion of the Virgin and a handsome trinket
box to hold it. He wrote, in a fine Italianate script, the card, as
Isabel had ordered: "The little virgin you gave me has made me
very happy. I send you her image, so you will not be lonely without her. I send it in gold to thank you for becoming my sister.
Pray for me as I shall pray for you. Isabel Ortega."

He asked the sales assistant to take great care with the
wrapping, since he would be asking the new pope to bless it. He
paid the bill, acknowledged the fictional discount "for our distinguished prelates," shoved the package into his pocket, and
strolled like any tourist down toward the river. As he walked, he
found himself haunted by an irrelevant tag of verse which Piers
Hallett had tossed at him over a dinner table.

*Think you, if Laura had been Petrarch's wife,*
*He would have written sonnets all his life?*

Back in his own apartment, he began instructing his small household. Tonight at eight, he would dine at home with Piers Hallett for company. Tomorrow he would enter the conclave. His luggage should be packed for what could be a week's sojourn—more or less, according to how well the electors cooperated with the Spirit working among them!

His daily uniform would be the black cassock with scarlet piping, the scarlet skullcap, and his pectoral cross. He would need enough underwear to accommodate any breakdown in laundry services at Saint Martha's House. He would need a pair of white surplices and his miter for the ceremonial aftermath, because, although he was a cardinal presbyter by rank, he was also a titular bishop of the Church of San Sebastian on the Palatine.

He would need his diary and some private stationery. No mail could be sent or received during the conclave, but private communication within it was permissible, if possibly indiscreet. On the heels of these thoughts came the vagrant impulse to write to Isabel and to Luisa. Instantly, he suppressed it. That, too, could be another indiscretion. Raul Ortega had care of them now; all Luca Rossini could do was wait for news.

His thoughts turned back to the events of the morning: the eloquence of the Japanese cardinal, and the unexpected silences of the camerlengo and the secretary of state. His resentment had died as swiftly as it had surged. This was, after all, the name of the political game in the hierarchy of a papal court. Silence had a thousand interpretations and carried no penalties. Words were subject always to gloss, interpretation, and altered emphasis. They were weapons for the hostile but defenses frail as gossamer against a determined attacker. Neither Baldassare nor Turi had attacked him; they had simply withdrawn themselves to watch how their junior colleague might fare in his joust with the Grand Electors.

There would be more jousts to come inside the conclave itself, when the grand electors and the outsiders met together in the lounge and the coffee bar and the smoking room in Saint Martha's House, or as they walked in procession to the chapel where the votes were cast, four times a day, until a new pope was named.

Alone, now, and cold at heart, Luca Cardinal Rossini reasoned with himself. He had walked thus far on his own two feet. He would walk the last mile and leave the future to God—provided God was still present in the cosmos and the human chaos.

# 14

Luca Cardinal Rossini and his personal confessor, Monsignor Piers Hallett, presented themselves at the reception desk of Saint Martha's House at four in the afternoon.

Named for the bustling biblical housewife, sister of the resurrected Lazarus, the building had been planned in 1993 as a hotel-residence for visiting church officials and semipermanent Vatican staff. The funds, according to report, had been furnished by the Knights of Columbus in the United States. Now it was turned over to the conclavists and their small army of attendants, from scullions to sacristans. The architect of the conclave and his technicians had been working desperately to make it secure against intrusion by outsiders, or escape by its inmates, who would be held there incommunicado until they were able to announce the election of a new pontiff.

The building had not been without its problems. The Green Party of Italy had protested that it would block the view of Saint Peter's dome from the Street of the Light Cavalry Gate. So the architects had lopped off one story and built a subbasement area. Then came the difficulty of providing a secure entrance and exit into the Vatican confines for the sequestered cardinals. So, a temporary sealed passageway had been provided through the basilica itself to the Sistine Chapel where the votes were cast.

When they came to register, with a long line of international colleagues, Cardinal Rossini was assigned a chamber among his peers on the second floor, while Hallett was relegated to the basement. In this place, some servants of God were more equal than others. Their baggage, however, was searched with equal thoroughness by Vatican security staff to make sure that neither was carrying a mobile phone, a bugging device, or any other suspicious electronic item. Clearly the Church had small trust in the ultimate integrity of its princes. It was specifically pre-scribed, for instance, in the apostolic constitution that the crime of simony, the buying or selling of the papal office, would not invalidate the election. It was further prescribed that any promises made to procure an election were unenforceable after-ward. In earlier times, the office had been bought and sold. Sometimes, murder had been done for it. It was clearly ac-knowledged that ancient tricks might be repeated in this mil-lennial age. Each guest was presented with a folder which contained all the necessary information for his stay: the facili-ties of the house; its restrictions; the names and telephone numbers of its residents and service personnel; a chart of its public rooms; precautions in case of fire; the texts of the oaths of secrecy which would be administered in public that same evening, both to electors and conclave staff; and a list of con-fessors, secretaries, and medical attendants. All these items were embossed with the *sede vacante* symbol, the red and yel-low striped umbrella called the *pavilion.*

There was a momentary confusion when Rossini sought to confirm the special arrangements which had been made for him to receive news of Isabella from New York. There were the usual Roman shrugs, pursed lips, fumblings through papers, misin-formation punched up on computer screens. There appeared to be no record of such arrangements.

Rossini stood over the desk, menacing as an Andean con-dor, until the relevant directive was located and the approved contact was presented to him and to Hallett. Then he demanded that a copy of the directive be provided immediately for himself and Piers Hallett. Could it not wait, Eminence? No, it could not. Tomorrow would be another day. There would be someone else behind the desk, and the conclavists would, in any case, be denied access to this part of the house. So, please, my friend, just hand over the papers—in duplicate.

When the documents were passed to him, he responded with a thin smile of thanks; then permitted the porter to show them through the foyer to elevators which led to their temporary prison house. Piers Hallett celebrated the moment with a Cromwellian quip.

"I like the way you do business, Eminence. Trust in God and keep your powder dry!"

"Your first duty, Piers, is to check the vicariate office three times a day. I don't want messages lost or filed away until doomsday."

"Trust me, Eminence."

"I do, Piers! It's the others I worry about. We'll meet in my room after the second afternoon ballot each day for a libation and a chat."

"How long do you think the election will take?"

"Hard to say. I have the feeling this could be a long process. The rifts between the parties are wide. The stakes for the conservatives are very high. The fears of the liberals that we may have another ice age run very deep. There's no way of making a forecast until the voting begins tomorrow. They'll be administering the oaths at seven tonight. The secretary of state will deliver his message on the state of the Church. I'll say my piece. Then we'll dine like good brothers together. There will be one vote on the morning of the first day and two that afternoon. Thereafter there will be four a day, morning and afternoon, until a new pope is named. You'll have a lot of free time on your hands. Keep your ears open and let me know any gossip you hear below stairs!"

"For shame, Eminence!" said Hallett with a grin. "This is a sacred enterprise. What could there possibly be to gossip about?"

"As you say, Piers, what could there possibly be?"

"Meantime, apart from the gossip, what am I supposed to do with myself?"

"Pray, if you can, and think a lot," said Rossini soberly. "This is the underside of the tapestry, my friend. You'll see the best and the worst of this Church of ours. There are no illusions here and you have a decision to make. As, indeed, have I."

"I wish you light and courage, Eminence!"

The porter carried Rossini's luggage into the elevator, while Hallett, carrying his own bags, descended on foot to the lower depths.

After settling himself in his quarters—a compact but comfortable bedroom with its own shower and toilet, a desk, an armchair, and a prie-dieu with a crucifix set above it—Rossini scanned the list of conclavists, ticking off the names of those he had met in his travels, making his own cabalist notations on the career background of each one and the dispositions of each in terms of character and personal loyalty.

They came from all over the world: Ethiopia and Africa, Lebanon, India, China, the Philippines, the Americas, Asia and the East Indies and the Pacific islands. Their skins were black as ebony, yellow and brown, and pale as old porcelain. Their names made a polyphonic litany. Their languages were a motley of tongues, helped out by the Latin of their schooling, colored by the vestiges of regional and tribal accents from their mother tongues. They were all high in dignity. In normal times their power was measured by the size of the populations they governed, by their nearness to, or their distance from, the seat of power in Rome, by the weight their counsels carried in the papal court.

The courtiers themselves—the cardinals of the Curia— moved among them with a certain patronizing ease. They were, after all, the castellans of this Roman fortress. They knew all its winding passageways, all the adits to all the congregations and councils and committees, and where the tentacles of power twined, and how—swiftly or by a lifetime of slow circuits—an outlander might arrive at a personal dialogue with the pontiff. They were not all Italians, as they had been in the past. The Curia had been internationalized to include British, Belgians, French, Germans, Slovaks, Spaniards, South Americans, Africans, Asians, and Australians.

There was another group, also, peripheral to this one; smaller but still powerful—the metropolitans of the big Italian sees: Milan, Bologna, Venice, Naples, Florence, Palermo, Turin. They were clothed with another kind of authority: pastors of great cities with long autonomous histories. In the election itself, they were men to be reckoned with because they were known as pastors and not as bureaucrats, and their lives were set among ordinary folk.

The archbishops from the United States were—as one wag put it—mutants of earlier migrants from Europe: Irish, Italian, Polish. Any one of these was a possible candidate, but all were marked with an invisible sign. They were the offspring of a democratic revolution, which, in historic terms, was still too recent for comfort. More importantly, they were members of an aggressively capitalist society in which the profession and practice of any religion was a free option, while its imposition was outlawed.

Strangely enough, the largest contingent of electors came from the former colonial territories of Africa: Angola, Benin, the Cameroons, Kenya, Nigeria, Senegal, and the rest. The image of an African pope was a seductive one. It would revive the image of a universal Church, a House of all Nations. It would rebut forever the charges of a racist religion, a Eurocentric Christianity. But, in the cold light of modern history, it could also emphasize the bloody tribalism, which still bedevilled the African continent.

For his own part, Rossini was convinced that they must find and elect a man on his own visible merits and virtues, a good man, a simple man—which did not signify a stupid one, but one who could speak from the heart to the hearts of the people of

God. The politicians of the sacred college were a necessary evil, but their shifts and stratagems matched ill with the stark simplicity of the Gospel. The clerical moneymen were ever present in the precincts of every temple, but they should not control the Holy of Holies. The censors and inquisitors should be held where they belonged: in service to the sacred deposit of faith. They should not—not ever again—be appointed as judges over the people, or usurp the primacy of their consciences.

So, as he moved casually from group to group, saluting old acquaintances, introducing himself to new ones, Luca Rossini tried to decide on whom to cast the first vote in the first ballot the next morning. This first ballot was always a trial run to establish, if possible, the spread of the candidates and to identify, if possible, the voting blocs which were pushing them. This evening, however, was simply prelude and preamble: a reunion of the smallest but the most powerful club in the world. Drinks were served. Canapés were offered. The talk was temperate, the exchanges were tentative. The members were more eager to hear opinions than to offer them.

Rossini did not linger too long with any individual group. He knew that he was being courted, solicited, studied, not merely for his single vote, but for what influence he might exercise after a quarter of a century of survival inside the Vatican. There were occasional jokes about his recent notoriety in the press. He could read them as he chose: jibes, or gestures of respect for a seasoned campaigner. He paused for a moment with a pair of prelates from the United States. One was the cardinal archbishop of Baltimore, the other was the man from Los Angeles who had been present at the previous day's meeting with the camerlengo. He had a large constituency of migrants and refugees from the South Americas and a fluent command of Castilian and dialectical Spanish. He seemed eager to make good his lost opportunity with Rossini.

"That interview with Guillermin in *Le Monde*, a splendid

performance. I liked your stand-up style on the sex question. *Muy viril!* It helps us all. You know the firestorm we've just been through on the sex issues! I thought Gruber was way out of line when he suggested you resign your candidacy. I was tempted to intervene, but—"

"As well you didn't." Rossini was smooth as honey. "Our colleague from Tokyo said what was needed and still avoided contention."

"He's an impressive guy. A shade exotic in his theologies, perhaps; but that's a personal opinion. We of the West are much more comfortable with Aquinas, wouldn't you say?"

"It depends on how we teach him," said Rossini. "We've had some dangerously narrow theologies in recent years."

"Are you suggesting"—the man from Baltimore intervened in the talk—"are you seriously proposing we should change our teaching?"

"Rather that we be prudent in the choice of our new leader," said Luca Rossini.

"How would you feel about a pope from the United States?" He said it with a smile, but the smile was not in his eyes. "This time, it's probably too early; but the Americans, North or South, will have to make, sooner or later, a bid for the See of Peter. After all, the United States still holds the world in military and financial balance."

"Spiritually," said Rossini, "you seem often much divided. You profess freedom of speech and conscience; but you still train killers for counterinsurgency in the South Americas. You claim right to life, but you still conduct state executions. You claim freedom of conscience, but you conduct violent blockades of abortion clinics. I should hate to be the first American pope."

"Someone has to make a start." Lacey of Los Angeles had a sense of humor. Baltimore was less tolerant. He challenged Rossini.

"So, whom would you propose to us?"

"I propose no one," said Rossini amiably. "I cast my vote and let the Spirit take care of the outcome. Excuse me, gentlemen."

As he faded back into the gathering crowd, Baltimore said tersely, "There's another arrogant son of a gun. What does Rome do to these people?"

"I don't think he's arrogant," said Lacey of Los Angeles. "He's a hard man who knows the name of the game. He might be the best protection we've got against Opus Dei and the Grand Electors."

"And what, pray, is wrong with Opus Dei?" demanded Baltimore. "We've done very well working with them."

"I'm sure you have," said Lacey. "But I'd reserve judgment until you've seen their final bill."

Rossini's next encounter was a more agreeable one, with his former professor and biblical scholar, who was now the archbishop of Milan, the most important diocese in Italy. He was a man of quiet warmth and rich scholarship, who, when he was not on the road among his parishes, conducted seminars in his own cathedral for Christians, Jews, Muslims, and secular scholars of all faiths, to whom he offered an open forum for discussion and debate. With him was the archbishop of Montreal, who had just put the question:

"Whom do we have who can overleap the centuries and take us back to the simplicities of the Apostolic Church?"

"No one," said Rossini. "We all carry too much history on our backs, and the history qualifies everything we do or say. The Holy Father went to Paris to greet the young. Great demonstrations, great fervor and enthusiasm—until suddenly the massacre of Saint Bartholomew's Day loomed up like a black cloud out of the past!"

"That's the whole point, I believe," said the studious man from Milan. "We can't change history. We make our worst mistakes when we try to gloss it or rewrite it. The captivities in Babylon and Egypt are as permanent a part of Jewish history as the Holocaust of our time. Our problem is that we believe that time will wipe some of the dirt off us before we have to acknowledge our own misdeeds. It never does."

"Public confession is, to say the least, a disarming process." Rossini felt comfortable with these men. His whole manner was different, open and unconstrained. "For myself, I know I could not have survived in this city if I had tried to live by concealment and pretense. But too often we reduce ourselves to absurdities. Now it is proposed we have glass-sided confessional booths, so that the faithful can monitor the conduct of confessor and penitent! At the same time, we try to suppress the most ancient practice of a public reconciliation by all the faithful at Mass! I don't know what we or the people gain from that."

"Little enough," said the man from Milan. "Privacy is available to those who need it. Reconciliation has been a public act from the earliest days when Christ came to the Baptist at Jordan Ford. The problem is that we, the pastors, cannot be seen to break the Roman rules, and we can only bend them so far."

"That's one of the problems we're here to solve," said Luca Rossini. "We have to open the windows again, let fresh air blow through the House of God."

"The windows have been closed too long," said the Canadian. "The shutters are stiff and warped. It will take a strong man to force them open again."

"Or a simple one," said Rossini. "A plain country carpenter who isn't afraid to use a chisel and a crowbar to break through useless timber."

When he drifted away a moment later, the two senior prelates looked at each other. Their looks conveyed the same unspoken question: 'Could he do the job?' For Rossini, the question posed itself differently. The Church needed a conciliator, a man with an open mind and an open heart and a sense of history. Sixteen centuries before, Milan had been the capital of the Western Empire; and Ambrose, the governor of Aemilia and Liguria, had come to the city to mediate a dispute between the candidates for the Christian bishopric. According to the historians, he himself had been proclaimed the bishop even though he was not yet a Christian. Ambrose had been a phenomenon in his own time—and perhaps, Rossini thought, a prophetic paradigm of the future. He had been born and bred to a senatorial service in the twilight of an Empire; yet he had managed to preserve and pass on to succeeding ages the best of the yesterdays: a belief in continuity, in basic justice, a respect for civic order. He was a man who had straddled the world of spirit and the world of sense, and kept his foothold firm in both.

Rossini found himself wondering whether his own onetime mentor, a man of most eminent reason, wise in history, hopeful for the future, might well be the man to lead the Church into the twentieth century. It would certainly be a battle to elect him. He had no taste for intrigue. He was a Jesuit, and the Jesuits had been a long time out of favor. The men of Opus Dei had been long entrenched in their posts of observation and financial control.

Even so, this was a man to have hope in, a man on whom to risk his own personal vote.

By six-thirty in the evening, Saint Martha's House had been cleared of all unauthorized personnel. The conclavists and their attendants were locked inside, and the members of the Vatican Vigilanza were posted at entrances and exits. At seven o'clock, the first oath of the conclave was administered to all participants and staff.

I promise and swear that I will observe inviolable secrecy about each and every matter concerning the election of the new pontiff that has been discussed or decided in the congregations of the cardinals, also about whatever happens in the conclave or place of election, directly or indirectly, and finally about the voting and every other matter that may in any way come to my knowledge.

I will not violate this secret in any way, directly or indirectly, by signs, words, or in writing, or in any other manner. Moreover, I promise and swear not to use in the conclave any kind of transmitting or receiving instrument, nor to use devices for taking pictures; and this under pain of excommunication *latae sententiae* (that is, automatically) reserved in especial manner to the apostolic see.

I will maintain this secret scrupulously and conscientiously, even after the election of the pontiff, unless special permission or explicit authorization be granted to me by the same pontiff.

In like manner, I promise and swear that I will never give any help or support any interference, opposition, or hostility, or other form of intervention, by which the civil powers of any order or degree, or any group of individuals, might wish to interfere in the election.

So help me God and these holy Gospels, which I touch with my hand.

After this, the electors themselves made a separate oath to adhere to the apostolic constitution, to defend the rights of the Holy See, to refuse all vetoes by any secular power on the election. Once again, secrecy was enjoined and affirmed.

Above all, we promise and swear to observe with the greatest fidelity, and with all persons, including the conclavists, the secret concerning what takes place in the conclave or place of election, directly or indirectly concerning the scrutinies; not to break this secret in any way, either during the conclave or after the election of

the new pontiff, unless we are given explicit authorization from the pontiff.

At 7:20 precisely, the secretary of state rose to deliver his formal
report on the condition of the Church. It began with a brief vale-
diction to the dead pontiff.

> . . .We have mourned him. We have prayed for him, we
> have commended him to God as a good and faithful ser-
> vant. For us the work goes on. First, we have to follow
> the apostolic tradition and elect a new pontiff. Let me
> show you the world he will face . . ."

Briefly, he led them on a tour of the world's powder magazines:
resurgent Islam, China exploding into the twentieth century,
America watching jealously for incursions into her markets,
Africa dying a slow death by AIDS, India and Pakistan building
their nuclear arsenals, Arabs and Israelis still at war over
pocket-handkerchief patches of dirt, the tribes of Europe bat-
tling still to maintain their ethnic and religious identities, the
resources of the planet—forests, oxygen, and water—being
consumed at a profligate pace while the Church still refused to
reason with the stark realities of overpopulation. Then, in the
same dry fashion, he dropped a live grenade into the assembly.

> We, my brothers, bear our own share of blame for all
> this. We, too, have fomented our wars, compounded our
> massacres in the name of God. We repent our misdeeds
> too slowly. We make our reformations too late. We have
> fostered within the Church a powerful organization of
> clergy and laity, a wealthy and secretive organization,
> pursuing in the name of God, programs that, however
> they are formulated in documents and expressions,
> belie in practice the message of the Savior. We are not a
> secret sanctuary. We are not—though some would like

to believe we are—the privileged faithful of a remnant
Church, persevering to the end of an apocalyptic age.
We are a city seated on a mountain, visible to the whole
world. Think on this! Think on the scandals in which
our secret money dealings have embroiled us . . ."

Listening to him, Luca Rossini was amazed at how little he had
guessed of the man, on how much he was prepared to risk in
this charge against the windmills. His discourse took on a new
tone as he thrust toward the end.

Think on these things. Try to discern the signs of the
times, which are God's continuing message to us. Try to
discern where we, as the people of God, must repent
and change. I remind you that until you elect a new
pontiff, the writ of the old one still runs. There are those
who say it should run from here to eternity. Not so! It
runs until the wisdom of a later pontiff and of his collegial bishops changes it.
    We have all been shocked by the publication of the
diaries stolen from the late pontiff and sold to the press
by his valet. Yet, even here, there is something to be
discerned. The pontiff himself, old and ill, was troubled
about certain of his own decisions and policies, and
wished he could reverse them. He has already passed
beyond our judgment into the merciful hands of God.
But we have our judgments still to make, and we must
make them with sober wisdom. God help us all!"

He sat down in an unreadable silence. The time was exactly
twenty minutes to eight when the master of ceremonies summoned Luca Rossini to deliver his homily to his peers. The text
was already in their hands; but none of them were reading it. It
was coming up to dinnertime. The cardinal electors were hungry. Luca Rossini had the sudden macabre thought that if he

bored them or angered them, they might well eat him for dinner. He crossed himself.

In the name of the Father and of the Son and of the Holy Ghost. I did not seek to address you tonight. I was commanded to it; but what I speak to you, I speak from the heart. I ask you a simple question: Whom shall we choose for our pope?

In theory, it is any male Christian. In fact, he is now sitting in this room. For good or ill, that is the way it happens in our Church today. It is a measure perhaps of the centralism into which we have lapsed, of the ignorance of our own diversity. Let me put to you the questions I ask myself about our next pope.

How old a man? If he is too young, he may last too long, and the arteries of the Church will harden along with his own. If he is too old or infirm, we may have what we have just narrowly escaped, a constitutional crisis in the Church, a crisis of conscience for faithful Christians. Already we are a deeply wounded community.

So next, we need a healer, a man of compassion, one who will have compassion on the multitudes as Jesus himself did. Unfortunately, words of compassion and comfort have not been easy to decipher of late in Vatican texts. All too many have been intent on dogmatic exposition than on the confused but plangent cries of the human heart. Our charge is to spread the good word, the simple word. "Consider the lilies of the field, how they grow . . . Mary's sins are forgiven her because she has loved much. Love your enemies."

For this so-simple exposition, we need a man calm in his belief in the ultimate good purposes of the Creator: "Now there remain these three: faith, hope, and charity, and the greatest of them is charity." The wisdom of love sees and accepts the whole mystery of creation, bright and dark. Love mediates the mystery with those who live in pain and fear and unknowing.

Our new pontiff must be open. He must listen before he pronounces. He must understand that language is an imperfect instrument, that it changes all the time, and that it is the most inadequate means we have to express the relations between human creatures and the God who made them. This is the crux of our problems. Our people do not believe us when we propound a morality of sex. They know that we are ignorant of its language and its practice; that we are forbidden to learn either in a marital relationship.

So, our man will be very careful whom he permits to speak in his name. He will remember the respect he owes his collegial brethren whom, like Peter, he is charged to confirm and strengthen. He will remember that, although the principle of petrine primacy has been acknowledged down the centuries, he is not, and never has been, a sole pastor in the Church. Those who, out of mistaken loyalty or partisan interest, have sought to inflate the office or the authority of the occupant have always done disservice to the Church.

Finally, secure in his own faith, he will respect the philosophers and theologians. He will encourage open inquiry on difficult questions. In the freedom of family life, he will encourage debate between the sons and daughters of the house. He will put an end forever to secret denunciations and secret inquisitions into the orthodoxy of honest scholars. He will protect them in charity against detractors.

Charity! Love! It all comes back to that, doesn't it? "Charity is long-suffering and kind. Charity envieth not, charity boasteth not, is not puffed up. Charity bears all things, believes all things. Charity never fails." Do you see this man of charity among us? Do you know him?

Do you, in the ancient sense of the word, discern him?
If you do, elect him boldly and let us all be about God's
business!

Once again, there was a silence, out of which the master of ceremonies recited the closing prayer. Then with a certain relief,
he announced, "There will now be a five-minute toilet break
before dinner is served. There are no place cards; please sit
where you wish. You are all welcome in Saint Martha's House.
Good appetite!"

Luca Rossini spent a restless night, haunted by a frustration
dream in which he wandered through the labyrinthine corridors
of a hospital, looking for Isabel. All the doors were closed. All
his questions were answered in dumb show by faceless people,
who pointed him deeper into the labyrinth.

He woke, sweating and gravel eyed, at four in the morning,
and decided, as he often did, to banish the nightmares by an
early morning walk. Then for the first time, the situation became real to him. There was no place to go. The house of Saint
Martha was a prison house, locked down tight until the inmates
had discharged their task.

As he lay musing in the darkness, he asked himself whether
his sermon had meant anything to anyone. He doubted very
much that it had. These elders in the assembly had heard all the
words before. They were armor-plated against eloquence, as
sceptical of simplicity as of serpentine cunning. He judged—if
a verdict at four in the morning had any validity at all—that Turi
Pascarelli's calm impeachment of secret partisan movements in
the Church had shocked many in the audience. Turi was not an
augur studying the entrails of birds. He was a man of respect: a
diplomat who read the large print, and the small, in every document, then picked at every loose thread of argument or language
and finally called for the dossiers on the negotiators themselves.

Perhaps Turi had left his intervention too late, or perhaps he had timed it just right. Technically, he was already out of office. All his functions were in suspense. Factually, he was still subject to the edicts of a dead man. He had breached none of them, but he had called them all in question. Without doubt, he had made enemies; but he was invulnerable to them. He had no ambition to rule. He was that most powerful of persuaders: the man with nothing to ask and nothing to lose.

As he drifted back into sleep, Luca Rossini asked himself a more radical question: Once Isabel was gone from him, who would he be, what could he be with any conviction or certainty? Then, quite inconsequently, he found himself thinking of Angel-Novalis. On the death of his wife, he had opted for the absolute certainty offered by the authoritarian sectaries of Opus Dei. He had served with a single mind and a loyal heart; yet at a crucial moment he had betrayed himself in a professional folly. To defend the memory and the policies of a dead man, he had begun an unauthorized pursuit of the faithless valet who had filched his papers. He had sought the help of his own colleagues, and, thus, set in motion events that he could no longer control.

It was the problem of all intrigues. It was also the tangled fabric of the dream into which Luca Rossini lapsed in the pre-dawn hour. He was a fugitive now in the lanes and alleyways of a sinister city. He was stalked by assassins who laughed softly in the dark and called in mockery: "Who'd like to fuck a priest!"

The ceremonies of election began with a celebration of the Eucharist and an invocation of the Holy Spirit. The cardinal electors then moved in procession to the Sistine Chapel, where they sat, each in his own stall, under the awesome gaze of Michelangelo's Christus, renewed and revivified by modern restorers financed by the Nippon Television Corporation.

Each elector was supplied with a small pile of ballot papers inscribed with a preamble in Latin: "I choose as Supreme

Pontiff . . ." The elector would write the name of his candidate in block letters. He would not sign the ballot paper.

The altar of the chapel was set with a gold paten and a large golden chalice. As each elector marked his ballot paper, he folded it in half. Then, in order of precedence by rank, each man advanced to the altar, knelt for a moment in prayer, and declared: "I call as my witness Christ the Lord, who will be my judge that my vote is given to the man who in the sight of God I believe should be elected." He laid his vote on the paten, tipped it into the chalice, and returned to his stall.

When all the votes had been cast, three scrutineers, chosen by lot from the electors, made the count. Their count would be checked by three others, similarly chosen. Luca Rossini was one of the first group of scrutineers.

There was a solemnity in the ceremony and its setting which touched everyone; yet there was a paradox as well. The repeated oaths, the duplicated checks, the immediate destruction of paper after each unsuccessful ballot, bespoke a distrust of human beings even when they were acting, as they swore they were, in the Spirit, whose abiding presence had been guaranteed until the end of time.

The first ballot was what everyone expected. It showed a spread of ten candidates, of whom the highest received eighteen votes and the lowest eight. The ballot was significant only in that it floated a raft of possibilities, South American, North American, Spanish, Belgian, Italian, and African. There were no middle Europeans, no French, no Orientals. None was within shouting distance of the required majority of two thirds plus one. Two of the South Americans, the Spaniard, and the North American had been appointed by the late pontiff. The African was a longtime Curia member. The two Italian candidates were from Venice and Milan. The name of Luca Rossini was nowhere to be seen.

That afternoon, there were two more ballots. By the end of the day, the battle lines were drawn. The number of candidates had been reduced to eight. One of the South Americans had dropped off the list, along with the African and the North American. Luca Rossini made his first appearance in the voting.

It had been a long, dragging day. By the time he returned to his room at five in the evening, Rossini was convinced that one of the most lethal threats in the life of any Roman pontiff was the deadweight of ceremony and protocol that he had to carry every day. The thought was prompted by his own unexpected appearance as a candidate, although he knew—or thought he knew—that he was being introduced as a spoiler, whose presence would shake out other unlikely pretenders and concentrate the minds of the electors on the strongest possibilities.

It was still too early to determine who they might be, but Milan had strengthened to twenty-five votes, the Spaniard had risen to nineteen, and the man from Brazil had taken a three-vote lead on the Mexican candidate. Politically, both were positioned firmly on the right of center.

At five-thirty, Monsignor Piers Hallett came to the room with a bottle of Scotch in one pocket of his soutane and a packet of peanuts in the other. He set them down with a flourish.

"Talk about a scramble! Their Eminences make a lethal tribe at the water hole! I'm afraid there's no ice. Shall I pour? You look as though you could do with a drink."

"I have small taste for rituals. How was your day?"

"Long but full of interesting gossip. The buzzwords now, courtesy of Opus Dei, are stability, continuity, fidelity. The Spaniards, homegrown or colonial, are the standard-bearers. No! Don't take it lightly! Spain's the power base, the money base, and it has a stable monarchy that still makes a kind of sense to the traditional Arab world, which remembers Alhambra."

"They're taking a hell of a risk," said Luca Rossini.

"They're prepared to take it."

"Who is their favored candidate?"

"Gossip says Chile. The smart money says the Spaniard's already ensconced in the Curia. Word is that they'd like to run you as pacer for the money horses."

"I'm on the wrong side, Piers. They know that."

"That doesn't worry them. They're sure you'll run out of steam just as their own people hit the front."

Luca Rossini laughed.

"What can I say to that?"

"I wasn't expecting a comment," said Hallett, "but I'd welcome one on my next item, which is me. I know this is only day one and I'm stuck here for the duration of the conclave; but the point is I've pretty much made up my mind."

"To do what?"

"Quit the priesthood and go back to work as a secular scholar."

"Do you want to tell me why?"

"I do. Your knowing is important to me. You have always been my eminently good friend. You took me as I was, as I am: a scholar of some worth, an indifferent cleric, passionless enough, I thought, to stay out of trouble and enjoy the pleasures of learning and friendship. So far, it has worked out well enough. But it can't any longer. The clergy are too much in the spotlight now. I'm vulnerable, and one day I could be too desperate for companionship to be discreet. Besides, if I want to seek gainful employment, now is the time to do it. There are a couple of jobs on offer: one at Harvard, one at the Getty in Los Angeles. The money's better at the Getty, but there's tenure at Harvard. So, that's where I'll address myself first. Any comment from my eminent friend?"

"Not too much. I think it's a wise decision. I'll do the best I can to facilitate your laicization; but if we get a hard-line pontiff, you may have some procedural headaches, which, on balance, I'd advise you to wear and ignore."

"And that's all?"

"I can't think of anything else. It's a simple situation. You don't have to turn it into a desperate one. You might, however, pour me another whisky."

"With pleasure," said Piers Hallett. "I can't tell you how much I've dreaded this moment."

"Which part of it? The decision or the telling?"

"Both. A lot of people would have fallen back to some prepared position. You know . . . take a little time, get some counseling, find a wise confessor, take a cold shower!"

Luca Rossini smiled and shook his head.

"There are no prepared positions; none that last very long, anyway. Sooner or later, we come to a final standing place from which we fight or die. *Salud*, amigo!"

When they had drunk the toast, Piers Hallett set down his glass and remarked, "I checked for messages, as you asked. There were none."

"It's too soon," said Rossini. "It's much too soon. I'm praying we'll be out of here long before anything happens to Isabel."

"And when it does?"

"That's my standing place."

"To fight or die, you said."

"That's right."

"It's a drastic choice," said Piers Hallett. "But you didn't offer it to me. Why not?"

"I have an argument with God that needs to be settled."

"'And Jacob wrestled all night with the man,'" said Piers Hallett. "'And Jacob came away limping.' If you don't mind, I'm going to have another drink."

"It's your liquor," said Rossini. He raised his glass in a toast. "To health, money, and love—and time to enjoy them. I wish you every good fortune, my friend!"

# 15

fter dinner that night, Luca Rossini was invited to take
coffee with the secretary of state and the camerlengo in
the camerlengo's private office. Now that his name had suddenly shown up in the voting, he wondered whether he was to
be wooed or warned. He decided to preempt the question.

"Who's running me into the ballot?"

"Fifteen voters, according to the count." The camerlengo
was suitably vague. "You're a scrutineer, you checked the figures yourself."

"Who are the voters? Yours or theirs?"

The camerlengo shook his head.

"No way to know; and it's the wrong question, anyway. Both
sides see a certain merit in your candidacy. Your sermon moved
a lot of people."

"You're also a splendid symbol," Turi Pascarelli said it with
a smile. "You're a penitent survivor, now leading a blameless
life, uncorrupted by power. You'd be a very popular choice with
the people."

"But the people have no voice in the election—and imagine what the press would do afterward!"

"We're not thinking about afterward," said Turi Pascarelli.
"We're thinking about now—the next few days."

"What are you thinking?"

"Strategy," said the camerlengo. "The strategy for the old guard is to push the conclave as far as it will go, without having to invoke the rule of absolute majority—which, in our view, they may not attain. Their best chance is to hold out to the final stage of stalemate when the electoral college will agree to an election by simple majority—in effect, a simple head count: first past the post."

"How long before that happens?"

"With a small field and four ballots a day, it will not be too long before the pressure builds up for a resolution. Don't forget all those people waiting in the piazza outside, all the millions watching television around the world. They are our constituents. We're in a fantasyland here. We like to believe we're the arbiters of human destiny, but we are not impregnable. We never have been."

"So tell me now, my friends; tell me plainly. What's your preferred outcome?"

"This time around? An Italian pontiff, politically clean, calm enough to settle things down and create an atmosphere of confidence in the Church again."

"Milan, in other words."

"Yes."

"He's my own choice," said Luca Rossini.

"Would you step aside for him?" It was the camerlengo who asked the question. Rossini stared at him in disbelief.

"Step aside? I'm not even in contention. There is no chance at all that I can be elected. All my history speaks against it."

"Your history speaks for you." The secretary of state was emphatic. "Don't you see? You're a charismatic man, Luca. Your very weaknesses recommend you. Who is more appealing than the penitent Peter, or Saul struck blind on the road to Damascus? You're quite unaware of the power you radiate, even among our most sceptical colleagues. You are much admired by many pastoral cardinals with whom you have dealt in your various missions. I'll make a wager that your voting tally will rise at each ballot from now on."

"And you, of course, will contribute to the inflation?"

"No guarantees; but yes, we'll contribute."

"And you're expecting Milan to rise, too?"

"We're sure he will."

"But you're equally sure he's a better choice as pontiff than I am."

"Don't you agree?"

"Of course I agree. So why bother playing out this comedy? I've already told you Milan is my candidate, too. I have neither ambition nor talent for the office. If it helps, I'll withdraw my candidacy before the next ballot."

"We beg you not to do that," said the camerlengo. "We need you in the ballot. We hope we can build around you a voting bloc that will eliminate the old guard and bring us swiftly to a runoff between you and Milan."

Rossini stared at him in total disbelief. Then he burst into laughter, a huge gusty bellow, with a hint of gallows humor at the high end of it.

"I can't believe what I'm hearing. You know me better than any other men in Rome. You know my past, my present—even the cloud of uncertainty that hangs over my future in the Church, and in the Faith itself. Yet you are lobbying for me with the electors, even putting me in a position to challenge Milan in a runoff ballot. I can't take this seriously."

"Why not?"

"Because you are risking too much on my fidelity. Give me enough voters, I could turn rogue and filch the Fisherman's Ring for myself."

"We risk less on you than on the ambition of certain other colleagues, who shall be nameless."

"Perhaps you judge them more stringently than you judge me."

"We believe," said the camerlengo, "that you would make a better pontiff than they. Your faults commend you more than their virtues."

"But," the secretary of state was swift to add the postscript, "we still believe that Milan is the man who will do best for the Church at this moment. There is strong opposition to him. He is a scholar. He is a Jesuit. He has welcomed alien voices into his pulpit. He could bring new light and new hopes into the Church. Nevertheless, we need more leverage to lift him to the chair of Peter. We need you to remain a candidate until we tell you the time is right to abdicate. Will you do it?"

"Suppose you misjudge the situation? Suppose Milan falls out of favor and I become the favorite? Suppose my nearest rival is a man we all disapprove, where does that leave me?"

"Alone on the Mount of Temptation." The secretary of state was somber. "With all the kingdoms of the earth spread below you like a carpet."

"And both of you would leave me there, alone?"

"You would not be alone, Luca, my friend."

"Why not?"

"Think about it," said the secretary of state, and then abruptly changed the subject. "This is terrible coffee, Baldassare. Can't you do something about it?"

"It's tradition," said the camerlengo cheerfully. "Members of the conclave must be kept in reasonable discomfort to encourage them to finish their work!"

The coffee kept him awake, and the conversation haunted the long, sleepless hours until midnight and after. For all his protestations, there was a curious seduction in the thought that he, Luca Rossini, might succeed to the See of Peter. The seductive imagining turned subtly into a temptation that insinuated itself like a vapor into the closed fortress of himself. This was where the vestigial hatreds lurked, the long memory of unrequited wrongs, the revulsion from every image of tyranny inside the Church, and out of it.

He began to play a mind game with himself. He set the rules carefully. I, myself, do not wish to become a tyrant or a brute. I wish only to balance the scales of justice. As a putative pontiff, I have power in my hands. I have seen how far that power stretches, how potently it can be used, how good men and good women can be persuaded to serve it, how others equally good can be oppressed by it. Where do I begin? What pieces do I remove from the board? To whom do I grant patents of power? Who will be my counselors, who my pursuivants?

He was surprised how much the permutations and combinations of the game intrigued him. He was shocked by the intensity of the primitive lusts they evoked in him.

There was a moment when images of reprisal became so overpowering that he could not close his mind against them, nor even summon any resolution to do so. His scarred back began to itch and burn. His heart was racing and he was sweating profusely. He forced himself to get out of bed, strip off his sodden pajamas, and take a long shower to wash away the dirt of the past that still seemed to cling to him. He wished for music to charm out the demons. There was no radio. He remembered that he was in prison, as much enslaved as the early Pope Pontian exiled to quarry labor in Sardinia.

He picked up his breviary and tried to read. The words swam before his eyes. He tried to meditate, and the first text that came into his head was that of Paul to the Romans: "O man, who are you to rail against God? Has not the potter power over the clay to make one piece into a vessel of honor, the other into a vessel of dishonor?"

His late patron had urged him many times to think upon it. He had chewed it like a grass stalk until there was no juice left in it; but still he found himself in dispute with his maker. Still he demanded to know, "Why, why me? Why her? Why is your world made thus and not otherwise? I have wrestled with you too long. I'm going to call off the bout and send you home— wherever your home is. All that clutter of galaxies, and they tell me you extend to fill all the emptiness between!"

Somewhere in the small, still hours, he lapsed into sleep.

The first two ballots on the following day showed a slight shift in the voting pattern. Milan secured more votes. Rossini registered a modest gain. The Brazilian and the American lost support and retired. The losses and gains in the rest of the list reflected the overnight discussions and maneuverings of the grand electors and a rival group of mid-Europeans.

Gossip over the luncheon tables reflected certain anxieties. A prolonged election would underscore the rifts within the Church. It would suggest that the victorious candidate might be a compromise choice. It would make the task of reunification more difficult. Like it or not, every new pontiff had to be provided with a public image, which he would wear, perforce, for the duration of his reign. If the image makers botched their job, or if the subject himself were difficult, the faithful could be alienated even more.

As they left the dining room, the secretary of state passed a swift word to Rossini.

"The last ballot today should give us some reading on how the currents are running."

"I'm glad someone can read them, Turi. In spite of all the crowds waiting in St. Peter's Square, I wonder how relevant we really are to the People of God."

The secretary of state gave a very Roman shrug.

"Who knows? I'll tell you one thing, Luca. If we weren't here, and all that we stand for, there'd be a big, blank space in human history and a great empty well in the human psyche."

Then he was gone, and Luca Rossini strolled over to a private corner of the Vatican gardens to read his breviary and offer the ancient prayers for the beloved who was now beyond his care.

As the secretary of state had predicted, the last ballot of the day provided, if not an earthquake, at least a tremor strong enough to shake out a batch of weaker candidates and confirm Milan and Rossini as the front-runners, with the Belgian and the Chilean still possible contenders.

Three hours later, Rossini was again bidden to meet with the camerlengo and the secretary of state. The camerlengo delivered the first installment of the news.

"We can finish this tomorrow at the first ballot. Chile and Belgium will step down. The decision between you and Milan will be made by a simple majority of votes."

"Is that legal?"

"It's a de facto situation," said the secretary of state. "It doesn't please everybody, but nobody in the electoral college is prepared to challenge it."

"There is, however, a problem," said the camerlengo. "There is a solid core of opposition to Milan. There are people who don't like the Jesuit connection. There are others—God help us!—who mistrust his liberal scholarship and his openness to nonbelievers. So, both Turi and I judge it could be a close-run thing. You could win the election."

"And lay the responsibility on the Holy Spirit!" Suddenly he was laughing, a happy, schoolboy laugh that welled up in his throat and shone in his eyes. "Forgive me, my friends! I did warn you, didn't I?"

"You did," said the secretary of state.

"And you also made a promise," said the camerlengo.

"Which I shall certainly keep." Rossini was grave again. "But you must instruct me how best to do that. Do I abdicate my candidacy before the vote is taken?"

"In that case," said the camerlengo, "you would have to ask

that the electors signify their agreement to Milan by acclama-
tion. It would be embarrassing if they declined to do it."

"If, on the other hand, I am elected and I decline to accept?"

"Then a claim could be made that the process was tainted
or rigged, and we might have to begin it again. Stranger things
have happened down the centuries."

There was a long moment of silence. Then Rossini stood up.

"I have no solutions for you, gentlemen. I shall do as I
promised. I can say no more at this moment. We should pray
perhaps to be infused with the wisdom of the Spirit while we
sleep."

He was awakened by the shrilling of a telephone—a suspect
sound in the house of Saint Martha. He had to grope to find the
instrument, and rub the gravel out of his eyes to read his watch.
It was eight in the morning. The voice on the line was that of
Piers Hallett.

"Can I come up, please?"

"Of course. I'm glad you called. I had a bad night. I overslept. Give me fifteen minutes to make myself presentable. If
it's not too much trouble, bring me some coffee and a *pannino*."

"No trouble at all," said Hallett, and rang off.

Rossini hurried through his toilet, but he was still in his
shirtsleeves when Hallett came in with his breakfast tray on
which was a copy of the *ordo* for the day. There was nothing new
in it: two ballots morning and afternoon, the usual list of doctors, sacristans, and confessors. Rossini scanned it quickly, then
gulped down the coffee. It was a couple of minutes before he
asked Hallett, "Forgive me. I'm still half asleep. You wanted to
see me about something?"

"This," said Piers Hallett and handed him a fax message for
the vicariate office. "It was received at seven this morning, sent
at one o'clock New York time."

Rossini stared at the paper for a long time, then read the message aloud as if to assure himself that it was authentic.

Senor Raul Ortega and his daughter Luisa ask me to inform Your Eminence that the Senora Isabel Ortega, a patient in this hospital, passed away at 2230 hours this evening. She was under heavy sedation and her end was peaceful. The family will be in further contact with you in due course.
>    Signed
>        Olaf Wintergroen,
>        Memorial Sloan-Kettering Hospital

"I'm sorry," said Hallett. "If there's anything I can do?"

"There is," said Rossini. "Show the message to the camerlengo and the secretary of state. Ask them to keep the news to themselves. Tell them I'll see them at the first ballot."

"Yes, Eminence," said Hallett, then went out, closing the door behind him.

Rossini stood staring after him. Then, slowly, he turned to the prie-dieu. He did not kneel but stood, staring at the figure of the crucified, nailed to the white wall above it. In a tone flat and almost conversational, he addressed himself to the Christus.

"So, she went without pain. Thank You for that, if You arranged it. Now, if You're so disposed, I'd like You to talk to me—given, of course, that You are truly there and not a cosmic fiction. This is our last chance at a dialogue, You see. I've run out of words, and blood and tears. I'm emptied out of everything. If You have nothing to say to me, let's not talk anymore. Let's make no more arguments. I'll play out this pompous drama and be gone from here. I'm only human. You know what that's like, don't You? We're limited creatures. You can't blow us up like balloons to infinite dimensions. Even You gave up at the end, didn't You? You said: 'Enough is enough. It's finished!' That's

what I'm saying now. Except I still owe You a debt for Isabel. I'd
like to settle that. So, if You're there, talk to me, please!"

"He's in shock!" Monsignor Hallett, the languid Englishman,
confronted the two most senior prelates in the Universal
Church. "He won't admit it. He can't admit it. You'll never read
it in that great stone face of his; but, gentlemen, you'd better believe it! He needs help, and in this Church of ours, we're not
very good at giving it anymore."

"You're out of order, Monsignor Hallett." The camerlengo
was offended.

"No, he's not," said the secretary of state. "He's reminding
us of simple charity. Rossini needs brothers and sisters to nurse
him through the loss. We've lost the art of doing that. Our sisters are too busy claiming back the rights we've denied them.
Our brothers are too busy putting the remnant Church together.
Listen to me, Hallett! Stay close to him. If you have to, break a
few rules to do it—look after him. Please!"

"I'll do the best I can, Eminence," said Hallett gravely, "but
this is a man who has had his heart torn out twice, while he's still
alive. What's the remedy for that in the Rituale Romanum?"

"There's a formula but no remedy," said the secretary of
state. "Go back to him. Stay as close as you can all day. Baldassare and I will talk about this."

"I don't know what there is to talk about," said the camerlengo curtly. "People die every day. We offer our sympathy, our
support, our prayers, our share in the saving merits of Christ.
What more can we do?"

"For Christ's sake!" Hallett cursed softly. "For Christ's
sweet sake! How we Christians love each other!"

"You are dismissed, Monsignor Hallett." The camerlengo's
tone was cold. Hallett bowed and walked away without a word.
The secretary of state shook his head.

"You shouldn't have done that, Baldassare. He's a faithful friend. He spoke his mind for our friend, Luca."

"I know! I know! I'll apologize later. I'm worried, Turi. What happens now at our ballot?"

"Perhaps," said the secretary of state, "just perhaps this is the intervention of the Spirit we have prayed for."

"What do we say to Rossini?"

"Nothing, until he decides to open himself to us. He is a man of steel, this one! He will do what he has promised. We should not try to dictate how he does it."

"They'll be calling us to the chapel in twenty minutes. We have to have some kind of plan."

"Why not leave the outcome to God?" asked the secretary of state.

"I wish I had enough faith," said the camerlengo gloomily. "I think I've been too long in Rome."

Before the first morning vote began, the secretary of the conclave made an announcement.

"The apostolic constitution provides that, if after an extended series of ballots a candidate has not been elected, the election shall be decided by a simple majority of the voters. Now we have arrived at another situation altogether. Two candidates only remain in contention. I have a proposal to make to you which, I am advised, conforms to the Spirit if not to the letter of the apostolic constitution. I propose that this ballot be decided by simple majority. You are free to decide otherwise, and to work strictly to the rule of an absolute majority of two-thirds plus one. However, with two candidates it would seem to serve little good purpose. I ask you to signify your assent by a show of hands."

It took a little time for them to declare themselves, but finally all hands were raised.

"Good," said the secretary. "The scrutineers will be His Eminence from New York and His Eminence from Munich.

They will be assisted by their colleagues from Sydney and from Paris. Let us invoke the guidance of the Holy Spirit."

Luca Rossini raised his voice with the others in the solemn invocation. "Come, O Creator Spirit, fill the hearts of the faithful and kindle in them the fire of Your love."

It was a prayer that reached deep into the heart of the most ancient Trinitarian beliefs of Christianity and stretched out to include the most primitive apprehensions of a deity abiding in all creation. It called for light in darkness, fire in a cold world, healing for the wounds of life. Time was when Rossini related all that it signified to Isabel. Once, among the Greeks, he had preached a passionate sermon on the feminine elements implicit in the mystery. Now the memory of it rustled like dead leaves in a parching wind.

The solemn exercise in which he was engaged was a theatrical irrelevance. He could hardly wait to be done with it. He printed the name of his candidate on the ballot paper and took his place in the line to lay it on the paten and recite the affirmation that he had chosen in good faith the best possible candidate.

He watched, dull eyed and indifferent, as the four scrutineers checked and rechecked the ballot papers, and when the count was agreed, he initialed the figures and handed them to the secretary of the conclave. The secretary then turned to the assembly and announced that His Eminence Cardinal Luca Rossini had been elected Bishop of Rome and successor to Peter Prince of the Apostles by a majority of two votes.

There was a moment of stunned silence, then a burst of clapping, which was stilled instantly by the secretary of the conclave.

"Please! Not yet! There is still a necessary formality."

He walked down the nave and stood facing Luca Rossini, who sat rigid as a carved figure in his stall. Then, in a loud voice, the secretary put the question to Rossini.

"*Acceptasne electionem?* Do you accept election?"

Slowly, very slowly, Luca Rossini rose in his place and faced the assembly. The look of him, the rigid stance, the lift of

his head, the fall of the light on his lean and anguished face reduced them all to silence. His utterance was that of a doom-
sayer pronouncing his own damnation.

"My answer is no! I do not accept. I cannot accept. I am not
fit for this office. I know that I should crack under the burdens
of it. You may ask, as you have a right to do, why I presented
myself as a candidate in the first place. The answer to that
is very simple. Certain of my brethren, your brethren, wanted
me to withdraw because of a brief association with a married
woman who saved my life in Argentina and for whom ever since
I have had a deep and constant love. The late Holy Father was
aware of these things. They were not secrets of which I was, or
am, ashamed. I accepted the penances laid upon me: a permanent exile from my homeland; honors beyond my deserving; a
discipline of silence about what had been done in my country
and the connivance of my Church, your Church, my brothers, in
what was done. My rank made me a candidate in this election.
I would not consent to any further abridgements of my rights in
the Church, or out of it. I did not expect to be chosen. The anger
you hear in my voice disqualifies me from the office you offer
me, because although I have learned to control it, I have not
purged it altogether.

"One more matter, the woman I have loved so long in absence died last night in New York. I was given the news at
seven this morning. In my first agony many years ago, I had
little time for healing and grieving. Now, I confess, I need it.
That need is measure of my weakness and not of my strength.
The very ground of my belief quakes under my feet. I am not the
man you want. I am not the man you need. He stands opposite
me: our brother from Milan. I do not know what formalities are
needed to ratify him but I know I have a right to acclaim him
and to urge you to confirm him in the place you have offered to
me. He is my old master. He is a wise man. I believe he can
heal the wounds which afflict the Church, and reunite us all in
the charity of Christ. We need that. We need to rule a line under

the past and begin again what is our true task: to demonstrate in our own lives the saving gospel. I beg you all to accept this man. Give him the votes you dedicated to me, who is so much less deserving. Rise and proclaim your acceptance. Let yourselves be seen and heard."

The camerlengo and the secretary of state were the first to rise, then the demonstration began. The others rose by fives and tens and twenties, until no one was left seated and everyone was applauding as the secretary repeated the question he had put first to Rossini.

"*Acceptasne electionem?*"

To which the answer came back, firm and clear.

"I accept."

They applauded him again, but this time he stilled them with upraised hands, conferred briefly with the camerlengo and then announced: "I should like this to be seen as my first act as head of this family. Let us pray for our departed sister, Isabel Ortega, whom God has already welcomed home. Let us pray for our grieving brother, Luca Rossini, that he may come soon to peace, through Christ our Lord."

The murmured *Amen* rippled through the chapel like a homing wave. Then, the new pontiff crossed the floor to embrace Rossini. The secretary to the conclave hurried to intercept him.

"Please, Holiness! There is still the question of the name by which you wish to be called. We have to make the announcement to the people and to the world."

"First I need a moment for my friend, Luca."

The secretary stepped back. The other prelates kept their distance, noting every detail of the scene, trying without success to hear the quiet dialogue.

"How are you feeling, Luca?"

"Very strange! Like the blind man in the tree, hearing the crowds moving and shouting as Jesus passed, but seeing nothing."

"But He will see you and He will open your eyes again."

"I hope so. I have no certainty anymore."

"My door will be always open to you, as it was in the old days. You put me here. I'm going to need your help."

"Thank you, Holiness, but for now I need to go away and be quiet and unknown. Will you grant me leave?"

"As much as you need. Later, when you are ready to come back, tell me."

"Thank you, Holiness."

"Is there anything else?"

"A speedy release for a cleric whom I have been counseling. He's a good man, but he is not happy in the ministry. It will be better for him and for the Church if he is out of it."

"Send me the papers. I will expedite them. Anything else?"

Rossini fished in the pocket of his soutane and brought out the package with the gold medallion in it.

"Would you bless this, please. It's just a medallion."

"For someone special?"

"You could say that, Holiness. She's a campfire girl from the Via Flaminia. I'm sure she'll be back there one day; she's just as sure the Madonna will protect her. That's only part of the story."

"The rest of it you will tell me when you come back. Be sure I am expecting you. Go with God and come safely home."

"Be kind to your people, Holiness," said Luca Rossini. "They live in a rough world. They are often afraid and lonely. They need a caring shepherd."